About the Author

Alex S. Bradshaw grew up in Kent in the UK and spent much of his childhood hiding (sometimes under tables) and reading a book.

He has always been a fan of epic stories (as well as dinosaurs) so it came as no surprise to anyone that he went on to study Classics and Ancient History at university.

Now Alex works in publishing and has turned his hand to making epic stories of his own.

For my brother.

Are you happy now?

A WINDBORN SAGA

TROLLGRAVE

ALEX S. BRADSHAW

Chapter One
Weak Runes

My runes were too weak to save her.

The woman's shallow breath rasped as she slept. I let her cold, skeletal hand slip from mine and pushed it back under her fur blankets. A cloth curtain kept us hidden from the rest of the family in the longhouse. I was sure they were grateful that it kept most of the smoke from my spells escaping into the main room of the house.

I watched Frida sleep. Her skin was stretched tight as her illness slowly drained her of vitality. It made her look much older than her thirty-five years. Every sharp outline of bone sliced me. She hadn't stirred as I'd placed my carefully chosen rune-stones along her bed and painted sigils on her arms and chest. Her breathing hadn't changed when I burned the sage and lavender. She had not heard the prayers and chants that drew on my strength and the power of the gods to weave my spell of healing.

For hours, I had prayed and infused my power through the sigils and into Frida's body. My strength was drained, leaving my chest hollow and my head light.

Still, she was insensate. Something was eating her from the inside and my spell had slowed it, but it was too deeply rooted and I could not defeat it.

I hung my head and rubbed my eyes with the heels of my hands until I saw stars.

I needed stronger runes.

Frida slept on. Her eyes fluttered as though she was caught in a perpetual dream, but I knew she would not wake.

I picked up my rune-stones, each one worn smooth by

years of use, but left the sage and lavender to smoulder. The healing smoke might help to ease her pain a little more.

With the stones gathered and my staff retrieved, I could no longer put off facing her family. I brushed a sweaty strand of hair from Frida's face then stood and took a breath. I tried to summon my god-speaker's bearing, standing straight and tall, wisdom and kindness in my eyes and the strength of the gods behind me. It took me a moment, but I found the familiar weight of my experience and the gods' strength within myself like a tree's heartwood, strong and deep.

I took up my sigil-laden staff and ducked under the curtain and into the main room.

Frida's husband, Sten, stood to face me as I entered.

"God-Speaker Alvir," he said. "How is she? Is she getting better?"

Fear soaked his red-rimmed eyes and he clenched and unclenched his fists with worry.

"I have eased her pain," I said. I put my hand on his shoulder and squeezed to try and give him some comfort. "She needs rest now."

"Of course," he said, the words nearly shattering into a sob. "Is there more you can do?"

"Perhaps."

I broke away from his pleading and looked over the house. It was much the same as the countless other homes I had visited across the Fjalmark. A dying fire glowed in the long hearth in the centre of the room. Woollen blankets stained with memories of spilled food and drink were draped across the furniture. A half-prepared meal lay on the table, forgotten when I had appeared.

The door banged open and their teenage son clomped into the house. He tossed a wooden mallet onto the floor as he came in.

"Dad, I've fixed the—"

He stopped when he saw me, hurriedly shoving a bunch of flowers behind his back. I could not blame him. Many paused, unsure how to react when they first saw me. At a glance, they saw a tall, cloaked stranger with runes tattooed across his arms and face. People relaxed once they saw my arm-ring—cunningly crafted from three interlocking pieces of wood—that symbolised my status as a god-speaker.

"Leif," Sten began, coughing to clear his throat. Now that his son had returned home, he straightened and wiped the tears from his eyes. He took up the mantle of the strong father as best he could, no longer the grieving husband from a moment ago. "This is Alvir Einarsson. He's a god-speaker. He's here to cure your mother."

I winced at the introduction. I helped wherever I could as I travelled from place to place, whether it was a simple homestead or a lavish mead-hall, but I was still not sure if I could cure Frida.

"I will do what I can," I said and stepped forward to shake the boy's hand. "It's good to meet you, Leif."

He shook my hand but the concern did not leave his face.

Sten coughed and drew our attention. "There's food, Leif. Not as good as your mother's, but…"

The words bounced around the room which suddenly felt too large and empty.

"It smells good," I said, cutting across the silence before it turned into grief and swallowed them whole.

"Oh. Thank you, God-Speaker. You're welcome to join us, of course." Sten dragged a stool to the table.

I looked from the stool to the bench. The stool was well made and looked comfortable enough, but the bench and table had long been worn smooth by countless dinners. For a moment, I felt a stab of jealousy. No matter how far I travelled across the Fjalmark—whether in the shadows of mountains, at the edge of the ocean, or beside long-ranging forests—my seat was always hastily found. It was always gladly offered but I knew that as soon as I left it would be put back in its place, forgotten. It was hard not to feel like some sort of instrument, taken up when needed and discarded when it was done. It twisted at me and I felt a familiar hollow yearning to have somewhere I would always have a seat.

"Thank you," I said, forcing a smile. "But I still have work to do."

He looked like he wanted to argue, to tell me to sit, like he knew that was the right thing to say, but if there was something else I could do to save his wife he would not stop me. There was an awkward silence as we were caught between what we wanted to say and what needed to be done.

Sten looked away first, passing an empty bowl to his son who found a place at the table.

I left them to their meal and dragged myself outside, pulling the door shut as I went.

The chill of winter still hung in the air, not quite chased away by summer, and I pulled my cloak tight. The valley where Sten had made his home was beautiful. Steep mountains watched over the fjord as ships cut through its calm, flowing water. Trees bristled over the mountain's low slopes, painting the world in clear bands of blue, green, and snow-mottled grey before being capped by the bright, endless sky.

Such beauty ahead of me and such grief behind.

I took a deep breath and closed my eyes. The wind brought the scent of the forest as it tussled my hair. I pushed my senses down, felt the slippery mud under my feet, and opened myself to the magic. The gods' power suffused the world: strong and stable. It felt like I stood on solid stone rather than slick mud. The surety of it centred me. My breath came steady and slow. My thoughts calmed.

I needed stronger runes to save Frida. We were close enough to the halls of the High King that I could journey there and back within a few days. His personal god-speaker, Eylis Gudrunsdottir, was a powerful and experienced rune-weaver. She may have the knowledge to save Frida.

I watched a gull cut across the valley and noticed something grey and unyielding trapped within the treetops dancing in the stiff breeze.

A colossal stone by the fjord's shores. A god-stone.

I tapped my staff against the ground as an idea began to form.

I could not save Frida, but perhaps I could give her more time. I glanced back at the longhouse then set off to the god-stone.

ᚠ

Once I was free from the cloying emotions of the longhouse, the urgency prickling against the back of my neck eased. I had softened Frida's pain and knew there was nothing else to be done from inside their home. Sten's well-intentioned but suffocating concern left no room for me to think. The god-stone was the perfect opportunity for me to centre myself and find another way to help.

I followed the well-trodden path down to the fjord. It wound through the edge of the forest but never so deep into the woods that the glistening water disappeared from sight.

The path curved towards the shore before I reached the god-stone. I imagined Sten's family often wandered down to the water to skip stones, swim, or watch the longships pass. The thought strengthened my resolve and I prayed to the Wanderer that I could use the god-stone to give Sten more time with his wife and Leif more time with his mother.

I walked parallel to the shoreline but kept to the edge of the woods, stepping over old pine needles and rotting twigs and before long, the god-stone appeared between the narrow tree trunks. The trees fell away as I approached, as though the woods themselves kept a respectful distance from the colossal monolith at the edge of the beach.

The god-stone was, at first glance, a pillar of rough-cut stone about ten paces wide that stretched taller than any tree I had ever seen. As I drew closer, the runes etched across its surface became clear. Each one a carved line that had been layered upon countless others. Years ago, I had tried to decipher all the runes on a god-stone by the Black Lakes. I had spent days muttering, memorising, and drawing the runes I could see, but it was still not enough. I could not translate the runes. I could not understand them. Some found the unknowable magic saturated into these gargantuan stones unsettling, but they were wrong. It was reassuring. The legends said that god-stones had been made by the gods to protect us from the savage spirits that haunted the wild parts of the world. The gods had pressed these colossal monoliths deep into the earth like pins into cloth and saturated them with their endless power to ward off the feral and unknown spirits that stalked the wilds. It showed us that the gods' magic was endless, undefeatable, and that they used that strength to defend their mortal children. The legends told us all this and if we could never understand it, then so much the better. If the gods' magic could never be unravelled then the gods' enemies would always fail.

I paused to drink in the sight of the god-stone and felt the last echoes of my doubt fall away.

Excitement shivered up my spine as I came up to the ancient monolith. Its magic thrummed through the air, making the hairs on the back of my neck and arms stand on end. When I lay my hand against its smooth surface, it was warm as though it had absorbed a day's heat. This was a quiet strength: invitingly warm with a depth of power that seemed infinite and inexhaustible.

The gods were with me. They were with us. With their help, I would ease Frida's pain.

I set to work, pulling things from my pack and laying them beneath the god-stone with meticulous care. I threw some ingredients in a bowl—dirt from under Frida's home, sprigs of rosemary, salt taken from the Black Lakes—and added a splash of water from the fjord.

As I mixed them together, I noticed a silhouette flitting in the sky above the fjord. I glanced up, wondering if it was some seabird caught on currents that cast it inland, then frowned.

It was a woman. Her cloak fluttered as she watched me work from her sky-perch. A Windborn. One of the unlucky few who were resurrected by the Winds, the gods' ancient enemies, and given strange, unpalatable powers.

I turned my attention back to my preparations. I did not need distractions.

By now, the ingredients had coagulated into a dark, viscous tar. I took a small bundle of cloth from my pack from which I unwrapped a lock of Frida's hair. I had not used it in the spells I had cast at the house and was grateful that I had some left. I stared up at the god-stone. From where I knelt at its base it seemed to take up the entire world. Usually, a spell must be woven again as the magic that sustains it fades. If I could cast a spell that drew its magic from the ageless, infinite strength of the god-stone like a river powers a mill, then even if I could not cure Frida, I could at least ease her pain.

I closed my eyes, rested my fingers in the bowl, and began my spell-work.

"Hear me, Father, wisest of gods and master of the secrets of magic. Lend me your strength so that I might ease the suffering of Frida Eirsdottir."

Pressure built against the back of my eyes as the magic started to flow through me. My bones grew warm and my hair stood on end. The gods were listening.

"Lady of Runes, falcon-cloaked and bright-eyed, grant your blessing to me, your faithful acolyte.

"I call to the Fate-Spinner and the Death-Weaver, let Frida Eirsdottir's thread spin on."

The strength of the gods churned in my head like thorn-filled water and I wove it into my spell. Magic pressed against my eyes until stars blossomed in the darkness under my eyelids. When I felt like I could not take any more I fed it through my arms and out of my fingertips. It flowed like a stream of crackling embers and the bowl began to heat, the viscous mixture began to bubble and steam.

With the spell ready, I stood and opened my eyes.

The tar-like substance in the bowl shimmered in the dim afternoon light. The sunlight seemed to fall into the liquid, far deeper than should have been possible. The bowl seemed so infinitely deep that it made my head spin. The knot of anxiety in my chest eased as I looked between my spell and the god-stone.

Sometimes, caught in the rain on a long and lonely journey between homesteads and mountains, I might wonder if the gods still listened and cared. Faced with the fresh bubbling magic and the immensity of the god-stone, I wondered how I could ever doubt that the gods were with me. In runes and magic, the gods had given us the strength to protect and help ourselves. In the god-stones, they had long ago set their timeless guardians.

I set to work slathering the spell-tar onto the god-stone. It hissed as I painted the runes with my fingers, then cooled and hardened. Once I finished, I would return to Frida and draw runes on her arms and head to mirror the ones on the god-stone. It would link the magic to her and, I hoped, ease her pain for a week or two, maybe more.

I lost myself to the runes for a time. I was a conduit for the gods, a rune-weaver, and this was my calling. I sank into the work like a long-beached ship returning to the waves.

A shadow fell over me.

I frowned and turned around, but there was no one there.

Then I looked up with a scowl.

The Windborn floated nearby, her head cocked to the side, watching me with interest. When she realised I had caught her gawking she held up her hands.

"Please, don't stop, god-speaker. I wish for a prayer but I don't want to interrupt."

She gestured for me to go on. I turned back to the god-stone, still scowling. The first half of the spell was not yet done. To stop now would weaken the weave.

For a few minutes more I drew runes on the god-stone, circling it to paint them in a ring around its base. Muttering prayers, I tried to stay focused on the spell and not let the hovering Windborn distract me. She knew who the gods were. She could pray for herself.

The bowl was nearly empty by the time I finished, but I would draw Frida's runes more finely so I was not worried. I flicked the last of the spell-tar from my fingers and set down the bowl before I turned back to the Windborn. Behind her, a longship carved a sharp path towards the sea in search of distant shores to plunder.

"What did you want?" I demanded.

She swooped a little closer, her head bowed as though in deference.

It was strange to see a Windborn so unsure. All Windborn were given supernatural strength and ungodly powers and with that always seemed to come a relentless arrogance. Yet here she was, her boots barely brushing the ground, nervously rubbing her hands together.

"A blessing, God-Speaker." She glanced back at the longship. "Or perhaps a spell on our longship? You are clearly a talented rune-weaver. The storms were bad this winter. I would be glad of the protection in case any of their fury lingers in the waves."

I frowned, rubbing my fingers together to get rid of the last of the spell-tar. I had always avoided Windborn if I could. They had their own kind of power. Whatever happened when they were joined with the Winds meant that they were rejected by the gods. Now, most of the magic a rune-weaver might weave on them—the gods' magic—would slough off like water from a stone. So many Windborn—traitors to the gods as they accepted strange powers from the gods' ancient enemies—used their resurrections for glory. I did not see why I should help them if the gods abandoned them.

"Why would a Windborn want the gods' blessings?"

She chewed her lip and looked at the longship again. "It's not for me. If we get caught in a storm, I can save myself easily enough." She gestured to the gap between her and the ground. "I would struggle to save my companions, though."

The woman's iron arm-ring glinted as she twisted in the air. An iron arm-ring to show she was Windborn. I toyed with my arm-ring, woven from three pieces of wood—one for each of the trees planted to mark the end of the god-war: ash, oak, and elm—and looked to her longship. It had twisted and paused in the water, waiting for their Windborn.

"Why did you not get the blessing from your god-speaker?" I asked. I tried to keep scowling, but the thought of those god-fearing warriors sailing into deadly storms softened my anger.

"Our god-speaker was seeing to a difficult birth, but our raid leader wouldn't wait." She splashed down in the fjord's shallows. "We gave our prayers, of course, but it would make me feel better if we could get a proper blessing."

Something twisted in my stomach at the mention of a god-speaker visiting a difficult birth. A memory, too often revisited in my darkest moments, of my first, most difficult birth and the scars my failure left behind.

I looked again to the longship and sighed. I could make out the crew's faces—some bearded, others with long, braided hair—and their grey-haired raid leader leaning against the carved dragon figurehead. I could not keep the gods' blessing from them because they, like so many, had a Windborn among their crew. How many stories told of raids saved by a Windborn's strength or enemies broken because of the fear a Windborn inspired?

"Get them to the beach and I will work a charm to bless your journey."

Relief washed over her face. "Thank you. Thank you. I... Thank you." She grinned at me as she shot off towards the longship as quick as a stone from a sling.

In the short time it took me to gather fresh ingredients and create another bowl of spell-tar, the Windborn had pushed the longship onto the shore with a tearing crunch of soil and pebbles.

"Hail, God-Speaker."

I looked up to see the raid leader, a middle-aged woman with silver beginning to thread through her hair.

"Hail, warrior," I replied, raising my hand. "Please, stay aboard. I will make a sigil to help with safe passage. It will not take long."

"Ah, good. We are grateful for the help, God-Speaker. The seas look calm today, but who knows how the rest of the journey to Ertland will be?"

I nodded and offered my agreement before taking the fresh spell-tar, glittering with sea salt and gritty with crushed charcoal, and used two fingers to daub it onto the keel, hoping it would last long enough to soak into the wood. With every movement of my hand I uttered a prayer and soon the lines became a six-spoked symbol. The *sjorgata*, a sigil for a safe ocean passage. At the end of each of the spokes I drew runes, to strengthen the casting, and then I moved to the other side of the keel and mirrored the sigil. I pushed a little magic into each grainy painted line, layering the gods' protection on the longship like varnish.

When I was done I leaned back to examine the sigils, satisfied.

The Windborn swung around to hover behind me. I waved her off, unsure if the Winds trapped within her would somehow sully the casting and unravel the carefully woven threads of my magic.

I looked to the crew. At first they had tried to watch me work, but soon realised the keel blocked their view and now they were bored, picking at their nails with knives or braiding each other's hair. The raid leader watched me expectantly and when she caught my eye she shot me a look that asked for more than silent sigils. I forced a smile. The gods did not need pageantry, but it seemed these raiders did. I took a breath and stepped back, raising my hands to the sky. The crew all shifted and turned to watch me with keen eyes.

"Father," I called, my voice sending a jolt through the raiders, "watch over these travellers as they brave the whale-road in search of plunder. Mother, grant these souls your protection as they prove themselves on distant shores. Warrior, strengthen these warriors' arms as they charge into battle and sharpen their blades. Hear me."

As I ended my prayer I pushed a final thread into the bindings to seal the spell. A fizz rippled through the air as the gods' power flowed through me and into the runes. The raiders cheered and pressed charms to their lips or offered prayers of their own.

The raid leader leaned over the side of the longship and grinned. "There's no way we'll sink now," she said and turned to her crew. "Let us sail! The gods have blessed us and the waves are calm. Let's show those fucking Ertlanders what we're made of!"

"A strong binding," the Windborn called from behind me, barely heard over the noise from her crewmates. "And a worthy prayer. Thank you, God-Speaker."

I nodded and forced a smile through pressed lips as I packed away my components and ignored the Windborn as best I could. When she realised that I was not going to respond, she set herself to the figurehead and shoved the longship back into the fjord.

Water sprayed up as the keel sliced through the shallows and then out into the calm waters. More cheers as they unfurled their sail and pulled away, carving a path to the sea.

The Windborn hovered a little way from the shore, watching me. I raised a hand, half a wave and half a dismissal.

She was too far for me to see her expression, but she stayed a little longer before swooping to her longship. I heard another distant cheer from the crew.

I put the Windborn from my mind and turned back to the god-stone. The black runes glittered, each one nearly dry between the evening sun and the warmth from the god-stone itself. I picked up the bowl of spell-tar and started back up the path to Frida's bedside.

ᚠ

It was dark by the time I made it back to the longhouse. Sten and Leif sat by the hearth, now warm and crackling, and barely looked up as I came through the door. When I showed them the bowl of spell-tar Sten stood, his eyes shining with hope.

I walked to Frida without saying anything.

She lay, breath too shallow, with eyes closed. Sten had brushed her hair. Instead of a sweat-clogged tangle, now her dark hair flowed over her shoulders in smooth, midnight waves. A bunch of flowers lay on a stool by the bed.

I moved the flowers to one side and sat.

I set the bowl on my lap and pulled a raven feather quill from my bag—it was etched with minuscule runes along its shaft to call upon the power of the Father and the First Ravens—and with it, I began to draw fresh runes across Frida's skin. Each one a gentle mirror to the broadly painted runes on the god-stone. As I scratched each rune onto Frida, I called upon the Father, the Lady of Runes, the Fate-Spinner, and the Death-Weaver, repeating the incantation I had made at the god-stone.

The air thickened as though with the promise of a thunderstorm as the gods turned their gaze to this home. Under my fingertips, the runes grew hot as the spell took hold.

When I was done, I put my hand over her chest and closed my eyes. With a grunt, I pushed power into the runes and there was a hiss of steam and fizz of smoke as the magic rushed through the spell-tar.

It was done.

The weight in the air eased. The runes glittered.

"Will she be okay?"

I started, nearly falling from my stool. I had not noticed Sten step through the curtain.

He wrung his hands together and leaned over to stare at his wife with tear-soaked eyes.

I stood and put my hand on his shoulder. A softly spoken truth does better than a well-intentioned lie. "I have done all I can for her, but it will not be enough. The illness is too far gone. The spell will ease her pain."

He looked at me and opened his mouth, then closed it as though if he tried to speak it would break the dam of sorrow in his throat. He swallowed, wiped at his eyes, and nodded.

"Sten?" A voice from behind us, as weak as a falling leaf.

"Frida?" Sten barged past me to kneel by the bed. "Frida, it's okay. I'm here."

He put a hand on her head and stroked her hair. Frida smiled and looked at her husband with watery eyes.

"Be careful of the runes, friend," I said, squeezing Sten's shoulder.

He shot me a mixed look of thanks, then nodded and turned back to his wife.

"It's okay, Frida. You're going to be okay. Do you need anything? Can I get you..."

I stepped back into the main room and left them to their reunion.

Leif stared at me with wide eyes. I shot him a soft smile and nodded at the curtain blanket. "Your mother is awake. She is still weak so try not to overwhelm her. Give her a moment before you go to see her."

"Will she be okay?"

I swallowed and looked into his eyes, so full of fear and hope. I shook my head. "She will feel better for a while. You will see the runes on her. They are to ease the pain."

Leif sniffed and stared at the curtain.

Both husband and son were fixated on the opportunity to speak with Frida one last time. I was forgotten.

I nodded and made to leave. There was nothing more I could do here except impose myself upon this private moment and I would be comfortable enough camping on the roadside.

As I reached the door I heard Sten's voice.

"Leif, your mother wants to see you."

I glanced back as the boy shuffled under the blanket Sten held up for him. Sten looked at me and nodded his thanks. I returned the gesture and stepped out into the night.

The air felt cool and light after the heavy atmosphere inside the longhouse. I took a deep, shuddering breath and looked out at the world as colours faded and night took their place.

No matter how many times I had healed someone—or failed to—I always picked up a sliver of their grief and hope. They were so sharp, cutting off pieces of me and leaving scars across my soul.

Memories welled as I walked away from the longhouse. I thought back to my own motherless years and those I had inflicted on others, despite my best efforts. At least I had given Leif the gift of a farewell.

I shook my head and pushed the memories away. I looked back. The longhouse glowed like a lone ember in the night. I prayed that the spell was strong enough to give Frida and her family a few more days together. Those days would feel like a poor consolation for the years that would stretch ahead without her, but I hoped that as time went on they would become a treasured gift.

A gift they might be, but they would never be enough.

I gripped my staff, its carved sigils digging into my palms, and set off with fresh determination. It had been a long time since I had visited the High King's hall in search of knowledge, but I had to believe that his god-speaker knew of more runes, stronger runes, that could have saved Frida.

Eylis Gudrunsdottir had been serving the High King for decades and had used her position to learn from the most powerful and knowledgeable spellcasters and rune-weavers that visited the High King. I would demand them from her so I never had to leave a fractured family behind again.

Chapter Two
A Task for a God-Speaker

My journey curved along the coast and I watched the sea grow crowded with longships. Their keels frothed against the water as though the ships themselves were eager to sink their teeth into foreign shores. My destination, however, was closer at hand.

After a few hours, I found the familiar paths that would take me to Konvald and God-Speaker Eylis. I settled into an easy pace and let the hours and miles pass without worry until the afternoon burned down to evening and I had to stop for the night.

I made camp close to the road, picking a spot where I could look out across the open valley with the dawn, and settled down with some cool water.

These quiet nights were precious to me, especially after a challenging day when my spells were not enough. They gave me the space to centre myself. I summoned my second sight and the shadows beyond my campfire were banished, replaced with shimmering opalescent colours. The trees around me glowed with slow-moving emerald light and small figures of pearlescent light hopped from branch to branch or scuttled through the undergrowth. Spirits. I smiled and made a note to leave a small offering in the morning.

I stood and looked out into the valley.

Magic wavered beneath me like fields of candles with every flame a different colour. In the distance, there were two beacons blazing so powerful they looked like splinters of the sun.

God-stones.

I sighed and some of the tension left my shoulders. The gods were with us. They would never abandon us. They would protect us.

As I turned away the hairs on the back of my arms stood on end. I dropped my second sight and looked around. I couldn't see anything. An itch between my shoulder blades. A tension settled on me as though someone held a knife to my throat. I spun around, trying to see what caused my creeping unease.

Colours blossomed in the sky. Tendrils of blue and green light whipped across the night. I scowled. These burning lights that lived in the place between the stars and the sky were called many things by traders and foreigners: the dancing sky fire, the star serpents, the northern lights. I knew them for what they were; the imprisoned spirits of the Giants who had tried to overthrow the gods and were now trapped as the Winds in their sky-prison.

Their fiery presence dwarfed me and all the power I had seen with my second sight suddenly seemed inconsequential.

I recalled my second sight and turned back to the god-stones so that I could remind myself of the gods' true power.

As I turned, I felt something shift in the air. All the tension that had been pushing against me crackled then disappeared and at the same time the bright, colourful power across the valley blinked out in a great wave of darkness. Even the blazing light from the god-stones stuttered.

Terror gripped my heart for the blink of an eye at the sudden suffocating blackness.

I swallowed and looked up.

The Winds still squirmed in the sky.

Then, one by one, the magic in the valley came back to life.

It took long minutes for my breathing to return to normal and I could not take my eyes from the valley and the god-stones' light, terrified that the magic would disappear again.

It wasn't until the Winds finally faded, an hour later, that I managed to convince myself that whatever had happened would not happen again. I returned to my campfire, calm but still shaking.

I picked up my waterskin with trembling hands and took a

draught then coughed and spat it out. Mud filled my mouth. I had taken this water from a clear river stream this morning and now it was poisoned with dirt. I looked out at the valley again.

What had happened? I had never heard of anything like this happening before. What had the power to disrupt so much magic? I glanced at the sky, filled with stars, and thought of the Winds. They were the gods' ancient enemies—defeated in the god war and imprisoned in the sky—surely they no longer possessed the strength necessary to make a god-stone stutter?

These questions circled ceaselessly in my head as I tried to get some sleep. The memory of the wave of darkness resurfaced every time I closed my eyes. It took me hours to fall into a troubled sleep and even then it was because I knew I was close to Konvald and Eylis. She had to know what had happened.

ᚠ

I woke still troubled and hastily packed my things. The road along the fjord was quiet and it was not long until Konvald—the seat of the High King and capital of the Fjalmark—loomed in the distance, squatting on the shore.

As I crested a rise, the quiet, insistent noise of hundreds of lives came to me, carried on the wind, as well as the smell of people and animals confined to close quarters. I wrinkled my nose and took a steadying breath. I already missed the quiet of the wilds. Then I shivered as I remembered that dark wave.

Most of the buildings were stuffed inside raised-earth palisades, all dwarfed by the High King's mead-hall. Its long roof curved above the rest of the city like the underside of a god's longship. Somewhere within the mead-hall's shadow, Eylis waited.

As I drew close to the walls, my path—which was barely wide enough for a horse—joined the broader main road. I moved to the side as merchants, farmers, and other travellers jostled their horses and wagons for prime position in the centre of the track, away from the sodden muck at the side of the road. I was happy enough to wander along the road's slick edge and use my staff to steady myself. I had walked through worse when visiting lonely farmers and fisherfolk on storm-ridden days. The crowd thickened as it came to the gates, thrown open to allow the eager early summer trade through, and I squashed myself in with them. One traveller among many.

Even though some new buildings had been raised since I had last visited Konvald, it was easy enough to make my way to the High King's mead hall and the longhouses where his servants lived. I passed the edge of the city, waving a hand to dismiss the merchants hawking food and drink, and wandered through the market. I let my eyes linger on the stalls, curious about the clothes, jewellery, and spices, but not interested enough to barter.

Soon enough, I came to the High King's mead hall. I paused to look at the entrance. The path was flanked by pillars, each one a whale-rib carved with intricate detail telling one saga after another. I took a step forward and ran my fingers along the images carved into the first pillar. Its base was black-stained, the chaos before creation, and rising up from it were figures carved from the bright bleached bone. The gods.

My fingers lingered on the image of the Father, still with both his eyes, before he had woven the First Ravens from the deepest shadows of the sky. It gave me strength.

A clink of metal.

I glanced up and saw the two huskalar flanking the mead-hall's door. Huskalar were the best trained and equipped warriors of any chief. The High King's personal huskalar were no exception. Their armour and weapons glinted in the morning sun. One of them took a step towards me and tipped his head, trying to see what I was doing.

I raised my left hand in greeting, deliberately turning my rune-tattooed fingers to face him and hoping my god-speaker arm-ring would catch his attention.

The huskalar nodded and returned to his post.

As I made my way from the lavish, open avenues and into the smaller, discrete pathways a tension settled in the air. I was no longer walking through spaces made bright for visitors and merchants displaying the wealth and power of the High King. Now I walked the servants' paths of scuffed earth lined with half-eaten food and toppled buckets. My path took me around the High King's impressive mead-hall, its roof bulging like the belly of a fat giant, and I heard a ragged cheer. I paused, craning to see down a narrow alley to the yard behind a nearby longhouse. People had crowded into an abandoned garden, forming a ring around two warriors circling one another. I was about to turn away when one of the fighters summoned a glove of flame and threw it at their opponent. Another cheer from the crowd.

"Easy, Bragi," shouted one of the spectators. Their nose was crushed like a bat's and patchy fur covered their neck. "If you burn down the house, this is over."

"The High King will kill you," called another voice. "Then I won't be able to make money off you losing no more."

The fire-thrower Windborn tried to look chagrined. It didn't last long as he had to throw himself out of the way of a grapple and the fight continued.

I scowled. I shouldn't have been surprised to see back-alley fights at the capital, but so close to the High King's hall? And with Windborn?

I watched the fire-throwing Windborn wrap his thick arms around his opponent and try to throw them to the ground, but the opponent disintegrated into ash before solidifying back into a tattooed warrior with a fresh grin etched on her face.

"Come on," muttered the fire-thrower. "I can't use fire but you can do the ash thing?"

"I ain't gonna burn the place down, Bragi."

The fire-thrower growled and threw himself at his opponent with fresh vigour. I spat on the ground and moved on.

The calm I had gathered from the carved images of the gods fell away with every thump and cheer that echoed through the streets. I clenched my fists until my nails cut into my palms.

Why were there Windborn so close to the High King?

After a rogue Windborn had crippled his daughter years ago, no one blamed him for his grudge, which I thought had long solidified into hatred. So why were they allowed to use their wretched powers so close to the king of the Fjalmark? Worry twisted the pit of my stomach and I hurried on, more eager than ever to find Eylis.

The closed alleys and paths suddenly gave way to a clearing bubbling with birdsong. The space was bordered by a thicket of bushes and shrubs and in the centre three ancient trees towered above me. Konvald's sacred grove. Each one represented the forces that had come together to end the god-war. Oak for the gods. Ash for the Giants, now trapped in their sky-prison. Elm for the Sea Giants, who had fought on both sides of the god-war but whose power had not been blunted.

Eylis' home was little more than a dilapidated hut at the edge of the grove. I let my eyes wander along the swaying branches and sucked in the dirt-scented breeze. After the body-clogged air of the markets and alleyways it almost felt like I was back in the wilderness. I pressed my hand to the oak's trunk and muttered a prayer before I ducked into Eylis' hut.

"Welcome," she called from somewhere out of sight. Her voice was thin, quiet, but strummed with power. Eylis had toughened with age like hardened leather.

"God-Speaker Eylis," I said.

The space around me was a mess of half-filled bowls, plants, and animal bones. Each one, I knew, could be woven into some spell or ritual, but even so, my nose pinched at the smell and chaos.

"Oh. Alvir. It's you. It's been a while. Sit."

I moved a half-cleaned fox skull from a stool and sat. Eylis scuttled out from behind a workbench. Her limbs were all corners and edges as she rushed out to meet me but did not disturb any of the strange items strewn about her home. She threw an empty bowl into a pile of crockery and nodded as she wiped a hand on her shirt. Her taut skin pulled against her muscles which highlighted the rune tattoos etched onto every part of her leaving no doubt about her power and wisdom.

"You finally tired of bouncing between farms?"

I shot her a tight smile. A denial pressed against the back of my teeth but I thought of the worn bench in Frida's home, waiting for her, and my heart ached for somewhere, someone to wait for me.

"There are Windborn in the city," I said.

"More and more." She scowled at me as she lit the candles stood along the table.

"Has the High King abandoned the gods?"

"What? Don't be a fool. Of course he hasn't. Since last winter, he's been plucking Windborn from wherever he can."

"He can't have forgotten what happened to his daughter?"

"He is reminded every time he sees her," Eylis said with a snort. "Have you not heard the skalds? There was a commotion up north and thanks to some Windborn woman, the High King was saved some bloodshed." Eylis shook her head as she poured some watered mead. "It seems that was enough for him to soften his prejudice."

From her tone, Eylis wasn't pleased but seemed to have come to terms with it. For me, this news was unwelcome and shocking. The High King's disdain for Windborn had been something that had given me strength in the quiet places out in the wilds. I trusted the High King's judgement because I knew he held the gods close and used Windborn when he had no other choice. If he could so easily forgive what the Windborn had done to his daughter, would he eventually look to the Winds for power? My thoughts turned to the wave of darkness from the night before and a shiver went up my spine.

"But he still worships the gods? He asks for your counsel?" I asked as I took a proffered cup from Eylis. Candlelight flickered on her skin, making the runes and sigils tattooed over her arm quiver with a life of their own.

"What? Of course he does. Just because he's eased up on the Windborn doesn't mean he's going to tear down any groves, boy. The years have blunted his anger and this business in the north proved their usefulness to him. They're tools, Alvir. They will not replace the gods."

I chewed my bottom lip. Eylis had known the High King

for decades and knew his mind better than most, but even so, my thoughts flitted back to the Windborn scuffling in the alley like restless youths. Could any of them be trusted? Then I thought of the magicless dark of the night before. How much did we really know about a Windborn's power? Could one of those Windborn have had something to do with the wave of power?

"I saw them brawling in the backstreets," I said, hoping that this revelation might bring Eylis' condemnation. "Do they have any supervision?"

"They're a bit boisterous at the moment, I grant you," she said with a shrug. "The High King's away. He's gone south to the Drektonn Sea. There's a delegation from some Daendrec king. Those bog-worshippers have been banging their shields, complaining about the summer raids. Calling them acts of war. The High King's gone to deal with it and the Windborn he's left here are excited, like children left alone for the first time. We keep an eye on them though," Eylis looked at me over her cup. "Do not worry, Alvir, Vigdis is keeping order. She will not let things spill over.

I stared into my cup and swirled the last sip before gulping it down.

"Did you feel it last night?" Eylis asked, her voice barely above a whisper.

Cold claws of fear scratched at my stomach. A small part of me had hoped that what I had seen was overblown in my memories. A scratch that, in darkest midnight, could be a murderous intruder but in the light of day is a branch scraping at the door.

I set down my cup amid a pile of animal teeth. "I did. I saw it."

"You saw it?" Eylis raised an eyebrow.

I explained what I had seen: the wave of shadow that swept across the valley, the stuttering god-stones, the dirt in the water.

Eylis nodded along with my recounting. A deep frown furrowed her wrinkled face. "I have never felt anything like that."

"You don't know what it was? You've not felt this before?"

"Never. The only thing that came close to that are the powerful rituals I performed with other rune-weavers. The kind of magic you need to call a tidal wave and even then, there is a taste to it. You can tell what the spell is supposed to do even from a distance. Last night..."

Eylis shook her head. I knew what she meant and said as much. The prickling air from the night before had been charged, but there was no sense to it, no direction. It had been a great amassing of power but no way for us to tell what its intention was.

Eylis sighed. "Let us put these things to one side. What brings you to this old woman's den?"

I pursed my lips, unhappy to let the topic slide but there was little we could do now and I explained why I had come. I told Eylis about Frida, her illness and my attempts to heal her. The old god-speaker nodded along, sympathetic but offering no consolations. She shook her head when I explained how I had laid a healing spell onto the god-stone.

"God-speakers have tried to break into the god-stones' magic before and it never works. I even tried for a whole summer before I came to Konvald. It can't be done."

"I didn't try to crack into it and drain it," I said. "The weave pulled on the god-stone's power to renew the spell's strength. It won't last forever, but it will ease her pain."

Eylis grunted and shrugged then took a drink from her cup. I looked over the myriad trinkets cluttering her home. Bones and teeth, dried sprigs of countless plants, strips of leather and bark, finely ground powders. I saw dried sage and lavender. Just like I had used in my spell for Frida.

"Could you have done it?" I asked, my voice barely audible over the hiss of the candles. "Could your runes have saved her?"

Eylis stared at me with pursed lips. Her eyes were ringed with age but still as piercing as a raven's beak. I had to look away.

"Perhaps," she said. "Likely not. It's not all about the power of the god-speaker, nor the strength of the magic they weave. If she lived nearby and I'd healed her before, spent time familiarising myself with her and knew how her body would react to my spells and healing..."

She trailed off as she saw my expression and shook her head.

"It may hurt less to fail strangers, but—"

"It still hurts," I said.

"I know," she said, holding up a spindly arm. "What I mean to say is that getting to know the people you help will strengthen your spells, it means knowing that they react to one rune or herb better than another. But sometimes that isn't enough. Sometimes you can never do enough."

I looked up and met the god-speaker's gaze. It was tinged with sympathy but there was no room for platitudes. Eylis had always been a practical woman. People often confused her forthright attitude with rudeness or callousness. That wasn't true. She didn't have time to waste with useless words.

"Do you remember the first birth you helped with?" she asked.

My grip tightened on my cup. "Of course I do."

"You knew them well, didn't you?"

I nodded, unable to speak, and put the cup down on the table before it splintered in my hands.

"Floki told me about it. It was a terrible thing. I know it hurt, but the gods placed you there for a reason."

Memories surged in my mind. I clenched my eyes shut and shook my head. Still, the smell of blood and sweat and fear suffocated me. The sheen of my wet hands clasping a newborn flashed in my mind's eye. My stomach fell as I remembered the baby's first stuttered breath. Then she cried out for a mother who would never hear her. My father had been quiet for a short while, brushing the sweat-drenched hair of my stepmother, then his grief had collapsed under the weight of his rage. His accusations echoed in my mind, as loud as they were then despite the years between: it was my fault, I was too young, not yet a god-speaker, my arrogance had doomed his new family.

I pressed a fist to my eyes to stop the tears.

"Floki could have saved them," I said, my voice thick with a sorrow and guilt I had never managed to shake. I had been an apprentice at the time and Floki, my teacher, had been away dealing with an emergency at another farmstead. "If I could have—"

"You did the best anyone could have asked," Eylis said, cutting me off. "You knew them and that connection gave your magic strength. You saved the child."

I blinked away my tears and looked at Eylis. She met my gaze with the same implacable, practical empathy. I nodded and sat up, taking a deep breath to shake loose my sorrow.

Eylis poured us more drinks and we sat in silence. I turned back to look at the strange ornaments covering Eylis' home. Hung on the back wall was a collection of dirty raven feathers bundled together with sticks. The skulls and teeth of various animals were strewn about the room collected into piles. Eylis had even used a deer skull as a bowl to hold scoops of wood shavings.

"I am jealous of your collection," I said, forcing some levity into my voice. "It is difficult to find half of these things in a farmer's stores."

"Another reason not to be running around the wilds from place to place," she said with a smirk. Then her expression turned serious. "Perhaps you should spend some time in one place, Alvir. You are not getting any younger."

I choked on my mead. "I've got a few years on you yet."

"Everyone has years on me, Alvir. You can't hide the grey in your stubble."

I scratched my chin as she stood and gathered our cups.

"My latest apprentice is leaving this summer. I do not have the energy to teach another. So full of questions. Why don't you stay here and deal with them?"

The question took me by surprise. I frowned at Eylis as she waited for my reaction.

Many god-speakers dreamed of such an offer. To be positioned at the capital, beside Eylis, would put you close to the most powerful people from across the Fjalmark and beyond. Not only the High King, but also chieftains, thanes, and foreign dignitaries.

Then I thought of the Windborn scuffling in the alley.

Perhaps, if I stayed in Konvald, I could convince the High King to distance himself from those unnatural warriors once again.

I glanced around and took in Eylis' house. The weight of years had smoothed its edges and softened its colours. It was a home, cluttered and carved through long, well-lived years. All Eylis' furniture was worn and welcoming, the benches dipping in the middle as though they had loosed a great, relaxing sigh.

My mind flitted back to the worn bench in Frida's home.

Who would care for the distant homesteads if I abandoned them?

"Eylis, that is a generous offer—"

"Generous?" She scoffed. "I'm trying to save myself some trouble, boy." She looked at me, then went on, her voice softer: "Think on it."

I met her gaze and found that same candid softness. I nodded, not an agreement but neither was it a dismissal.

"Good. For now, seeing as you're so good at walking, I have something to ask of you."

"And what's that?"

"There's a god-speaker in the town of Vidsetr, to the south. Ulfrun her name is. She sends me smoked honey mushrooms to use in healing draughts. She collects them from the Trolbjolvid. I've always found those to be the best for potions. I don't use them often, except for Vigdis' healing draughts. The poor girl's arm is almost always giving her trouble. Ulfrun hasn't sent any for a few months and I am nearly out."

"So you want me to go and get some for you? Couldn't you send one of the Windborn to do it? I've seen plenty of Windborn who can fly. They'll be there and back before I could even leave the city."

Eylis scowled at me. "Even under normal circumstances, would you trust a Windborn to tell the difference between honey mushrooms smoked with wood from the tree it grew on from dried funeral bell?"

I couldn't argue with her.

"It's more than that. I don't mind a few months between parcels of mushrooms. It's the silence. We have been sending messages to each other for years but I've not heard from her in weeks, which is unusual, now with the strange snap of power last night I am beginning to worry."

Eylis tapped a finger against the table and frowned at the middle-distance. I chewed my lip, lost in thought. I was not sure if I could take up her offer and stay with her, but something stopped me from turning her down. I put my hands in my lap and ran my fingers over the rune tattoos across my knuckles. This task would give me time to properly consider her offer. Those distant families in their isolated homesteads deserved that much.

"Wait," I asked, as something fell into place in my mind. "Ulfrun Valdisdottir?"

"The same." Eylis turned back to me and cocked an eyebrow.

The name was familiar, tied to rumours of a woman obsessed with stretching the limits of runecraft. Many god-speakers were dismissive of her efforts, some openly derisive and fearful when they whispered the darker stories. Tales of ghosts tethered to runestones or claims that her fingers were always blood-crusted. Little wonder that Ulfrun lived beside the sprawling, ominous Trolbjolvid, The Forest of Broken Trolls. Legends said that at the end of the god-war many trolls who fought against the gods fled into that forest, but one god followed. The Warrior, furious with the trolls for their part in the scheme that killed his wife, spent a summer and a winter hunting them until all that was left was splintered stone and shattered rock. Perhaps she had found some forgotten magic when wandering the shadowed woods. Perhaps that would be enough for me to save Frida.

"I can fetch the mushrooms and check on Ulfrun."

"Thank you, Alvir," Eylis said, her cheeks wrinkling as she smiled at me. "When you return we can talk about your future as a god-speaker."

I returned her smile and stood.

Eylis' expression turned serious and she locked her eyes onto mine. "Ulfrun is a talented spell-weaver. She may be able to shed some light on whatever that was last night. If you were able to raise your second sight, perhaps she was able to raise some spell in time to glean its intention."

I nodded and ducked out of Eylis' den.

If Ulfrun had somehow gleaned long-forgotten secrets of

runecraft and was able to show them to me, then I could never remain in Konvald or anywhere else. There were too many homes hidden in the folds of valleys and fjords. Too many families waiting to break.

Chapter Three
Night by the God-Stone

I left Konvald before midday with a pack full of provisions from the market and ingredients from Eylis' generous stores. As I walked beyond the walls, I felt a tension ease from between my shoulders. Many would be nervous to leave the protection of the city, but I was pleased to be away from the crowds and the Windborn lurking in the alleys. The road bulged with jostling traffic and moved to the side of the road to trudge through muddy grass. Soon enough, my route took me away from the crowds and the gentle presence of the wilderness swelled around me: birdsong, the scratch of the wind against my cheeks, the first swaying flowers of the season.

Hours passed and once the afternoon began to wane, the shrubs and bushes by the road twisted and grew until they became a forest. My eyes were drawn back to that verdant mass over and over again, scanning the dark shadows that the sun could not dispel. The forest sprawled over hills and mountains and in sunken, distant valleys. Most named this wood the Trolbjolvid, but this sprawling expanse was the same as any other forest. It was not until you reached the forest's centre that you found the true Forest of Broken Trolls. It was hidden far within the greenery of the forest: a place of shadows and spirits and ancient sorrow distant from the sight of mortals or gods. No one ventured there without being forced. I shivered and looked away.

Thankfully, the forest was soon hidden behind a rising slope that turned into a hill and into a mountain.

The hours rolled on and I let my feet take care of the journey. Eylis' offer churned in my chest like a foaming whirlpool, moving in all directions and going nowhere. Part of me longed to be rooted and to help familiar faces. It would make healing easier. Often, in the lonely homesteads to the north, I had to give small doses of potions and medicine to my patients to make sure they would respond positively. If I knew the person and was familiar with their history, then I could ease their pain so much faster.

Nonetheless, slow magic still healed.

If I abandoned those distant homesteads—the families often separated from their nearest neighbour by hours—who would help them?

I sighed. This was a conversation I had had with myself many times over the years. Whenever I sat alone by my campfire, days from another human and yearning for a community that would welcome me. I would slowly convince myself that soon, this winter, I would put down my roots.

I never did.

Sooner or later, I left a home without a mother, father, son or daughter. Eventually, there was a sickness that I could not heal and I would feel the guilt of my failings, that I had not known enough to save them, like a knife stuck between my ribs.

I barely survived these deaths of strangers. How could I hope to survive failure when I knew the person? How would I face the family I had splintered if I had known them for months, years?

A glaring spear of sunlight snapped me from my thoughts. The sun wallowed against the forest-covered mountains, slowly sinking beneath the distant canopy. I watched the day burn amber under the setting sun.

Vidsetr was still hours away and a rogue root or loose stone on the road could lead to a sprained ankle or worse. I was better off finding somewhere to camp rather than risking injury by travelling in the dark.

I shifted my pack and kept on. As the shadows lengthened, the colours faded from the world, and the landscape became a mess of blocky black shapes under the bruised sky. The mountains were ragged teeth biting the sky like the jaws of the world serpent. I looked up to watch the stars spark into life, and something else flickered across the sky like moonlight reflected off the sea. Blue and green tendrils of horizon-wide flame danced in the sky. The Winds.

I scowled. Queasiness settled in the pit of my stomach as I remembered the wave of power from the night before, but there was no tension in the air. This, I prayed, was not the same. Perhaps I could find some cover so I would not have to witness the gods' ancient enemies slither across the sky.

The forest was too far and the black shadows of the distant trees leading to the Trolbjolvid sent a shiver down my spine. I could not rest there. As I turned a corner, I saw something jutting from a nearby hill. A singular stone rising from the ground.

A god-stone.

The mighty stone would not block my sight of the Winds completely, but the weight of the monolith and the heat of the runes' ancient magic would offer me solace. Perhaps resting in the lee of the gods' power would help me decide if I should stay with Eylis.

I set off with fresh determination, taking careful steps as darkness seeped deeper into the world. The flickering light of the Winds suffocated the stars and I felt the weight of their gaze on my neck like a wolf's wet fangs.

"The gods protect me," I said, one hand clutched my arm-ring and the other to the rune-stone hung around my neck. "With the Father's wisdom I will know the way."

The Winds' slow movement seemed to follow me like an adder watching its prey. In Ertland they called the Winds the dancing sky-fire and it was easy to see why. Their movements might be slow as clouds, but they lit up the sky as surely as a hearthfire lights a home.

"With the Warrior's strength, I will not be defeated."

I pulled some kvanne root from my pack and stuffed it in my mouth. I used the herb in many potions and unguents to ease the suffering of others, to soften their pain and prayed that it would soothe my anxiety to be travelling alone with the gods' ancient enemies for company.

A gust of wind snapped across the road as I followed it up a hill, churning the treetops into a frenzy. The edge of the woods crept up on me, lurking in the middle-distance and ready to envelop me in ghostly shadows if I wandered too close.

The forest loomed beside me and the Winds pressed down from above. The hair on the back of my neck prickled.

"The Mother protects me."

My voice was a whisper now as I searched for the god-stone's silhouette. My breath came too fast, too shallow. My heart thundered like a rabbit sprinting from a fox. I would be safe by the god-stone.

I stumbled as my boot caught on a rock. I managed to fling out a hand in time to stop myself falling flat on my face but the rough ground tore into my palm. Wincing, I hurried to my feet, wiping the grit from the wound. Looking around, I saw that the path was covered in rocks and boulders.

Then, ahead: the tall stone.

My heart skipped a beat and I sucked in a deep breath. The gods were here. Warm relief flooded my body. They would protect me.

I used a small boulder on the path to pull myself forward. My fingers caught in grooves carved into the stone.

Frowning, I looked at the boulder. It appeared to be half-shattered, like it had been torn from some larger stone. A curved groove ran along its length which disappeared off its cracked edge. I looked at the other stones. Some were as small as pebbles, but some were as large as barrels or even cattle. They seemed to have fallen from the top of the hill. A burst of sickly green light from the Winds picked out their edges and the lines carved into them.

I put a hand against the nearest stone, tracing its cross-hatched carvings with a finger. The lines echoed the channelling rune tattooed on my knuckle.

Chill seeped into my bones.

I spun around but the broken stones blocked my view of the god-stone. Rushing up the hill, I kicked rocks out of my path until the stones were too large to move, then squeezed between shattered boulders. My skin scraped against rough stone and sharp edges and blood glistened in the Wind-light as I fought my way to the god-stone.

All at once, I stood before the monolith.

I reached out and took a slow step forward as though any sudden movement would break it into pieces. My hands pressed against the rough, rune-carved stone. I smiled. It was warm and slick under my bloody, sweaty hands.

In the distant night sky near to the horizon, one of the Winds—a long burning strand of blue light bruising to purple—kicked its tail like a striking snake. The light cut behind the god-stone and cast the shattered tip of the lopsided monolith in stark relief.

My heart sped up as talons of fear crushed my chest.

"No..." I clutched at my wood-woven arm-ring, squeezing it until it creaked. "It can't..."

I took half a step back and tripped on a stone. I looked at it and saw the long, shattered line that had once been a rune. That had once been part of the god-stone...

Bile burned the back of my throat and I twisted onto my knees, hands pressed against wet soil. I wretched and vomit splattered onto the gravelled ground.

Was this what the terrible ritual had been for the night before?

I had to see.

I pawed through my pack and pulled out flint, tinder, and kindling. I wiped my sticky hands on my tunic and chipped at the flint until the pile of dried moss and twigs began to burn. Blowing on the embers helped steady my breath and I focused on it until the night was pushed away by the burgeoning flames.

The clean light of my small fire revealed the god-stone's horrific state.

It was lopsided, leaning as though a great force had torn it apart. Rocks and boulders were strewn down the slope as though fleeing the once proud monolith, their runes still clear where they had not sunk into the ground. Wilted yellow mushrooms and moss were smeared over the churned earth with their roots torn like a ripped tapestry. I rushed between them, placing my hand on each one as though they would speak at my touch. My feet caught on the smaller stones and I stumbled. More blood on my hands as I hurriedly clutched at razor-edges. Without meaning to, I smeared my blood across the shattered god-stones. The trail of detritus led down the slope, falling like a dead body in the direction of the forest.

My heartbeat caused a landslide in my chest. With each pounding beat, a falling boulder crashing against my ribs, threatening to shatter me.

This couldn't happen. The god-stones were infused with the power of the gods. Monoliths that stood beyond mortal understanding and power. How could it break?

My thoughts turned to the wave of darkness that I had seen wash over the world the night before, suffocating magic as it went. Had I witnessed the death throes of a god-stone? Why would anyone do this? More than that, how could anyone do this? I knew of no spell or creature save the gods who could influence a god-stone's power.

As I tried to clasp at answers, fresh bile burned my throat. It felt like the earth was dissolving under my feet and I swayed, lightheaded.

The light faded as my small fire, untended, died. Darkness suffocated me. Then, as my eyes adjusted, I saw the Wind-light dancing over the world. I wretched again.

I couldn't bring myself to move for fear of tripping over some shattered, sacred rock. Instead, I closed my eyes, muttered a prayer, and summoned my second sight so that the night would be illuminated with the power of the gods and all sight and thought of the Winds would be banished.

I kept myself pointed away from the god-stone—if its magic was still intact then it would blind me—as the light pressure of magic settled on my eyelids. I opened my eyes. The world was painted with bright shadow as the world's magic smeared everything in dull colours. The god-stones scattered around swirled with the clear, wild power of the gods but it was dim and poisoned. The emerald light was fading, draining into the ground, and muddy streaks of black ran through them like rotten ivy suffocating a tree trunk. I ran my hands over the broken rocks, trying to sense what the poison was, but only succeeded in smearing more blood across the stones. My blood sparkled with my energy, but faded quickly. It was nothing compared to the pieces of shattered monolith. All I could sense was their slow-fading strength. It was impossible to pick the weave of the god-stone from the poison. It was as though I stood at the centre of the ocean, trying to unravel the tide from the current of the rivers feeding into it.

I fell back against a boulder and looked at my hands. Blood and magic glittered on my palms.

The ground around me was a swirling mass of power. The god-stone's power bled into the earth. Magic poured downhill like a flood. I followed it, unable to look away. At first, it followed the slope of the hill, but it disappeared into the distant trees beyond the valley. As I watched, the magical light pulsed and flashed and I felt the Winds respond hungrily above.

I blinked away my second sight, afraid of what I might see if I looked up. The world faded back into darkness highlighted by the writhing Winds but I knew their attention was elsewhere. They did not care for me, no matter that I was sprawled amongst the shattered remains of an aeon-ancient god-stone. The world was still and silent as though nothing was wrong.

My breath was deep, ragged, and I felt the sharp teeth of terror gnawing at my insides. With raw, bloodied hands I scrabbled at the stones around me, pulling them close as I crawled back to the god-stone. And as I pressed my back against the once-proud monolith, a fearful shiver scraped down my spine and rocks tumbled from my lap in a clattering avalanche.

I sat like that until an uneasy, broken sleep took me. Whenever I woke—nightmares of cracking stone whipping me from my slumber—I snapped my head around and looked into the night. Always toward the same place. The darkness where the god-stone's power disappeared at the edge of the forest. The spot where the magic was hungrily drawn into the shadowed depths of the Forest of Broken Trolls.

ᚨ

The next morning I couldn't bring myself to move. It felt as though I had slept in a broken barrow. Rough stone surrounded me, encasing me in walls of shattered god-stone and it took time for the sun to chase away the bleak shadows.

As the sun coaxed the world back into life with gentle warmth, I stared at the valley and forest ahead of me. Birdsong filled the silence. Mist danced in the breeze even as it burned away. It was as if nothing had changed.

I scowled.

I lay in a god-stone's shattered bones and yet the sun rose without qualm. The birds continued to sing their joyful chorus.

My hollow chest blossomed with heat.

How could life go on without grief? Where was the mustering horn, the flaming beacon to rally against whatever had done this?

My rage faltered as quickly as it had bloomed. What could have done this? I tried to run through the legends I knew, the prophecies that echo between god-speakers. Was this a sign that the world was ending? Was the prophesied Final War upon us?

I swallowed and looked out at the Trolbjolvid. The sun could not burn away the shadows in the Forest of Broken Trolls. What monstrous things were hidden there? What if there were troll-ghosts feeding on this god-stone's magic? Could they use it to fuel their revenge on the gods?

My breath came quick, shallow. I felt myself tipping to panic and closed my eyes before it could take me completely.

I pushed my hands as deep as I could into the mud around me, past the scattered gravel, and felt dirt catch under my fingernails.

For a moment, there was only the cool darkness of wet earth.

My heartbeat slowed.

I pushed my senses into the earth. I sought the gods' power.

Magic thrummed beneath me.

At first, I felt only the tattered flow of the god-stone's power. Broken, bleeding. My stomach twisted.

I pushed deeper.

Then, an endless churning force like living bedrock.

The gods' magic.

Eternal, impenetrable, terrifyingly powerful.

I pressed against it like a snake resting on a warm rock in the morning sun. The power seeped into me, restored me. The exhaustion pulling at my eyes eased and the aching cuts across my palms soothed.

Time faded as I knelt on the wet ground and lost myself basking in the gods' ceaseless strength. It had been a long time since I had needed to lean on the gods so overtly. Normally, watching the world with my second sight calmed me. Seeing the power of the gods blatantly painted across the world made me feel safe. Not this time. Something had shattered the god-stone. The gods' power had not been enough to save the ancient monolith they had placed here for our protection. If a god-stone could be broken then—

No. I shoved the thought away.

The gods' powers were not broken. Their strength would still aid me and with the gods' power blazing against my soul I knew I would find out why the god-stone had fallen.

I opened my eyes.

The sun had burned away most of the shadows and, as I pulled my hands free of the ground, I realised that the mud around the god-stone was too wet, too black. It dripped from my fingertips, silt-thick and shining. I stood and stared down the slope and saw the dirt, away from the god-stone, was dry and light as clay.

A fresh wave of fear surged in my chest, but it washed up against the gods' power.

I gritted my teeth and looked out over the valley. The Trolbjolvid swayed in the breeze.

To the south, thin swirls of chimney smoke floated through the sky from behind a low hill.

Vidsetr.

If the village was this close to the god-stone then perhaps Ulfrun would know what had happened. I chewed my lip, remembering that Eylis had not heard from Ulfrun for months. How long had this god-stone been broken? Not long, surely, otherwise the news of it would have spread across the

Fjalmark as fast as a raven flies.

I bent to shove chunks of god-stone into my pack, ignoring the crunch and snap of whatever was already inside. Some of them were as large as spearheads and just as sharp. I cursed as they sliced at my fingers.

When it was as full as I could make it without being too heavy to carry, I made my way back to the road, wiped the black mud and dusty gravel from my tunic, and pressed on to Vidsetr.

Chapter Four
Videstr

THE GOD-STONE SHARDS BLUDGEONED MY BACK with every step I took. Once, I thought to abandon my terrible cargo by the side of the road. When I stopped and shoved a hand in my pack to toss the shattered rocks into a ditch I found them warm to the touch. There was still magic in them. My second sight showed no hint of the rotten magic that infested the god-stone's roots in these shards. I could not part with them. I settled for taking out a pebble to clutch. It was warm against my skin, melting the scabs on my palm until it began to slip in my tight grip, but the warmth came from the god's magic and I would not let go.

Soon after midday, I came to Vidsetr. My thoughts became a crowded, half-heard whisper as I saw the turf-roofed houses beneath the edge of the forest. I had hoped that when I reached Vidsetr I could huddle under the cloak of civilisation and be protected from any worry of what had shattered the god-stones, but the trees stood tall like giants in verdant cloaks. The canopy shifted in the breeze as though the wilderness was watching.

I squeezed the shard in my hand.

A giggling child ran across my path, oblivious to me as it was chased by a barking dog. Indignant chickens squawked as they rushed out of their path.

The child and dog rounded a corner. Their noise faded and the animals relaxed, returning to scavenging scraps. The few figures I saw going about their morning errands glanced at the child as they zipped by.

A stillness hung over the town like the held breath before

dire news. I looked down at the god-stone in my hand and squeezed it one last time before I put it back in my pack. In the quiet, it felt like I walked over new-formed ice on a river. Even the smallest falling stone might shatter the silence and plunge the town into freezing despair and panic. I wondered if someone had found Ulfrun and whether that news—good or bad—caused the tension in the air.

The town was a rough gathering of houses with turfed, angled roofs. The houses were sparsely placed so there was enough room for vegetable patches, tool sheds, and drying racks for skins and meat. People appeared at their doors as I walked by. They watched me from within the safe shadows of their homes. Animals wandered between the houses, a goat nosed at a small fence built around a vegetable garden until the garden's owner rushed out and frightened it away.

I raised a hand to greet the goat-scarer, but they stepped hurriedly away from me and said that the god-speaker's house was by the edge of the forest before scurrying back inside.

More people appeared as I walked further into Vidsetr, though the same quiet tension surrounded them. They carried sacks from one place to another, leant on houses to watch me pass, or leaned close to one another to gossip.

I frowned. Usually, a few people would speak with me. Either they wanted to get help for their ailing family and friends or wanted a blessing. I had not wanted an adoring crowd, but I had expected more than this.

Beyond the houses, there was enough fresh-cut timber and drying animal skins to show that the townsfolk used the forest for most of their trade. I thought of the usual dangers of the forest—wild animals, outlaws, even accidents if your woodcraft was poor—and knew that there was a new danger to add to that list. A danger threaded with black magic. Did the people of Vidsetr already know? Had they found Ulfrun's body—broken and faded as she tried to combat this new threat?

I shook myself. Speculation would solve nothing. I prayed that Ulfrun had been found safe and hurried on through town, pulling my pack up to keep it from bashing me.

My heart sank when I arrived at Ulfrun's house.

It was obvious which house was hers. Set between the town and the edge of the forest, it looked much the same as the rest of Vidsetr except for the patches of wildflowers and herbs that grew around it, some creeping up the turf roof, and the tumbledown collection of bones and antlers hanging above the door. It could only be the house of a god-speaker.

A small crowd gathered outside. They murmured amongst themselves. I could not make out any words, but the tone was full of fear and sorrow, upset and worry. Some of them were draped in mud-hemmed cloaks, a few were armoured and carried spears, and one massive, hooded figure stood as tall as Ulfrun's house and as broad as three people. He must be Windborn. I ignored him and focused on the crowd. Had news of the god-stone brought them to Ulfrun's house? To seek comfort from their god-speaker?

As I approached the house a raven fluttered onto one of the antlers hanging from the roof and cocked its head at the people beneath it. I let my pack drop to the ground when I reached the edge of the crowd. People turned at the heavy thump and their eyes widened. Without a word, they parted for me and I realised that their attention was focused on a few people arguing by the door.

One—with his back to me—was a man dressed in heavy furs and a thick leather cloak wrapped tightly around him despite the warm morning. He turned and I saw his pinched nose and realised his fur was not clothing, but actually part of him. It was the bat-nosed Windborn from Konvald. I pursed my lips.

"Ah, finally," he said. "God-Speaker."

There was a sharp intake of breath from the edges of the crowd. Hope lightened their expressions until they realised he had announced me, not Ulfrun's return.

As the bat-nosed Windborn stepped towards me so did a stocky, finely dressed woman. Her cheeks were flushed with irritation and she kept pace with him as he walked away.

"That's not our god-speaker," she said. "I told you she—"

"I know," the Windborn replied. His smile became brittle but he did not take his eyes from me. "God-Speaker, Eylis sent me to find you and collect the mushrooms. Vigdis has had a flare-up of pain since she spoke to you. She said that if Vidsetr's god-speaker"—he nodded at the house behind him—"wasn't here that you, God-Speaker Alvir, would be able to help."

From his tone, it was clear that Vidsetr's hospitality left him desperate to leave. I scowled.

"Ulfrun is not here?" I leaned around the Windborn to ask the woman behind him.

"No," the Windborn and the woman said together.

The woman glowered at the bat-faced Windborn and shoved past him. As the Windborn shifted I realised that he was not wearing a leather cloak. Rather, he had enormous, leathery wings clasped around himself.

"She's lost in the forest." Her face was creased with worry and she clasped her hands in front of her. "When this Windborn, Dromi, arrived I asked him to help us. He flew here, so he can fly around the forest and go and look for her. Then—"

"I told you, Chieftain Ormhildr, that I can't," Dromi said, pointedly using her name and title to draw attention back to himself. When she turned, he drew himself up to tower over her. His furred shoulders and wing-clad form making him seem more monster than man. "God-Speaker Eylis has given me specific instructions. I must have those mushrooms and cannot be delayed."

The chieftain shrank from him. There was a low rumble from behind us. Fear flashed across Dromi's face as the hooded, house-tall Windborn pushed to the front of the crowd. Dromi backed away from the other Windborn and slouched so he didn't loom over the chieftain. Instead, he looked to me.

"God-Speaker Alvir, can you please get me the mushrooms or whatever it is I need so that I can bring them to Eylis and Vigdis?"

Once again, all eyes turned to me. I swallowed. Focusing on the question of healing helped distract me from the whirlpool of thoughts about the god-stone and Ulfrun's disappearance.

"Give me a moment." I made to leave and collect my pack

and then, as an afterthought, turned to the stout woman. "Let me give this Windborn what he needs, Chieftain Ormhildr, and then we can discuss Ulfrun."

Ormhildr looked between me and Dromi. She seemed unsure about whether she should press the matter further, but in the end she nodded. "Please be quick."

"Let me fetch my bag."

I turned away and my eyes widened as I saw a child creeping up to my pack, eager hands reaching for the drawstrings.

"Get away!"

The child froze, hands still reaching for the pack. Everyone turned to me, shocked.

"I am sorry," I said, offering a weak smile, "but there are many things inside a god-speaker's bag. Some of them must be handled with great care."

This seemed to mollify the crowd and the child's father steered him away with rough hands. I heaved the pack over my shoulder then hurried into Ulfrun's house, edging around the house-tall Windborn that had growled at Dromi as one would move around a skittish wolf.

Inside, Ulfrun's house looked much like Eylis' hut. It was a single room dominated by a table covered with a gabble of items all mixed together. On the other side of the room was a bed, a blackened fire pit and a mess of clothes and sundry possessions. Animal skulls, hides, and pelts hung on the walls and teeth strung between roof beams wavered in the wind as I came through the door. One of the skins was pinned open with black marks drawn across its surface, a mixture of bold lines to show where the bones would have pressed against the skin and careful, delicate runes drawn on it. As I came closer, I realised that it was several hides stitched together with the seams half-hidden in the thick black lines. The top half of the hideous creation was a wolf's powerful forelimbs and the lower half the lithe legs of a deer. The runes were like anchors—I saw sigils to trap spirits and to steal power—and I felt them clawing at my skin, hungry for my strength. I shuddered and turned away.

I began sifting through the mess on the table: rune-stones;

sprigs of rare and common plants; knives rusted with blood; a mortar and pestle; feathers from songbirds, ravens, game, and eagles; seeds of all kinds. It was clear the god-speaker's possessions had not been moved in some time, but the floor was clear of dust and a bowl of fruit and nuts—a few days old—had been set by the hearth. A family member, perhaps, or an apprentice to keep things tidy whilst Ulfrun was off on errands? One end of the table had been carved with runes to form a small circle for strengthening spells. A pang of jealousy shot through me to see such a well-made, dedicated space for spellcasting. It was my choice to not settle so I could help those distant, lonely homes that needed it most. Although that choice came with many benefits, it meant I could never have a permanent rune-circle like this. This was part of Ulfrun's home, it was strengthened through repeated use and her ambient power had soaked into the grain of the wood. I sighed and turned away from the table.

Instead, I studied the other half of the room. The hearth-side chair, the mess of clothes, and scattered debris from a hurried life.

There were bowls and buckets near the fire and half-hidden under the bed. I tipped each of them to look inside. Berries. Dried wildflowers. Something black and viscous. My nose crinkled as the thick ooze shifted in the bucket and it took me a moment to recognise it. Spell-tar, like I had used for Frida's spell. I glanced to the closed door. Many god-speakers who had dealings with Windborn used the tar to keep them accountable. Not only was it one of the few ways that the gods' magic could affect a Windborn—the divine power would otherwise find no purchase on a Windborn's soul—but it would also sap whatever gave the Windborn their powers, rendering them sick and weak. God-speakers could also imbue spells into the tar and then paint them on a Windborn and I knew of several bounty hunters that had used these tar-spells to track rogue Windborn. I hoped that Ulfrun had not needed to use this against the colossal Windborn outside, but I was pleased it was there.

Soon, I found a bowl filled with honey mushrooms, some smoked and dried and some waiting their turn, lying on a bed of broken sticks from the tree they had been harvested from. I quickly tipped it all into a sack. The dried mushrooms would likely be enough for Eylis, but with the wood she could smoke more as needed.

With my task done, I left the house, stepping out to an awkward silence and from the crowd's expressions, I knew that Dromi and Ormhildr had been re-treading their argument. The crowd had thinned, though I could still see people performing half-hearted tasks at the edge of earshot, no doubt hoping for some glimmer of gossip to take with them.

"Do you have it?" Dromi asked.

"Here." I passed him the pouch. "The smoked mushrooms are in there, as well as some unprepared mushrooms and the wood from their tree."

"Thank you, God-Speaker Alvir. I know Vigdis will be grateful."

His wings unwrapped and he took the pouch with the clawed hands at the joint of his bat-like wings. It took him a moment to secure the pouch to his belt and then he nodded curtly to everyone and walked away. As Dromi hunched and raised his wings, ready to take off, he seemed to remember something and looked to me.

"Oh yes, God-Speaker Eylis also wanted me to ask if you had found the source of your worries. She was not any clearer than that so I am hoping you know what she is talking about."

The weight of my shard-laden pack dragged at my shoulders.

I chewed my lip, unsure of how much I could say with so many listening, nor how much I could trust a Windborn. I dropped my pack and jogged over to him. "I think I have. Tell Eylis that I will look for Ulfrun in the forest. Tell her..." I trailed off. "Tell her there is too much stone on the road. She should look into it."

"Of course, God-Speaker." He failed to keep the confusion from his voice. "Now, I would step back if I were you. I need room for this."

I did.

Dromi stretched, letting his wings unfurl. They sprawled

so wide that he blocked the sun from me and I shivered in the brief shadow. Then, he sprinted forward, leapt, and pumped his wings. A gust battered me. I threw up my hands against the billowing dust. When I looked back Dromi was little more than a silhouette above the treeline. No bigger than a bird.

The crowd had swelled to watch Dromi's departure, but now seemed to be finding their way back to their usual routines. The few people who stood with the chieftain and the huge, cloaked Windborn peeled away from them as I arrived. I looked to the colossal, hooded Windborn as he bent to say something to Ormhildr. His hood was still pulled over his head so I could not make out his features. His voice was deep and thick, almost slurred, and I wondered what the Winds had demanded to give him such strength and stature.

The chieftain nodded and waved him away before turning to me.

"Chieftain Ormhildr, as Dromi mentioned, I am God-Speaker Alvir. Eylis sent me."

The stout woman offered me a hard glare. "Did she send you for more than just fetching mushrooms?"

"She did." I smiled, trying to dissolve the tension but guilt churned at the pit of my stomach as I stepped up to my pack full of god-stone shards. "Eylis hasn't heard from Ulfrun in some time and she's worried. She asked me to help."

Orhmildr's expression softened and she sighed, her need for help overcoming her annoyance. "She's been gone for weeks. She has disappeared into the forest before to forage for things, only ever for a few days. Nothing like this. There are more than simple beasts in the Trolbjolvid." Ormhildr's brow furrowed. "I worry she has been overcome by the outlaws. She would not be the first."

"And you don't have any way to contact her?"

Another flash of irritation. "We're not spell-weavers, god-speaker. We can shout and scream or try and track her down, but we look to you for anything else."

I turned away from the chieftain and looked to the treeline. At the edge of the forest, the trees were scattered but they soon crowded close to each other and became an impenetrable twist of shadows, leaf, and branch. A good place for outlaws. A good place to set an ambush. Perhaps the outlaws needed a healer and could not resist the temptation of a lone god-speaker. I thought back to the shattered god-stone, to the sparks and flashes of dark threads with my second sight. Perhaps something worse had taken the god-speaker in the Forest of Broken Trolls.

A woman with braided blonde hair and clad in light armour walked into my unfocused gaze and approached, slow and cautious. Someone who needed to discuss something with their chieftain, I assumed. I nodded as she approached and realised that the woman was looking at me.

"Alvir?"

Her voice gave me pause. I felt like I should know it, but any recognition was buried under years of absence.

"Yes?"

She frowned, edging closer as though unsure if I would snap at her like a rabid dog or envelop her in an embrace. We were matched in height, which was uncommon as I was taller than most, and there was something about the shape of her face that scratched at the back of my mind.

"Alvir..." She said my name slowly and recognition hit me like a landslide.

For a moment, I was twenty-seven years younger, still an apprentice god-speaker and too young to be dealing with a difficult birth on my own. But there was no one else. My teacher had been called away and could not return in time. I remembered the pained screams of the mother and the cries of the baby. I remembered how they should have overlapped. I saw my father in the corner, the horror on his face mirroring the gnashing pit of terror in my gut as the child squirmed but the mother fell still.

"Sigrun..."

I looked at a woman I had seen twice. Once when she was born and then again when our father died. My half-sister. The daughter of the first family I had fractured. The first child I had left without a mother.

Chapter Five
Rune-Sticks and Ravens

Sigrun watched for some reaction. Her expression was guarded. She took a step forward. I flinched. Her arms fell back to her sides and hurt filled her eyes. Too late, I realised, she had been reaching for me with hesitant affection not long dormant resentment and fury.

"What are you doing here?" she asked.

I looked between the chieftain and my half-sister. "I was sent to help God-Speaker Eylis with something and now I need to speak with your god-speaker, with Ulfrun."

"She's not here."

Sigrun's response was clipped. She took half a step back, shrinking from us.

"This is your brother?" Ormhildr asked.

Sigrun bit her lip and nodded.

Ormhildr's worried expression softened and when she looked at me there was a gleam of hope in her eyes. "Please, God-Speaker Alvir, help us find Ulfrun. Sigrun's told us so much about your skill at rune-weaving. If we have to search the forest on our own it could take us weeks to find her. It would be easy for you, I'm sure."

I looked between the chieftain and my half-sister and then back to Ulfrun's home. Suddenly, I felt like I was surrounded. The weight of the god-stone shards pressed against my back and Sigrun's gaze cut into my chest. I wanted to speak to Sigrun alone, to apologise for flinching, but Ormhildr waited for my answer and the Windborn loomed over us all. I had no space.

There were spells to find lost things, even people. I would

need something of Ulfrun's, a strand of hair or thread from her clothes, to weave into a finding spell. It would be like a compass pointing a direction for us to follow. I glanced up at the trees and the never-ending darkness beyond them. Even with a finding spell, it might take days—weeks—to find Ulfrun. From a distance, the magic would be weak and may not work at all. I would be like a drop of rain dripping a jagged path down a mirror, heading in the right direction but not knowing the quickest path. My back itched at the weight of the god-stone shards. I couldn't wait that long.

Something squawked above us and I saw the raven perched on the roof of Ulfrun's house. My thoughts turned to a rune-weaver I had met years before and heard many tales of since: Viggo Hallrson, the Bear Father. Perhaps there was something I could do.

"I will help you, Chieftain. Is that Ulfrun's raven? Did she keep others?"

Ormhildr's face lit with my promise of help, then clouded as she pondered my question.

"I think so. She sometimes threw seeds for the birds at the edge of the forest. I think there were usually a few ravens among the flock."

"Did she have an apprentice or anyone who might be able to get those ravens into cages?"

Ormhildr's frown deepened. She glanced at Sigrun and the enormous Windborn beside us, who both shrugged at her. "She was teaching Tjorvid a few things."

I nodded and turned to my half-sister.

"Sigrun," I said. She looked at me warily. I reached out my hand, but let it fall when she did not move to meet me. I swallowed my disappointment. "Could you find Tjorvid and collect some ravens for me? Three would be best."

She glanced at Ormhildr for confirmation before she agreed. She walked away with long strides and did not look back. Something twisted at the pit of my stomach as she left. It urged me to chase after her, to talk to her, but it could not tell me what to say, or even what I wanted my half-sister to say.

"Do not mind her," came a soft, rumbling voice from

behind me. The enormous Windborn nodded his cowled head at Sigrun. "She speaks well of you."

"Fafnir's right," Ormhildr said when I did not respond. "Everyone knows about Sigrun's powerful God-Speaker brother."

She smiled at me as though her words would soothe the tension, but they reminded me of how long it had been since I had seen Sigrun. How long it had been since I had thought of her. Sickening guilt bubbled in my chest.

I sighed as I watched Sigrun walk back into Vidsetr.

"So, how can we help, God-Speaker?" asked Chieftain Ormhildr.

I sucked in a breath in an effort to hide my discomfort then forced a keen expression onto my face. I gestured for Ormhildr to head inside Ulfrun's house. The enormous Windborn shifted as we left him, unhappy that he couldn't fit through the door.

"I need something of Ulfrun's," I said once we were inside. "The spell will use it to point to her so the closer its connection to Ulfrun the better. The best thing would be her hair, if you can find any. I will gather whatever else is needed."

I went to the cluttered table and began gathering ingredients and components into a large bowl whilst Ormhildr searched the other side of the house.

Once again, I felt a twinge of jealousy as I examined the runes etched into its surface. The clear lines had been carved into the table years ago. Their once-sharp edges had smoothed as Ulfrun's hands had moved over them countless times. It was one of the ways that showed me how long Ulfrun had lived there and that in those years the house and Ulfrun had folded into and over each other and together had become a home.

I shook my head to clear it and threw myself back into gathering what I needed for the spell. There were sticks of ash, elm, and oak split down the middle for a god-speaker to draw runes on them. Bundles of yarrow stalks. Dried mugwort flowers. Sprigs of juniper complete with dried berries.

"Will this do?" Ormhildr asked as I finished my collection. She showed me a stained and tattered blanket. "She's had this for years. I must have told her to throw it away a hundred times, but she always waved me off. Will it work?"

"Let us pray it is enough," I said.

Outside, the looming Windborn straightened and stepped away from the house like a guilty child. He had been picking at the turf and moss growing on the roof. I frowned as I saw that on both hands, his fingers were bandaged into two meaty stubs, but otherwise ignored him. I had more important things to do.

I looked around, trying to decide where to perform the ritual. Part of me wanted to do it in sight of the town and let them see that the gods had sent them help when they needed it, but as I turned I saw my pack. Its lumpy outline sent a chill down my spine. I had to be swift. The power was draining from the god-stone. Who knew what terrors would be unleashed upon us if the gods' protection faded?

Instead, I picked up my pack and led Ormhildr to the edge of the woods. By now the sun had reached its zenith. Even so, as I looked into the trees it felt like the canopy caught the daylight and refused to let it penetrate the forest's black depths. I shivered.

We piled the components and blanket together in the grass and I lowered my pack onto the ground beside it. There was some flat ground a little way from the scattered trunks that marked the edge of the forest. As I surveyed the grass-patched ground, I noticed a boulder caught in the shadow of the trees. I might have ignored it anywhere else, but here—next to the Trolbjolvid, where the stone corpses of trolls littered the forest and so close to the shattered god-stone—something about it set my stomach fluttering.

"What is that?" I asked, pointing to the boulder.

Ormhildr squinted then shrugged. "Ulfrun made it. She was always doing strange rituals and I saw her with Tjorvid a few weeks ago doing something with that stone."

I nodded, a frown creasing my brow, and looked around. Sigrun was nowhere to be seen so, with nothing to do but wait, I went to investigate.

The stout stone was set into the earth a few paces from the edge of the forest, standing sentinel between Vidsetr and the wild darkness under the canopy. As I drew closer, I realized it was not a simple monolith. It tapered about one third of the way up its length in a smooth curve. It reminded me of a lower leg, the curve mimicking a calf muscle. There was no foot and it stood upside down, but the resemblance was there. Was this one of the fabled troll-boulders that the Forest of Broken Trolls was named for?

With a short prayer, I raised my second sight, feeling the familiar thrill as I saw the world as the gods must see it, and the boulder flushed with brilliant light in my magically enhanced vision. I squinted, trying to reconcile the bright magic with the now dull material world.

I ran my hands over the stone and my fingertips found the old lines scratched into it. Runes. They were lightly carved into the rock, almost invisible, but now that I had found them I was able to pick them out with my second sight like looking for single feathers of flame within a wildfire. They seemed to be striving to fulfil the same purpose as a god-stone. Wards of protection meshed with warnings and some other runes I did not know. Nothing of the black threads I had seen in the broken god-stone. I turned to gaze into the forest, to see what my second sight would show me: small, shimmering spirits hunched on branches and the natural magic that infused the world flickered between the trees and beneath the earth, but there was nothing unusual.

Had Ulfrun had some warning that the god-stone would crumble? Was this stone her preparation to protect Vidsetr?

I let my second sight fall and familiar disappointment flashed through me at how dull everything was without the pearlescent sheen of magic. I shook myself and bent to examine the base of the boulder. Its weight pressed it deep into the ground, but the earth all around it was smooth so I could not see where it had come from. The boulder, this imitation god-stone, seemed to mark the border between the town and the forest. Dark moss and yellow mushrooms crept up its forest-facing side and thick grass grew all around it. Not a recent addition, then.

I stood. My confusion smouldered into frustration. More questions.

"God-Speaker!" Ormhildr called.

Two figures, each with a wicker basket, came towards us. Sigrun and a young man. Ravens squawked from within the creaking makeshift cages. I made my way back, aiming a distant smile at Sigrun and raising my hand. I wanted to speak with her, to begin building some kind of relationship or see if she hated me for everything I had done. As they came closer, the enormous Windborn lurched off to meet them and bent his head to speak to Sigrun. She smirked and her reply made Fafnir guffaw. My smile twisted into a scowl as jealousy tightened in the pit of my stomach. I hurried over to Ormhildr.

"This is Tjorvid?" I asked the chieftain, a little too loudly. Sigrun and the Windborn fell silent like chastised children.

"It is."

She waved the young man forward.

"God-Speaker Alvir," he said, voice gentle and cautious as a rabbit stepping from its burrow. "Sigrun says you're here to find Ulfrun."

Tjorvid was a thin young man with a short beard that hadn't quite grown in and he would have been tall if he hadn't been hunched over his cage. I smiled, trying to put him at ease.

"I will do what I can, Tjorvid, and with the help of the gods, I am sure we will succeed."

He nodded, offering a smile in return.

Sigrun put her basket down next to us and Fafnir moved to crouch beside the cage and wiggled his enormous, bandaged hand at the two birds inside.

"What are the birds for?" he asked, his voice thick as though his tongue had trouble forming the words.

I scowled at him and was about to turn away so that I did not have to engage with a Windborn when I noticed Sigrun and Ormhildr's expectant expressions.

"Have you heard of God-Speaker Viggo Hallrson, the Bear Father? Or Bjorg Idunnsdottir?"

Slow, uncertain nods.

"There are runes that can let a god-speaker layer their mind upon the mind of beasts. Viggo and Bjorg have spent their lives perfecting these magics with their animal companions. Viggo has a snow bear, Kala, that he has looked after since it was a cub, and Bjorg a pack of wolves." I gestured to the ravens jumping indignantly in their cages. "If the gods are willing, I should be able to see through the eyes of these birds and, with the help of a seeking spell, I will be able to find Ulfrun no matter where she is in the forest."

"We won't need to go into the woods?" Fafnir asked as he pushed himself to his feet. He turned to Ormhildr and leaned forward, hands clasped as if in hope. The chieftain looked to me.

"With the gods' help we will find Ulfrun," I said. "But you said she has never been away for this long. We may need to send someone to help her."

Fafnir's shoulders tensed and he looked into the forest. Sigrun put a hand on his arm and some of the tension left his frame. Once again, I felt a stirring of jealousy at their easy companionship and guilt that I had not tried to build that with my sister. It mixed in my gut like silt kicked up in a stream.

"I can fetch her, if it comes to that," I said.

Sigrun and Fafnir turned to me. His expression was still lost in the depths of his hood, but his posture eased. Sigrun tipped her head a fraction as though unsure if I was being serious. I took half a step forward, ready to prove to her that I would go in, that I wouldn't abandon Vidsetr. I wouldn't abandon her again.

"Do you have everything you need?" Ormhildr asked.

"I... yes. Let me begin."

They cleared a space for me as I carved a sigil into the ground using an antler taken from Ulfrun's table and then passed me components as I needed them. I questioned everyone as we worked to try and find out where Ulfrun might be found. Only Tjorvid, also apprenticed to the town's foremost huntress, was able to give me some clues.

The sigil formed a circle with four spokes branching out at each compass point, with each branch ending in a different rune: *sight*, *dreams*, *air*, and *belonging*. At the centre I marked a smaller circle where I would sit. I took three of Ulfrun's rune-sticks—one of ash, one of elm, and one of oak—and began to inscribe them with the runes to bind the ravens to me, then placed them in the centre of the sigil. I took a moment to look upon the ritual and its components using my second sight and was rewarded with a low-burning light pulsing from the sigil's edges to the centre like a rippling wave.

My pulse quickened as I sorted the components into the order that I would need them and imagined the magics that would flow through me. Soon, I would be like the Father himself, commanding the First Ravens to scour the world for secrets, but instead of hoarding all the knowledge in the world—I would save this town's god-speaker and fix the god-stones.

"Tjorvid, please bring the ravens here, but do not let them free. Sigrun, could you start a small fire?"

As they moved to help, I saw that some of the townsfolk had wandered back over to us. No doubt eager to see the ritual and hear news about their god-speaker.

"Fafnir." The Windborn perked up as I addressed him and took half a step towards me, then stopped to avoid walking across my carefully constructed sigil. "Could you make sure the spectators do not interfere?"

"Aye, god-speaker."

He bowed his head, perhaps disappointed with his mundane task, but I could not risk involving a Windborn in the gods' work.

I checked the birds then placed them next to the newborn fire. Carefully, I plucked a feather from each raven—they cawed and pecked at my hands, but my fingers were swifter than their beaks—and used thread from Ulfrun's blanket to tie each feather to a different runestick.

"Sigrun."

She looked expectantly at me from beside the fire. I smiled at her as warmly as I could.

"Thank you, but you cannot be within the sigil during the ritual."

She nodded and pushed herself to her feet, making her way to stand with Ormhildr. I wanted to reach out and offer her some token of thanks, but my hands were full of rune-sticks and raven feathers and the gods waited for me.

I looked over the ritual with my second sight one last time to make sure that everything was in place. The magic fluttered like a flag in the breeze, but the weave was strong and did not falter. I took a breath then knelt in the centre of the sigil, looked from the fire to the ravens, and began.

ᚠ

Wisps of smoke trailed into my face. I closed my eyes and focused on the warm echo of magic. Noise fell away: the chatter of the spectators, the swirling whisper of the leaves, and the flutter and squawk of the ravens. I opened myself to the gods. Everything else was meaningless.

"Father, hear me," I called. "As you task the First Ravens to search the world, let me use these ravens to search for God-Speaker Ulfrun."

The air around me grew heavy. No wind dared bluster through the ritual. All was still.

"Mother, hear me. Let your wisdom show me the quickest route to God-Speaker Ulfrun so I can find the answers that I seek."

A murmur from the crowd. They knew I sought out their god-speaker, but perhaps did not realise I had motives of my own. My attention flickered towards my pack, set aside outside the sigil, and the god-stone shards inside it, but I wrestled my mind back to the ritual. If I did not then focus, the magic would not weave into the spell and all would be lost.

"Warrior, hear me. Let your strength bind these birds to my will and give me the courage to face the trials ahead."

The weight in the air pushed and shifted as though being pulled by some unseen tide. The gods had heard me. They were watching.

I opened my eyes and placed the rune-sticks, each with their raven's feather, on the edge of the fire. The ends of the rune-sticks began to singe and smoke. The feathers' edges curled in the heat. I moved my open hand over the fire and felt its warmth grasp at me. I sucked in the smoke from the rune-sticks. My chest felt full and warm.

"I call on the trees of the First Grove." Smoke trailed from my mouth like a dragon's breath. "Grant me the strength of oak, the protection of ash, and the wisdom of elm."

The fire flared. Gasps from the crowd and squawks from the ravens. I gritted my teeth against the roaring flame. Its heat tore at me like a raging animal and a column of flickering smoke twisted up from the fire's heart. I took a long breath, letting the smoke and the god-heavy air deep into my lungs then snapped my hand shut and drew all the heat from the flames.

The fire died. Heat rushed into me like a spear driven through my soul, I gasped and reared back, but kept from screaming. With deep breaths, the pain of the conflagration beneath my skin was let out piece by piece, until the heat merely burned.

With one hand, I plucked the half-burned rune-sticks from the glowing embers—each one was burned at one end, but the runes and feathers remained—whilst my other hand pulled a fistful of ashes from the dead fire. I uttered another prayer to the trees of the First Grove and blew the mixed ashes onto the ravens one by one, matching each prayer to the raven as their feather was tied to each rune-stick. The first raven screeched and flapped in its basket, knocking it along the ground. The second tried to hide at the back of its cage and spread its wings threateningly. But the third raven simply stood, silent, and let the ash cover it. The weave tightened.

To finish the ritual, I cut my hair and used it to tie the three runesticks together. Now, the three ravens were joined and they were connected to me as the First Ravens are connected to the Father.

I let out a breath and smiled. It was done.

A breeze flowed past me—the air light and agile once more as the gods turned their attention away, their gift given—and I looked around. The crowd watched me with worry on their faces, but also hope. The ravens beside me were quiet. They cocked their heads at one another, no doubt curious about their new connection. For my part, I felt the ravens like three darting shadows at the back of my mind that moved separately but together like a single reflection split over shimmering waters.

The wind cooled my still-burning skin. Part of me wanted to rest and let the wind chill me until I was as cool as stone, but there was no time. I wasn't finished yet.

I clutched at the rune-sticks and felt for the invisible threads tying my awareness to the ravens.

Fly. Into the forest.

The ravens made no sound, but their shadows fluttered in my mind. They understood and would obey. I freed them from their cages and they leapt into the air.

For my part, I closed my eyes, raised my second sight, and focused on the rune-sticks in my hand. Bright threads and images writhed over the rune-sticks as though the world was beginning to crack between them. I saw the leaf-feathered branches of pine trees, a man kneeling in a strange circle that had been gouged into the ground, a sideways glance at a raven flying by my side. Through my fingers I watched the world as the ravens did. I let myself fall into those images, using the connection I had built to jump from one raven's eyes to the next. A shiver of vertigo made me sway as I tried to make sense of the ravens' swift-flying sight and I nearly tumbled from my seat then I settled, and my breath caught in my throat.

I had done this only twice before, once with a trio of ravens and once with a sea eagle, and each time I was amazed at how different the world looked. The gods have blessed birds with better vision than a human could ever imagine. Even the shimmering magic visible through the second sight pales in comparison. One of the ravens looked at another and I gasped at the colours that flashed over it with each beat of its wings. To my human eyes their feathers were black, but with the eyes of the raven, it was as black as the night sky with deep-hued purples and blues flashing across its body and other colours my human tongue had no words for.

I put one hand to the ground and dug my fingers into the earth. The dirt under my fingertips, the bugs scurrying over my knuckles helped to anchor my soul to stop me from losing myself in the beauty of the raven's vision and the intoxicating power of the gods.

The ravens soared on. They flitted between the thin trunks, brushed against the leaves, and darted over foxes and elk. I used the gentle tug of Ulfrun's magic to guide them to the trails that Tjorvid and Ormhildr said their god-speaker often used. The ravens found the deer paths and streams and other landmarks I had been given, but no god-speaker.

The small flock passed stream after stream. Trees blurred as the forest climbed up hills and mountains. The chipped boulders the ravens saw sent a shiver of disquiet through me. I knew I should stop. Time passes differently through the mind of a raven than a god-speaker and if I spent too long with them, then I may not be able to pull myself free, but I could not wrest the shattered god-stone from my mind. Ulfrun must be found. With a thought, I sent the ravens spiralling out from one another to widen the search. They no longer searched for a figure wandering through the undergrowth collecting berries and twigs but rather looked for any sign of human passage.

As the birds flew further away from one another the tug of Ulfrun's magic became blurred and unfocused as useless for guidance as a spinning compass. The distance between us made it harder to keep the raven's dissonant visions clear. My mind's eye followed three different paths through the forest. They looked near identical to my human mind, especially as I struggled to make sense of the vivid and unknowable colours that the ravens took for granted.

A moss-covered trunk. Glittering streams babbling over small stones. A deer hopping over a toppled tree. The hiss and spit of leaves and branches snapping in the wind. An amber spear of sunlight stabbing into a glade. Blood. The snort and thump of a wandering elk. Hooting owls rousing themselves to hunt.

Blood?

With some difficulty, I found the raven that had spotted the blood—the raven bonded with the oak rune-stick—and forced it to circle back. It squawked with indignation as I cut short its joy in its swift passage but complied. I urged the other birds to join their companion. They were some distance away so would take time for them to converge on their flock-mate.

The oak-raven landed on a low pine branch and cocked its head to the side, searching.

There.

The iron-tang of blood in the air. The raven twisted on its branch, looking for the source. Evening had begun to settle on the world and the depths of the forest were drenched in shadows. I shivered, glad to be safe in Vidsetr. Below the oak-raven was a trail of small, snapped branches, ferns crushed underfoot, and blood sparkling in dying daylight.

I sent the raven along the trail to follow the blood and there, sprawled on their side in the churned mud, was a body.

It was difficult to make out details as I wrestled with the raven's desperate desire to peck at the eyes of this lonely victim. From their position on the ground it looked as though they had tumbled to the ground and died there. Their hands were bound and their face bruised. In the dark and through the raven's inhuman eyes I was not sure if they were a man or a woman.

I prayed that this was not Ulfrun.

Something moved.

Branches twitched.

Twigs snapped.

The raven leapt up to a low branch, away from any earth-bound predator. I told myself it was likely the wolf that the oak-raven had spotted earlier, but from the fear thumping through my bones and fluttering in the raven's chest I couldn't believe it.

A shape rose in the distant darkness. Too bulky and broad for a wolf. It rose, standing like a bear on its hind legs but too tall. It took a ragged step forward and shook itself as though getting used to its new height. It pulled at the nearby trees and the branches snapped, dragged in the shadow's wake like driftwood in a riptide.

The oak-raven screeched in fear and tried to fly away.

I held it in place.

Whatever this thing was, it could be the reason for the shattered god-stone.

The other ravens felt the oak-raven's fear through their new connection. They screamed and twisted in the air as though they had flown into a firestorm. I tried to push them but I could not force them on without releasing my hold on the oak-raven. After a few hasty beats of their wings, they threw themselves back to Vidsetr, to me.

I grunted with the effort of holding the oak-raven, distantly aware of the rune-sticks cutting into my palm, stabbing splinters into my fingers. We watched as the shadow-creature came to its full height.

It had a humanoid shape with a head like a boulder, shoulders wide as a river, and arms as thick as tree trunks. I watched through the raven's eyes as the creature's enormous silhouette—draped in snapped branches, nettles and thorny vines, with stones with dirt falling from its wide shoulders—took one shuddering step towards the body. Then another. The oak-raven screeched in terror. It was all I could do to keep it in place.

The shadow-creature, whatever it was, drew in an impossibly deep breath. Its chest rose and rose and rose and it felt as though it would suck in all the air from the world. Then it raised its branch-tangled head to look at the raven.

No, not to look at the raven.

Something slammed against my senses. The weave buckled. The ravens cried out, twisting in the air, throwing themselves against my mind desperate to be free.

It looked through the ravens and saw me.

Chapter Six
A Broken Connection

I fell back, scuttling away from the shadow-creature. My mind felt like a wave smashed against a cliff, scattered and broken but coming back to itself. I lay at the edge of the sigil, pushed from the centre both by the force of whatever was in the forest and my fear. As I looked around I saw gouges in the dirt where I had clawed myself away from the shadow-creature.

Sweat prickled my skin. Not feathers. Skin. I took a deep breath and stared at the ground, at my fingers and the mud seeping between them. Slowly, I came back to myself.

A shadow enveloped me. I flinched.

"Alvir, are you alright?"

I blinked. It was not the shadow-creature. Someone crouched over me.

"What's my name?"

The voice was familiar. I looked up. A woman stood over me. I knew her, though not well. Her round nose reminded me of my father's.

"S-Sigrun," I stammered.

Some of the worry left her face.

"Are you alright? What happened?"

She reached down to help me up. Mud squelched between our palms as I got to my feet.

"I'm fine. Just a little shaken."

I took a breath then raised a dirt-clogged hand to forestall any questions. The ravens were still a swirling presence in the back of my mind and I sighed with relief. They were winging their way to me—not only because they were tied to me but also because I was a point of strength to them—I let them both come.

Both?

I focused on those mind-shadows again. There were only two. Whatever the shadow-creature had done to me had wrenched the oak-raven from my spell. I pursed my lips, wondering what could do such a thing. I shuddered to imagine what the shadow-creature would look like through my second sight.

Night had fallen and the stars glimmered above. The only people that had been willing to wait this long were the chieftain, Sigrun, Tjorvid, and the massive Windborn Fafnir. He was still covered in his heavy cloak, his hood pulled low. Now that I had come back to myself and looked to be recovered the chieftain and Windborn came to join Sigrun by my side.

"You've been gone for hours," Sigrun said. "I was starting to worry."

"I told you, spear-sister," rumbled Fafnir, placing a shield-sized hand on Sigrun's shoulder. "Trust in the gods. He is fine."

I smiled thinly. The raven's terror still soaked my bones and what comfort I took from Sigrun's concern was diluted by Fafnir's closeness.

"What did you see?" asked Ormhildr. Her expression was one of carefully couched concern. She wanted to seem sympathetic but would not wait for answers.

I took another breath and ran my fingers along my wooden arm-ring. The gods were with me. They would protect me.

"I sent the ravens deep into the forest," I began. "The finding spell gave a rough direction from here, from me, so I sent them to search the places Tjorvid told me about. We didn't find anything, so I sent them deeper and I found..."

Suddenly, I felt the weight of Fafnir looming over me. I felt the power granted to him by the gods' ancient enemies like a charge in the air. I wondered why he did not want to go into the forest. Did he have something to do with the shattered god-stone? Could the answer be as simple as his Windborn strength? I had heard of Windborn who could crush pebbles in their palms. There were outlaws in the forest and worse. Perhaps Fafnir was in league with some shadow-Windborn haunting the Trolbjolvid. I remembered Fafnir's hand on Sigrun's shoulder and unbidden I wondered if Sigrun was involved in his Windborn conspiracy? I hated myself for thinking it, but it wouldn't go away.

"I found a body."

Ormhildr's expression hardened, Fafnir's hood twitched, and Sigrun's hand went to her mouth.

"I could not tell if it was Ulfrun," I said quickly, to cut across any questions I would not answer. "It was difficult to make out their face. Their hands were bound and their face bruised."

"A hostage escaping from outlaws?" Sigrun asked.

"Perhaps," said the chieftain. "It wouldn't be the first time. Where did you find them, Alvir?"

I explained the location as best I could and, with Tjorvid's help, we were able to figure out where the body lay.

Ormhildr's frown deepened. "We have to find Ulfrun. If she crossed paths with whoever did this... She's a strong woman, but she's no warrior."

I went to my pack. It had fallen at some point during the ritual. The god-shards were sharp lumps under the cloth and a mix of relief and fear settled at the pit of my stomach. No one had taken them but seeing them again sent fresh terror churning in my belly. Carefully, I checked inside for my waterskin and food then pocketed the rune-sticks. As I picked up my pack, the stones clacked together and I wondered how much more of the god-stone had crumbled.

I had to find Ulfrun.

"Do not fear, Chieftain Ormhildr," I said as I tightened my cloak. The ravens screeched as my anxiety and fear filtered through our connection. "I will travel into the forest. With the gods' help, I will find Ulfrun."

"You cannot go now," Ormhildr said, incredulous.

I looked back into the forest. The night seemed to swell and thicken beneath the canopy. Shadows curled around the black trees like monstrous fingers. I suppressed a shiver as I imagined the blocky, thorny hands of the shadow-creature closing around me. Was Ulfrun already trapped in those clutches?

"I can wait until morning," I said. "But any delay could put Ulfrun in more danger. If he is willing, Tjorvid can accompany me and we will find the body, and then Ulfrun."

The young man tensed as I called his name. Tjorvid picked up one of the wicker baskets as though that could hide him. Ormhildr pursed her lips and looked from Tjorvid to Sigrun and Fafnir.

"Tjorvid knows Ulfrun's routes," I said before Ormhildr could object. "With his knowledge and the raven's help, we should be able to find Ulfrun swiftly."

The chieftain stared at Tjorvid before she nodded, coming to a decision.

"Ormhildr," Sigrun stepped away from the Windborn. "You aren't going to let them go on their own, are you?"

"Speed is of the essence, Sigrun," Ormhildr replied, though the surety in her voice was crumbling. "Ulfrun's been in the forest too long already."

"I'll go with them," Sigrun said. "One more person won't slow them down."

Ormhildr turned to the Windborn, who had taken half a step back as though to keep himself out of the conversation. "How many can we send before their numbers slow them down?"

Fafnir shifted. He looked from the dark woods and then back to his chief. "Ten. Maybe a dozen."

Ormhildr nodded as though this confirmed her suspicions. I shifted, uncomfortable at the thought of being trailed into the forest by this enormous Windborn. If he was in league with the shadow-creature, then there would be nothing to stop him from sacrificing us to it as soon as he could.

"I appreciate your concern," I said. "Truly, I do, but I am not helpless. The gods will protect us." I looked at each of them in turn and smiled and tried to show them more confidence than I felt. "I have travelled the length and breadth of the Fjalmark. There are outlaws everywhere."

Sigrun looked to Ormhildr, waiting for the chieftain to force me to stay, but she couldn't. I answered to a higher authority than chieftains. Instead, she turned to Fafnir. The enormous Windborn looked from my half-sister to the forest. He tried to suppress a shiver then stepped beside me.

"We have lost one god-speaker," Fafnir snuffled. "If you would let me, Chieftain Ormhildr, I will be God-Speaker Alvir's shield."

"You would go so readily?" Ormhildr replied before I could make my sharp denial to Fafnir.

"Yes," he said in a tone that suggested it was the last thing he wanted to do. "But I will need my things. I will not go unready into the deep woods."

That seemed to make up Ormhildr's mind. She straightened and nodded. "There are many dangers in the forest and we will not simply add to the missing. I will speak with Erri and see who we can spare."

I opened my mouth, wanting to object, but the darkness of the forest pressed against my back and the ravens' terror flooded through me. I closed my eyes and felt beneath me for the warm bedrock of the gods' power. It hummed some distance beneath my feet and as the music of it thrummed through me, I felt my mounting frustration ease.

"We must be quick, Chieftain," I said. "We cannot wait for you to muster a warband. Ulfrun is—"

Ormhildr waved my objections aside. "I understand that, God-Speaker, but we cannot let haste overcome caution. We will prepare a proper escort for you and be ready to leave at dawn.

"Fafnir, find Erri and get him to pick some huskalar to send with Alvir. And I would not be against it if Yrsa also wishes to provide some additional protection. Tjorvid, go and speak with Drifa and see if she will gather some supplies and accompany them as well."

I ground my teeth against more objections as Tjorvid and the enormous Windborn nodded. I watched Fafnir as he left. Each hulking step sent a shiver through the ground. With him gone, I wanted to ask Ormhildr why he was so keen to keep us out of the forest.

As I turned, Sigrun stepped up to me.

"You can stay with me, Alvir," she offered. "If you'd like to meet your family?"

"My family?" I asked, incredulous.

"Well, my wife, Ljota, and our children, Ama and Raggi. They'd love to meet you."

My voice caught in my throat. I wanted to cry out and tell Sigrun how much I wanted to meet them and to be part of that family and at the same time I wanted to move her aside and tell Ormhildr about the shadow-creature.

Behind my half-sister, Ormhildr took one last look at the forest and then turned to go. In front of me, Sigrun's cautious smile became brittle, her brief hope calcified by my indecision.

I turned away from Ormhildr and smiled at Sigrun.

"Let's go and see your family."

ᚠ

Sigrun's home was much the same as any other house in any other small town. Its steep roof reached from the ground to a crossbeam at its zenith. Each carved beam stretched high until they became two dragons facing one another. The moss-covered thatch that covered the roof made it seem as though the forest's influence had begun to seep beyond the trees. I braced for an explosion of noise and questions as Sigrun guided me through the door, but it was quiet. We were alone. A flush of thanks washed through me immediately followed by a wave of guilt. I had not seen my half-sister in more than a decade and had met her wife once, yet here I was, thankful to avoid her family for a little longer. Inside was one large room with a small firepit cut into the floor. Two storeys of beds were built into the building frame to the left as we entered and the right side of the room was given over to a table covered in toys, utensils, and small clothes.

"How old are your children now?" I asked, hating that I did not know.

"Ama's nine. Raggi's five. You can put your things over there."

Sigrun made her way to the hearth. The silence pressed against me like the air before a storm as I put my pack and staff beside one of the beds. Dust fell from the roof as the ravens hopped on the thatch and their muffled screeches seemed to draw attention to the awkward quiet inside the house.

"Is that yours?" I asked, pointing to a battered round shield hung on the back wall. Given how Ormhildr had spoken to Sigrun and her friendship with Fafnir, I assumed she was one of Vidsetr's husksalar.

She glanced up and her expression clouded when she looked at the shield. "No. It was Astrid's. Raggi's mother. She and her husband went raiding last summer. They were desperate and needed the money. Only her shield came back."

A raid orphan at five years old. My heart twisted.

I looked back to the shield. Would I have wanted my mother's shield hanging in my home after she died? I did not think so. There had been a constant churn of rage in my heart when my mother's raid companions came back and she didn't. Although I would be grateful for some reminder now back then I may have tried to destroy it in the heat of youth, blaming my mother for her own death. Raggi was five years old. I wondered how much he understood what was happening. Perhaps he thought his parents were still somewhere across the sea making their way back to him. I sighed and prayed that Raggi would treasure the shield and not use it to vent an orphan's frustrations.

I shook off the thought and moved over to the hearth. Sigrun huffed on the embers of a freshly sparked fire.

"How is…" I trailed off as I struggled to remember her wife's name.

"Ljota?" Sigrun kept her eyes focused on the fire. "She's fine. Running around with the children most of the time."

We fell back into awkward silence. Sticks and charcoal crunched as Sigrun placed wood onto the hearth's growing embers. The muffled call of ravens came from the roof and their presence fluttered in the back of my mind. They were still uneasy so close to the forest and it set me on edge.

I sat on the bed, my leg pressed against my pack. The

sharp stones inside prickled my skin and stoked the fear that smouldered at the pit of my stomach. I closed my eyes and tried to focus on the power of the gods, like I had at the god-stone, but the raven's flighty panic kept me distracted.

I shifted, moving away from the pack, and looked around Sigrun's home again. The table had old food stains on it, rough animals were carved into the beams, there were toys scattered across the floor. A few runes had been carved into the beams, but no shrine or space dedicated to the gods. This was a house that had been well lived in. This was a home that was full of tears and laughter and love.

Suddenly, the silence was too loud. I felt a burning ache in my chest to be part of the noise that echoed under this roof.

"Sigrun..." I started.

She turned. Her expression of polite interest turned to serious concern when she saw my discomfort.

"What's wrong?" She stood and took a step towards me, hand outstretched.

I wanted to apologise for everything—for shattering her family as soon as she was part of it, for only appearing when our father died, and for avoiding her in the years after—so that we could start again, so that I could be part of this home and be a part of this family. Now that I sat by my sister's hearth all the lonely years spent wandering the wilds felt cold and hollow.

"I… I should have visited you sooner," I said.

Something sharp came into her eyes, but she smiled. "That would have been nice."

I took her still-outstretched hand and squeezed. It was calloused but still warm and soft and it eased the god-stone fear in the pit of my stomach.

"I'm here now," I said. Sigrun wrapped her other hand over mine and suddenly all my choices seemed clear. "God-Speaker Eylis has invited me to stay with her in Konvald, once this is done."

For a heartbeat, Sigrun's face lit up, then she schooled her expression into polite interest. "You'd always be welcome if you did."

I smiled and squeezed her hands again then she pulled herself free. She looked to the fire and then back to me. It felt like she had more she wanted to say, but instead she puffed out her cheeks.

"Ljota will be back soon. She's probably been running the children around outside collecting firewood or berries or something. Would you help me with this?"

Sigrun motioned to a large pot that was set out of the way and we placed it over the fire. For a while, we pottered around the house, collecting what she needed for whatever meal she was preparing.

It seemed that our brief conversation and the promise of future visits was enough to thaw most of our awkwardness. As we wandered around, Sigrun pointed out the various artefacts of her family. Here, a wooden horse that had been a gift from Ljota's father for Raggi. There, a tapestry that the family was working on together. And there, clumped in the corner with a spear and shield, the sword Ljota gave her on their wedding day. She offered to find the sword she had given to Ljota—our father's. I frowned at that, I could not remember my father owning a sword, but I waved it off. I had no interest in dredging up talk of our spiteful father.

A mixture of pride and guilt swirled within me. The friendly, joyful woman before me seemed to be just as comfortable with her weapons and armour as she was at home. She was a far cry from the reserved fisherman's daughter I had left behind.

I looked back at my pack, stuffed with broken stones, and wondered if I should tell Sigrun about them. My mind bounced between the shattered god-stone and the shadowed forest. The ravens squawked above us.

"What do you think of Fafnir?" I asked.

"Fafnir's great, especially if you need to lift something heavy," she said with a chuckle. "He doesn't rush anything so he can be a bit slow, but he's a good man."

"It doesn't bother you that he's... Windborn?"

Sigrun shrugged as she tipped some water into the pot. "I knew him before he was Windborn. He's had a tough time but he's made the best of it."

"I'm surprised that you have a Windborn here." Given the High King's new enthusiasm for Windborn and that Vidsetr was about a day's travel from the capital, I would have thought any Windborn would be dragged to Konvald.

"We have two," Sigrun said. "Fafnir and Yrsa. She's a bit pricklier than Fafnir, but still a good woman. She's been here forever. Fafnir was offered a place in some king's hall somewhere, but he turned them down. He refused to leave Nal. That's his little sister."

The fire crackled between us. Sigrun tipped vegetables and dried meats into the pot and the soon-to-be-stew began to steam and bubble. With nothing to do but wait. I kept my peace, letting Sigrun choose the pace of conversation as she stirred the pot and then poured us both a cup of ale. Water hissed as it splashed on the hot sides of the pot.

The darting movements of the ravens scurried in the back of my mind. I glanced over to my god-stone stuffed pack.

"Sigrun—"

The door to the house burst open. I leapt to my feet, my empty cup clattering to the floor, and reached for my staff. Two children rushed past me. Sigrun had enough time to move away from the pot so it did not topple over as the children leapt on her. They all fell over in a jumbled heap of laughter, questions, and kisses. I leant my staff back against the bed and picked up my cup as a dark-haired woman stepped through the door. She smiled at her wrestling family but her words fell away when she saw me, whatever softness she reserved for her own home lost in the presence of a stranger.

"Ljota," I said and bowed my head. "It is good to see you again."

The worry did not leave her face and she took a step towards Sigrun, away from me.

"Sigrun...?"

My half-sister spluttered under the landslide of children and managed to surface long enough to explain who I was. The suspicion in Ljota's features softened as I offered her my hand, though it did not disappear.

"Sorry, I was surprised to see you," she said, shaking my hand. "It's good to have you here. Ah, Sigrun's already got dinner started. Excellent. I'm starving. Let me get you a fresh drink."

Ljota plucked my cup from the floor as the children untangled themselves from Sigrun. They giggled and took stock of the room, finally noticing me. Ama was a head taller than Raggi, with dirty blonde hair that matched Sigrun's, and Raggi—wiry and with one of his front teeth missing—narrowed his eyes at me.

"Children," Sigrun said. She clambered onto her knees and put a hand on each of their shoulders. "This is your Uncle Alvir. He's a god-speaker, remember?"

Ama's expression softened, though not completely, and her gaze flitted over my rune tattoos and then to my wooden arm-ring. Raggi edged closer to Sigrun.

"It's alright, Raggi," she said. "He's my brother. He's come to see us and he's going to help find Ulfrun."

I smiled as best I could as Sigrun's words speared through me. The mention of Ulfrun sent the ravens squawking through the thatch and the numb fear in my gut writhed and twisted. The forest's black shadows surged in my mind and I thought I heard the creak and snap of branches.

My fear may have shown as Raggi folded himself into Sigrun, hiding his face, and Sigrun shot me a questioning look as she stroked his hair.

"He's still a bit nervous. He'll come around."

Before I could mollify her—I had seen enough nervous children in the homesteads I visited—Ama hopped up to me. Her hands were clasped in front of her and she leaned forward, staring at my cheeks.

"They're special runes," I said, anticipating her question about my tattoos.

"What are they for?"

"They protect me and give me special gifts."

"Like a Windborn?"

I forced a smile and nodded thanks to Ljota as she passed me another full cup. "No, not like that. They help me do the gods' work. These runes," I touched a finger to my left cheek, "help me weave magic into things for spells and rituals, like your god-speaker. The runes on this side are to protect me from evil magic. And this one," I pointed to the sigil tattooed in the centre of my forehead, "means I can see magic and magical creatures."

Ama's eyes widened. "Like trolls and spirits and dwarves and elves?"

Another knife-twist of fear in my gut. "Well, I've never seen any dwarves or elves, but I have definitely seen spirits."

"Wow! Where were they?"

"Everywhere. Some are small. Some are big. They live in the rivers and the trees and the stones. They are part of everything."

Raggi, inspired by his step-sister's questions, unfolded from Sigrun and came to stand with his sister. I offered him my staff. He reached out nervously as though it would turn into a snapping viper at any moment, but his fear soothed as I pointed out the runes on it and explained each one.

That broke the dam and the evening passed in a chaos of questions, playing children, and a small banquet's worth of food and drink.

Some time after the dinner had been served and whilst the children were being calmed and made ready for bed, I slipped out of the house with my pack. The night outside was brisk, the wind still edged with winter, but my cloak kept me warm. I found a place to sit amongst the scattered debris of a busy life and parenthood and took some of the god-stone shards from my bag.

They clacked as they fell against one another in my hands. I had saved seven chunks and shards of stone from the god-stone of various sizes. One, still in my pack, was the size of my closed fist. A couple were heavy against my palm, just fitting into my hand, but the rest were finger-slivers and spearhead shards. I turned one of the largest over and ran my fingers across the rough rune-grooves. It hardly seemed possible that this had once been part of a god-given monolith. I wracked my memory for some hint of a myth that would help me, but there were no tales of breaking god-stones. The gods had made them not long after the first mortals had been made, when the echoes of the god-war still bounced between mountaintops, and everyone knew that the god-stones would remain until the end of days.

They were timeless sentinels against the wild unknown.

Silent. Unknowable, unbreakable, infallible.

Not unbreakable.

Holding the shard of god-stone in my hand felt like I held the first echoes of the end of the world as though this small stone was the first flutter of dust before an avalanche that would bury all mortals beneath its fury.

I thought back to the shadow-creature in the forest. All the legends said that the Warrior had smashed the trolls' bodies but what of their souls? Perhaps trolls still wandered the dark beneath the trees and had learned to make themselves new bodies using the forest itself.

The door to the house opened and Ljota stepped out, smiling. I shoved the god-stone shards back in my bag, slicing my finger on an edge as I did. Ljota called something back into the house then turned to smile at me.

"Are you alright?" She frowned at me as I sucked the blood from my finger.

"I'm fine, just caught my finger on something. Please, sit."

Ljota smiled and found a seat on a nearby barrel. "Sigrun's putting them to bed. It's my turn but she has to do it whenever she goes away." She looked fondly at the house, door ajar with light spilling out. "Sigrun is always volunteering to accompany the traders to market or the Althing. She says it's to get me or the children presents, but I know you were the reason. She wanted to look for you. She'd always end up talking to other god-speakers to see if they know where you are or what you've been up to. I don't know if the stories get more elaborate on the way home, but from the way she tells it you're some kind of hero, wandering between farms healing the sick."

"I do what I can," I said with a chuckle but didn't meet her gaze. Guilt and regret prickled my cheeks. I thought of the years spent wandering between homesteads, barely a thought given to my half-sister, as she travelled to every gathering she could in the hope of meeting me. "I didn't realise she was looking for me. I thought she would never want to see me."

Ljota frowned at me. "Why wouldn't she? She's always wanted a proper family, Alvir, and you're her family."

I clenched my fists and looked at my white, rune-tattooed

knuckles. "How could she want to see me after what I did?"

"What you... Oh." Ljota shifted and looked out into the night, staring at nothing. "Sigrun's childhood wasn't easy, Alvir, but I don't think she ever blamed you for that. You saved her. If you hadn't been there, she wouldn't have survived."

I didn't say anything. I kept my eyes locked onto the runes tattooed across my hands, runes I didn't have when Sigrun was born.

A giggle escaped through the door beside us.

"She's getting them excited again. They'll never go to sleep at this rate." Ljota sighed and pushed herself to her feet. "Don't be too long, Alvir. You'll catch a chill."

She disappeared inside. There was more laughter and then the quiet murmur of soothing voices.

I pulled my cloak tight as the cold night seeped into me.

The darkness deepened. Somewhere out there was a monster made of shadow and splintered forest. I rubbed my thumb over the cut from the god-stone, wondering why this shadow-creature, perhaps the long-lost ghost of a troll, had appeared over the body in the woods. Perhaps Ulfrun had been captured by outlaws and those outlaws were directed by something older and more dangerous than any mortal. If it had lost her perhaps it had felt my magic, the touch of Ulfrun's blanket in the weave, and appeared to make sure she was dead...

I thought of the legend of the Líkrifa, the axe smithed by powerful troll-mages that was so sharp it had severed the Winds' souls from their bodies, enabling the gods to trap them in the sky. Trolls were masters of magic. If one of them had survived then surely over the centuries they could have figured out how to make the god-stone crumble.

Why now?

I flexed my fingers and watched the runes stretch. Was Ulfrun the key? If this shadow-creature had captured her that might have been the final piece to shattering the god-stone, ending its protection and letting all the myriad forces of the wild and chaos sweep over the gods' mortal children.

I shivered again as fear wormed its way into my heart and

closed my eyes. I let my senses drift down into the earth and brush against the magic there.

It was strong and warm. The gods were still powerful. The god-stone may have shattered but the gods still gave me strength.

The magic soothed my anxiety and warmed my soul in the cold night.

Something clattered from the house and I jerked back to myself.

A fresh, freezing dread seeped into me as I heard Sigrun's voice whispering through the door.

I had just found my half-sister and we had so much time to make up for, yet tomorrow I would drag her into the Forest of Broken Trolls. A place teeming with predators, outlaws, and strange creatures that could rend my magic with a look.

Before I went back inside, I took a deep breath to steady myself and prayed to the gods that I would not be leaving another home without a mother.

Chapter Seven
Into The Forest

I woke up early and was glad for it. I did not mind sleeping on the blanketed floor, I was used to that, but my mind and soul were agitated. Broken dreams of tree monsters and shadow creatures had woken me several times and the constant flutter of the ravens at the back of my mind had kept me from easily falling back to sleep.

The house was quiet but filled with the low tension of someone trying to move silently. I blinked and saw Sigrun carefully placing something under a fur blanket draped across a bench. She froze when she saw me.

"Sorry, I didn't mean to wake you," she whispered.

I waved her off and sat up. "I'm a light sleeper. Why are you awake so early?"

"Just a little ritual before I take a trip." She glanced over to Ljota and the children then shot me a gleefully conspiratorial look. "Come on, let's not wake them."

She led me outside, waiting as I wrapped myself in my dusty blanket, and closed the door behind us as carefully as she could. We sat on a couple of logs that lay near the house.

"What were you doing?" I asked.

"A little fun," Sigrun whispered, a smile curving her lips. "Every time I go away I hide a gift for the children. It keeps them from wondering if I'll come home."

I raised my eyebrows but didn't respond. I didn't know what to say. The casual way Sigrun talked about not returning to her family chilled me far more than the cold morning air.

We sat in silence for a little while and watched the town.

It was early enough that the sun just strained over the mountains. Our only companions were a few errant notes of birdsong, some huffing livestock behind a nearby house, and the rune-linked ravens that fluttered down to join us. The houses, blurred beneath the chill morning mist, faded against the looming forest and I felt a now familiar fear prickle at my skin. Without thinking, I reached out to the gods' power all around us. The ground was soaked with it like mud clogged with water after a storm, the air steamed with the strength of the cold night as it was burned away by the sun, and the sun warmed my skin like a wildfire beginning to take root.

"I like to watch the town before anyone wakes up," Sigrun said. "It's so peaceful."

One of the ravens hopped next to her on the log and she stroked it. The raven clicked its beak and I felt its happiness through our connection.

I thought back to the rune-sticks still in my pack. Three sets, though one was now useless thanks to whatever strange creature I had seen in the forest. I pursed my lips.

"Sigrun," I started.

My half-sister turned to me, smiling. For a heartbeat, I saw something of our father in her. A crooked reflection of his smile, when he had still smiled. My voice caught in my throat at the thought of the time lost to grief and regret and worry. We sat together, for the first time in years, enjoying each other's quiet company. I smiled back and put my hand on hers.

"I'm glad I found you."

Sigrun's smile widened and she put her other hand on mine.

"I am, too."

I kept silent for a few more moments. Sigrun's long, relaxed breath overlapped my own tense breathing.

The mist withered as the day burned brighter and I pulled my hand out from under Sigrun's. "I saw something in the forest yesterday."

A frown creased Sigrun's brow and she cocked her head at me. "What do you mean?"

"By the body. There was something else in the forest.

Something... massive. Whatever it was threw me out of my spell. It cut me off from one of the ravens."

Sigrun kept her serious expression locked onto me as she pursed her lips. "And you don't know what it was?"

I hesitated. "No. It looked like it was made of the forest. It was all broken branches and leaves, but it's hard to make sense of what a raven sees."

She frowned and turned away, looking at the pointed canopy in the distance.

"Do you think the body was Ulfrun's?"

"I don't know." I tried to conjure the image of the body, but the memory was hazy, blurred by the magic of my link and the unknowable colours seen by the raven. "I don't think so."

Sigrun nodded and seemed to consider this. I was impressed by how calmly she processed this information, but I supposed living beside the Trolbjolvid, she was used to dangerous happenings and living with Windborn must acclimatise you to things you did not truly understand. I thought of the god-stone shards in my pack and how worried I had been that any mention of them would cause widespread panic. Perhaps I had been too hasty.

"And there's something else." I sighed and hung my head. "Do you know the god-stone on the road to Konvald?"

"I've seen it from a distance," she said with a shrug. "I've never been there. The kids want to see it someday. They're desperate to visit Konvald."

I watched Sigrun, wondering if I should burden her with anything else, and noticed her staring at the dark forest beyond the homes of her friends. Her eyes narrowed and focused on something I couldn't see.

"Whatever it was you saw," she said, "do you think it has anything to do with Ulfrun's disappearance?"

I chewed my lip and nodded. "I think so. There is something going on in the forest. I don't know what it is but it is dangerous. I think it shattered the god-stone."

Sigrun's head snapped around and she stared at me, wide-eyed. "What do you mean shattered?"

I bent and pulled one of the shards from my pack. It was warm to the touch and if I closed my eyes I could almost believe that I had my hand pressed against a complete, hale god-stone. I passed the stone to Sigrun. She took the shard, cradling it in her arms like it was a newborn. The whites of her eyes shone in the early morning light.

"How?"

The terror I saw in Sigrun's eyes sparked through me and it began to shake my bones. I closed my eyes against it but it kept coming like the first pebble of a landslide and it began to overtake me. Instinctively, I reached out for the gods' power. It swelled with the morning and cradled me in its strength. I took a steadying breath then looked back at Sigrun.

"I don't know." I raised a hand to forestall more questions. "I think Ulfrun may know more and, gods willing, she may be able to help fix it."

Or, I thought to myself, stop the magic from draining away into the depths of the Trolbjolvid.

Sigrun looked from me to the god-stone shard, panic barely constrained behind her eyes, then she shoved it back at me. I placed it back in my pack where it clacked against the other shards.

The mist was almost completely burned away by now and people had begun to wander out of their houses, checking on animals and greeting neighbours. We gazed out over Vidsetr as the townsfolk started their days, unaware of the true danger that lurked in the forest beside them. Then, I saw a lumpy silhouette in the distance.

Ulfrun's rune-woven boulder.

Sounds started from inside the house. Yawns and sleep-thick voices and then the clattering of clumsy hands.

"Sounds like it's time for breakfast," Sigrun said and shot me a hollow smile.

"You go," I said. "It won't be long until we are to meet with Ormhildr and I have something I want to do before we set off."

"If there's something that needs doing I can—"

"There's nothing you can do to help," I said, softening my words with a smile.

Sigrun looked like she wanted to argue, but she settled for pursing her lips. "The children would like to see you," she said. "I'm sure whatever it is can wait so we can have a meal as a family."

I closed my eyes and clenched my jaw against the stab of white-hot guilt as the desperate desire to be part of the family I had just found my way back to collided with the sharp weight of the god-stone shard still heavy in my mind.

"I can't," I said, not daring to look at Sigrun and instead, staring at Ulfrun's distant boulder. "I have too many questions."

ᚠ

As I walked through Vidsetr, I nodded at those few awake at this early hour. They returned my silent greeting with looks of wary deference as my rune-linked ravens swooped along with me, screeching over the soft morning birdsong. I felt my soul settle as though I was coming home after a long journey. How many times had I wandered through new towns and seen that same look on strangers' faces? I strode between their houses as a manifestation of the gods' protection, an extension of their power. This was what I was made for, how it should be, and with every step I felt my old confidence returning. The gods would guide me, no matter what lurked beneath the shadowed canopy of the Trolbjolvid.

I glanced at Ulfrun's home and the edge of the forest but there was no one there. It was too early. Thankful that I would not be spotted by any of my soon-to-be companions, I turned and made my way over to the imitation god-stone at the edge of town.

The stone looked strangely fixed against the ever-swaying branches of the trees. It was as though the stone stood fast against the forest and refused to be pulled into the dance of leaves. Mist still clung to the base of the boulder, despite the strengthening sun, and I felt a shiver run up my spine. The stone loomed over me, perhaps an arm's length taller than myself, glistening with condensation.

I raised my second sight and the magic near-blinded me. The stone shone with a steady but powerful glow and its magic extended down into the soil like roots. I squinted at the ground, trying to follow the magic. It quickly blurred and shivered amidst the power saturating the earth like a weed caught in a muddy river. I knelt and ploughed my fingers through the wet soil. At first, all I could feel was the reassuring weight of the gods' power soaking into the earth, then I caught the strange, but almost familiar thrum of magic from the boulder. It felt like a shuddering reflection of the god-stone magic but flushed with some other strange power like a reflection seen on the surface of a churning river. I dug my fingers in an arc in front of me and frowned. The stone's power spread from the base but quickly funnelled itself in a single direction.

Now that I knew what to look for I could follow the stone's magic without needing to dig at the wet earth. I circled it. On the other side, the magic was the same. As it seeped into the ground it seemed to find a path and flowed down it like a coursing river. The path led from one side of the boulder to the other. It skirted the edge of the forest.

I let my second sight drop and rubbed the dirt between my fingertips. The grainy earth broke apart leaving my hands covered in black spots and the stained water ran down my palms. There were minuscule roots caught between the muddy water and I realised that there were withered mushrooms growing on one side of the boulder. I frowned and plucked one of them from the silty, sodden ground. It was dying, despite the fertile earth around it, and it had faded to the bleached yellow of old teeth. I wandered around the monolith and realised that the mushrooms and the wet earth were only on the forest's side. As soon as the mushrooms stretched across that invisible line, they turned to husks and the mud was dried and cracked.

With a growing sense of unease, I pulled one of the god-stone shards from my bag. This marker at the edge of the forest was big, but nowhere near as large as the god-stone was—or should have been. I looked down at the shard in my hand and then to Ulfrun's boulder. There was a stark contrast in the stones' colours. The god-stone shard was a deep shadow-grey similar to slate, whilst the rune-stone I stood beside was a pale grey and more akin to limestone. Any worry I had that this was a stolen piece of the god-stone faded, but was replaced by fresh fears.

The god-stones protected us from the dangerous magic of the wilds. What dangers were we exposed to now that this god-stone had shattered? I stared along the edge of the forest where this imitation god-stone's power flowed. Why had Ulfrun made this? Did she know that the god-stone would break? If she had, why wouldn't she have told Eylis? The darkness of the forest pressed against my senses and I shivered as I remembered the shadow-creature's sight on me. Had Ulfrun tried to contain and fight that monster herself? My rune-linked ravens screeched as they remembered their terror brought on by the shadow-creature.

"What's got them riled up?"

I jumped at the voice and spun to find Sigrun beside me, her hands raised in surrender.

"Sorry, I didn't mean to sneak up on you."

"It's fine," I said, more harshly than I meant to as I stuffed the god-stone shard back in my bag.

Sigrun frowned at me. "Is everything alright? Did you find your answers?"

"Some." I sighed and stayed crouched over my pack. "And more questions."

Sigrun shot me a look as I stood up as though she didn't know what to say. I waved my hand in an effort to move the conversation on. The only place I could get the answers I needed was from a god-speaker lost in the woods.

I threw my pack over my shoulder and made my way back to town with Sigrun falling in beside me. She was dressed for battle. A shield bounced against her back, an axe slung in her belt, a spear resting on her shoulder.

"What's that?" I asked, pointing to something tied to the spear shaft. It looked like a broken stick covered in randomly daubed lines of bright paint and it clattered against the wood as she walked.

"A gift from the children. Sometimes they like to give me something to keep me safe. A good luck charm, you know? Oh!" Her eyes widened and then she dug a leather-gloved hand into a pouch at her belt and shoved something at me. "They made you one as well."

She held out a small stick for me with string tied around one end. When I picked it up I saw that one side had been scraped clean of bark and burned onto the bright wood were two crude runes. If I squinted then they looked a little like the runes *protection*, and *home*.

"I know the runes aren't good, but they wanted to do something for their uncle. Ama did that rune and Raggi drew that one."

I stared at the wavering black runes. I knew there was no magic in it. How could there be? Even so, I felt the weight of the trinket, the magic of children.

"Thank you," I said and tied the stick onto my belt.

Sigrun's face split into a wide, warm grin. "You can thank them when we get back."

I tried to return the smile but the mention of our journey soured my expression and we walked on in silence for a few moments.

Morning was well underway by now, though it was still early, and the town roused itself awake as people began their chores. A cold breeze swept up from somewhere in the forest and in that instant I desperately wanted to be surrounded by people and let the noise of their lives wash away the fear that gnawed at the pit of my stomach. Instead, we skirted the broad open space at the edge of town and aimed ourselves at the dark trees.

The ground shuddered and, for a heartbeat, my gnawing fear sank its terror-fangs deep into my heart.

"Sigrun. God-Speaker."

I spun to face the voice that rumbled across the open ground like a rockslide. The colossal Windborn Fafnir nodded as he stomped up to us.

The sight of him crunched the fangs of terror deeper into my chest. His face was still shadowed under his hood and with the sun behind him his towering, hulking presence reminded me of the shadow-creature.

"Are you well, God-Speaker?" He planted his mast-tall spear in the ground and shifted the shield—which was as wide as I am tall—on his back. With those subtle movements Fafnir's silhouette returned and the spell was broken.

"I... yes, I'm fine."

He stared at me with his featureless shadow-face then swept his hood towards the forest.

"They have not yet gathered. We should wait here."

"Here?" I asked, incredulous, looking around the clearing of grass. "Shouldn't we wait by Ulfrun's home?"

Fafnir shifted half a step back and his spear clacked against the shield on his back. "Haste is a poor travel companion, friend, especially when we must travel the Trolbjolvid. We should wait for our chief before we step into the woods' shadow."

I was ready to snap at the Windborn, but Sigrun stepped towards him and placed a hand on his barrel-thick arm.

"It's okay, Fafnir," she said. "We'll be fine."

I looked from the horse-broad Windborn to my half-sister, questions surging against my teeth, then Fafnir grunted and set off with clomping steps towards the god-speaker's house.

"What was that about?" I hissed at Sigrun.

Her eyes, ringed with concern, followed Fafnir as he abandoned us. "He died in the forest," she whispered before she trailed in Fafnir's wake.

My heart lurched, my cheeks blanched, and I felt a chill run up my spine as a cloud covered the sun. I thought of all the times I had seen death in my travels across the Fjalmark. It always left a mark on the people who were left behind—the empty spaces, the question half-spoken before they realised there was no one left to answer it, the fear that it could happen to you—and I wondered how deep the mark would be if you survived your own death. What would it take to ask you to face it again?

I shook myself and the god-stone shards dug into my back. Whatever price the gods asked of Fafnir must be paid. It was the price to find Ulfrun and fix the god-stone.

As I hurried to catch up with Fafnir and Sigrun, I took up my rune-sticks once more. With a prayer and a push of will, I pulled the ravens from their lazy circling above me. They descended in a flutter of black feathers, one landing on my staff and the other on my shoulder. They cawed a raven's laugh at Sigrun and Fafnir as the warriors stared at me. Let this be a reminder to them that the gods were with me. The gods would protect us.

The air was thick with tension as we waited. Fafnir wandered to and fro, shifting his spear from hand to hand, until he sat on some barrels beside Ulfrun's house that creaked under his weight.

After a while, Ormhildr strode purposefully from the town with a small crowd in her wake. Her head was bowed in conversation with a man with short-cropped grey hair. He walked confidently and with grace despite the weight of his shield, spear and sword. An experienced warrior, then. Behind them came two more huskalar dressed for war, then a middle-aged woman trailing Tjorvid, Ulfrun's would-be apprentice, both laden with hunting gear.

I watched them with gritted teeth as their weapons, armour, and voices shattered the peaceful morning. The more people that came with us the slower we would be, the less likely we were to find Ulfrun, and the more the god-stone would crumble in my absence.

"Do we need so many, Chieftain Ormhildr?" I called when she was within earshot. "We will travel faster with a smaller party."

The chieftain smiled. "These woods are full of dangers, Alvir. I won't take the risk of losing you as well. What would the gods do to me if I lost two god-speakers?"

I tipped my head at that, forcing myself to admit the truth of her words. Something powerful enough to break my connection to the oak-raven loomed in the forest. I should not be so hasty to turn down an armed guard. If nothing else, Fafnir could wrestle with it long enough for me to get Ulfrun to safety.

Now that the whole group had arrived, we made our way to the edge of the forest and everyone made their final preparations. Fafnir checked a bag so large that it would have fit on a packhorse, Sigrun had brandered over to the huskalar and they checked each other's armour, the hunters checked their bows and knives. Ormhildr kept herself between her people and the forest, watching them prepare with grim determination.

The hunters set themselves a little way away from the rest and I went over to them.

"What is that stone?" I asked the huntress, pointing at Ulfrun's monolith.

"Ulfrun made it a few weeks ago," she said with a shrug. "Said it was to keep Vidsetr safe from something in the forest. I'm Drifa, by the way. Alvir, right?"

She offered me her hand and I took it.

"Did she say what it was?"

"No. I haven't seen anything strange in the forest, and I'm hunting there most days. Ulfrun always was a bit mysterious though. Liked to separate herself from the rest of us."

I nodded as Drifa went back to checking her equipment and stared at Ulfrun's boulder. The weight of the god-stone shards pressed against my soul. A memory surged in my mind of something colossal, powerful, and fractured seen through a raven's eyes for a few heartbeats. I shivered.

"Are you alright?"

"Hm?"

Sigrun stood next to me, concern furrowing her brow.

"You were standing there with a storm on your face."

"Yes, I'm fine, just thinking about... the journey."

"You don't have to come with us, Alvir. Drifa is an excellent tracker and we've got the best warriors Vidsetr can offer. You point us in the right direction and we'll find her. You can stay. Rest with Ljota."

I shook myself and turned so I was no longer facing the distant stone and instead aimed myself at the forest. "I have to go, Sigrun. I need to find out why..." I looked around to see if we would be overheard. "I need to find answers and I think I will find them in the forest."

Sigrun's mouth twisted to show she disagreed but nodded and took a step back, her armour jingling. It was strange to see my half-sister dressed as a huskalar. My mind jarred every time I caught her smile, a smile I had known from its earliest days. I knew huskalar were all edges and blood and splinters. I also knew Sigrun was too joyful for that.

"Oh, no," she muttered. "She's not coming with us, is she?"

Before I could complain that even more people were

joining our expedition, I saw who Sigrun was talking about. Another huskalar approached us, but it was not him that drew the eye. Stalking beside him was a tall, older woman with silver streaks running through her hair like sword slashes. She glanced over the crowd with heavy-lidded eyes as though none of us were worth her concern. An iron armband flashed in the morning light. Another Windborn.

"Yrsa," Sigrun supplied. "Oh gods, she makes me nervous."

"I thought you didn't mind Windborn."

"Well, no, not usually, but she's different. Fafnir's a big guy, but he's straightforward. Her? She can read your mind. It makes me shiver." She turned to me and her eyes raked the runes tattooed on my cheeks. "I don't suppose you have anything that you can do to protect me from it? That's what your runes are for, right?"

I chewed my lip and watched Yrsa and the huskalar join the others. My tattoos should protect me from any incursion into my mind and I muttered a prayer of thanks. If this Windborn could rake my thoughts and know what I had seen in the forest then there would be panic and I was sure Ormhildr would want to delay us so she could summon even more warriors. I turned back to Sigrun, to tell her to stop being paranoid, but the stricken look on her face gave me pause.

"I can do something," I said. "Give me a moment."

I turned away from her and rummaged through my bag, careful to use my body to block the shards from view of everyone else and pulled out my pestle and mortar and a few herbs. It took a few moments as I mixed the herbs with my own blood, but soon, I had worked all the ingredients together into a viscous syrup. The mixture fizzed when I muttered half a prayer to the Lady Syf, the Queen of Spells, and the magic took hold. I dipped my thumb into it and then pressed it hard onto Sigrun's forehead.

"Father, bless this casting. As you guard your knowledge from your enemies guard this mind from those who would seek its secrets."

Sigrun looked up as though she would be able to see her forehead then took a deep breath.

"Thank you," she said with genuine relief flooding her voice.

By now the sun was well on its journey and the chill morning was replaced by the promise of a warm, still day. Townsfolk meandered at the edge of Vidsetr, no doubt to nose a look at the strange god-speaker and his unwanted retinue. They were soon ushered along by other huskalar that wandered between the buildings. It seemed we would not be leaving the town defenceless.

"Okay," called a man's voice. I turned to see the grey-haired warrior raise his hand at us. "Time we were moving. Everyone, get your—"

Suddenly, someone sprinted through the milling crowd and dashed towards us. Everyone turned as a woman called out, and then Ljota was chasing Ama and Raggi as they rushed over to their mother.

Sigrun let her spear and shield fall to the floor and she ran out to meet them. She knelt and the children leapt into her open arms. Sigrun tumbled backwards with the force of it then Ljota was there, breathing heavy and caught between laughter and recrimination.

"What are you two doing here?" Sigrun asked when she managed to get upright. "We said our farewells."

Ama wiped a runny nose against the back of her hand then tucked a lock of hair behind her ear. "Raggi wanted to see you again before you went."

"Yes, it was definitely Raggi," Ljota offered with half a smile.

Ama stuck her tongue out at Ljota then turned back to Sigrun and took her hand. Raggi, for his part, kept his face pressed against Sigrun's chest.

Sigrun turned around to the rest of us, an apology on her face. Everyone was smiling at her but their patience wouldn't last forever.

"One last hug." Ama squeaked as Sigrun dragged her back in for another bear-tight squeeze then she let them both free, although Ljota had to help unpeel Raggi from Sigrun's chest.

"You be good, my sweets," Sigrun said as she stood. "I'm going to make sure Uncle Alvir is safe in the forest. Listen to Ljota and do as you're told."

"Will you bring us back a present?" Ama asked, now clutching to Ljota's side.

"Maybe," Sigrun laughed. "Who knows what strange gifts the forest has for us. Maybe I'll find a tiny troll-brother for you."

Ama's eyes widened and her mouth dropped open. "Gross!"

Sigrun laughed and kissed her again.

"Are you coming back?" Raggi asked, voice almost a whisper, his pale eyes glistening and downcast. My stomach twisted as I remembered the shield at Sigrun's home. Raggi's mother's shield.

"Hey now." Sigrun knelt to face him and cupped his cheek with her palm. "I am coming back, I promise. It's just a walk in the woods. And anyway, I've got your Uncle Alvir to keep me safe, right?"

I looked from Sigrun to Raggi and offered a blunt smile. "The gods will protect us, little one. Who could ask for better than that?"

Raggi nodded, but his expression remained the same. As Sigrun stood and kissed him on the top of his head, Raggi clutched at Ljota's dress. She gave one final smile to her family and collected her shield and spear.

Everyone shifted as they performed one last mental check of their equipment and then turned to face the forest. Ormhildr smiled at us, still standing between us and the dark woods and gestured for us to gather around her. We did. Ten of us in all: a god-speaker surrounded by huskalar, hunters, and two Windborn.

"Friends," she said, looking at each of us in turn. "It is a brave thing that you do. The Forest of Broken Trolls is restless. We have lost many people within its borders this year. Whether this is because of outlaws or something worse, I cannot say. I do know that somewhere in there is our god-speaker. Ulfrun has helped all of us. She's set broken bones, offered us prayers for the lost, and kept us in the gods' favour. She is the heart of this community and I will not abandon her to the woods.

"Erri and I have called upon you to accompany God-

Speaker Alvir because you are our bravest and strongest. We know you will not baulk at whatever lurks in the forest shadows, whether outlaws, wild beasts, or trolls.

"Go with my blessing, for whatever it is worth. May the Father guide your steps, the Mother grant you her protection, and may the Warrior lend your spear-arm strength."

There were murmurs as people touched talismans, necklaces, and uttered their prayers alongside Ormhildr's blessing. I noticed that Fafnir murmured along with everyone else and seemed to be trying to shrink behind the huskalar, but Yrsa remained scowling and silent.

Then, the only sound was the rustle of leaves. It was as though the forest dared us to step into its shadow. I looked at my companions. None looked eager to step into the Trolbjolvid, each waiting for someone else to make the first move.

"Well said, Chieftain Ormhildr," I said, projecting my voice. The ravens squawked and blustered into the air. "The gods are with us. They will guide us and we will soon return with God-Speaker Ulfrun. I swear it."

Ormhildr nodded and stepped back to let us pass.

I shifted my pack, the god-stone shards dug into my back like scrabbling claws, and led the way forward. I strode past Ormhildr, away from Vidsetr and from the broken god-stone and took my first steps into the Forest of Broken Trolls.

Chapter Eight
A Body

At first, the trees kept their distance. The ground was still slick from the morning's mist and there were myriad hoof prints pressed into the wet earth from the cows and pigs that the people of Vidsetr let forage on the undergrowth. Tools leaned casually against trunks or hung on branches for jobs still half-finished. Slowly, we left behind any reminders of civilisation and we walked through the quiet, still forest.

For the first hour or so, the trees were still sparse enough that the warmth of the sun filtered through the canopy and bright light lanced between branches, guiding our way. My ravens swept around us in long, lazy arcs and I bounced between my eyes and theirs as I tried to use them to find our way.

In their eyes, the woods were painted in a strange beauty. It kept my spirits level as it reminded me of the gods' power and the strength that they had gifted to me. Berries flashed like wet stones in the branches. When the ravens looked at each other their feathers were darkest black and saturated with an unknowable rainbow of colours that I knew my human mind would not remember.

Despite the ravens' help, it was not long until I lost my way in the forest. My years of travelling had been over open roads, rivers, and mountain passes, only skirting the forests. On top of this, whatever the shadow-creature had done to my spell had ruined any connection to Ulfrun. No matter how well the ravens could see in the forest I was suffocated by its swaying greenery. Every time I thought I had found a clear path a thicket of gorse soon clawed at me and blocked our way. The fourth time this happened, the stout huntress Drifa pushed her way to the front of our group and asked me where I was taking them. I ground my teeth against an explanation at first. The ravens settled on a branch and laughed at us, but even as I looked through their eyes I couldn't find a way through. The birds had no use for footpaths. They were doing what I asked of them, returning to the body, but as a bird flies. Hadn't they flown over a river and seen a waterfall? How would we cross it? I sighed and tried my best to explain to Drifa where the ravens had found the body. She frowned, but nodded when I mentioned the waterfall. Then she gestured for us to follow her and, after we had backtracked a little way, we were moving.

We fanned out as we travelled and settled into a rough marching order. Fafnir followed a little behind Drifa as she led the way, pushing through the undergrowth like a longship clearing a path through thin ice-sheets. His bandaged hands clutched his spear and shield tight, though no one else had readied their weapons. Then Erri led the huskalar, talking amongst themselves. I followed them and behind me Yrsa, Nal, and Tjorvid made up our rear guard. I shuffled along as quickly as I could, keen to keep myself closer to the huskalar than to the Windborn Yrsa. Her bleak expression made the hairs rise on the back of my neck and I wondered how many thoughts she could hear. Did she hear any impression of my thoughts? Was I silent to her or were my thoughts more like something viewed from a great distance, blurred and unclear but still visible? For his part, Tjorvid's expression was a swirl of dread and excitement which looked almost comical next to Yrsa's stoic scowl.

Every so often, Sigrun fell back from her companions to ask me a question or to try to introduce me to one of the other huskalar, to which I would offer a grunt or half-answer as I focused on my ravens and then she would get pulled into some fresh topic of conversation and rush back to her friends.

More hours passed and the forest closed in around us. The shadows deepened as the sunlight lost the battle against the canopy. The rustle of leaves grew louder as though the trees, furious with us for our trespass, demanded we turn back to leave them in peace. The further we walked the quieter the forest became. Our footsteps crunched on twigs and shards of bark. Branches clawed and snapped as we pushed our way between the sentinel trees.

My mind turned to the shadow-creature. It had looked colossal through the ravens' eyes but, now that we walked the forest and I recognised some of the trees the ravens had flown past, I wasn't sure how large it truly was. To the ravens, everything was bigger. All of us, Fafnir more than any other, looked massive when seen by a raven perched on a low branch. Their sense of size was warped. I ground my teeth as I considered it. Could the figure have been a man? A powerful spell-weaver, certainly, but perhaps nothing more than a man. I clutched the rune-sticks and pulled the ravens closer, setting them circling to keep watch over me and alert me if this man—or whatever it was—appeared.

By mid-afternoon, we came to the low waterfall. A wide, shallow stream bubbled and gurgled over a low, ragged stone shelf. In the dim light, the waterfall looked like threads of magic being pulled down by some water spirit further downstream.

"We're here," Drifa announced over the thrum of water.

"Which way now, god-speaker?" iron-haired Erri asked. He stood straight, unafraid or unaware of the pressing weight of the forest air.

I looked around, though I could barely tell one direction from another, then reached for my rune-sticks. "I will summon the ravens and they will find the body."

"Wait." Fafnir put a gentle, giant hand on my shoulder to stall me. His bandaged fingers must each be as thick as a sapling. "There is blood in the air."

He lifted his head, still hidden by his heavy hood despite the shade, and sniffed. I shook his hand from my shoulder and summoned the ravens. They landed on nearby branches and stared at us with dark, hungry eyes. I prayed to the Father to lend me his wisdom. I told myself that, in this, Fafnir was simply a tool for us to find the body and soon I would send him back to Vidsetr.

"Old blood," Fafnir muttered.

"Weapons ready," Erri said. "Fafnir, lead the way."

The huskalar tightened their grips on their spears and kept the points low and ready. Drifa and Tjorvid nocked arrows to their bowstrings. Yrsa pulled two axes from her belt. I found my knife for whatever good it would be against a shadow-creature. No. There was no shadow-creature, it was the ravens' eyes. Surely all I had seen through their eyes was an outlaw, a mortal man, and a knife would work on any outlaw.

"Come," Fafnir rumbled.

Fafnir led us through the stream and waterfall, which soaked the hem of our cloaks and made them heavy at our backs, and through the undergrowth. We left the deer paths and easy tracks that Drifa had favoured and moved straight through the forest, battling against brambles, ferns and fallen branches at every step. Though we had stalled when I had tried to lead us straight Fafnir's bulk carved through the undergrowth like a plough through soil. I gritted my teeth. Fafnir was a tool for the gods to use.

After a few minutes, Fafnir brought us to a stop with a raised hand.

"We are close," he whispered and pointed to a fern rusted with dried blood.

We glanced around, looking for the body or hidden enemies, and Fafnir, with his Wind-given height, shook his head to show he could not see the body.

"I will find the body," I announced too loudly in the tense quiet. For a moment, everyone held their breath, but there was no change in the forest.

With a moment's concentration, I sent the ravens circling out from us. They cawed with joy, pleased to take to the wing, and once more I saw the forest with their unfathomable vision. I swayed and someone grabbed my arm, though I could not tell who, I muttered a thank you.

The ravens carved a path through the air, weaving through tree trunks and over branches, but for an agonising few heartbeats I found nothing. Then the ravens saw something. A glint on a leaf. The elm-raven cawed. It landed on a nearby branch and cocked its head, bringing the plant into focus.

Dark droplets on a fern's feather-leaf. Blood.

The ash-raven circled the bloody fern and spotted a break in the undergrowth. A line carved by the ritual passage of deer or something similar. It swooped down and I saw that some of the stems of the ferns had been snapped and trampled. Then, there, half on the path, a human figure lying too still.

"I found it. Follow me."

Without waiting, I pushed through the undergrowth and followed the thread of my raven-weave. Without the bulk of Fafnir, I had to snake between the bushes and double back to stumble onto the track further than I would have liked. Even that small diversion turned me around and, without the eyes of the ravens, I nearly tripped over the body in the deep shadows under the leaves.

They lay face down in the dirt with both hands caught under them. Their legs were splayed as though they had tripped and fallen and their head was twisted and pushed into the ground. I crouched beside them and rolled the body over. It was a young man, not long out of his teen years, blond hair caked to his cheeks with a paste of mud and blood. There was thick, rough rope wrapped around his wrists that had once bound him but been roughly hacked through and there was some sort of talisman hung around his neck.

The others came up behind me. Erri and Drifa came to kneel and crouch beside me as everyone else fanned out to form a rough perimeter to keep watch on the forest.

"What killed him?" Drifa asked.

I looked over the body. There were myriad bruises and cuts over his skin and his clothes were torn.

"Exhaustion, perhaps," I said. "His hands were bound, though he seems to have freed himself, and he has many wounds. It seems likely to me that he fled from his captors and eventually succumbed to his injuries."

Erri nodded. "Look." He pointed at the body's side where the ribs sunk like rotten fruit. "Whatever hit him, hit hard.

Maybe that's what did him. Drifa, search around for tracks. Anything that will give us an idea of what happened and where he came from."

Drifa nodded and called Tjorvid over. As she gave him his instructions, his eyes landed on the body. His eyes widened. His face paled.

"That's Arvid," he said. "He went missing a couple of weeks ago. He'd occasionally help Ulfrun with her foraging."

"You sure?" Drifa asked.

Tjorvid knelt beside the body and wiped some of the muck from its face. He opened his mouth, then closed it, and nodded.

Shock rippled through the group. Some of the huskalar, torn from their guard duties, turned to study the body before muttering a prayer. From the look of horror plastered across Tjorvid's deathly pale face, he had known Arvid well. The death shook him and he did not move until Drifa helped him back to his feet.

I closed Arvid's eyes and spoke a prayer for him, hoping that the gods would hear me, even in this dark place.

As Drifa and Tjorvid fanned out to look for tracks the atmosphere of the forest pressed against us. The ravens cawed from their perches above our heads. They shifted from branch to branch. Their heads whipped around at the smallest sound. They were terrified. Every twitching twig could be another shadow-creature and they would be lost, like the oak-raven.

Their terror seeped into me with each broken squawk. The shuffle of leaves around us suddenly felt deafening as though it could hide the approach of outlaws or wolves or monsters as they slithered through the undergrowth.

Panic rose in my chest. I took a deep breath but my lungs weren't large enough to hold it so I sucked in another and another but it still wasn't enough.

I closed my eyes and the ravens' vision flickered inside my eyelids.

The forest glittered with unknowable colours. It was like my second sight. My god-granted power.

That was enough to dam my swelling terror.

The gods were with me. They would protect me.

When I opened my eyes I was alone by the body. Drifa and Tjorvid had fanned out to look for tracks as Erri went to speak with his huskalar. I looked at the talisman around Arvid's neck. It was a cord of rope strung through a hole worn into a pebble. A simple rune-stone, I thought, then I saw the dark stain of old blood and something else.

I summoned my second sight. Magic clung to the rune-stone like heat to charcoal in a dying fire, swirling with a complexity that belied its small size. Whoever had made this was a skilled and powerful rune-weaver.

The blood on the stone was Arvid's and it had mixed with the rune painted onto the pebble and concealed the smaller runes scratched into it. *Darkness. Deception. Forest. Shadow.* The runes' magic twitched and pulsed together like a beautiful tapestry. The magic here helped to hide Arvid from sight, magical or otherwise, but with his death his life no longer fed the spell. Not only that, but the rune-stone also had been created to hide him within the forest. If Ulfrun had made this for him she had done so specifically to keep him hidden whilst he was within the Trolbjolvid.

"I found some tracks," came Drifa's voice. "It looks like Arvid's and... something big."

We crowded over to Drifa. She knelt a little way off the deer-track and pointed to a depression in the ground about the size of a roundshield.

"Those can't be tracks," I said, praying that Drifa was wrong. "It is too big."

"Whatever made it was bloody massive, I'll give you that," she said. "But it's definitely a footprint. There's more. Going deeper into the forest. And you see the branches over there? Snapped like something crashed through. The trail goes the same way as Arvid's. It looks like it was chasing him."

Muttered prayers and oaths bounced between us.

Erri knelt beside the footprint, scowling. "Where did it go?"

"I don't know. We followed the trail a little way, but it starts up from nowhere. They lead here and then they... stop."

Drifa showed Erri the trail, its mysterious beginning and

abrupt end, and I let the group jostle me out of the way as the last of the huskalar came to see the enormous footprint. Sigrun's eyes were wide. With one hand she gripped her spear and with the other she clutched the charm her children had given her. We locked eyes and she stepped over to me.

"What is it?" she whispered once we were away from the others.

"I... I don't know." I glanced back at the footprint and the shattered foliage around it. "Sometimes spirits can make bodies out of objects, like feathers or stones or even ice, but it needs the help of a rune-weaver and an incredible amount of power to bind them even for a short time."

Sigrun chewed her lip. Her eyes darted from the huskalar to the footprint then to Fafnir's distant, boulder-silhouette—perhaps wondering if they would be able to fend off whatever monster made that footprint.

"Could Ulfrun have done it?"

I shook my head. "If I wanted to give a spirit a body, say a cat-sized one, I would be bedridden for days afterwards. To give a spirit a body of that size? You would need the strength of the gods to do that. And however skilled Ulfrun is with runes, she cannot have that much raw power."

Sigrun did not look convinced. She looked around into the darkening forest and said, more to herself than to me: "But who knows what's hiding in the Trolbjolvid?"

Her voice faded as Erri and Drifa returned, but Sigrun's words echoed louder and louder in my mind. I went back to the footprint and felt fresh fear run up my spine. The shadow-creature's feet were as thick and round as tree trunks, though more roughly shaped. Leaves and twigs had been crushed into the ground and yellow mushrooms were squashed at the edges of the footprint. I thought of the monolith at the edge of Vidsetr and how much it had looked like a leg. According to the myths and sagas, trolls were legendary spell weavers, almost a match for the gods in skill and power. It would be an easy thing for a troll to snap my magic like a dry twig. Surely, if a troll-spirit still wandered the heart of the Trolbjolvid, it could build itself a new body from wood and stone.

The huskalar whispered amongst themselves as Erri,

storm-faced, looked between them. His eyes found me and he gestured to the colossal tracks.

"Do you have any idea what this is, God-Speaker?"

I looked at Arvid's rune-stone, still clutched in my hand: a talisman that had proven too weak to save him.

All eyes were on me. I saw in their faces the same fear that clawed at my heart, but theirs was etched deeper. They stood in a forest that had grown from the darkest legends and now there was something out there killing their friends. Every face pleaded with me for reassurance, desperate for me to name whatever this was, to solidify this formless threat into something they could comprehend.

"I'm not sure," I said.

Wood creaked as hands tightened on spear shafts, but no one said anything. They let the silence stretch, hoping, praying I would fill it.

I locked eyes with Sigrun. She knew these people better than I did. Would they cope with the fact that deathly legends now walked the forest?

I prayed that Sigrun knew what I was asking her. We stared at each other before she gave me the slightest nod.

I swallowed and turned back to Erri.

"It could be a troll."

Chapter Nine
Forest Spirits

There was a wave of furious whispers at my announcement. The huskalar shook their heads. They asked me if I was serious. They asked Sigrun if I could be trusted, if I was telling the truth. She looked at me, fear still brimming in her eyes, and said I could and I was.

Erri kept his gaze locked on me as everyone else milled around in a miasma of confusion and fear and anger. After a few moments, he raised a hand and the voices faded to quiet, leaving only the creak of the trees and the hiss of wind.

"How could it be a troll?" he asked.

I straightened, trying to dampen the fear that pummelled inside my chest and project an aura of authority. "It is possible for spirits to be given bodies." My voice faltered under the weight of everyone's eyes and the pressure of the forest around us. The gods were with me. I cleared my throat. "It takes great skill and considerable power to make a body for a spirit. I have seen one skilled rune-weaver achieve the feat twice. A body made of bird bones and feathers for an air spirit and a pile of pebbles for an earth spirit. These were small things, though, and the power needed to bind the spirits to their new bodies—even for a short time—left the rune weaver bedridden for a day."

Erri frowned and glanced back at the footprint.

"I know," I said. "There are spirits in this forest, but they are the same as spirits everywhere. Small, difficult to direct, and hesitant to leave their home. But the trolls of legend... Their skill and strength in magic was nearly unmatched. If one of the spirits survived, then..."

I trailed off and gestured to the crater.

"Why?" Erri asked, shaking his head. "Why would they kill him?"

No one answered. The ravens shifted and screeched. Their minds stabbed at the back of my skull as I fought their instinct to peck out Arvid's eyes. I sent them away with a twist of will and the forest silence smothered us.

"He had rope around his wrists," Drifa said. "Maybe they wanted him alive but he got free. Maybe they killed him to keep him quiet."

A blood sacrifice. Did they want to use Arvid to bind themselves to their new bodies? The thought curdled to nauseous terror within me.

I glared at the blood-smeared rune-stone in my hand then offered it to Erri.

"Ulfrun could have freed him. Someone was trying to hide him with this rune-stone. It is bound to Arvid and the runes hide him, but only in the forest. Perhaps she sent him to find help."

Erri looked down at the bloody stone and then back to me. He squeezed it.

"Can they use the body?"

They. The trolls. I could not blame this stout-hearted huskalar for not being able to say the word. I could still barely believe it.

I shook my head. "They left the body once. Why would they return for it?"

Erri nodded, his gaze unfocused as his mind wove plans for us. I looked at my companions. Sigrun hovered nearby, one hand still clutching her charm, and the other huskalar churned about uneasily. They kept their weapons ready and their eyes darted between the countless shadows.

The Windborn made their way back to us. I hadn't noticed any signal to recall them but perhaps they had grown weary of wandering alone.

Yrsa, sharp-limbed and scowling, glanced over the crater footprint without so much as a flicker in her expression. Surely she had heard the fear in her companions' minds like the never-ending whisper of a distant river. When Fafnir approached the footprint I heard his sharp gasp. Even beside his enormous frame, the footprint looked colossal. He muttered something that I couldn't make out in his strange, half-slurred voice then his head whipped around as though the shadow-creature was creeping behind him and he gripped his spear hard enough that the wood creaked.

"What do we do now?" Yrsa snapped. She clipped off each word as she spoke, as though she were annoyed she had to speak at all.

Erri's jaw clenched and he looked over at her but said nothing. He looked from the Windborn to the footprint to the huskalar then to me and back to the Windborn. His muscles bunched when he looked at the footprint and I could imagine the terror-soaked thoughts swirling in his mind. I glanced at Yrsa, but her expression revealed nothing.

Erri sighed and straightened. No longer a hesitant man but a steady leader. Everyone caught the change in the air and they gathered around him.

"I never thought I'd see something that could go toe to toe with Fafnir but the Trolbjolvid is a strange place. From the looks of that footprint and what it's done to Arvid, it would kill us as quick as we could make a shield wall." He paused, scratching the silver stubble on his chin. "But it could have Ulfrun somewhere out there along with the gods only know how many others."

People shifted, unsure if they were being asked to charge headlong into the Forest of Broken Trolls after some half-mythical enemy. From the hardness in some of the huskalar's eyes, some were willing to go on but the tracks and Arvid's half-crushed ribs had blunted their enthusiasm with fear. Most, however, had terror writ clear on their faces and were ready to flee.

"It will do us no good to die out here in the forest. So we head back. We can bring Arvid's body back to Vidsetr and lay him to rest. Then we gather all the warriors we can. Maybe Ormhildr will be able to convince the High King to send another Windborn. Then we can come back and rescue Ulfrun."

Tension leached out of everyone like air from a sail. No one looked more relieved than Fafnir who sagged and let out a long breath.

Slowly, the group shifted, hefting their spears as they half-turned back in the direction we had come.

I looked down at the crater footprints filled with crushed roots and flattened leaves and with yellow mushrooms sprouting from its side. My heart thundered at the thought of facing that shadow-creature, the troll-revenant, but I could not turn back. If the shadow-creature was responsible for the shattered god-stone, if it truly was a troll reborn after countless ages, then what damage might it do unchecked? There was no time to waste. I could not abandon this. Perhaps alone, weaving myself a rune-stone to keep me hidden, I could escape the notice of the shadow-creature. I could find Ulfrun and together we would fix this.

I let them make their small movements to leave and waited until two people crouched next to Arvid's body, looking at how best to bundle him home. I let the decision settle in their bones, hoping they would not rescind it.

"I cannot go with you," I said. "You go back—Arvid's body must be recovered—but Ulfrun must be found. Alone, I will travel faster and be harder to track."

"Fuck that," Sigrun snorted. "I'm not letting you go off on your own."

"Sigrun, please," Erri said, raising a hand. "God-speaker, this is not something for a person to do alone. Not even one so favoured by the gods as you."

My jaw bunched. I looked around. Sigrun's shoulders were tense as she gripped her spear, looking between Erri and I to see who would win out. The other huskalar stood nearby, eyes alert to any danger from the forest and with one ear on our conversation. Yrsa stood next to Fafnir, who was at the front of the group already ready to leave.

"Fafnir," Erri called. "Can you find a trail?"

The Windborn did not react. He stood, hooded face turned to us, before he dragged himself back to the footprints. He knelt and leaned his head close to the ground. I heard him sniff.

"There is no scent. Only the smell of stone and tree."

"I can find her." I tried to keep the frustration out of my voice. The gods were with me and I did not need the help of a fearful Windborn, no matter how large he was. How could they not see that I was their only answer? The gods chose me. "The rune-stone she made for Arvid is a powerful charm to keep him hidden, linked by blood. I can use the same magics to hide myself and to find her."

Silence.

Erri looked at me then to the tracks and finally to Arvid's body.

The buzz of insects and hiss of leaves scratched at my ears. I ground my teeth in frustration. The god-stones in my bag dug into my back with my every movement. The press of them an accusation that I was moving too slowly.

"I know the danger now. Ulfrun was likely caught unawares. If I—"

"I am sorry, God-Speaker Alvir, but no. I will not abandon you in this evil place. We have lost Arvid and Ulfrun is still somewhere in the forest. What if this creature finds you too? You must come back with us."

Sigrun came to stand next to me and put a hand on my shoulder. "Come back with us, Alvir. We can gather our strength and you can spend some time with your family."

I smiled at her and squeezed her hand. She smiled back at me, but it faltered when she saw the resolve in my eyes. I shifted the bag on my shoulder and the shattered stones inside it clacked together. I hoped that she understood why I could not stop.

"I cannot go back," I said, turning away from Sigrun. "The gods have set me on this path."

Sigrun squeezed my shoulder. She turned to Erri. "I'll go with him. You can go back if you want, but I'm not going to abandon him."

Erri pinched the bridge of his nose. "You can't go off into the forest on your own."

Sigrun bristled and snapped a retort but I let their voices fold into the hum of the forest.

I looked around at the men and women around me.

How much longer could we stand here and argue? How long would it take for the High King, travelling as he was, to send help to their little wood-side town? Their caution would doom them, but I could not tell them that their god-stone—the gods-given anchor that protected civilisation from the wild spirits and revenants and trolls—had shattered. They would break down in terror. Reason would disappear like water boiled away in the sun and there was no telling what they would do.

We could not debate any longer. I needed to find Ulfrun and, with her, undo whatever had happened to the god-stone. I could not delay.

"I will send word to Vidsetr," I said. Everyone turned to me. "I can send one of the ravens back. We can write a message and let the raven carry it to Ormhild then it will guide them here to Arvid's body when they are ready to claim it. If you will not let me press on alone, then we must go together. The forest holds many secrets, the Trolbjolvid more than most, but we cannot let it force us into inaction. Your god-speaker is out there somewhere and we must find her. We cannot run from this. The gods would curse us for our cowardice."

My words bounced between the trees and the only sound was the sway and hush of the leaves and skittering birdsong. Sigrun looked uneasy, but everyone else had turned to see how Erri would receive my speech. He looked at his companions and then to me, caution and fury warring in his eyes as he balanced the need to care for his people over my accusation of cowardice.

He sighed.

"Perhaps you are right, god-speaker. I would not be able to live with myself if we found Ulfrun's body like this, knowing that we could have saved her if we had moved more swiftly. If you can get a message to Vidsetr, to tell them of our plans and show them to Arvid's body, then we continue. Agreed?"

Everyone nodded. Fafnir's shoulders slumped then he picked up his spear from where it lay against a tree and stood to attention. The huskalar all wore serious expressions but none backed down. Despite the indecision and uncertainty caused by the enormous footprints, these were warriors and now they had been set to the task they took to it with grim determination.

As the warriors and hunters prepared to follow Arvid's tracks I pulled apart my rune-sticks. Once three, I now had two and I was even abandoning one of those. I plunged the ash rune-stick into the earth next to Arvid's body. The ash-raven fluttered down and cawed at me, interested in what I was doing with its rune-stick. I pulled a scrap of cloth from my bag and drew a quick message into it with a lump of charcoal. There was not much room, but I wrote of Arvid's body and instructed whoever read the message to follow the raven into the forest. Then, as I pushed magic through the ash-raven's rune-stick, I gave it my final commands: fly back to Vidsetr with the message and then lead the people there to the body. The raven would be inexorably pulled back towards its linked rune-stick and the draw of the magic would overcome its fear-drenched memory of the shadow-creature.

By the time I had done that, the others were ready. Erri nodded to me and called out fresh instructions.

"Drifa, Fafnir, follow Arvid's trail, but be wary. Everyone else, keep an eye out for trouble."

"Tjorvid, follow me." Drifa nudged the young man as she walked past. Throughout all this, Tjorvid had stayed close to Arvid and the footprint, sometimes wandering away in disbelief but always drawn back to them. Some of the colour had returned to his cheeks, but the harrowed look had not left his eyes. Drifa nudged him and he started, then followed her without a word.

Sigrun sidled up to me as we all made our way away from Arvid. "Are you going to be okay with one raven, Alvir?" she whispered. "We can always try and find you another bird on the way."

"It's fine, Sigrun. With this raven and the gods' help, we will prevail."

She looked unsure but didn't press the issue.

Our trackers moved to the front of our pack. Drifa kept her eyes focused on the ground with Tjorvid trailing her like a shadow. Fafnir walked behind them, pausing to sniff the air every so often. I clenched my jaw at the slow pace, but then I passed the footsteps of the unknown creature. Once again my mind whirred back to the stone stood outside of Vidsetr and the looming shadow-creature. As we walked into the forest's depths, I felt a flash of cold terror in my belly at every clump of branches and overgrown boulder, waiting for another shadow-creature to raise itself and attack.

I took a breath. The gods were with me. I could not fail because they were with me and their power was my power. They had defeated all trolls that stood against them and I would prevail with their help.

Even in my mind, the words felt small against the vast, shadowed reaches of the woods. I swallowed and forced myself to steady my breathing. I pushed my awareness into the earth, reaching for the gods' power. It was there, as I knew it would be, and my heart slowed its panicked pounding. The gods' magic hummed in the earth, low and powerful veined like marble with flashes of the smaller power of other spirits. My breathing eased.

It spread out beneath me and lifted my soul like the warmth from the hearth after a long, cold journey with the small spirits' magic leaping like a fire's sparking embers.

As I let myself bask in the familiarity and safety of the magic around me I realised there was something else within it. A ragged, torn thread within the weave. It felt like cold, fetid water dribbling across my skin. I shivered and focused on the gods' soothing and familiar strength, but this skein of discordant power flowed across my skin and I felt like I was drowning.

With a gasp, I pulled myself free. I swallowed and looked furtively around. Now I had no doubt there was a dark power hiding deep in the woods.

ᚠ

Hours passed as we wandered through the thin trunks and stretching boughs of the trees. The forest seemed unending, unchanging. More than once I wondered if we were walking in circles as the trees began to blur and meld together in my mind. The endless green surrounding me felt like it did not change, no matter how quickly or how long we travelled. I was stuck in a moment between bark and pine needles. More than once I raised my second sight to make sure there was no spell upon us to force us to travel in circles. There was no weave keeping us in place, only the bright life of the forest all around us and the frightful flashes of that dark, stagnant power.

We walked past tree after tree, trudging through the undergrowth, the bark began to blend together in my mind and the longer all I saw was bark and shadow the more I began to feel as though we were frozen in a moment, like we were trapped inside an ancient glacier and the only sense of movement came from the light rippling through the ice.

Each time my bag hit my back I felt the god-stones' sharp edges. They cut against my soul. My breath came a little faster and heat rose to my cheeks.

The trees passed. We walked on. We made no progress.

Some unending time later Erri raised a hand. He had called the hunters back and now he turned to us.

The forest was dim. An early dusk had settled, although true night would not be upon us for some time, and the green around us was soaked in amber twilight and dusky evening.

"Time we made camp," Erri said. "I'll not have us crashing through the undergrowth in the dark. Drifa and Tjorvid will find us somewhere to stop."

Fafnir fell back, some tension falling away from his shoulders, and let Tjorvid take his place. Drifa and Tjorvid melted into the undergrowth.

Sigrun appeared at my shoulder. "Are you okay, Alvir?"

"I'm fine. The forest feels like it will go on forever, that's all. Do you think we are close to the end of Arvid's trail?"

She shrugged. "I don't know. Let's ask."

She turned away from me and before I could stop her she had called over the massive Windborn.

"What is it, spear-kin?"

"Do you think we're close? Alvir's wondering."

Fafnir turned his deep-hooded face towards me and shrugged his mountainous shoulders. "I do not know. The trail winds and breaks. It is hard to track or say how long it may last. It feels like the land denies us. It tries to shake off any mark of Arvid's passage."

"Do you have much experience tracking?" I asked. I had never heard of the land denying the marks made upon it. "Perhaps you are not used to tracking so deep in the forest."

"I do not come into these woods, but I hunt. I track." There was a tension in his voice and he clenched his half-bandaged fists. Sigrun put a hand on his arm and he let out a breath and tapped his hidden nose. "Few can flee my nose, god-speaker. Do not fear. We will find Ulfrun. Haste will not aid us, but we will not slow."

I looked between my sister and this Windborn and shifted the weight of my bag on my shoulders. Stones clapped together. "Haste may be the only thing that saves Ulfrun."

Nearby, leaves and branches crackled. All weapons snapped to the figures emerging from the darkening woods. Drifa held up her hands as she stepped through the foliage.

"I've found a place a little way off," she said. "It's a bit cluttered but it's hidden."

Erri nodded and we followed her to a clearing overshadowed by a fallen tree trunk. Half-dead bushes littered the clearing along with long-dead branches from the fallen tree.

"This'll make a good camp."

Without any further instruction everyone set to their tasks. Some began to collect dry wood for a small fire, whilst others set about clearing a central space for us to sit. Even Tjorvid had something to do as he began to prepare a couple of rabbits he had caught on the day's travel for the cookfire. I stood, watching, leaning on my staff, but with nothing to contribute. The young huskalar Nal, who it turned out was Fafnir's sister, and the older huskalar, Laufey, laughed as they hunched over the fire so I strode over to help, eager to show them I could be of some use. Even as I reached for my tinder and flint they coaxed an ember from between the kindling and soon the flames wriggled their way free of the shadows.

"Alvir, sit by me."

Sigrun gestured me over to where someone had dragged a

heavy branch, angling it towards the new fire like a bench. For lack of anything better to do, I made my way over.

Laufey pushed himself up from where he crouched by the fire and sat on my other side. For a moment, we watched the camp, Fafnir and Yrsa had been sent to watch the perimeter, Nal and Tjorvid sat off to one side, their shoulders almost touching, and the bustling wave of activity calmed as everyone else took their places around the fire and made ready to rest.

"Sigrun tells me you're a powerful rune-weaver," Laufey said as he nudged me with an elbow.

"I have what powers the gods see fit to grant me."

"He's being modest," Sigrun said from my other side. "You saw what he did with those birds. He's one of the best."

"I'm not the only god-speaker who can form a link with animals. Have you heard of Viggo Hallrson? He has spent years perfecting his rune-weaving to connect himself to a bear he found as a cub."

"Oh yeah!" Laufey rocked back in his seat. "You remember, Sigrun? That skald sung that song about his bear, Kala. It smashed all those soldiers in the Spinefell."

"That was a good song," Sigrun admitted. "But you know how exploits get exaggerated when you sing them. We've seen what Alvir can do with his birds. We know that's true."

"Can you do it with other birds?" Nal asked. "What about an owl? You could send it to find Ulfrun while we slept." She wore the open expression of youth, trusting and eager, but I still saw how easily she handled the spear in her hands.

"It can be more difficult with other birds," I said. "Ravens are blessed by the gods so take to magic more easily."

Nal nodded, disappointed.

"He can do more than that though," Sigrun said and pointed at the rune I had painted on her forehead. "This is so that Yrsa can't read my mind."

Nal frowned, but Laufey's eyes widened with awe as he leaned around me to see.

"Really?" he said. "Can you do one for me?"

"Of course," I said, raising my voice a little to be sure Nal heard. "It would be an easy thing."

Before anyone could respond Erri came and sat by the fire.

"What's an easy thing?" he said with a forced neutral tone.

"Giving us all runes so Yrsa can't read our minds," Sigrun said.

Erri frowned at the mark on Sigrun's face then looked to me. "You don't need runes to protect you from Yrsa," he said with the patience of a man who has said this all before. "She's fought with you how many times, Sigrun? And I don't know how many times she's saved my life because of her Windborn gifts. Alvir, I appreciate you wanting to help, but if we all wear that rune then we will lose one of our greatest advantages. If Yrsa can hear our thoughts she knows how we're going to fight and if we're struggling and she can come and save us."

"Do you not trust the gods to save you?" I said. I picked a twig from the ground and rolled it between my fingers. "It is their gifts I share with you. Not poisoned power from the Winds."

Nal flashed me a sharp look and Erri offered me a tired smile, something hard in his eyes.

"I pray to the gods every night, god-speaker," Erri said, "but they have never stood beside me in a shield wall. Yrsa has."

I snapped the twig and let its pieces fall to the patch of pine needles at my feet. I looked to Sigrun, hoping to get some support from my half-sister but she would not meet my eyes. A look of guilt and chagrin moved across her face as she pursed her lips. I ground my teeth.

We turned at a snapping of branches as Fafnir and Yrsa returned to our camp.

"We are safe," Fafnir rumbled then he slumped down onto a log with a creak of wood.

"There's no one about?" Erri asked. He had pulled a knife and used it to jab at the rabbit above the fire.

"No," Yrsa replied. "If anyone gets close, I'll know."

I traced the runes across my cheeks, glad for the gods' protection. Fafnir sat by Nal, his sister, and Yrsa sat next to Erri. The awkward silence stretched out, seemingly amplified by the crack and spit of the flames and the gossiping leaves above.

Yrsa sighed. She looked at Erri and he shrugged and I realised Yrsa was responding to his thoughts.

"I don't want to listen," Yrsa said. "I know you're private with your thoughts, Sigrun, and I keep clear of your mind whenever I can."

Sigrun kept her eyes locked onto her boots. "I know," she said, her cheeks glowing with embarrassment. "I only meant—"

"Is that what the mark on your head's for?" Yrsa asked. There was a quiet thread of something I did not quite understand in her voice, perhaps incredulity, perhaps hurt.

"It is," I said, loud enough to cut across Sigrun's stammered explanations. "I don't know what strange powers the gods' enemies have gifted you, but my sister asked for my help and I gave it."

My words stirred up a fresh tension in the camp and all eyes flitted between me and the Windborn. My pulse quickened, pounding through my veins. What if they decided to attack me? Could the Winds control them? Would the Winds use them to rid the world of a god-speaker?

Nal had tightened her grip on her spear and her frown deepened into a scowl. "Yrsa and Fafnir are here to protect us. There's gods only know what wandering around in this forest and I'm glad we've got their strength to help us. You brought along a couple of ravens and you've sent one of those away."

Nal's grip twisted on her spear and I thought she would try and stab the elm-raven, but Sigrun started to her feet.

"Don't talk to my brother like that," she growled. "His ravens found the body, didn't they? We wouldn't even know where to look if he hadn't done his ritual. You think, because you—"

"That's enough!" Erri threw a pebble into the fire and the flare of sparks, coupled with his shout, cut the argument short. "It's been a long day. We're all tense. Tove, Sigrun, you take first watch. Everyone else, eat and sleep."

Sigrun stood, hands clenching, then moved to join the other side of the fire. Tjorvid swapped the rabbit for the second and offered them both a leg as they made to leave. The air lay heavy across our camp. The fresh rabbit dripped fat and blood onto the fire making it sizzle and flare.

Fafnir stood, tearing up what was left of his bread and throwing it on the ground for the elm-raven.

"I will keep watch for a while longer," he said. "Tove, Sigrun, eat. Fetch me when you are done."

They thanked him and sat back down. Sigrun offered me her rabbit leg but I waved it away.

Fafnir's heavy steps clomped across the camp and as he passed me he let loose a great sigh and his shoulders slumped.

"It is not an idle thing we do, god-speaker, to go so deep into the forest. We have all lost things in its depths and we risk more with this journey. But we will go. We will follow you and your raven. We go to save our friends."

The words twisted in my gut. He was not the sharp, repugnant Wind-driven warrior I had expected. His voice seemed to rumble through the ground and thrum into me and with it I felt his earnestness. I wanted to apologise, but he was already moving away, I was being offered a drink, and the moment passed.

I took a swig from the waterskin then passed it along. Tension still hung in the air—clear from the hushed conversations full of forced jokes and too-quick laughter—but it was from more than my near-confrontation with the Windborn.

I summoned the elm-raven and as it fluttered onto my shoulder silence fell over the camp. I smiled awkwardly at Nal from across the fire and pointed to the runes on my cheek.

"My runes give me some sense of sight through darkness. I think I may be able to do the same for the raven. It won't be as good as an owl, but it will be something."

She nodded, but didn't meet my eyes, unwilling to forgive me completely, and went back to her food. The other huskalar watched with interest. I raised a hand to forestall any questions and set to adding more threads to the magical weave connecting me to this final raven.

As I lowered my senses to take in the weave of the spell, I winced. The slicing separation of the oak-raven had sundered many of the threads. These untethered strands of magic drained the power from the spell. The separation of the ash-raven was neater, but still weakened the casting. The spell had drawn from the power of the First Ravens, mirroring those three immortal birds with three of my own, but now I had one.

I folded the sundered threads back into the spell and felt my grip on the elm-raven strengthen. Then, with a careful application of will and adding a few runes to the already busy rune-stick, I gave the raven true sight in the darkness. I prayed to the Father, first of spellcasters, and to Lady Syf, the First Weaver, Queen of Spells, that this would work. The runes would give human eyes sight in the darkness, but a raven's eyes already saw so differently I could not be sure.

Everyone was staring now. I closed my eyes against the weight of their expectations and, hands gripped tight on the rune-stick, let myself fall into the elm-raven. It rose from my shoulder with a triumphant screech.

I took a deep breath, feeling both mine and the raven's chests swell with air. My lungs filled with the scent of woodsmoke, the sweat of my companions, and blood-soaked herbs. The elm-raven smelled clear, cool air laced with the sticky scent of pine. The gods' power thrummed through my mind. Caught within the weave there was no space for doubt. The gods had placed me here. I would find Ulfrun and fix the god-stones.

The raven's sight cut into the gloom, though not entirely. The trees were outlined in those strange, nameless colours and they shimmered with their own magic. I sent the elm-raven spiralling out from the camp, darting cautiously from branch to branch and tree to tree, and soon it found Arvid's trail.

The night-drenched forest passed under my raven wings and I felt my mind drifting from the raven's as the trees blended into one and all I could see was night.

A flicker of something between the trees. Light.

The elm-raven landed on a branch, cocked its head.

Some distance away a clear light flickered between the trees. Not the calm, dancing flames of a campfire but something different. Whatever it was undulated and pulsed with a ghostly blue light. It went out. No. It moved, momentarily blocked by a tree and then reappearing on the other side.

I sent the raven closer. A fluttering hop to the next tree then the next.

The flickering light kept up its steady pace, seeming to blink in and out as it moved through the trees. It was difficult to see its shape through the raven's eyes, though it appeared tall and scraped through the tree branches. Between the raven-colours and the extra layer of magic I had added, I could barely make out any details, but it seemed to be a tall figure. Arms swung as it walked and it made no sound.

I urged the raven on but something pressed against my mind. A pressure against the weave of my magic, pulling it taut. I thought back to the shadow-creature I had seen, those enormous footprints, and jerked myself away from the raven and back to myself.

My connection to the raven remained, it fluttered at the back of my mind, and now the bird swooped lazily towards me. Its ease a stark contrast to my stampeding heartbeat.

It took a moment for me to adjust to being back in my body. The world was suddenly silent with no rushing wind under my wings. Everything felt black, bereft of colour as my human eyes adjusted to sight without the beautiful raven-colours and I was left with the pale flicker of the campfire.

I frowned as I settled back into my human soul.

Animals often had an instinctive reaction to spirits. Cats hissed at malevolent spirits. Dogs barked at unsettled ghosts. When the ravens had seen the shadow-creature, they had tried to tear themselves away, but the elm-raven had no reaction to whatever this was. I had spoken with spirits before. Perhaps this was a forest spirit and it would have answers. It could help us find Ulfrun.

Most of the camp was asleep. The rustle of the trees was broken only by the spittle of fire and the hushed steps of those still awake. Someone had set some food by my feet and Sigrun, noticing I had come back to myself, looked like she wanted to ask me something. My expression warded her off and instead she nodded, happy I had returned from the raven without raising the alarm and went to find somewhere to sleep.

Once I had eaten I let my head fall loose between my shoulders. The long physical exertion of the day's march and the mental strain of riding the elm-raven's mind crashed against me like a tidal wave. I looked around for a space to lie down and cobble together some sense from everything I had seen.

I pictured the shadow-creature in the moments before it had snapped my connection to the oak-raven. Its limbs had tangled together with the branches and plants of the forest, pulling and snapping them as it loomed over the oak-raven. It was as though a chunk of the forest had come to life and torn itself from the ground. Could it be a troll? In all the legends they were deeply tied to the mountains and to stone.

And now this flickering, distant spirit.

I had some limited experience with the rituals to speak with lingering spirits. Every ghost looks different, as unique as the person that it once was, and some had been known to move objects. Spirits, though, needed a body to affect the physical realm.

All places had their spirits. No matter where you looked with second sight, you were bound to see some small spirit scamper away or watch you from a distance. Were the spirits here simply larger, more powerful, hidden so far from civilisation and mortal eyes?

I looked out into the darkness, squinting as though that would help my eyes penetrate the night, then stared at the rune-stick and the extra runes I had layered onto the raven's sight.

"Did you find anything?"

I started and turned to see Erri watching me from across the fading campfire.

"What?" I blinked.

"Did you find anything with your raven?"

"Oh." I paused. Had I found anything? I would not normally consider a spirit out of the ordinary. It was its size that gave me pause. "No. Only more of the same trail. It may be some time until we find Ulfrun."

Erri shook his head and poked a stick into the fire. "As I

feared. Best get some sleep. We'll push hard tomorrow."

I nodded and lay down but did not close my eyes. I heard Yrsa offer to keep watch. Erri dismissed her, demanding she be fully rested for tomorrow, and then the camp fell into silence.

Sleep did not come.

Every time I closed my eyes I saw the shimmering spirit in my mind's eye. I cast my mind over the rituals that summoned spirits and gave a rune-weaver the power to speak with them. I thought of the legendary skills of the troll rune-weavers who were powerful enough to fold the light of a rainbow into a bridge that could reach the realm of the gods. Would a spirit that walked the Trolbjolvid know some of the ancient trolls' spellcraft? If it did then perhaps it knew how to fix a god-stone.

I rolled onto my back and stared at the forest canopy, hoping that counting the stars would settle my mind. I scowled as my view of the night sky, already broken by waving tree limbs, became blotched with the writhing blue light of the Winds.

I had to do something.

As I got to my knees, I realised that Sigrun was asleep next to me. I chewed my lip, wondering if I should wake her. The forest was a dangerous place. The night but deepened that danger. Then Sigrun shifted and as her hand fell onto the ground her fingers loosened around a painted stick. The charm from her children.

My heart skipped a beat. No matter what I might face out in the forest, I could not bring Sigrun into more danger than I already had. I could not leave another family without a mother.

I looked around and saw there were two people missing, keeping watch. My steps through the forest had been clumsy during the day and a midnight trek be no better. Certainly loud enough to alert those on watch.

I rummaged in my pack and pulled out some herbs, crushing them in my fingers and muttering a short prayer. I felt the thrill of magic snap through me like a crack of lightning and threw the herbs onto the flames. There was a brief flash as the campfire clamped hungry flame-jaws over the herbs and then the smoke changed. It billowed out like fog and with it, brought a deeper sleep. The spell would not last long, but I did not need long.

I crept out of the now-silent camp and towards the blue shimmering spirit.

Chapter Ten
Stones in the Forest

The forest whispered to me. Slicing branches, the myriad calls and chirps of its night creatures, the hint of larger things moving in the darkness. It felt as though the forest was warning me to turn back, but I could not. The gods were with me and within the darkness ancient ghosts had answers.

I let the raven guide me to where it had seen the figure of light and, after half an hour, I felt a strange tension in the air. The raven hopped down beside me, uncomfortable and squawking at something unseen.

The only thing I could see was the dim shadows of the trees and the pinprick light of stars and the Winds above me. No spirits.

I raised my second sight.

The forest glowed with verdant light, a flickering echo of latent power, but from what? The heavy air was nothing new to me, it was the same kind of weight that any god-speaker felt during a ritual: the manifestation of the gods' power and attention. This was different, though. It was directionless, unfocused, as though part of the ambience of the deep woods.

I squinted at the shivering light. It was rooted by the base of a tree and glittered up the trunk like sunlight bouncing from a river. The tree's emerald echo slowly writhed, whipping around like a snake trapped in tar. Then, it blinked out before flickering alight once more.

No. For a heartbeat, the vibrant green was consumed by something black and still. My mind whirled back to the black scars running through the shattered god-stone's magic. Again, the viridescent light writhed then shivered to black before erupting back into pale, pine green.

The raven landed on my shoulder and I blinked away my second sight. The world returned to dim shadow and black night. I put my hand onto the tree and tried to push my awareness into it, in the way I had moved my sight into the ravens. It was a skill most god-speakers used with animals or people. By skating your awareness across your patient's, their ailments crystallised in a way that was clearer than any description, but the skill had its limits. Limits that ended in flesh and blood. What, though, were wood and sap but the flesh and blood of the forest?

My mind pushed against the bark. Its hard texture scraped my spongy skin. My breath filled and left my lungs. Too fast. A tree inhaled with the sunrise and exhaled as the sun set. My heartbeat was like a stampede against the arboreal thrum of the forest that was the tree's pulse. Its sap flowed like a glacier to my blood's tumbling waterfall. I took a breath, slowed my heart to fall into the rhythm of the pines.

Something in the roots watched me like a waking wolf watches a field mouse skitter across its paws. Too fast to catch. Too small to bother with.

Its gaze fell on me like a falling tree, pinning me in place. I stared back, felt it glitter with arboreal power. This entity was the pulsing heart of the forest. The green, flickering lights came from this and its power burned my mind like poison ivy wrapped around my throat. Then, a moment of blackness. It flinched and I lost my grip. I fell from the tree, tumbling to the ground.

My body shivered as I came back to myself. I was too cold. My heart had beat too slowly in an attempt to keep pace with whatever spirit lived in these trees and I lay corpse-cold, letting my body return to its normal warmth and rhythm.

Something hard formed in the pit of my stomach and my lungs suddenly felt too small. I sucked in a breath that was too short and tried again and again.

Whatever was happening to the god-stone was leaking into the forest. Was this black, ichorous magic infecting the

Trolbjolvid because of its proximity to the shattered god-stone or was this sickness the reason for the shattered god-stone? Would the forest die if the god-stone broke completely?

A flicker caught my eye.

Blue light.

I pushed myself to my feet, still shivering but strong enough to walk.

The raven hunched on my shoulder, beak open and wings akimbo as though to ward off the light.

I leant against a tree trunk and squinted into the night. Light bloomed against the bark of nearby trees and a bright figure appeared between them. Its outline blurred and swayed as it walked, but it looked vaguely human although its limbs were elongated and blunted, ending in a haze instead of hands or feet. Its steps were long and light as though it walked underwater. I held my breath as it walked by, seemingly oblivious to me, then I followed.

It was difficult to keep pace with the ghost. Its movements were slow and ponderous, as though it had no sense of time or had no need to measure its passing. Its head scraped through the branches without slowing and the leaves twitched as though caught in a breeze. Its long legs carried it easily over the roots and fallen trees that I tripped and scrambled over.

After a frantic few minutes trying to keep up with it, using its light as a beacon whenever I fell behind, I froze in my tracks and let out a gasp.

The figure stopped and turned to me but my attention was focused behind it.

Beyond it, painted with the spirit's dancing light, was a standing stone. Its angular edges were out of place and unexpected this deep in the forest.

I stepped forward, next to the spirit and reached out a hand to the monolith. As I drew closer the air grew heavier, the monolith's magic saturating everything around it. It looked like a god-stone in miniature. There were thick runes roughly carved into it, moss crept up its side, and the ground around it was dank and glistening with the beginnings of mushrooms growing at the stone's base.

My thoughts boiled with questions as I tried to decipher what the standing stone was—perhaps another miniature god-stone created by the shadow-creature, or something older from the time of the gods—but I shook my head and looked to the spirit. There were more pressing questions: Ulfrun was still lost in the forest; Vidsetr's god-stone still lay shattered.

"Friend..."

The spirit stared down at me.

My throat was dry. I coughed and swallowed.

"Friend, I seek your wisdom. Can you—"

Its head twisted, turning to watch something behind me. The raven screeched, its mind filled with the panic of a predator suddenly spotted and launched itself into the air in an explosion of feathers and dry leaves. I threw myself to the side in time to watch an axe bury itself in the tree beside me.

I scrabbled back as my attacker, outlined by the ghost's flickering glacier-light, tried to tug their axe from the tree. They wore a patchy cloak covered in mud and wet leaves over their ragged clothes and used a painted deer skull as a mask. Its broken antlers and yellowed teeth glittered with malice.

"Wait," I said as I crawled backwards. "I'm a friend."

The only response was a grunt and the splinter of wood as they wrenched the axe free.

They turned to me, charms clattering around their neck, and attacked. I threw a handful of leaves and dirt at their face, forcing them to flinch back, and clambered to my feet. I pulled my knife from my belt, a small thing meant for meals. I prayed to the Warrior for strength and held it out in front of me.

"I'm a friend," I said again, but they did not seem to understand or care.

They growled and leapt forward. I slashed wildly with my knife and sliced across their arm. Their growl twisted into a howl of pain. They managed to keep hold of the axe and I couldn't move fast enough to stop their other fist. It connected with my jaw in a blast of pain, sending me stumbling.

Before I could right myself they were on me again,

punching me in the stomach and then grabbing my hair and holding the axe blade to my throat.

I froze as the cold, jagged iron pricked at my skin. I stared at the face behind the deer skull mask.

Their eyes glittered with fury in the spirit's light, standing out bright against the dark mud caked on their face. The smell of fetid water filled my senses as their breath brushed my cheeks. Their eyes flicked over my tattoos and I sensed them holding back the last furious wrench of the axe that would have sliced my throat.

A twig snapped. Something tore my attacker away from me the same moment that the ghost-light vanished leaving me in darkness.

There was a cacophony of movement around me. Heavy footfalls, snapping branches, the hot stench of blood, and then, silence.

As my eyes adjusted to the black night I saw someone new standing over a still body. They straightened and came over to me, an axe in each hand.

"Are you hurt?"

Yrsa.

I let out a long breath. "No. Just shaken."

"Then get up," she snapped. She turned back to the dead man. "We need to show this one to Erri."

I opened my mouth, whether to thank her or justify why I had crept away from the camp, I wasn't sure, but Yrsa was already dragging the corpse back to camp. I struggled to my feet and hurried to catch up.

ᚠ

I gave up trying to talk to Yrsa as we walked back to camp. I peppered her with questions, demands, and accusations, but each was met with an indifferent shrug or a noncommittal grunt. And so we trudged through the starlit forest to the sound of our footsteps and the scrape of the corpse across the muddy ground. The only concession Yrsa made to my existence was when I pointed out that dragging the body through the mud would make us easier to track. The dead man's furrow through the soft earth would draw a line straight to us. She grunted and swept the body up and over her shoulders in one smooth motion.

My blood still pounded in my ears from being so close to the spirit, the revelation of the forest monolith, and the fight. I clenched my hands to try and keep them from shaking, then shoved them under my arms. I had seen violence before, even been in a few fights, but they were mostly fistfights started by the bereaved taking out their grief on me. This was different. We were deep into a forest haunted by things I was barely beginning to understand and if it hadn't been for Yrsa, for a Windborn, then I would likely be food for roots and mushrooms. Another ghost lost under the branches of the Trolbjolvid.

Eventually, the glow of the campfire came into view and relief washed over me, not only for the safety of the camp but also for the promise of a conversation that wasn't grunted at me.

The herbs I had thrown on the fire had long since burned themselves out but the magic still clung to the air. As we came into the firelight people stirred from their sleep but only Fafnir, next to the fire, was alert. He stood and took up his spear.

"You are safe," he rumbled and I saw the tension leave his shoulders.

"No thanks to him," Yrsa said and dumped the body on the ground.

Erri, who had been trying to rub the sleep from his eyes, leapt up at the sight of the corpse. He roused the rest of the camp and in moments everyone was awake, armed, and watching the forest for an attack, my magic finally burned away by their warrior instincts. I stood to one side, still with my hands under my arms, and watched their smooth precision and confidence, the deadly conviction with which they gripped their spears, and felt again that I was out of place here amongst warriors and Windborn.

"Are you okay?" Someone asked as they rushed at me from the darkness. Sigrun.

"I'm fine," I said. I kept my eyes down and stared at the corpse.

"You should have woken me." Sigrun put a hand on my shoulder. "I would have come. I would have protected you."

She sounded hurt, as though I had asked a Windborn to follow me. Guilt scrunched in my belly even as I thought it: without Yrsa I would be dead. And I could not meet Sigrun's earnest gaze. All my sister wanted to do was to keep me safe and I kept running away because I did not deserve her protection. Then I saw Sigrun's charm hanging around her neck like a pendant and any guilt I had at abandoning her dissolved. Her children needed her. Her wife needed her.

I opened my mouth, but Erri beckoned me over.

"Alvir. Over here."

I shot Sigrun an apologetic look as I went over to Erri and Yrsa as they crouched beside the corpse. Erri rolled them onto their back and pulled the deer skull mask free, turning it over in his hands.

"What am I looking at?" he asked, pointing to the paint scrawled across the mask.

I took the skull. At first glance the paint was randomly splattered across it, then I realised that the paint connected the runes that had been lightly carved into the bone. I picked at it and the paint came away in chunks, revealing the ingredients ground into it: berries, sap, rough flakes of bark, silty earth, and a few other components too finely crushed to identify. I raised my second sight, trying to decipher the runes, but there were too many overlapping threads of magic. Their power churned together with whatever strength remained in the paint so I could make out some of the magic's intention. It had been made to keep this person hidden, to help them move through the forest without being seen, and it was linked to my attacker and... something else.

I gave the mask back to Erri and explained what it did, though I did not tell him that the magic was linked to some power I could not identify.

Erri frowned. "Yrsa, could you sense anything from him before he attacked you?"

She shrugged. "Barely. I thought it was a rat or something."

Erri nodded and gestured for her to get back to watching the perimeter. He turned the skull over in his hands, pensive, and looked down at the dead man between us.

"What did you do?" he asked.

"I tried to defend myself with the knife, but—"

"No." The skull creaked in his hands. "What did you do to us? You left the camp and only Yrsa and Fafnir were unaffected. If not for them we would have been defenceless."

I sighed and looked down. The dead man stared back at me, unseeing and mouth agape, and I shivered. That could easily have been me. If Yrsa hadn't somehow resisted my magic or chosen not to follow me then my soul would be feasting in the gods' halls.

"I cast a spell on the campfire," I said. "I need answers that are in this forest and I left to find them."

"Then we're lucky that the Windborn didn't fall under your spell. We're here to find Ulfrun, Alvir." His voice was steel and the intensity in his eyes told me there would be no argument. "If there are other things for you in this forest, you will have to wait to find them."

I met his eyes, but his will was stone and the memory of the axe's edge at my throat forced me to look away and nod.

I looked at the deer skull in Erri's hand. The paint seemed to ripple in the freshly stoked firelight.

"Do the forest outlaws always have such powerful protection?" I asked.

Erri looked at the skull and shook his head. "They're as you'd expect. Half-rotten camps if they're organised at all and a lot of infighting. I've not seen anything like this before."

"It's a complicated weave."

"Do you think they found Ulfrun, then? Have they forced her to make this?"

"It could be. Or another skilled rune-weaver is with them. But if they are using Ulfrun to make more of these masks then they won't hurt her."

"A grim hope."

Erri shook himself, then set about checking on the others.

"We're doubling the watch for the rest of the night," he said, loud enough for all to hear but not so loud it would carry out into the forest. "We'll get what sleep we can and then head out to find out where this wretch came from."

The camp filled with lethargic bustle, which felt strange in the quiet forest as though in trying to defend ourselves from whatever threats lurked between the trees we were calling out to them in challenge. I helped move belongings to the fireside as we retreated closer to the centre of our camp. Once again I was filled with a sense of awkward uselessness as everyone else took to their tasks without a word and so sat by the fire, hoping that I could keep out of the way of the warriors shooting me annoyed looks.

After a moment, someone came to crouch beside me and I turned to see Sigrun's worry-creased eyes.

"You're sure you're okay?" she asked.

I offered a half-smile and nodded. "Sigrun, I shouldn't have gone alone, but I couldn't wake you. I couldn't ask you to come with me."

"You don't have to ask," she said with a sigh. "I'm glad that Yrsa followed you out but it should have been me. I owe you that much."

I frowned at her. "What are you talking about? You don't owe me anything."

"Without you, I wouldn't be here. I don't just mean here now. If it weren't for you then I wouldn't be here at all."

"I did what any god-speaker would have done. What any midwife would have done."

"Maybe, but you still did it. You saved me."

"But I couldn't save your mother." I looked at the dirt, unable to meet Sigrun's eyes. "My runes couldn't save her."

Sigrun put her hand on my shoulder and squeezed. She waited until I looked up and she met my gaze, staring deep into my eyes, seeking something. "But they saved me."

Deep inside my chest something shifted. I couldn't tell if, after decades of nursing the guilt from that night, the splinter of blame was sinking deeper into my heart or if it was starting to loosen. I put my hand on Sigrun's and squeezed.

"Our father blamed both of us for my mother's death, you know." Sigrun's voice was soft. There was no recrimination. Only the release of something long held back. "Whenever he was drunk, which was a lot, he would scream that you abandoned us. Then he'd move on to me and accuse me of being the reason he lost her."

I winced. My father had tried to drown himself in drink ever since my mother died. It had eased when he met Sigrun's mother, but I remembered spending days running through the woods or tending to the fishing nets in the pouring rain to avoid him. Guilt and empathy flared in my chest.

"I talked to Floki a few times after you left, Alvir," Sigrun went on. The memory of my teacher came easily to me: his stern expression, the rare smile, and his child-like enthusiasm for runes. "He might not have been around that night, but I talked to him about it. I couldn't talk to our father, could I? And Floki said he was proud of you. You did more than anyone could have expected of you."

I opened my mouth to protest but I couldn't find the words. Instead, I shrugged Sigrun's hand from my shoulder. She let her hand fall back to her side but did not shy away from me. I had often had difficult conversations, but I was usually on the other side of it giving poor diagnoses and verdicts. Now, though, Sigrun remained beside me, not forcing her presence on me but waiting as though to prove she would always be there.

"I should have done more," I whispered, half-hoping she would not hear me. "If I had known more runes, if I had been a better apprentice, then I could have saved you both."

Sigrun pulled me into an embrace, awkward as I was still sitting.

"No one blames you," she said. "You did so much more than anyone could have hoped for. You did your best. You saved me."

We stayed like that for a little while until Sigrun was called away to stand watch. Reluctantly she pulled herself free and, with one final glance in my direction, walked away.

I lay and curled up beside the dying fire, watching the embers slowly fade. Despite the night-black depths of the forest around me, I felt that sliver in my chest shift and as a calm sleep overtook me it felt like I had let out a breath I had held on to for far too long.

Chapter Eleven
A Wall Woven with Magic

I OPENED MY EYES AND SAW THE DARK UNDERSIDE of the canopy and shadow-drenched bark. Panic spiked as I felt the weight of an axe on my throat and I slammed my eyes shut.

No. I was safe.

I kept my eyes closed and pushed my senses into the earth. I felt the thrum of magic around me. There may be strange things in the forest, but the gods' power was still here. I was safe. The gods were with me.

I let myself bask in the fizz of magic against my skin for a few more moments then opened my eyes and sat up. The camp was bustling. Spears clattered against shields. Boots kicked up leaves. Voices called out. We were nearly packed and ready to move and people had begun to gather around the body of my attacker from the night before.

"God-speaker," Erri, crouched next to the body, called over to me. "Can you tell me any more about him now the sun is up?"

I went over and examined the corpse, but there was little more to be found. Sticks had been roughly stabbed into his cloak to help him blend into the forest, but there was no magic in them. His clothes were torn and rough as though he had been living in the woods for a long time. The strangest thing about him was the black mud slathered across his entire face. I ran a thumb over his cheek, it felt silt smooth like it had been dredged from a river, but there was no magic left in the mud if there ever had been any. I stood and said as much to Erri who scowled.

"Then we leave him for the wolves. Yrsa, you go with Drifa

and Tjorvid and make sure we don't get any surprises. Alvir, you're going to show us where you got attacked."

I frowned, but no one else questioned Erri. Yrsa and the hunters stalked off without a word, heading in the direction she had dragged the body from.

"We're not following Arvid's trail?" I asked.

Erri shook his head. "We've got a better lead now. Sigrun, Nal, you bring up the rear with Fafnir. Everyone else, you're with me and Alvir."

And so we went.

At night, the forest was a small thing. Only as vast as the nearest tree, but now it stretched out an endless parade of straight-backed sentinels that seemed to sway and watch us pass. The morning light could not pierce the canopy except in sparse, solitary spears and left us trudging through an unnerving twilight.

"What were you looking for?" Erri said after some time had passed.

"What do you mean?"

"You said there are answers for you in the forest and Yrsa told me there was light nearby when she found you, but it went out when she attacked the outlaw. Why were you out here? A deal gone wrong?"

"What? No!" Indignation swelled in my chest and I stopped, but Erri kept walking so I had to hurry to keep up with him. "What deal would I be making? I... I thought I saw a spirit."

"A spirit?"

"Yes. A ghost perhaps."

Erri stared at me. "That's not a good enough reason to spell everyone to sleep. It's a good thing your magic doesn't affect Windborn or you'd be dead. We might all be dead." Erri paused and jaw clenched. "You're sure this thing wasn't the same spirit that made those footprints? The troll spirit?"

I let Erri's words hang in the air. Erri could easily have decided that my spell from the night before was enough reason to send me away. I owed him an explanation, part of one at least, but how much could I tell him that would not cause him to panic? Outlaws with rune-woven masks was one thing, even malevolent spirits building themselves bodies—spirits could be appeased—but revenant trolls destroying god-stones? That might be too much.

I thought back to the raven's reaction to the shimmering blue spirit, or rather its lack of one. Surely there was nothing to fear.

"It was a different spirit, Erri. There are many powers in this forest and I thought I had found one."

"I know," he said, an annoyed edge seeping into his words. "We all leave offerings at the edge of the forest. It—"

"I do not mean spirits that can be appeased with a bowl of honey and a strip of meat. This forest is filled with monsters, Erri, alive and dead. And I have questions for them."

Something in my conviction gave Erri pause.

I think that was the first time Erri truly saw me and appreciated the world I inhabited. Perhaps I had only been Sigrun's brother until then, a god-speaker of dubious skill tolerated because of my half-sister. Given enough rein to be useful but not so much to canter away. Now, I felt that he understood what it was to be a god-speaker. Mine was not a world of blades and barked orders. I straddled the material world and the realm of the gods. My second sight let me watch the world beyond our own at the powers that could break a mortal with a breath. I had the strength to bind that magic to my desires. I was not someone whose soul had been stolen from the gods and saturated with the strange power of the Winds. I was a god-speaker, rune-weaver, hallowed wanderer.

"So be it, god-speaker. But no going off on your own again. If I let you get killed then Sigrun will kill me and if that happens I'll haunt the shit out of you."

I snorted a laugh and it shattered the tension between us.

Before long, Yrsa fell back and told us she had lost the trail. Erri sent out Drifa and Tjorvid and then Fafnir, but none of them could find it. Consternation rippled over the group. It should have been an easy thing to follow mine and Yrsa's footsteps from the night before. Though I had urged Yrsa not to carve a furrow dragging the body behind us we had not made any concerted effort to hide our tracks.

Eventually, Erri turned to me and I summoned the final raven. It fluttered from the low branches to my shoulder where it hopped from side to side. I brushed its feathers with the back of my fingers and whispered soothing nonsense to it which seemed to ease some of its agitation. It cawed and I sent it off into the trees, folding its vision over mine.

The dim forest became a coruscation of colour. Leaves shimmered with nameless colours and the heavy smells of sap and pine became tinged with the subtler scents of berries and grubs.

The raven swooped in a wide circle around us and at one edge it flinched as the air caressing its wings became thick and sticky. It cawed in irritation, but I pushed it on and some way behind, we followed.

I forced the raven deeper into the viscous air, praying it would lead us to the stone the spirit had guided me to.

A weight pressed down on us and there was a silence between the trees that made it feel like something watched us, glaring at each crunching step we took. People clutched their spears and moved closer to their companions.

The raven screeched in the back of my mind. A wind had picked up, dragging the thick air around it like chains. Its wings pumped furiously but the adversarial gale slowed its progress.

"We're close," I said.

Erri called for everyone to come together. Worry creased their faces. They knew we were getting close to something, though they could not feel the full extent of the magic pressing down on them. For those not schooled in the ways of magic, the atmosphere would feel oppressive and dark but there was not the same physical weight that I felt.

Between the blurry, jagged memory of the fight and the weak daylight breaking through the canopy, it was difficult to tell where I had fought the outlaw. The trees all looked the same and the wind swept the pine needles and dry leaves around our feet, killing any hope of finding tracks. The raven had swooped onto a nearby branch. I pushed at it to fly closer to the ground, to try and pick up any trail with its sharper senses, but it refused to move like a traveller refusing to go on in a downpour.

"Okay," Erri said. "Where now?"

I raised my second sight. Some of the tension left my shoulders as the dark forest blossomed into bright life. I had hoped to see some bright trace of blood, but the magic in the air made everything hazy. Colours swirled together and there was something else that darkened them like silt caught in a river current. I thought back to the wandering spirit. Perhaps we had stumbled upon a troll's grave and its power still stained the woods even as its ghost still patrolled the night.

I shook my head at Erri and he summoned Fafnir to the front of the group. The Windborn's hood flickered in the wind as he looked this way and that, sniffing, but he did not pull it down. Not for the first time, I wondered what deformity Fafnir hid under his hood. I had seen some Windborn that looked like half-breed trolls with stony skin and glowing eyes, but they usually revelled in their ferocious appearance.

"Over here!"

Nal waved us over and pointed. Between the trees some distance away was a lone monolith covered in carvings and moss.

I tried to examine it with my second sight but was forced to look away and blink the burning bright power from my eyes. I tried again, more cautiously, and saw that its magic wasn't quite the same as a god-stone. Where a god-stone was a solid mountain of magic, a firm beacon in the landscape, this stone's power reached and stretched like a living fortress wall throbbing in my second sight. Nearby, the soul-strength of individual trees and smaller spirits bounced up to the wavering magical wall and were thrown away. A bird fluttered past us and through the barrier. The monolith's magic flickered before stabilising with a sharp pulse and returning to its slow, swaying waves. I felt like I had witnessed a wolf watch a mouse wander by and decide it was not worth the effort to catch it.

This was not a sentinel standing alone in the trees, it was part of a larger weave. Something had created a barrier that cut across the heart of the forest to stop magic from crossing.

"It's a border," I said, blinking away my second sight. Everyone turned to look at me and I explained about the barrier. "It's a focus point for a powerful spell, like a fence post or watch tower."

I followed the others up to it, though no one got too close.

"To do what?" Erri asked.

"I am not sure. The small spirits that are trying to pass are simply bouncing off. Perhaps some spirit deeper in the forest is marking its territory."

My mind flashed back to the shadow creature that had shredded my connection to the oak-raven.

"Can we get through?" Erri asked me.

"I think so, but it's likely that whatever set the spell would know we had crossed into its territory."

Erri nodded and turned to Drifa, "Did you find any other tracks?"

"There's not much, but some churned mud heading out past this stone. I would have thought it's been too dry around here for that kind of thing but they're there."

"Great." Erri stood and chewed his lip, then sighed. "We've come too far to turn back now. Alvir, is there any way we can get through this without alerting whatever made it? Windborn aren't affected by magic, right? Maybe Fafnir and Yrsa could topple it. Break the spell entirely?"

"No!" My voice was harsher than I intended and Erri's eyes went wide. I took a breath before I continued. "You can't push against it," I near-whispered as though that would undo my outburst. "This is part of a larger spell. I think it's linked to other stones. If you push it over it would be like smashing through a city's walls. Give me some time. I might be able to find a clean way through."

Erri stared at me before he waved a hand to invite me to try.

I stepped forward, moving up to the wall of magic though I was still a good few paces away from the monolith, and as I came close to the swirling invisible barrier the raven swooped onto my shoulder. It cawed at me and hissed at the invisible wall in front of us. I brought up my second sight and, careful not to look directly at the rune-stone and blind myself, examined the barrier.

The magic blurred the world and flowed past me like a fast-coursing river. The rune-stone was acting as both fence post and waterfall, stabilising the barrier and giving it power and speed as it rushed onward to the next rune-stone, though I could not see it. After a few moments watching, I saw that there was a pattern to the weave. The same threads rippled and flexed. As they moved up and down they created a flat barrier in front of me like a churning spider's web, eager to catch anything it could. If I could pull on one of those threads then I could create a gap in the weave and allow someone to slip through. Or something.

The raven grumbled on my shoulder as it realised my intention and flew off to a nearby branch. I shot it a look. "It will be safe," I mumbled, half to the raven and half to myself.

I turned back to the weave.

The magic was linked to the forest, it was rooted beneath the rune-stone as a god stone rooted itself in the world. As I examined the runes carved into the stone, I realised that many were the same as had been on the outlaw's deer skull. The skull's magic was linked to this weave. I frowned, wondering what sort of creature held the outlaw under its thrall, then shook the thought from my mind. Now was not the time.

I picked up a handful of dirt and leaves and moss and rubbed them into my palms and between my fingers until my fingernails were caked in muck. With a quick prayer and a judicious application of my will, I began to feel the coursing magic as well as see it. At first, it was as heavy as mist. Then, as I pushed my hands forward it felt like sea spray and then the surface of a river.

I waited.

I let my magic mix with the earth and the trees and the weave in front of me. After a few minutes, the power rushing past my fingertips felt the same as the power I couched in my hands. I took a deep breath, praying that I would not set off the trap, and pushed into the coursing web of magic.

It felt both cold and still and warm and fast. The heat of the weave layered onto the cool, slow power of the forest.

The weave flowed over my fingers and, once I had waited a few cycles to follow its magic, I tugged at a thread. The magic kept flowing, but it shifted and parted. I heard gasps behind me as a window appeared in the air before us and we saw through the barrier. The forest beyond was much the same as the one we stood in, but the sound of rushing water came to us and as I pulled the window open further, I saw a stream burbling over a rocky outcrop and flowing down a hill we had not seen a moment before.

Curses and oaths from behind me. I made a silent prayer to Lady Syf and the Warrior. Whatever had made this was powerful. It was beyond any rune-weaver or god-speaker I knew. The strength needed to power such a spell would have left any mortal a husk of dry bone and skin. There was no way that Ulfrun could have made this. My mind went back to the shattered god-stone and the rune-laden deer skull. I suppressed a shudder. Something with the raw strength to shatter a god-stone could be using Ulfrun's knowledge and casting through her, but pushing such power through a mortal body would destroy it.

We needed to find her and save her from whatever had made this.

I summoned the raven back to my shoulder and urged it through the gap I had made. It resisted but I pushed until it relented with a squawk. Once the raven was through, I closed my eyes and let myself see what it could see.

The forest sloped up, a hill ahead of us where the stream began, and there was a clearing in the distance with some sort of ruined building in the middle of it and a pile of discarded clothes thrown against a nearby tree. The raven looked back and saw us, our forms blurred as though seen underwater.

Friction on my fingers. The weave was beginning to tear. I had held it open for too long. I slowly released the pressure, pulling my mud-stained fingers back, and the gap closed.

The raven disappeared from my mind. The connection lost.

I cursed and turned back to my companions.

"The raven got through. There's an old, abandoned building in the centre of a clearing. Whatever made this was powerful, but if we are quick I think I can hold it open long enough for us to slip through."

"Alright," Erri said and turned to everyone. "Looks like we're closing in on them. Any volunteers to go first?"

Feet shuffled and people looked at the ground. Sigrun looked at me and then the barrier. Her chest puffed as she gathered her courage. My heart lurched at the thought of sending her through first.

"Perhaps the Windborn," I suggested. "We know that normal magic does not work easily on them. I think they should be able to slip through the weave more easily."

Erri did not look convinced. He turned to Yrsa and Fafnir. She shrugged and he nodded slowly, face hidden in the perpetual shadow of his hood.

"I will try," Fafnir said. He came up to me and hesitantly reached one hand out, mimicking my own. "Just step through?"

"Wait for my signal."

Fafnir tensed and waited.

I stepped back up to the weave with my dirt-covered hand outstretched. After a long moment, I took hold of the coruscating weave. It rippled and flowed around my hand and then... there. I guided the weave away from us and there was a gap.

"Go."

Fafnir rushed forward in a stumbling gait, kicking up leaves and dirt. Then the weave fell once more and he was gone.

The world ahead of us looked the same as the world behind. A vast, shaded forest with the buzz of insects and hiss of leaves to keep us company. Fafnir was nowhere to be seen.

"Did it work?" Erri asked. He had a white-knuckle grip on his shield and his eyes darted from me to Yrsa.

"It should have," I said. "But I have lost connection with the raven, I can't see beyond the barrier. Give me a moment and I will open the gap. Then we'll be able to see through."

"He's fine," Yrsa said. "I can feel him over there."

I turned back to the barrier to hide my frown that a Windborn should be able to sense anything through this barrier.

"Good," Erri said with a relieved sigh. "Nal, you next."

The night-haired warrior stepped forward and glanced between me and the air blurred air in front of her.

"You're sure this is safe?" She kept her voice steady but I saw the fear and worry in her eyes.

"It's safe," I said as softly as I could. I pulled at the weave once more and the strange window began to slice through the air and we saw Fafnir's hulking form through the sliver-window.

Nal's shoulders slumped in relief. "Tell me when."

I nodded and pulled the window wider before beckoning her through.

After that, it did not take long. One by one they came up to me, waited for my signal, and leapt through the barrier. My fingers began to chafe against the weave's flow and the longer I touched the weave the more it felt like I was gripping thorny branches. By the time I ushered the fifth person through the gap, I had to clench my teeth to keep from screaming.

Sigrun waited until last. She smiled at Yrsa as the warrior disappeared behind the hazy air then turned to me. Her gaze met mine, worry creasing her eyes. She looked away and picked at mud under her fingernails.

"You're coming too, aren't you? You're not going to leave us?"

I smiled at her, strained under the weight and pain of holding open the weave.

"Of course I am." I hurried her with my free hand. "I can't hold this forever, Sigrun."

She looked at me, bit her lip, hesitant.

"Go. Now. Before I lose my grip."

Sigrun looked at the gap in the hazy air and then to me. She opened her mouth, closed it, and hopped through the barrier. The air swallowed her, churning her image into myriad splinters that disappeared like leaves on the wind, and she was gone. I let the magic go and the searing pain in my fingers eased.

I was alone.

I massaged my fingers and eased the pain in them with more cool earth and as the pain lessened guilt gnawed at the pit of my stomach. Sigrun clearly wanted to protect me, to include me in her family, and all I had done was snap at her. And now I was alone.

The forest closed in. What had been small noises a moment before—the hum of insects, the gossip of the leaves—pressed against me and I felt the vast distance between myself and civilisation. I shifted and my stone-stuffed pack banged against my back. There were answers deeper in the forest and I needed to find them.

I grimaced as I pulled the weave apart a final time and stepped into the dark heart of the forest.

Chapter Twelve
The Outlaw Camp

IT FELT LIKE STEPPING THROUGH A WATERFALL. There was a sudden rush of power and a crushing weight thundered around me then it was gone and I was on the other side. Sigrun threw her arms around me before I had managed to get my bearings.

I put my hands up, ready to push her off, but the thought of the empty forest stopped me. I could disappear here and the trees would not notice. Wolves would notice only so long as it took to gnaw the flesh from my bones. Sigrun would notice. She would mourn. I returned the embrace before pulling away.

"I told you I was coming," I said with a half-smile. "I'm not leaving you again."

Sigrun's smile was small, still thick with worry, but she smiled, nonetheless. After she fussed over me a moment more, I took in my new surroundings this side of the magical barrier. Erri crouched beside the pile of belongings I had seen through the raven's eyes, sifting through them with Fafnir and Drifa. The other huskalar had formed a rough perimeter as Yrsa and Tjorvid patrolled around us. I looked for the raven, but with our connection severed it was a normal bird once again and likely long gone. Despite the short time I had been connected with the ravens, I felt a pang of loss and vulnerability now that I had lost them all. There was no time to find new birds to help us in our search. I would have to rely on the huskalar and Windborn.

Behind us, the barrier-weave shimmered in the air. I could still see through it but it felt like I watched the forest from underwater.

The weight of magic still pressed on my shoulders, which was unexpected. I had thought that once we were through the barrier the air would return to normal.

Cautiously, I raised my second sight and sucked in a breath.

A faint light hung in the air all around us like a fog. It was the colour of old holly leaves and pockmarked with blackened spots that looked like rotten raindrops. My breath came short and sharp, every inhalation laced with stagnant water. The forest closed in around me. I could taste the moisture in the air. The spores filling my lungs.

"Alvir?"

A hand squeezed my arm. I dropped my second sight and turned to see a concerned Sigrun beside me. Without the oppressive haze brought on by my second sight the air felt clean again and my breath slowed.

"I'm fine," I said. I took Sigrun's hand and squeezed. "There's so much magic in this forest. I was shocked. I'm fine now, really."

She frowned at me but did not press the issue.

I took a few shaky steps towards Erri. He looked up at me, a question in his eyes, but I waved him off.

"Does this tell us anything?" I asked, gesturing to the pile of belongings.

"Not much," he said. "Likely from your outlaw. He left a waterskin and some food so seems to me that he wasn't out hunting you, just saw an opportunity and took it."

"The scent is the same," Fafnir rumbled. "He came here often. The air is thick with him."

"A lookout," Erri said. "He'll be missed. Drifa, you reckon you can find the trail?"

Drifa looked towards the forest depths. "The ground's wetter this side of"—she waved at the still-wavering air—"whatever that is. We'll be able to follow the tracks easy enough."

"Then let's go. It's getting dark and I don't want to camp anywhere near this thing. Everyone, on me."

Without ceremony, Erri led us deeper into the forest. I

stayed at the back of the group, feeling lost and vulnerable that I had no ravens to swoop ahead and show me what was coming. For a heartbeat, I thought to raise my second sight, but the thought made my chest constrict and I pushed it from my mind.

We splashed through the stream and clambered up a gentle slope until we reached the crest of a small hill. The forest swept out before as our new vantage brought a fresh gust of wind, it pushed at us as though trying to force us back and seemed to carry with it the myriad voices of the forest's denizens. Within the hiss of the wind I could almost hear the scuttering of countless insects beneath our feet, the whisper of feathers from birds circling in the branches above, and the near-silent pad of predator's feet unseen in the distant shadows. All this at the edge of hearing spoken in one voice. Something was watching us, warning us with the wind.

It was too late. We had come too far to turn back. I had questions for the spirits still wandering these woods. Vidsetr needed its god-speaker returned. I would seek out whatever was speaking to me through the wind and find my answers.

It took an hour of walking—trudging through the gloom where we jumped at the snap of every twig—until we saw it. Drifa called us to a halt and pointed out a shadow in the trees that was too uniform to be natural. At first I thought it was another monolith, but Tjorvid reported it was an empty camp.

Cautiously, we made our way to it. Night had descended and the darkness made it difficult to see clearly. Yrsa did not sense anyone within, but after examining the outlaw's skull mask we were not taking any chances. Fafnir sniffed at the air, but the wind still buffeted us and he shook his head.

"The wind is too strong and blows the wrong way. I smell only us."

We made our way into the small clearing where the outlaws had made their camp: huskalar with spears lowered, hunters with arrows nocked, and me with my hand clenched around the god stone shard.

The ground was scuffed and churned by boots all circling around a dead campfire. A canvas hung over some tree branches to give cover to half the camp—that was what Drifa had seen. Under the canvas were piles of half-eaten food thrown into the hollows between roots and even the glint of a discarded knife beside the fire.

"See what you can find," Erri said. He was forced to repeat himself for some of the huskalar as the wind carried his voice too fast for them to hear.

From what I could see, the camp had been long abandoned. My companions began sifting through the scattered belongings in search of some clue that would tell us where to go next or perhaps show us what had happened to Ulfrun. I had no idea what to look for and stood awkwardly at the edge of the camp. I twisted my arm-ring and clenched my fists as my feeling of impotence turned to gnawing frustration and irritation.

To give myself something to do, I wandered to the campfire and looked for something to light it. A fire would be welcome. It would give us all a chance to warm our bones and see each other's faces clearly. I huffed when I saw the state of the campfire. The charcoal was too cold, the kindling too wet. I hovered my hand over the hearth and called my will. I muttered a prayer to the gods and summoned an echo of the flame that blazed in the gods' hearthfire. For a moment nothing happened. Then I felt a chill in my arm as the heat left my body and dried the kindling, heated the charcoal, and flames burst into life with a snap.

I stood to gather some dry wood to feed the flames and flinched as someone rushed past me and kicked at the ground, smothering the burgeoning fire with mud and dust.

"What are you doing?" I cried, grabbing the huskalar's arm. But the damage was done. The fire was dead.

"I'd ask you the same thing," Nal hissed. "Do you want to send up a signal fire to everyone in the forest? Not to mention that the fire would have told us how long they've been gone. Now it's useless."

I stared at Nal. I was unused to having anyone speak to me so sharply, especially someone so young. Nal's black hair writhed in the wind as she stared daggers at me. I took a step back, hands up to show my capitulation. She shook her head and went back to searching the camp.

I waited by the useless fire though I wasn't sure what I was waiting for. Perhaps I wanted someone to grab Nal and reprimand her for speaking to a god-speaker that way, but I knew she was right. I had tried to help and had nearly set a signal fire that could have gotten us all killed.

At least we would have been warm.

Without meeting anyone's gaze, I wandered away from the competent hunters and trackers. I wanted to go far enough so that I couldn't hear or see the warriors and Windborn whose easy woodcraft put me to shame, but the battering wind and the oppressive gloom of the forest kept me close. Instead, I circled the edge of the clearing, letting my fingers run along the tree trunks as I passed them.

On the fourth tree, my fingers snagged on something more than the scaly bark. I paused. Something was carved into the tree.

A rune.

It was hacked into the bark in rough lines. Not lovingly made by a rune weaver. Whoever had done this had done enough to make it work, and only that. I looked to my companions, still turning over everything in the camp, and caught sight of the dead fire. With a frown, I looked back at the tree. It was the rune *air*. I wondered why someone would need that here.

I raised my second sight, trying to blink away the weight of the verdant, black-spotted fog that saturated the air. The power within the tree shone brighter than any other tree. More vibrant for its sudden brightness in the night. The rune's power was threaded through its soul and there was something else there, a shadow that seeped up from the tree's roots. There was something half-buried between the roots that held the power in place like a keystone.

"Hey." Sigrun's voice knocked my second sight away and I turned to her, blinking.

"Hi."

"Sorry about Nal. She can be a bit of a bitch sometimes. I think it's pressure, you know? Fafnir's little sister. That's a lot to live up to."

"I suppose," I said. "Look, Sigrun, there's something

carved here. Are there any other trees like this?"

"Er, I don't know. Oh look."

She snatched something hidden in the leaves and dirt gathered between the tree roots.

"Sigrun, no!"

"What?"

She straightened, shocked. She held her hands up in surrender but clutched a rabbit skull in her left hand. Dirt fell away from it, revealing the deep runes carved into the bone.

All at once, the tension in the air fled and the blustering gale fell away. In its place a gentle breeze blew from the other direction.

"What?" Sigrun said. "What did I do?"

"I don't know." I looked at the skull in her hands and then to the camp.

Everyone had stopped when the wind dropped. They looked around to try and see what had happened, weapons ready and shields high. Fafnir was boulder-still. He straightened and held his head high like a wolf scenting prey on the wind.

Then he crouched, shield up, spear ready.

"Ready yourselves," he shouted. "Ambush!"

ᚠ

Sigrun's smile vanished and suddenly my half-sister was replaced by a sharp-edged huskalar.

"Get low and follow me," she said, dropping the skull and unslinging her shield from her back.

Without waiting, she half-ran back to the clearing to stand with everyone else. I hurried to catch up and pulled my knife from my belt. Clutched in both hands it felt far too small compared to the long fangs of the huskalar's spears and the hunters' powerful bows.

Sigrun pushed me into the centre of a ragged shield wall that circled the dead campfire. The huskalar's heads whipped this way and that, trying to see the enemy that Fafnir had scented. Wind tickled the low branches, sending the leaves gossiping, and then even that small breeze died away, leaving no sound but the ragged breath of my companions and the wooden creak of their weapons.

I raised my second sight, hoping to see something to show where some hidden foe might be snaking through the undergrowth. It was better than squinting blindly into the darkness. Nothing. Only the spear-straight emerald spirits of the trees and the clotted green haze that seemed to suffocate everything else.

For a moment, there was silence. The huskalar remained as tense as a drawn bow with teeth bared in frustration that there was no enemy to charge, no opponent to skewer.

I eased my grip on my knife. How well could we trust a Windborn's nose? Whatever Fafnir was hiding under his hood, surely he could not smell danger? I bent to begin lighting the fire once again, to give us some light to see by, and Yrsa suddenly tensed, axes raised.

"There! In the—"

A pack of something burst from the ferns outside the camp. Bone shone as a strange light began shifting through the trees. Weapons glinted. More outlaws. All with skull masks that transformed them into savage monsters surging at us in the night.

"Brace!" Erri's voice echoed through the forest.

The huskalar pulled together, forging their shields into a wall of wood and iron. It would not be enough.

More skulls surged out of the undergrowth, highlighted by a strange blue undulating light. I looked up and saw a line of blue light, fading to green, whipping slowly across the sky beyond the canopy. I gritted my teeth. The Winds. Of course the Winds had come to witness this ambush. What powers had taken Ulfrun hostage?

The pack of feral outlaws smashed against the shield wall, opponents crunching together in a cacophony of splintered wood and bone.

The tang of blood in the air. The thunk of an axe against wood. The cry of the wounded.

I clutched at my knife, cringed away from the sounds and sharp movement. A body was thrown into me, I pushed against it and the warrior leapt back into the fray.

Battle raged.

I watched the shadows, trying to tell friend from foe, and prayed to the gods for protection. After a few heartbeats, my impotence coalesced into a coal of rage in the pit of my stomach. I had got us here, I had commanded ravens and pulled apart a god-like weave to bring us here and now all I could do was cower?

The gods were with me. Their power was mine.

I slammed my hand into the dead campfire. I pulled on the magic within me, the power of the gods, and shoved it into the ashes. My earlier spell still lingered and I grabbed hold of it and shoved my will back into it. Heat cascaded down my arm, making me shiver as the warmth left my body and erupted from the dead kindling in a geyser of pure flame.

For a heartbeat, the forest was illuminated by furious golden light. The outlaws stumbled back, blinded, and the huskalar seized their chance and attacked with renewed fury. Many of the outlaws fell to those iron-flashing blades, but some scrambled out of the way and disappeared between leaves and shadows.

The smell of burnt hair filled my nostrils as the flames singed my arms, but I stayed close to the fire as it fell from a raging bonfire to a spluttering beacon.

The battlefield tension that had engulfed the campsite fell away like sea spray returning to the ocean, but in its place a wind circled the campsite, kicking up dust that whirled around me and settled on my shoulders. The weight in the air shifted and became heavier. It focused on me.

"Have they gone?" I whispered.

Fafnir sniffed. "No," he said in his heavy-tongued voice. "They wait."

And so we waited with them.

The fire snapped and growled as though angry that it had been summoned only to smoulder uselessly between us. The huskalar kicked bodies out of the firelight. Part of me wanted to step forward and join them, but the attention of the forest kept me anchored in place.

The dancing amber firelight mixed with the writhing glacial glow of the Winds and covered the forest in a sickly shivering sheen as though oily algae covered the world.

"Does anyone have eyes on them?" Erri growled.

A chorus of negatives.

"There's enough light we should be able to see them move," Drifa said through gritted teeth. "It's like the forest is hiding them."

"They'll make a move soon enough," Erri said. "Stay sharp."

And once again, we waited.

Sigrun took half a step back and without looking at me asked, "Are you hurt?"

"I'm fine. What are they doing?"

"Waiting us out maybe. Waiting for reinforcements."

She propped her spear against her shoulder and passed me something. An axe.

"You need this more than I do."

"Sigrun, I'm not sure—"

The ground trembled. Not a landslide but a footstep. A colossal footstep.

Something tickled my skin, like a thorny vine creeping into a noose around my neck. I cried out as it snapped its hold shut. Sharp pain. The forest's attention on me. The force of it pushed me to one knee.

"Alvir, what—"

Too late. Another footstep shivered through the earth. The outlaws erupted from the undergrowth. Then more. So many more.

Sigrun leapt back to block the gap in the ramshackle shield wall. Her shield boss smashed into the head of one of the outlaws. Their skull mask splintered, their head crunched.

They swarmed the huskalar around the campfire. I crouched behind the shields, panting. Erri speared a deer-skull outlaw. A wolf-skulled outlaw grabbed Sigrun's shield as she was distracted stabbing an enemy I couldn't see.

I slashed wildly with my borrowed axe. It sliced through the outlaw's hand. They screamed, Sigrun shoved them back and finished them off.

The scent of pine was overcome by the campfire smoke and the iron tang of blood.

I moved up behind Sigrun, trying to do something useful but I could not swing the axe far enough and also keep myself safe behind her shield.

I don't know if it was because the forest had singled me out, or if they saw me as an easier target, but as soon as I stepped up to the edge of the firelight the outlaws surged up to me like a wave against a cliff face.

Sigrun toppled into me as three outlaws pushed against her shield. I steadied her. We tried to push back. They were too strong.

Fingernails scratched at my arm, too sharp for human nails. I howled in pain. My legs began to give.

Fafnir smashed into the outlaws like a charging boar. He swung his enormous shield and sent them tumbling away and like a viper's tongue his spear stabbed through one, two, all three.

He glanced at us, saw we were safe, nodded. His hood was down. I thought I saw elongated teeth jutting from under his lips and a snout-like nose. I blinked and he was gone, spear lashing out at more enemies.

Another outlaw leapt at us. Sigrun smashed her shield into their face but stumbled back as the body fell against her legs.

"Sigrun!"

I caught her arm and as I went to help her an outlaw tackled her to the ground in a crackle of twigs and jumble of mail. I heard Sigrun snarl but before I could help her someone wrenched me away.

I flailed the axe at them and its head sank into their side. The outlaw screeched in pain and retreated. As I straightened, two more outlaws grabbed my arms.

I stumbled. My feet kicked through the mud, unable to find any purchase.

Nal appeared, teeth shining in the firelight. She stabbed at the outlaws. One died. One fled, wounded. She shoved me back towards the camp, not waiting to see if I would follow before she sprinted back to the safety of the shields. I ignored Nal's direction and rushed back to help Sigrun, swinging wildly at the outlaws trying to grab me. Sigrun had dropped her shield and was using her spear to keep the outlaws away from her.

"Get back to the fire!" she shouted when she saw me.

"Not without you," I yelled back.

It felt like all the shadows of the forest had turned into a swarm of skull-faced monsters. We hacked and stabbed at the arms and hands that reached for us. The scent of churned mud and iron filled the air.

The ground shook.

They were gone.

My axe sailed through empty air.

Sigrun and I stood, side by side, panting into the suddenly-silent forest.

The still quiet pushed against my senses. The night felt frozen except for the flicker of the firelight and the slow, writhing Wind-light. I scowled.

"Come on," Sigrun said and dragged us back to the others.

The outlaws attacked before we could reform the shield wall. They crashed against the huskalar's shields like a tidal wave against a jetty. Fafnir stood firm in the centre of the attack, but all others were shoved aside. Animal skulls appeared in of front me, gaping eye sockets and grinning death. Hands grabbed at my shoulders, arms, and dragged me away from the campfire.

Sigrun screamed and dove at the outlaws.

They grabbed her as well. Their tactics, now that they had swarmed over us, seemed to be to grab as many people as they could and flee. My mind flashed back to those dark flecks of power I had seen with my second sight and panic gripped me. Were they the last remnants of human sacrifices powering whatever was happening in the forest? I kicked and writhed with fresh determination and threw off one of my captors. I swung my elbow into the face of the other, the dry wolf skull mask cracked and their head was thrown back.

Around me, some had managed to fend off the outlaws but others were being dragged away. The forest was a mess of screams, blood, and skulls.

Sigrun struggled ahead of me. Her spear forgotten by her feet. The charm her children had given her sinking in the blood-soaked mud.

I leapt forward and grabbed onto her cloak. The tangle of bodies trying to drag her away jerked to a stop. I punched one outlaw in the jaw, scraping my knuckles on the teeth of their boar skull mask. They stumbled away and Sigrun was free, scrabbling for her spear.

Something flashed in the sickly Wind-light and pain exploded in my shoulder.

A knife, hilt-deep in my flesh.

I screamed as someone threw an arm around my neck.

Sigrun leapt forward as I was dragged backwards. She dropped her spear and grabbed hold of my tunic.

A wordless snarl from my captor.

They yanked me roughly back.

Sigrun's fingers slipped. I tripped and fell. The outlaw let me fall as Sigrun tackled them, trying to keep them off me.

Another shuddering step shook the ground. Then something distant screamed, a sound halfway between creaking wood and a landslide.

Terror rippled through us as the ungodly noise echoed between the trees.

Our skull-masked enemies drained away once the screaming stopped. What few were left alive disengaged from their skirmishes, some had squirming prizes clutched in their hands, but others simply fled into the night.

As Sigrun rolled on the ground, trying to pin her opponent, another outlaw grabbed her. I tried to push myself up but my shoulder screamed at me and I fell.

Sigrun was overpowered. She kicked but they dragged her away. I heard her scream my name.

I glanced back at my companions. Through the haze of pain in my shoulder it was hard to tell who was left. The only person I could make out for sure was Fafnir. He was down on one knee, his clothes stained with blood and sliced in a thousand places.

They could not give chase.

I would not abandon Sigrun.

With a cry, I got to my feet. Every movement shook the wound in my shoulder, sending agony shivering through my entire body. I had cost Sigrun her mother, I would not cost her children theirs.

I ran. Desperate to catch up with the outlaws. I heard them crashing through the undergrowth, but as I left the firelight it was hard to make them out. I saw the impression of animal skulls highlighted in the green and blue of the Wind-light.

There.

They crossed a clearing—how had they crossed the clearing already?—and there was Sigrun, still struggling.

She saw me as I reached the edge of the trees. I pulled on the power of the gods, dragging whatever strength they could give me. The runes tattooed on my cheeks scorched my flesh as the magic found its way into me. I surged forward with new strength.

"Sigrun!"

As I called out, my foot caught a root. I tripped. Stumbled. Righted myself. They were almost lost in the darkness. I sprinted on.

Another root. This time it sent me flying forwards. I held out my hands to catch myself, but my right hand slipped from a moss-covered rock and my left would not stand against the pain of my shoulder.

The stony ground swept up to meet me.

Something smashed against my head.

Chapter Thirteen
Lost Power

I PUT A HAND TO MY THROBBING FOREHEAD. My hair was plastered to my head by something sticky. I kept my eyes closed and tried to breathe through the thumping agony behind my eyes.

Memories came to me in flashes of weapons, the copper taste of blood, and the blurred movement of outlaws in the darkness of the forest. I opened my eyes to stop reliving it and saw the canopy above me, dappled in sunlight. Morning.

More memories surfaced and panic coiled around my heart. They had captives. They took Sigrun.

I jerked to my feet, ready to chase after my sister.

Or I tried to.

Pain sliced through my head. Stars and black spots exploded across my vision. I couldn't find my balance and fell back to the ground.

I closed my eyes again to try to stop the blinding stars and stem the overwhelming panic. I took a deep breath and reached out to the power of the gods. Their steady strength would calm me and then I could help Sigrun.

I pushed my senses out, down.

Nothing, only the throbbing pain behind my eyes.

I frowned, took a breath, and tried again. This time I reached my fingers down into the mud to help with the connection. The mud was warmed by the sun but the heat faded to a deathly cold as it squelched through my fingers.

My breathing came more quickly now. I tried to slow it but the panic filled my chest. There was no room for air.

I sent my senses further out and... there. There was power

nearby, but it felt... wrong.

It was too distant, too singular, too unstable. This was not the steady, unending power of the gods. This power writhed and coiled about itself and as I reached out for it responded and reached for me.

"You are awake," came a rumbling voice.

I opened my eyes. Fafnir sat on a nearby rock, carving a chunk of wood. He looked over to me, hood covering his face once more. We sat in a clearing. Sunlight dried the mud churned up by the outlaw's stampede. Next to me was a stone streaked with dark red.

I sat up, my shoulder ached and as I put my hand to it I remembered the knife wound. The flesh had closed though it was still sore to the touch under my slashed tunic. I frowned. There were magics that could be weaved to close wounds, but I had never heard of a rune-weaver doing so whilst unconscious. Was it something I had done without meaning to? Had the gods healed me? Perhaps when I pulled in the magic to chase Sigrun across the clearing I had healed myself.

"I found you lying still," Fafnir said, waving with the woodchip-covered knife. "Yrsa kept up the chase. I brought your things."

I grunted at Fafnir, moving my arm to work some of the stiffness out.

"Who did they take?"

"Most. Drifa is injured, but with us. She tracks with Yrsa."

I grunted again, trying to push that writhing power out of my mind. Getting up, pain flashed through my head, lights peppered my vision, bile surged at the back of my throat.

Once I blinked the pain and light away, I looked around the clearing. There was a body at its edge, an arrow in its back and an animal skull lying nearby. I shuffled over and rolled them onto their front with a boot.

A woman, her expression caught half-way between pain and serenity. She had a necklace with threaded pebbles and a jawbone complete with yellowed fangs. A wolf's jaw to match her skull mask. Her clothes were ragged, covered in mud and with twigs threaded through her sleeves. Much like the outlaw that had attacked me.

Her wolf skull mask was covered in the same runes and swirling paints. I picked it up and felt a flash of power like a miniature lightning strike. I threw the mask down. Its fangs sank into the soft earth and its eyeless stare bored into me.

I thought back to that first mask: the power in it had been older, faded and it had not stung me like this. Had these outlaws prepared fresh magics for their ambush? Or was I more sensitive to the magic after calling on the gods' power so carelessly during the chase? The eyeless skull-wolf watched me, daring me to touch it again.

Carefully, I knelt and reached for it. As my fingers drew close to the paint I felt that power. Gentler now. Less lightning strike, more hearthfire. The warmth seeped into me, running up my arm, making me feel dizzy but also giving me strength.

This wasn't right. Usually, I—

Writhing power.

My attention snapped away.

Something was coming through the trees. Its power squirmed against my senses. I suddenly realised I did not have a weapon.

I opened my mouth to shout for Fafnir, to call on his Windborn strength, as Yrsa appeared between the trees.

She was covered in mud and bloodstains and stopped as she came level with me. Our eyes met and she raised her eyebrows.

The writhing power was in front of me. It reached for me.

Yrsa.

I felt around and that second squirming presence came to me from within the clearing.

Fafnir.

I frowned. I had not felt any power or presence from him before. There was no magic in any Windborn for a god-speaker to sense.

My eyes went wide and panic twisted my soul as an answer came to me. Suddenly my chest felt scraped raw and filled with terror. I retched.

I half fell, half ran away from the clearing. Before I had gone twenty paces a root caught my foot and I toppled onto my hands and knees. I retched again.

I pushed my hands deep into the earth and searched for the gods' power. I had not searched hard enough before. My head still ached from the knock against the boulder. Hard enough to crack into my skull. I could not have been thinking clearly.

Insects scuttled over my knuckles and I clawed my way deeper into the mud until my fingernails scraped across worms and stones. I took a deep breath, closed my eyes, and pushed my senses down. I felt for the space between the world of mortals and the power of spirits and gods.

Cold seeped into my fingers.

A spider crawled up to my hand, flinched away and scuttled off to the safety of leaf mulch.

Nothing.

The earth was empty.

I was dizzy. The world was hollow. There was no power to buoy me, to keep me grounded.

I pulled my hands up and shoved them under my arms.

My chest felt tight. There was no room for air in my lungs. My breath came in short, sharp bursts.

If my head injury had somehow made it more difficult to feel the magic around me, then perhaps I could still see it. I pulled up my second sight.

Nothing happened.

I tried again, scrunching my eyes so tight there were stars behind my eyelids, but whenever I opened them, all I saw was the forest.

The mundane, sunlit forest.

I could not see the haze of power hanging in the air. I couldn't see the flitting lights of small spirits dancing from tree to tree.

Panic stabbed at my heart.

I tried to breathe, but there didn't seem to be enough air in the world. The ground beneath me felt hollow. My stomach roiled and I thought if I opened my mouth I would vomit. I stood but it felt like if I took a step the dirt would crack beneath my feet and I would fall into an endless void. I stumbled to the nearest tree and clutched its trunk as I fell to my knees.

The rough bark gave me something to focus on. The physical sensation of its firm, calloused wood anchored my mind and I stayed like that for some time.

A hand on my shoulder brought me back.

"Alvir?" Drifa knelt beside me. Her hand was wrapped in torn cloth and her face was covered in dirt and scratches. "Are you alright?"

I focused on her worried expression, and that human concern anchored me. The ground began to feel whole again and the world stopped spinning.

I nodded and let Drifa pull me up. I felt lightheaded, but not like I was going to throw up.

"I'm okay," I said. "I'm still reeling from last night."

"I hear you." She held up her bandaged hand and then gestured for us to head back to the clearing.

"Is there anyone else?" I asked, trying to shift the focus from whatever had happened to me.

Drifa shook her head. "Only the Windborn. Too much trouble to take, I bet."

We came back to the clearing. Yrsa and Fafnir sat on a fallen tree with their heads pressed close together. When they noticed us they sat straight and shuffled away from each other.

The writhing presence resurfaced at the back of my mind.

"Do we know where they went?" I asked, aiming my question at Drifa but with my voice loud enough to encompass the Windborn as well. "Fafnir said you and Yrsa were chasing the outlaws."

Drifa slumped on the boulder with my blood streaked on it and sighed. "Oh yeah, we chased those bastards alright. There was something strange about it though. No matter how fast we ran and believe me Yrsa can move when she wants to, they were always ahead of us. They'd run through some trees and then when we went to dive through the same part of the forest it was all gorse bushes and roots tripping us up." She looked at me. "Do you know any tricks for tracking someone with magic?"

Fafnir shot a look to Yrsa, but she ignored him.

"There are spells," I said. "Perhaps I can work something

up to find the rest of them. We should head back to their camp. We're more likely to find something I can use to track them there."

Drifa nodded and looked to the Windborn for confirmation. Fafnir shrugged. Yrsa made no comment but followed us as we left.

The walk through the forest felt like it took forever. I quickly fell to the back of the group, trudging through the mud and keeping a careful eye on the roots and rocks on the ground. I still had an echo of a headache and I did not want to provoke it. I reached out my arms and ran my fingers along each tree we passed. With every touch, I thought I felt the spirit of the tree, but it was faint and felt nothing like the magic I was used to. Magic I knew was there. I gritted my teeth against a feeling of helplessness. It felt like I was suddenly blind. I was adrift without an anchor or safe harbour.

Ahead: writhing.

I swallowed the bile rising at the back of my throat.

Then we were back at the camp.

Bodies were strewn across the clearing and the ground was stained with red. More bile at the back of my throat.

"What do you need for the ritual?" Drifa asked.

I looked around and waved my hands, already exhausted. "Something that will point us to the rest. Is there some possession they all have?"

"Let's see."

Drifa strode to one of the bodies and bent to examine it. Fafnir and Yrsa wandered between the dead without checking them properly as though they didn't trust me to cast the spell. I gritted my teeth and stomped over to the nearest outlaw's body. My eyes lingered on the animal skull. There was still a tingle at my fingertips from the skull in the clearing. Perhaps some defensive magic I had set off when I picked it up. Still, I ignored it and sifted through the rest of the outlaw's clothes. They had a knife and a necklace on them. The necklace was a jawbone with stones, much the same as the outlaw from the clearing.

Drifa came to crouch beside me. She saw me looking at the

necklace and prodded it. "They're all wearing something like that," Drifa said. "What do you reckon?"

She pulled the necklace free with a snap and held it up to the light. The jawbone had been snapped in half and threaded through the necklace to lie lightly on the outlaw's chest. Centred between the jawbones there was a stone. It had a hole with a cord threaded through it and as the stone twisted in the air I saw the runes lightly carved into its surface. We quickly checked the closest bodies and saw the same stone with the same runes on their necklaces.

"I think this will work."

I took the necklace, careful to only touch the cord, and found a patch of earth that was easy enough to scrape clear of blood and leaves.

"Here." Fafnir's thick voice from behind me.

He held out my pack in one meaty, cloth-wrapped hand. Instinctively, I snatched it from him and saw that Fafnir's fingers were wrapped together. It was almost as though he had two thick fingers on each hand rather than four nimble ones. The weight of the god-stones jerked my arm down and my bag thunked on the ground. Fafnir dipped his head and wandered away.

Had he looked through my things? Did he know why it was so heavy?

I shook my head, putting the Windborn out of my mind as I took some ingredients from my pack.

Rosemary, downy feathers, and a bird's skull.

There was no time for delicate lines: I ploughed a rough circle into the ground with my fingers then carved some basic runes around it. *Yearning. Distance. Sight.*

I took a breath, tried to focus on the gods' power—it was still beyond reach—and pushed some of my will into the runes.

Nothing.

I pushed again.

There was nothing.

The nearby squirming presence seemed to reach out for me but I shoved it away. I couldn't sense the solid, god-granted magic within me that I needed for the ritual.

I shook my head and retraced the lines in the dirt, more carefully now. I needed to finish the ritual, put everything in its place, and I would be able to draw on what power I needed.

This time I placed the necklace in the centre of the circle and arranged the components around it.

A deep breath.

"Father," I intoned. "Hear my prayer."

The words felt empty. Where was their usual power?

I closed my eyes.

"Father," I said again, straining to put all my willpower into the words. "Hear my prayer."

This wasn't right. Where was the weight of the god's attention?

"Father." This time my voice cracked and I choked on the rest of the words.

"Alvir, are you okay?" Drifa's voice from somewhere nearby.

I looked at her. "I'm fine. It's just... I need... I need some air."

I stood and took an unsteady step away from the ritual. I couldn't look away and it made me lose my balance.

Drifa caught my arm. "Are you sure you're okay?"

I shook her off. "Yes."

Fafnir had taken a step towards me. I kept my face turned away.

"Alvir," he said, his voice impossibly calm.

He reached out an enormous, bandaged hand to me and as he did I felt that presence reach for me too. The hairs on the back of my neck stood on end. It felt like there were a thousand invisible tendrils within Fafnir all trying to touch me.

I took another step back, my eyes widening in horror, then ran into the forest.

Chapter Fourteen
Beyond Mortal Hands

My tears blurred the forest as I ran. I bounced from one tree to another, kicking up dust and stones, and I soon stumbled to a halt. I was spent.

In vain, I tried to summon my second sight. I knew it wouldn't work, but I couldn't stop myself. I knew that there were spirits here. I knew there was a mist of blotted power hanging in the air. Why couldn't I see it?

I fell to the floor and scrabbled at the ground, clawing chunks of mud out from between the roots of a tree. Deeper and deeper, I gouged until my hands were caked in cold, wet earth and my fingernails were bloodied by sharp stones. I pressed my hands as hard as I could into the earth and closed my eyes.

I opened myself as I would for a prayer to the gods, but this time I opened myself to whatever powers were out there. Gods. Spirits. Troll-ghosts. I tried to pull them all into myself. Anything that would be able to tell me what was wrong with me. How to fix me. I stretched my senses, the ones I had spent years training and honing as a god-speaker, trying to feel something, anything...

The sound of the forest. The smell of mud and pine. The rough touch of bark. Only the physical world.

Then, like a river at the edge of hearing, I felt a quiet, relentless magic.

I hadn't noticed it at first. My heartbeat rattled like a war drum and it had drowned out this careful presence, this deliberate power.

It shifted, perhaps realising I had noticed it. It was like a plant turning to follow the sun, slow but intentional. It was a deep power and now that I had focused on it I thought I could feel myriad other things latched on to it like leaves on a branch or crows on a carcass. And there was something else. Something black and stagnant glittering across it. If those small powers were feasting crows then this dark presence was a jealous wolf.

Slowly, I brought my senses back to myself. Whatever this fetid wolf was I did not want to attract its attention.

I had never felt more useless than I did in that moment. Trapped in the middle of a forest full of outlaws and magic and severed from the power of the gods.

I opened my eyes and I felt something edging towards me in the forest. I felt it squirm against the edge of my mind. Not something. Someone.

"Alvir."

Fafnir's rumbling voice floated through the forest and soon after I felt his plodding footsteps. I pulled myself free of my hastily gouged pit and fell back, sprawling, onto the ground, heedless of the cold damp the forest floor spread through my clothes.

I stared through the branches above me.

I could not run from this.

The Winds were gone now, though I would never again be without them.

"I am here, Fafnir."

The enormous Windborn shuffled over and crouched next to me. That writhing sensation fizzed in my ears.

"For what it is worth, I am sorry," he said.

I kept my eyes on the sky. Could the Winds still see during the day? Were they watching us even now, laughing at me, at what they had taken from me?

"It is not so bad to be Windborn."

I glanced at him. He twisted a twig between his enormous, bandaged fingers. The hood was still up on his cloak, hiding his face, and for an instant my future flashed before my eyes. I would be forever shunned. The god-speaker turned Windborn. Who could possibly want to know such an abomination? What possible use could there be for someone so clearly thrust out of the gods' graces?

"Vidsetr is a good place for Windborn. We are too far from the shore to send longships across the sea and Chief Ormhildr does not demand too much of us."

The squirming fizz in my ears hissed louder with every half-slurred word out of Fafnir's mouth. He was no comfort. His words only proved that my life was over. I was—had been—a god-speaker. Wanderer, healer, friend to all. Now I was Windborn. I was only good for spilling blood.

"True, becoming Windborn is not all good. My hands are not as nimble as they were and I so liked to carve toys for the children."

Carving trinkets for children? What loss was that? I had lost any connection I had to the gods. My soul was lost.

"I am not some warrior gifted a second life and stronger arms," I snapped. "Do you think people will look on my face, the runes I have tattooed there, and welcome me? You can keep plying your deathly trade. I wandered wherever the gods sent me and I channelled their power. Now that is severed from me forever and I am to be chained to some petty chieftain. Everyone will see my tattoos and laugh at how far I have fallen."

Fafnir nodded. His hood twitched in the wind. He let the twig fall from his fingers and he flexed them, examining them slowly as the bandages crinkled. Somehow his silence sliced at me more deeply than any rebuttal.

"I know your anger and pain, Alvir. You are owed your fury, but they have taken your sister. They have taken mine. We cannot linger too long and you still have strength. We need your help."

Fafnir stretched his arm out as though to reach out for me, then changed his mind and instead reached up and slowly pulled down his hood.

I couldn't stop my intake of breath.

His face was monstrous. His nose was pinched up into a wide-nostrilled snout and his teeth were too big for his mouth. No, they weren't teeth, they were tusks. Two tusks curved out of the bottom of his mouth, pressing his lips into strange forms, and two more tusks jutted out at odd angles from under his top lip.

He looked at me and, for the first time, I could truly look back. Amber eyes stared at me and there was more compassion there than I deserved.

"Do not be long, brother," he said and I saw how those tusk-teeth forced his words to slur. He pushed himself to his feet. "If you cannot help us find our sisters then we will have to rely on this." He tapped his snout-nose.

We looked at each other for a moment more, then he turned and walked away. His crunching footsteps faded into the forest and the fizzing faded from my ears.

I sat for a little longer and the silence between the trees enveloped me. I looked at my hands. Dirt caked my fingernails and my forearms were covered in pink lines. Yesterday, those had been thorn-scratches, bleeding and bright red. I shrugged my shoulder. The knife wound now reduced to a dull ache. I was healed by whatever powers the Winds had used to bring me back from the dead and drag my soul from the gods' halls.

My head was still sore, but my headache was gone. I rubbed at the place where the rock had smashed against my skull. My fingers came away dusted with scabs. I tried to think of any Windborn stories that were not vicious blood-soaked tales. I could not.

Was this to be my life? To be alone and covered in quick-healing wounds?

That was a question for another time.

I looked out at the forest and had never felt more alone. The trees disappeared into infinity and I knew I would never again see the spirits dance along their boughs or sparkle in the fjords. I reached out my senses, one last time, but there was nothing until I pressed against the squirming power of the Winds from Fafnir's receding presence. I closed my eyes and pinched the bridge of my nose to clear the tears from my eyes.

Somewhere in this dark, verdant expanse, Sigrun was a prisoner. My mind travelled back to a warm home in Vidsetr where her wife and children waited for their spouse and mother. I remembered a day, years distant, when I had struggled to shepherd a woman through a complicated childbirth and had pulled Sigrun into the world, bloody and helpless. I had not known enough then to save Sigrun's mother, but I would not leave Sigrun out there to die. I would bring her home to her children with or without the gods' help.

ᚠ

They had been busy at the camp. By the time I returned, they had dragged a few of the bodies together and laid out their weapons and skull masks. Fafnir had left his hood down and when he noticed my return he offered me a crooked smile. I nodded, trying to match it but I could only muster a grimace. Drifa crouched beside a tree at the edge of the clearing, checking arrows. Yrsa sat nearby sharpening her axes. I moved to where Fafnir knelt beside the bodies.

"I have a scent," he said, waving a meaty hand at the collection of bodies. "What can you tell from them? Any information will help."

I felt my stomach twist to look at the butchered bodies of these once-men and women. There was nothing that so clearly cut the line between a person and meat than the slice of a blade. Swallowing the bile at the back of my throat, I bent to examine the grisly collection. The outlaws all wore the same thing—old, ragged clothes combined with twigs and leaves to let them melt into the forest—and their animal skulls were all scratched and daubed with runes and paint. The runes were all the same. All woven to hide them in the forest and shield their minds from any magic that might find them. Perhaps not only magic...

I picked up a wolf skull to examine it. A flare of heat at my fingertips from the power in the runes. As I flinched from the sudden warmth and dropped the mask as the heat fled into my hand and up my arm. I grimaced as the heat swirled in my chest. It felt like I had swallowed a burning coal. Slowly, too slowly, the pain and heat dissipated. The weave reminded me of the border-stone at the edge of Vidsetr, but it felt more akin to the god-stone. It was slow and deep but threaded with something sharp. A rotten root wrapped in thorns.

"This is intricate work." I clenched and unclenched my fists in frustration. "All these masks are linked to the person who wore them. If I had... if I could use magic it could have led us to them."

"What's the magic for?" Drifa asked, leaving her arrows to join us.

"To keep them hidden."

"Makes me feel better about not realising we were being tracked," she said.

"It's more than that," I said. "It's not about hiding in the forest. You see these two runes? They protect the mind, like I did for Laufey. It's a complicated weave to maintain. They must have known Yrsa would be coming, otherwise why bother?"

Yrsa paused her sharpening and shrugged. "I am not a secret."

"Even so. It means they have forced Ulfrun to work against us and that might mean she's left clues, or weaknesses for us to exploit."

Yrsa cocked an eyebrow at me. "Then why make these masks?"

"I don't know. If she's captured then there's only so much she'll be able to do without risking her safety."

Yrsa scoffed and went back to sharpening her axes.

"What else can you see?" Fafnir said as he shuffled up to me and the bodies.

The others were scrawny, their muscles tightly bound with no gap left for fat. My gorge rose as I caressed the dead. It was nothing I had not done before, but that had been as part of the final blessings to send a soul to the gods' halls or to figure out what ailment had caused the person's death. This felt different. They were my enemies. Men and women hacked down the night before. If the Winds hadn't been writhing in the sky then I could so easily have been like them. I could have been meat for crows. My stomach twisted. How could I be grateful to the Winds? They severed me from the gods and now, with these bodies barely cold, I'd nearly thanked them for keeping me alive.

I went to push the closest body away, disgusted, when

something sharp caught my fingers. I frowned and lifted up the man's shirt. Paint swirled on his chest, the same colour as the paint on the mask, and something sharp had been pushed between his ribs. Shattered bone and chips of stone jutted from his chest like seeds pressed into fertile earth, each one anchored between two ribs. Grimacing, I put my fingers to one of the stones. It was as cold as the flesh it was mounted in and though I could not feel any magic in them, the runes and paint told me these scattered stones were part of something bigger. From the look of the archaic patterns painted across the grey flesh it was linked to something ancient.

"Has..." I trailed off, worried about sounding foolish, but I could not shake the thought. "Has anyone ever seen any trolls in the forest? Even stories of your parents or grandparents seeing trolls?"

"No one has seen trolls here since the Warrior killed them all," Drifa said. She raised her eyebrows as though I was a child asking what held up the sky. "Are you sure he's alright? He hit his head pretty hard."

I chewed my lip. Of course the Warrior had destroyed the trolls. We had walked by their corpse-boulders. But was that truly all that was left? I thought back to the shimmering spirit, the shadow-creature, the ungodly scream during the fight.

The trolls' bodies had been destroyed. What of their souls? The Winds were the trapped spirits of the Giants who stood against the gods in the god-war. Why wouldn't the spirits of the trolls wander the Trolbjolvid? Surely it was possible that the Warrior had cursed their spirits to forever wander the shadows under the trees and now, with the shattering of the god-stone, they sought their revenge.

I continued my examination of the bodies for a few more minutes though they did not reveal any more. If anything, I became more confused as I traced the stone-studded chests and the runes and marks painted there. If I had tried to weave a spell like this it would have faded to nothing within moments or else killed the host in an effort to sustain the weave. Whoever had made this had done so with old magic that mirrored the carvings of the god-stones like a hearthfire imitates the sun. There was something else there. Something deliberate that lay at the bottom of the weave like black silt.

"There's nothing here that I can use to track these outlaws," I said, eventually, and pushed myself to my feet. "This runecraft is beyond anything I have ever seen."

"You couldn't stab someone in the chest with a pebble and cover them in paint?" Yrsa said with a sneer.

"It's more than that," I snapped back. "I could recreate this spell, as brutal as it is, but it would either fade too quickly to be useful or it would kill whoever I put the spell on. Whoever did this must be terrifyingly powerful."

"Ulfrun is a skilled weaver," Fafnir said as though that settled the matter.

I bit my lip, letting the comment pass. I had no doubt that Ulfrun was a competent spell-weaver, but this was beyond mortal hands.

For a moment, there was only the ambient sound of the forest. Birds, leaves, and the hum of insects. If I closed my eyes I could almost ignore the bodies around me, the squirming Windborn presence pressing against my mind, the aching once-wounds in my head and shoulder. I could almost pretend that I was in the forest and everything was as it was.

"It looks like it's up to you and me, big man." Drifa rolled her shoulders and picked up her bow.

Fafnir nodded, a slow bow of his deformed head. "I am ready."

"Then let's go."

They packed up their things with an efficiency born from long, necessary practice. I wandered over to my pack and paused. Inside: a change of clothes, components for spells I would never cast again, and the god-stone shards. My mouth went dry. Should I bring the pack? I had reacted to the magic from the skull-mask. What would happen if I touched the god-stones?

Fafnir came to stand beside me, making the leaves by my feet shake.

"Come, brother," he rumbled, a soft smile twisted on his face. "We must save our kin."

I looked up at him, furious and jealous of his strength and purpose that he could simply point himself at the unknown and not waver. But the emotions dissolved as quickly as they had appeared and I felt ashamed. Fafnir was offering me peace and companionship, to be a guide to the new world I had been resurrected into.

I smiled at him and threw my pack over my shoulder.

"Then lead the way."

Fafnir's smile expanded and it was unsettling and reassuring in equal measure.

As Fafnir went to join Drifa at the edge of the clearing and decide on our course, Yrsa tossed a knife to me then shoved a spear at my chest. "You're Windborn now. That means you fight."

She didn't wait for a response before she swept off to join the others.

It was Sigrun's spear. The charms from her children clattered against the ash shaft. I stared at the shining spearhead and gripped the spear until I felt splinters prickle my palms. I went to join the other Windborn and we few began our hunt.

Chapter Fifteen
Distant Ghosts

THE FOREST LOOKED MUCH THE SAME TO ME as it ever had. Fafnir and Drifa led us on a twisting trail over hillocks, through gorse bushes, and clambering over rocky outcrops. There was no chatter, no banter amongst the group as there had been when we first entered the forest. The only sounds were our footsteps, the caress of leaf on leaf, our passage upsetting the undergrowth, the endless hum of unseen insects, the flutter of feathers from passing birds, a hoarse elk-cry in the distance, burbling bird song—

"You said you couldn't catch them," I said, to break the relentless forest-silence.

Yrsa shot me a look. "It's not a problem I've had before. It must be the forest putting me off."

"They were too quick," Drifa called back. "I can move in the woods if I want to. I know how to look out for the roots and rocks. I've chased game through the forest without missing a step. But I couldn't keep up with them..."

"They know the forest," Yrsa said, gruffly. "That's all it is. We'll find them."

From her expression, Drifa did not agree but she kept her silence.

Drifa fell back to walk with me. Together, we scraped leaves across our footprints and tried to make it as difficult as possible for anyone to find our trail. "The gods can see everything, can't they, Alvir?"

I glanced at Drifa, surprised by the question, then shot a look at the two Windborn ahead of us whose power squirmed against my skin.

"The gods do not see everything all at once," I said after a moment. "But they can turn their sight to most places."

"Most places?"

"Well, there are certain places—like the cavernous depths of the Ever-Rotting Queen's realm—that even the gods cannot scry into."

"What about this realm?" She chewed her lip. "What about the Trolbjolvid?"

It was a question that had been pawing at the edges of my mind. We had journeyed into the depths of this cursed forest and there were powers here, certainly, but how much sway did the gods have in this place? The spells I had woven had been slowly picked apart the deeper we travelled and worst of all...

My heart turned to ice, each beat sending a shiver of pain through my chest.

Worst of all, my connection to the gods had been severed. If ever there were likely to be a place in the world the gods could not reach it would be the Forest of Broken Trolls.

I glanced over at Drifa and saw the same need for reassurance in her that I had seen countless times across the Fjalmark. I tried to shake off my misgivings and show her the fatherly face of a god-speaker but my expression was strained.

"Even if something did have the power to prevent the gods from watching over us—and such a power would need to be strong enough to rival the gods themselves—the gods would not stand for it. Anyone or anything that might try to challenge the gods' might and stand in their way would find themselves the subject of a swift lesson. The god-war may have been a long time ago, but the gods are still the supreme force of this world."

"Until the war that ends the world," Drifa muttered.

I forced a chuckle. "That is centuries away. We are hunting outlaws. They might have some strange magic, but they cannot hurt the gods."

Drifa looked at me and slowly her uncertainty unravelled and was replaced by a cautious optimism. She nodded and shot me a shy smile. "Thank you, Alvir. What with being surrounded by all these shadows and everything that's happened... I needed that."

"It's what god-speakers are for," I said and tapped my wooden, thrice-threaded arm-ring.

Drifa smiled, seemingly reassured. She pushed on ahead of me. Something twisted in my stomach as I realised that I no longer deserved to wear my god-speaker arm-ring. The thought of losing it was like losing a part of myself. To take it off would be to admit what I had become. I thumbed at the rune tattoos on my cheeks. At least I would never lose those.

Ahead, Fafnir and Yrsa had stopped.

"Look."

Fafnir gestured for us to join him. He crouched at the edge of a path made by some passing beast, perhaps a bear judging by how wide the trail was.

"Did the outlaws use this trail?" I asked.

"Not only outlaws," Fafnir said and gestured to a puddle in the wet ground.

"Gods above," Drifa gasped and muttered a prayer of protection.

"What are you—" My voice fell away as I realised it was not a puddle, but a heavy footprint. It was rounded like a tree trunk, about a pace across, sunk about a finger's length into the ground and filled with muddy water. More of the circular footprints led down the trail. Whatever had made these footprints had been heavy, colossal.

"Did they come this way?" Yrsa asked.

"See there." Drifa pointed to a chain of leaves that were crushed into the dirt leading to mud churned with boot prints. "That's the clearest trail we've seen all day."

Fafnir nodded along with Drifa's comments and confirmed that the outlaw's scent followed this trail. Drifa assured me that with all the churned mud and other tracks there was no longer any need for us to hide our passage and so we moved on as a tight group, clustered in Fafnir's wake with Yrsa behind me.

This close to the other Windborn I felt suffocated by the whirling force of their powers. I tried to fall to the back of the group so the Windborn would be in front of me, but as I slowed, Yrsa pressed a hand against my back—the writhing boiled and sparked against my mind—and pushed me on.

"Keep up," she said. "You need to stay close."

I took a deep breath, thankful that it tasted of moss and dirt and pine—scents of the forest—and was not laced with some ethereal Windborn scent. I sucked in a few more lungfuls of fresh air and my stomach stopped squirming, though nothing seemed to be able to quell the sense of the Windborn powers reaching for me.

Along the trail there was one enormous sunken footstep for every five paces that I took and every three of Fafnir's. I glanced at the massive Windborn and shuddered. These steps must have been made by the shadow-creature and now that we were following its trail I realised how large it truly was.

We followed the tracks for an hour before Drifa noticed a smaller trail that cut across it. I was left with Yrsa as the two trackers crouched together, trying to decipher which path we should follow. I looked at the mind-reading Windborn. She swept the forest with a bored expression. I opened my mouth to try and break the awkward silence. I knew I should try and connect with this person, this Windborn with whom I had suddenly become joined but my mouth went dry when I tried to summon the words.

"What can you do?" Yrsa asked.

I frowned. "What do you mean?"

She gestured vaguely in my direction and I felt her power press against my skull. "You're a Windborn now. You must have something you can do."

"I... I don't know. I don't think I can do anything."

Yrsa snorted. "Doubtful. All Windborn can do something, even if they're bigger, stronger. Like Fafnir. You have to do something. There's something about you..."

She trailed off and I realised this was the longest I had ever heard her speak. Now that I was Windborn, it seemed she had let her defences down.

"What about me?"

Yrsa crossed her arms and looked off into the forest before shooting a glance back at me. "You can feel me, right? Feel the Windborn power in me."

I gritted my teeth and looked away. I knew what she

meant. Of course I did, but I couldn't bring myself to utter the words. Even the thought of it made my tongue feel slick and rotten.

The writhing presence beside me intensified. It felt like a cyclone of wind filled with maggots. Then it reached out and brushed against me, indiscriminate at first, then the maggot-tendrils caressed my head and pressed against my mind. She was trying to read my thoughts.

I clenched my jaw and kept my gaze locked on the forest.

The writhing washed over me again. Power scraped across my skull like scuttling insect legs.

"Stop it!" I waved my hands to fend off the feeling.

The writhing fell away and I turned around to see Yrsa smirking.

"Can you feel it now?" she asked, amustment clear in her voice.

I gritted my teeth, thought about not answering, but I didn't want to feel that scuttling power again.

"Yes. I can feel it."

"Good." She nodded. "You'll feel Fafnir too when he gets close but there's something different about you. It's like my Windborn power forgets you're there if I'm not looking at you."

I frowned. "Is that... normal?"

"No. Maybe you can turn invisible. You tried that yet?"

"No," I said with a scowl and turned away again. "I don't have... I don't know what I can do anymore."

"Fine." Yrsa's voice feigned disinterest. "Just get your head on straight. If you get any of us killed because you're still crying about being Windborn then you'll have me to deal with."

I kept myself turned away, trying to suppress a shudder. I had seen what Yrsa could do, how swiftly her axe-fangs bled the life from her enemies, and I did not want to feel their sharpness.

"They went this way." Drifa's voice cut through the air, saving me from Yrsa's terse threat. She pointed down the smaller trail where Fafnir still stood a little way down. "It's hard to tell as the trail is so well used, but a group went this way not too long ago and, judging from the depths of the footprints, they were carrying something with them."

"We are getting close," Fafnir rumbled. "The smell is stronger."

I gripped my spear—Sigrun's spear—and muttered a prayer to the Warrior to give me strength. As I stared into the green depths around us, I was sure that every branch twitching in the breeze hid some outlaw ready to leap out at us or summon whatever monsters were hidden in the depths of the forest.

"Should we be using the same trail as the outlaws?" I said. "What if they use it to find us?"

Fafnir rolled his shoulders and shook his head. His knotted face scrunched into a thoughtful expression, teeth twisting as his lips pursed. "We cannot leave the trail to wander the forest. We risk losing the trail. We will follow until we know where they have gone. Do not fear. We will not be caught."

I frowned but could not offer any alternatives. My ravens were long fled and the thought of trying any fresh spells filled me with a cold dread, though that was nothing compared to the drenching terror I felt as something in my chest responded to Fafnir's closeness. A squirming power that turned my stomach.

"They're not the only ones using the trail, there's animals using it too, so if we're careful they won't be able to tell it's us either," Drifa said. "It's the strangest thing. Usually, if people start using a deer track, then the deer will stop. They'll smell the humans and find somewhere else to wander. But there's fresh hoofprints here. It's like the forest is ignoring them."

We all shifted uneasily at that. Our eyes scanned the shadowed, infinite greenery around us, but we could see no enemies.

I let our trackers lead us away from the crossroads and soon, with the foliage pressing closely against us along the smaller trail, I felt suffocated. As the wind pushed through the trees, the frustrated hiss of the leaves clawed at my back and every patch of darkness puddled under a fern's open leaves felt like it hid a predator.

Once again, time was lost to me. Trees and stones and

ferns and bushes all faded into one another. The sentinel trees all identical. The only thing that anchored my sense of direction was the track we followed, leaving me with forward and back.

For hours, forward.

Eventually, the tracks and footprints became deeper and more numerous. Wherever this path was leading us it was busy with outlaws.

"Okay," Drifa said. "We need to get off the trail now. Our passage is pretty well hidden by everyone else's movements, but these prints are fresh and they're overlapping backwards and forwards. They're using this trail frequently. We need to move off before someone sees us."

I breathed out a sigh of relief and let my grip on the spear loosen.

"Where do we go from here, then?" I asked. The track was my guide through the forest. If we wandered away from it then I would be lost in moments.

"This way," Fafnir said, pointing into the forest to the right of the track. "The scent of humans is thicker this way. We will find a safe space and make camp."

No one else had a better plan, or any plan at all, so we pushed our way into the overgrowth. Drifa hid our passage as best she could, making sure Fafnir did not snap too many branches on his way past the saplings and twigs scattered on the ground.

Within five paces, I was lost in the depths of the forest. If I had not seen the trail with my eyes then I would not have believed it was behind us.

Yrsa moved me on with a grunt and a shove. As her hand came close to my body the echo of the Winds within us both squirmed and writhed. As she touched me I felt a similar burst to when I had picked up the mask. Some sliver of power slipped between us and I gasped as a whisper of Yrsa's voice echoed in my head.

...get us killed...

Then it was gone and I was left stumbling at the force of her touch.

I turned back to Yrsa and found her looking from me to

her fingers, her expression clouded with uncertainty and hostility.

"What is it?" I asked. I knew I would be an outcast when I eventually left the forest, the god-speaker who had been severed from the gods. I could not bear to be an outcast from Windborn as well.

"Nothing. Get moving."

Drifa found us a hollow under a fallen tree in which to make camp. The tree trunk was as wide as Fafnir and lay over the hollow like a roof beam stolen from a giant's home. We made ourselves as comfortable as we could as the bark collected moisture and rained it down on us.

It wasn't long before the forest's first false dusk came to us, earlier than usual as the shadow of our hollow enveloped us, but this time the darkness made me feel safe. The world shrunk around us, slipping out of existence as it was swallowed by night, and I was swaddled by the swirling Windborn powers around me.

We were hidden. We were protected by two powerful warriors. We were safe.

I swallowed and looked at the tattoos across my fingers and the back of my hands and I felt a traitor.

ᚠ

I startled awake during the night. The Windborn writhing enveloped me and pressed against my chest and I sat bolt upright, fear wrapping tight around my lungs until my memories settled in place. When they did a deep sorrow soaked into my bones but still the Windborn power swirled around me.

Something was wrong.

I looked around. All I could see was the black, flat column of the fallen tree and the lumpy shadows of my companions. Fafnir and Drifa lay next to me, breathing steady and slow, and Yrsa had clambered up the side of the hollow and leaned against its lip, looking out. It was her. I let out a breath. Power wriggled out from her like heat from a bonfire.

"What are you doing?" I whispered.

"Trying to feel if there's anyone out there."

"Is there?"

"Nothing close enough to be a problem."

She slid back down the side of the crater until she lay next to Fafnir.

"But there are people out there?"

"Foxes, a bear, maybe a person," She shrugged.

I shifted, trying to get comfortable and go back to sleep.

With the urgent churning of Windborn power around me the darkness around me was suffocating. Beneath me: black earth. Above: night-dark trees. I was surrounded by an abyss of oak and dirt and all I could feel was Windborn power pressing against my senses as though it was trying to creep inside and poison me.

I needed to escape. I had to get out.

This was a familiar suffocation. I had felt it whenever I stayed too long in a village or distant homestead and had become too attached to the community. I knew then it was time to move on. To become the Wanderer once again. But here, I could not escape. I could not flee into the predator-filled forest, could not disappear on the road and reappear once I had faded into fond memory to be welcomed back. I pushed myself up, desperate to see the night sky, to see anything.

Yrsa shifted, raised her head to watch me.

"I need to relieve myself," I said.

"Don't go far."

"I'll be fine, I need to—"

"I know what you need to do. Don't go far," Yrsa said. This time her voice was firmer, a command rather than a concerned comment from a comrade.

I grunted as I scrabbled my way out of the hollow, clawing my way up the cold wet earth.

The world opened up as soon as I stood on flat ground. There was enough weak starlight pushing through the canopy to see the impression of the forest around me. The woods were daubed in shadow-paint, but the light was enough to walk by.

I walked until the Windborn writhing was nothing more

than a whisper at the back of my mind.

I rubbed at my eyes until stars exploded beneath my eyelids. When I looked back at the forest I thought I saw something glimmering in the distance.

A spark between the trees. Then another.

A wildfire? No. The forest was still damp with the memory of winter and the distant glimmer shifted from blue to green. Spirits then.

I fiddled with my god-speaker arm-ring.

Perhaps being a Windborn was not so different from being a god-speaker. I closed my eyes and reached out with my senses as I would have when I prepared any spell or ritual.

The fizz of Yrsa and Fafnir rose up against my ears. I pushed them to one side.

I had to be able to feel something of the magic that I knew surrounded me. I had to.

There. Something small or distant. A vibration like a fly heard in another room, a hammer strike from across the marketplace, a tree falling on a distant hill. It was as though I could hear the trees growing and breathing in the night.

I opened my eyes, now thick with tears. I was not locked away from the spirits and power that the gods had once bestowed upon me. I could still feel it. A blessing from the black-hearted Trickster, no doubt.

The distant spirits flickered between the trees. Once again, I wondered what they were. Troll-ghosts? I thought of the Lífraka, the legendary troll-forged axe that had sliced the Winds souls from their bodies. What secret, powerful knowledge could those troll-ghosts have? If they could create a weapon to slice the Winds souls from their bodies could they draw the Winds from me like poison from a wound?

I watched the ghosts for some time. I could not fathom how far they were from me. In the depths of the night, they felt close enough to touch and then, with the blink of an eye, so distant that I could barely make them out. They could have been small enough to hide beneath the fern bushes or large enough to scrape the canopy with their heads. I thought of rushing to them and demanding they teach me their secrets. Then I thought of the skull masks. The outlaws leaping from the darkness like wolves. I turned away.

The hairs on the back of my neck stiffened as I felt something scratch at the back of my mind. A Windborn power. Yrsa. It pressed against my skull for a heartbeat or two then, apparently satisfied, it retreated back to our hidden camp.

I looked at my hands, tried to ignore the rune-weaver tattoos encasing every knuckle and crease otherwise I might have wept. They were Windborn hands now, but still so different to Fafnir's. I thought of his bandage-wrapped fingers and how easily those fingers gripped a spear, took lives. That was what Yrsa had said. I was Windborn. I had to fight. When we had been ambushed at the outlaw camp, I had been terrified. The thought of being forced into battle after battle twisted my gut. When I held a spear I held it like my rune-woven staff. It was something to lean on and perhaps to be used as a club if the worst came to the worst. My spear lay back at our camp. Sigrun's spear.

I sighed and pushed myself to my feet, then made my way back to our camp using the tug of the Windborn power to find my way through the shadow-trees.

Yrsa shifted as I half-slid back into the darkness. She grunted, the best she would do for a greeting. I pawed my way back to Sigrun's spear and clutched it as I lay back down. The children-given charms clattered on the spear shaft. I knew I would have to fight again. It wasn't about being Windborn. It was about saving Sigrun and protecting her—my—family.

I could not shatter another.

Chapter Sixteen
Summoned Enemies

THE FIRST THING I SAW WHEN I WOKE was a grey-haired woman, cross-legged, eyes closed, and meditating. For a moment, I thought it was Eylis and my heart lifted that I should be able to seek answers from a wise god-speaker. Slowly, the world came back to me and I realised I was not in the God-Speaker's home in Konvald. I lay on the dirt underneath a fallen tree in the middle of the Forest of Broken Trolls. Windborn powers pressed against my skin like a heavy mist and my sister was somewhere in the forest, a prisoner.

Yrsa shifted where she sat and tilted her head as though listening to some small, distant sound.

Fafnir leaned over to me and offered me food and drink. I took both and gestured to Yrsa.

"What's she doing?"

"Reaching," he said, voice lumbering through the word. "She sends her mind to find others. She will tell us where the outlaws make their camp."

I nodded and sipped at the cold water and tore at a strip of dried beef. It came to me how much like a god-speaker she looked, cross-legged and reaching out to sense something beyond sight. A shiver ran up my spine that she could look so similar and yet be so separate.

Yrsa opened her eyes as Drifa slid into the hollow, back with full waterskins from a nearby stream and confirmation that there were no sneaking outlaws nearby. Yrsa stretched out a hand for one of the waterskins and drank deeply.

"They are about a league away," Yrsa said.

"You're sure it's them?" I asked.

"Yes. It's too far to get much detail. There are people and what feels like animals. A few minds are familiar."

"Who?"

Fafnir and I asked the question at the same time, both leaning forward in tense expectation.

Yrsa shrugged. "Too far to tell. Could be Ulfrun. Could be Nal."

"What about Sigrun?" I pressed.

"Maybe," Yrsa said. "It could be everyone. Like I said, I can't tell."

"Then we go," Fafnir said. He stood, so tall that his hair brushed the bottom of our tree-roof. "We cannot wait."

We all muttered our agreement and made our hurried preparations. I took up my spear and a thrill went through me. It was an echo of the much-storied battle-lust, a keen anticipation at the conflict to come and the blood soon to be spilled by the narrow tooth of ash and steel held in my hands. I watched the sun flash off the spear's iron fang then caught myself.

My face dropped and my stomach twisted. I thought of all the battle-wounds I had stitched up and all the tears I had seen that accompanied bloodletting. For so many years, I had worked to preserve life and keep it. How could I now look forward to the spilling of blood, slathering like a wolf? Guilt and horror crept up my spine as I glanced at the rune tattoos on my knuckles. My connection to the gods had been severed for barely a day and already my darker nature was overwhelming me, begging me to sate its hunger with blood. I shivered and cursed the Winds for what they had done to me.

I could not wait to give Sigrun back her spear and step back behind the battleline.

"Can you keep up?" Yrsa asked, looking back as we clambered out of our crater-camp.

I opened my mouth to reply, but saw she was looking at Drifa. The huntress's smirk was fit for a wolf.

"Just try and lose me."

Yrsa's mouth twitched into a smile and we were running.

The forest blurred.

Trees swept past nearly as quickly as I could dodge out of their way. Fern, heather, and nettles whipped at my legs. Birds exploded out of the undergrowth as we smashed through their perches in low branches.

We leapt over a stream and paused, Yrsa raised her head in the air like a dog trailing a scent and then we were running again. Twice more we stopped like this, pausing for the briefest of moments for Yrsa to find her bearings and the third time Yrsa pulled us to a halt she unslung the axes from her belt.

"We're here."

I looked at my companions. Fafnir sniffed at the air then locked his gaze onto some point ahead of us, his expression as intense and sharp as a spear point. Yrsa cocked her head to the side as though listening to a distant conversation. Drifa was kneeling on the ground, panting with sweat dripping from her nose.

"Are you alright?" I whispered, alarmed that she would let Yrsa push her so hard.

"I'm fine," she said between breaths and shot me a ragged smile. "It's tough keeping up with Windborn but I'll be alright once I've got my breath back."

Ice down my spine. I had not run like that in a long time. I should not have been able to match Fafnir and Yrsa's pace. Yet here I was, huddled in the undergrowth with a few drops of sweat on my cheeks despite racing through the forest with a spear in hand and a god-stone-laden pack at my back. My smile faltered.

"The smell is thick," Fafnir rumbled. "Nal is with them."

"What about Sigrun?"

Fafnir paused before he answered, sniffing at the air. "I think so. The scents begin to mix."

Relief washed over me. She was there. I could save her. Her children would have both their mothers.

"What's the plan?" Drifa's breathing steadied. She looked between Yrsa, Fafnir, and me. My stomach twisted when I realised she was looking at the three Windborn for some direction for the fight.

"They don't know we're here," Yrsa said.

"We surprise them," Fafnir added. "We hit them hard. Kill them and save our friends."

I looked at the two Windborn next to me and a sense of unease crept over me. It could not be that easy.

"How many of them are there?" I asked, determined to try and introduce some tactical element to our plan.

Yrsa closed her eyes and we waited. The quiet forest sounds rose up like a tide, buzzing and hissing all around us. Yrsa frowned and tilted her head.

"At least twenty. Maybe more. It's still hard to tell. I think some of them are wearing masks."

"Twenty?" I hissed. "Against four of us? How can we possibly hope to win against those odds?"

Fafnir turned to me, as though seeing me for the first time. "Alvir."

He put a hand on my shoulder but quickly removed it as our Windborn powers crackled. I had a heartbeat of vertigo as images flashed through my mind. *Teaching a black-haired girl how to use a spear. A boar hunt. Blood.* I blinked them away. Fafnir looked from his hand to me, frowning. Then he shook it off and grinned at me with those spear-sharp tusk-teeth.

"Alvir. We are Windborn. We are as wildfire and they are kindling. How can they hope to win against these odds?"

"We move in as quiet as we can," Yrsa said. "Fafnir and I will get their attention. Drifa, Alvir, you find Nal and the others. When we get close enough I'll give the signal."

"What's the signal?" I whispered.

Fafnir glanced back and shot me another spear-grin. "If you miss hers, you will know mine."

After that, there were no words.

We crept through the undergrowth, guided by Yrsa's directions. Soon we heard the noise from the outlaw's camp. Quiet voices, the clatter of plates and cups, sniggered laughter. We made our way to the edge of the undergrowth and saw their camp.

This was much larger than the camp we had found before. If that was an outpost then this was a homestead. There were makeshift buildings made from old planks, woven together with the tree branches to make walls and rooftops. Hammocks swung between tree trunks and there were barrels and boxes strewn about, plundered supplies. From where I crouched behind a wilting sapling, I saw outlaws wandering to and fro. Some whispered beside fires, others drank together, but none seemed to have noticed us. I craned my neck to find Sigrun but the ground was too cluttered, the homestead too crowded and spread out.

My heart thrashed against my ribs. Whatever Wind-given excitement I had felt before was gone. Now there was only fear. I had never charged into battle before. The fight at the clearing had been a cacophony of confusion and blood and I had barely escaped unscathed. Now, I crouched at the edge of a skirmish where the enemy outnumbered us at least five to one. I wiped my hands on my tunic to clear the sweat so I could grip my spear properly. I glanced from side to side. Everyone else looked serious but unafraid. I swallowed.

A flash of Windborn pressure against my mind

The signal.

Fafnir and Yrsa crashed out of the undergrowth like boulders in an avalanche. Some of the outlaws scattered, others scrambled for weapons, the rest froze. Fafnir's spear struck out, quick as a snake-tongue and two outlaws fell in the blink of an eye. The spear shone with slick black-red as Fafnir loosed a roar worthy of the Warrior himself, so loud that it shook the branches. Yrsa sprinted past him, chasing down outlaws with unerring steps and flashing axes. In the space of two heartbeats, the quiet camp had been transformed into a battlefield.

I rushed in alongside Drifa. We skirted the killing field as we tried to find where Sigrun was being kept. The outlaws ignored us as they charged to stop the Windborn tearing through their camp. We ducked past barrels and crates, only to find a pile of old animal bones. I cursed.

"Come on," Drifa hissed and tugged at my cloak. "This way."

We edged around the camp and I couldn't help but look at Yrsa and Fafnir. As they drew on their Windborn power their swirling presence crashed in a tidal wave against my senses.

Fafnir had ripped a wall from one of the makeshift buildings. He smashed it into one of the outlaws sending them flying backwards. They snapped like a twig and fell limp to the floor. Fafnir was already facing another outlaw. This one dodged around his spear only to find Yrsa's axe deep in his chest. Fafnir was already gone, grabbing an outlaw by an arm and smashing him into another.

Where Fafnir was a raging wildfire, Yrsa was a whirlwind. She slid through the outlaws swift and fatal, demonstrating the danger in her quiet power. Her movements left her a hair's breadth from sharp edges, but never cut. She paused her charge and an arrow flew through the space where she would have been. Without looking Yrsa leant back and dodged a spear thrust. She took hold of the spear with one hand and yanked it forward, throwing the outlaw off balance and sinking her axe into his chest with her other hand.

Drifa and I edged around a pile of firewood and I gave an involuntary cry of triumph as I saw Sigrun, trussed against a tree, together with Nal, Tjorvid and some others I did not recognise.

I hurried forward and fumbled my knife from my belt, dropping my spear in my eagerness to cut the ropes. Drifa grabbed at my cloak and tugged me back as a spearhead stabbed through the air where I had been.

The outlaw stumbled forward with the momentum of their swing. They recovered and swung their spear butt into my stomach. I doubled over and dropped my knife.

As the outlaw tried to dance back, out of reach, I grabbed his spear and yanked it towards me. The outlaw stumbled forward again and my eyes widened as I realised my strength. Without thinking, I threw a punch. It connected with his jaw with a crack and the outlaw went down. I shook the pain from my knuckles and looked down, wide-eyed, at the unconscious outlaw.

"Come on," hissed Drifa, sliding her knife between the ribs of the outlaw with a hunter's efficiency. "Let's get them out of here."

"Right." I hurried over and began sawing through Sigrun's ropes. Drifa started on Tjorvid's.

Fafnir's battle cries echoed against the tree trunks and the screams of the outlaws rose and fell like waves in a storm.

Before either of us could cut through the ropes a bloodied outlaw stumbled by. I froze, but he did not seem to realise we were there and so I kept cutting through Sigrun's bonds. The outlaw tore off his deer-skull mask as he fell to his knees next to a collection of bags and then began rummaging through them.

"What's he—"

"Ignore him," Drifa whispered, her voice hot with urgency.

I watched the outlaw pull some tangled sticks from the pack. He clutched it to himself and closed his eyes, muttering something. Instinctively, I tried to raise my second sight. Nothing happened, but I sensed a glimmer of power in the outlaw's hands. It was a rune-stick. Like the ones I had used to bind the ravens but far larger and clotted with fur.

I pushed myself to my feet. I had to stop him.

"Alvir, what are you doing?" Drifa shouted, her urgency overtaking any need for quiet.

I ignored her and rushed up to the outlaw. He noticed me a heartbeat before I reached him. The whites of his eyes shone bright in his mud-splattered face. As I reached out to him, he held the rune-stick away from me but did not stop his muttering. I grabbed onto his arms and pulled.

Something inside me answered the call of my urgent fear. A whirl of writhing power twisted in me like a vortex and I felt something panicked and vital surge into my arm.

Before I could register what had happened the outlaw slumped bonelessly to the floor. Dead.

I picked up the rune-stick and its hot power flowed into me. I sensed something large, close, furious.

I turned back to Drifa, holding the rune-stick up. "This is—"

Something roared.

Everyone froze.

I looked around the campsite-turned-battlefield. Some of the outlaws had managed to put on their masks and surrounded Yrsa. The skull-magic seemed to be blurring her Windborn powers as she had bloody slices through her clothes.

Fafnir's spear was blade deep in a body, standing straight like a standard. In one hand, he held an outlaw by the neck. They scrabbled at his fingers, trying to pry them free as their legs kicked uselessly in the air.

Another bestial snarl and something huge, furred, and white-fanged crashed through the trees.

As the brown blur rushed towards him, Fafnir snapped the outlaw's neck with a pulse of his hands then charged forward to meet his fresh adversary.

Fafnir and the bear crashed into each other like two wrestlers, arms slamming against each other with enough force to topple trees.

Outlaws scattered as the two colossal figures tore at one another and tumbled across the camp. Fafnir bellowed in rage and pain and the bear did the same. Paint matted its fur and there was a rope looped with rune-stones around its neck.

It roared at Fafnir, almost a challenge, and Fafnir roared back.

I snatched up the rune-stick. I pushed my will into it and commanded the bear to stop fighting and flee. Magic flowed out of me and into the rune-stick. A thrill went through me and for a heartbeat I thought that I wasn't really Windborn, after all, I could command magic as well as any god-speaker. The power flowed out of me and into the rune-stick.

The rune-stick heated in my hands. Its runes glowed.

Something wasn't right.

It exploded.

I cried out and fell back. I put my hands against my face as though that would stop the pain from the volley of wood-shards impaled in my cheeks.

"No," I half sobbed. "No. No. No. No."

Until that moment, I had held some sliver of hope deep inside me—despite everything—that I was not Windborn. That whatever had been done to me could be undone, but the way that the magic had reacted to my touch was my final proof that I could never be the same. I was Windborn, severed from the gods and everything I had known.

"Alvir, stop fucking around and help me," Drifa hissed.

I crawled back to her, blinking away tears, and went back

to sawing at the bonds tying Sigrun to the tree.

The bear's cries had changed. There had been something in its voice before, something intelligent and taunting. Now there was nothing but rage.

One of the ropes fell away from Sigrun, then another. I caught her as she fell forward and lay her on the ground before sawing through the ropes at her ankles. Her eyes flickered open as Drifa cut through Tjorvid's bonds and began cutting Nal free.

"Wha... what's happening?" Sigrun said, her voice thick with sleep.

"It's okay," I whispered. "We've come to save you."

"Alvir?" Sigrun tried to look at me, but her eyelids were too heavy and struggled to keep them open.

"Yes, it's me. Now save your strength, we're going to need to move quickly if—"

A pressure against my skin. Not Windborn this time but something far more powerful, something far older. It was a shimmering reflection of the gods' strength and power, but somehow distorted. The power brushed past me and I sensed regret, powerlessness, and rage.

Then the forest fell around us.

Branches toppled from trees and rocks began to churn out of the ground as though caught in some unearthly current. The fallen branches bounced and, piece by piece, something formed from the rubble. Two of the branches fell against each other and stayed in their crooked shape, suspended in the air. Then more of the forest clung to that shape. Leaves, moss, dirt, stone, twigs and branches. They came together in a hunched, humanoid figure as tall as a longship's mast.

The shadow-creature.

It twisted its great, leaf-browed head to look at me and I felt a wave of power like a landslide.

Nothing happened.

For the first time, I felt a sliver of gratitude that I was Windborn and immune to whatever magics this monster was capable of.

The hunched shadow-creature sighed with the whisper of leaves and I felt the distant flicker of annoyance and then reticence before it stomped to join the fight.

"Sigrun," I said, whirling around to grab my sister. "We have to go."

She was unconscious. Whatever magic the shadow-creature had thrown at us looked to have knocked her out cold. I looked around and saw that Drifa, Tjorvid, and Nal were the same. Most of the outlaws were still standing, some clutched at their runestone necklaces as though channelling whatever magic was imbued there. Some protection against the shadow-creature's magic then. Other outlaws, those that had been injured now lay sleeping against the muddy ground.

The shadow-creature swept up to Yrsa. The outlaws around her fell away like stones in the ocean and let her stand alone against this forest monster.

She screamed and leapt forward.

Branch-limbs shook under the onslaught of her axes but they merely twitched, apathetic to the Windborn's rage. It bent as though looming over an errant child, and reached for her. She renewed her assault and chips of wood flew from the shadow-creature's limbs.

It was not enough. Its arm unravelled like unfurling roots as it came at Yrsa and as quick as a falling branch it had surrounded her in a cage of living wood.

Yrsa screamed in frustration and tried to tear her way free but the cage twisted and tightened around her. She screamed again, this time in pain as thorns blossomed over the wooden cage and sank their teeth into her.

The shadow-creature stepped towards Fafnir. Its arm was still anchored to Yrsa's cage. It kept moving. The sound of cracking, splintering wood and its arm was ripped free from its body, leaving Yrsa trapped in thorns.

Fafnir had managed to wrestle the bear to the ground and had his arms around its neck. He snarled at the shadow-creature and the bear scrabbled beneath him to try and find some purchase.

As the shadow-creature approached, Fafnir roared, this time screaming a challenge at the monster and rolled, putting his shoulder underneath the bear's belly and using his momentum to launch the bear at the shadow-creature. The bear snarled and pawed at the air as it smashed into the summoned monster, crashing through it like a boulder through the undergrowth.

Branches, leaves, and stones exploded out from the shadow-creature and it wobbled where it stood. One side of its chest was now a torn, gaping hole of snapped branches.

It looked down with its stone-branch face and the hole began to repair itself. Branches snaked out from what was left of its body and wove themselves back into an oak-thick chest.

Fafnir, bloody bear-claw gouges all over his body, roared again.

The bear, seemingly free of whatever spell held it captive, picked itself up from the ground and fled.

Fafnir thumped his chest with both bandaged hands. He picked up a log from the ground and charged.

The shadow-creature let Fafnir come. Roots and stones rippled up out of the ground in Fafnir's path. The Windborn stumbled and fell.

He tried to leap to his feet. More roots pulled themselves free and bound him as tightly as a trussed pig.

I pushed myself to my feet and took up Sigrun's spear. I knew I should make a stand and fight as Yrsa had, but fear rooted me to the spot. I had faced this creature from behind the safety of a raven's eyes and felt its power then. What hope did I have now? I was without my magic, wielding an unfamiliar spear that clattered in the wind, and this shadow-creature had defeated two other Windborn—each more fearsome than I—without breaking its patient stride.

The wind picked up. The shadow-creature, still one-armed, turned to me.

Its leaves flickered in the breeze and I felt the ripple of magic as the forest turned against me. Branches twisted around my arms. Roots gripped my feet. The spear was wrenched from my grasp. I strained against my living bonds. I clenched my eyes shut and pulled with my body and soul.

Suddenly, I felt the mind of the shadow-creature. Its magic flowed into me like the magic from the skull mask. Its power was slow as tree sap. It was ancient and verdant and flowed throughout the forest. Black spots floated within it like algae on water.

I opened my eyes and looked at the shadow-creature. It had straightened, standing so tall its head was lost in the low branches but I knew it was staring at me.

It felt as though we were the only two beings in the world. This powerful, ancient spirit tried to push something back along our connection but it was lost to me in a burning vision of bubbling black water.

I retreated from our connection and then the outlaws covered my head in a mouldy sack and began to beat me.

Chapter Seventeen
An Outlaw's Memories

THE WORLD WAS ONLY SHADOWS AND PAIN. The outlaws took the fact that I was the last one standing as some kind of challenge and continued to beat me long after the forest fell silent.

I heard the spirit disappear, falling apart in a clatter and clap of tumbling wood and stone. From the sounds of Fafnir's muffled shouts and Yrsa's constant cursing, their root-prisons held them long after the shadow-creature had left.

Eventually, once the outlaws had become bored with beating me, I was dragged away. I heard what sounded like preparations for a journey and it was clear that we were the cargo. Various voices called out to make sure that the big one was tied up properly and that the woman was gagged. The grunt and snarl of the bear. I was shoved and barely kept from stumbling then we were on the move.

For a long time, we trudged through the forest.

At first, I was terrified that I would catch my foot in some unseen root or stone and tried to walk slowly, sliding each foot carefully forward, but the outlaws shoved at me to keep me moving and I was forced to hurry on. My fears were unfounded and I found the invisible path clear. Perhaps their forest spirit ally kept the ground clear for us.

Within the darkness of my sack-hood it was difficult to tell how much time had passed by the time our strange caravan had arrived at its destination. The sliding, grinding sound of Fafnir being pulled along the ground stopped and someone tapped my chest with a stick to bring me to a halt.

People called out to each other. Some of them greeting

friends, others calling for drinks, and the last were soft voices marking those who would not be returning.

"Untie the big guy from the bear." A shout from beside me. "Take him and the woman, make sure they're tied up properly, and throw them in the shed until the chief decides what to do with them."

"What about the boar? It's still drying out in there."

"Do I look like I give a shit if these Windborn fuckers get boar blood on them?"

"Gerta's going to be pissed if she can't get to it when it's ready to butcher."

"Just do what I fucking tell you."

Without being able to see who was talking, the voices started merging together. I tried twisting my head from side to side but that made it worse. As people came and went I noticed that some of the voices had a twist to their words, an accent from beyond the Fjalmark.

"What about these ones?"

"Put them in the usual place. Wait, what's his story?"

"Him? Last one standing. After they ambushed us up at the outpost and... after reinforcements arrived, the Windborn got taken down and he was tangled up but still standing."

"You see his arm-ring?"

"So he's got jewellery."

"You bog-worshippers really are clueless, huh?" Someone grabbed at the rope binding my hands and pulled my arms up. "That's not jewellery, that's a god-speaker's arm-ring. That means this one could be useful. Put him over there. Let me get that sack off him, we can use it for someone useful."

The slap of flesh on flesh. "Leave it. Limbstitcher won't want to be seen by him. Not yet."

"Suit yourself," the native outlaw grumbled as they walked away.

The other one tugged at me, dragging me harder than they needed to. They manoeuvred me away then shoved me against a tree and told me to sit. I leaned against the rough bark and slid onto the ground to wait.

The bustle of this camp, outpost or whatever it was, washed over me. I heard laughter, the clatter of cups and plates, the tang of hammer on anvil, shouts and voices. If I had not known we were deep in the Trolbjolvid then I could have imagined that I was in any village throughout the Fjalmark.

Then, silence flowed through the outlaw village like a cold stream. Heavy footsteps came thudding up to me as though each foot was a boulder smashing into the ground. For a terrifying moment, I thought the shadow-creature had come back.

"He's another god-speaker. See his arm-ring? Now, look at his hands," one of the outlaws said. "All tattooed like a proper rune-weaver. We thought he might be able to help."

"Perhaps." A voice that burbled like a boiling bog. "We can use him to ensure that the ritual does not fail again. One way or another." A cold hand grabbed my head and tipped it back. "Are you a rune-weaver?"

I nodded, my tongue frozen in my mouth. Sharp nails dug into my scalp as the cold hand squeezed.

Silence for a heartbeat. The wind dragged the stench of dead things over me.

"Put him to work. She can inspect him and decide how best to use him."

The hand lifted from my head and I felt my hair damp with moisture, then those boulder-heavy footsteps receded.

Someone pulled off the sack covering my face and I blinked in the sudden sunlight. Finally, my eyes adjusted and I found myself staring into a cheery, grime-ridden face.

"Looks like you're working for me now." The woman's dark hair was tied loosely back and strands flew around her face. She shot me a vicious, gap-toothed grin. "Come on."

She pulled me onto my feet by tugging at the ropes binding my hands and dragged me off again.

Their camp was closer to a military outpost than a village. My captor took me through an open space dotted with buildings all topped with a living thatch of pine branches. Many looked to be homes, but from my brief glance I saw a blacksmith, a fletcher, and someone tanning leather. The space was enclosed by walls made from fallen trees. The trees had been tipped over, their roots still sticking out, but they were still alive and thorny bushes had been thickly woven between the upright branches. It was difficult to distinguish where each building ended and the forest proper began. It was no wonder these outlaws had eluded capture for so long.

As we came to the edge of the camp, I saw someone shoving Yrsa into a ramshackle shed. The Windborn growled but she was bound too tightly to fight back. I craned my neck to try and see the other captives, to see where they had taken Sigrun, but I was dragged in a different direction.

My captor took me to an alley between two houses, piled high with stones and skulls and broken branches. She looked around and told someone to come over and guard me. They didn't look happy with their new assignment and they glared at me as they took off their mask, burns across their face now clear to see, and my captor grabbed the mask to show me.

"Can you figure out how to make these?"

I nodded, afraid that if I spoke they would realise what I really was and pack me in with Yrsa and Fafnir.

"Then get on with it," she said and tossed the mask at me.

I caught it with shaky hands. As soon as the skull touched me the magic hummed through my skin and the weave on the mask unravelled. The magic fizzed through my veins and the weight of my exhaustion lifted a little. Then nothing. The magic in the mask was spent. I looked at the painted mask and examined the rune-scratched bone and prayed that they couldn't tell that it was now useless.

"Wait," I called after the outlaw.

She half-turned back, annoyance plain on her face. "What?"

"I need my pack." My heart thundered as I asked for it. What if it was now lost out in the forest? What of the god-stone shards? "It's got everything in it. I'll need it to cast the spell."

"Ugh. Fine. I'll get it. You, get his hands free but tie up his feet."

I offered the disgruntled outlaw an apologetic smile as he came over and did as he was told, moving my bonds from my hands to my feet.

"Where are you from?" I asked. "It sounded like some people here aren't from the Fjalmark?"

"Don't break my mask," the outlaw growled and went back to his post at the end of the alley.

"Here you go." The woman had returned and tossed my bag into the alley. It landed with a crunch a couple of paces away from my outstretched hands.

I scrabbled over my pack and looked inside. Some of the sticks had broken and a bowl had been cracked, but the god-stone shards were still there. My brief surge of relief was quickly flooded with worry as I wondered what would happen if I took the magic from the god-stone shards. The image of the collapsing god-stone flashed through my mind. Would I speed its collapse? Would I strengthen the shadow-creature?

My captor spat into the alley, dragging me back to the present. "I'll never understand how a load of rocks and moss can come together to make magic."

"The gods bless us," I said, the litany automatically rolling from my tongue. "We use the tools they provide. It is they who truly know how to weave the world into new patterns."

"Ha, maybe it used to be. Just you wait till you see what we've been putting together."

She was gone before I could ask her what she meant.

I looked at the piles of bones and wood that surrounded me. There seemed to be no order to the pile. It was simply a collection of everything that the outlaws needed, or thought they needed, to make more of their masks and strange deadwood armour. Careful not to touch the god-stone shards, I drew out some of the other components then picked up the skull of a small deer, still stained with blood and stared at it.

Any spell that I tried to weave would fail. I knew that, but I couldn't sit here and do nothing. The guard would get suspicious and they might decide they had no use for me after all. Here, in this alley, I had my hands free. I could escape and rescue Sigrun and everyone else.

I was quick to fall into a rhythm, going through the motions of scratching runes into the bones. Runes I had used for most of my life: *mind, hidden, forest*. Before they had been keys, gateway sigils to a power bigger than myself. Now, they were meaningless lines. Letters for a language I understood but could no longer speak.

I kept one ear tuned to the bustle beyond my bone-ridden alley. There was plenty of noise from people moving and dragging things from one place to another. Too much for me to risk trying to overpower my single guard and so I took a breath, took out a few components from my pack, and started crafting skull masks.

On my fourth or fifth mask, a wolf skull, I couldn't help but try and infuse it with magic. I closed my eyes and tried to draw on the power of the gods, as I would have for any other weave or ritual and draw that magic into the pattern of my spell.

Nothing.

The breeze dragged at the hairs on my arms, the sharp edges of the wolf's teeth against my fingers, and something humming at the edge of hearing.

It was like I was locked in a room drenched in darkness when I knew that there were colours and sunlight just out of sight.

The outpost was quiet now. The shouts had died down and the conversations were quiet enough to be drowned out by the shifting leaves all around us. I looked down at the half-finished wolf mask. This was getting me nowhere. Who knew what was happening to Sigrun and the others as I scratched nonsense into these bones? If I could get the outlaw's spear or his knife then I could get out of my bonds and find them.

I grabbed the paint and swirled it across the mask in a random pattern that I hoped would make the mask look magical enough at a glance.

"Hey," I called to my outlaw guard. When they looked at me I held up the boar mask that they had been forced to give up. "You can have this back. I don't need it anymore."

"About time."

He came to stand in front of me, out of sight of the rest of the camp, and bent to take the mask from me.

I threw it into his face and grabbed the end of his spear.

The outlaw flinched away from the mask and toppled over as I yanked the spear out from under him.

"You fucker," he growled.

I tried to pull the spear from his grasp, but he held tight and pulled a knife from his belt with his other hand. He stabbed at me and my only Windborn reflexes saved me.

I slapped the hand away, quicker than I'd ever been before. As my hand connected with his, something fizzed between us, a quieter version of the reaching, squirming Windborn powers.

The outlaw's eyes went wide and he looked at his hand, perhaps trying to see what spell I had cast on him. I grabbed his leg and the fizzing returned, blunted by the material between our skin. It felt like my soul was a ravenous vortex and the life caught in this man's flesh and bones was the only thing that would sate my hunger.

I drew that life into myself.

The outlaw gasped, went pale, and collapsed.

Strength flowed into me. Images streamed through my mind.

I sit in a longhouse, my arm around a woman's shoulders, laughing. Everyone else has gone to bed, but we are still up. I watch the firelight dance over her cheeks. Our heads lean close and our lips meet.

The last of the onions are picked and I am on my way home. Solveig will soon be done with dinner and I can finally play with my son. My longhouse comes into view and my heart lifts at the sight of it. Firelight from inside promises a warm evening with my family. Solveig kisses me when I come in. I missed you, Hofi, she says. My son, barely old enough to walk, cries out and runs to my arms.

The longhouse is on fire. The smell of charred meat. I clench a knife in one hand and an axe in the other. Solveig tries to hold me back. I scream at the Windborn floating in front of me. He shrugs, tells me it is how things are. It is the raiding season. Strength is all. I charge. He shoves me aside with one hand. I fly away as though kicked by a horse. The Windborn lunges at me. Solveig tries to stand between us.

The forest. The burns on my face are cool and tight with the years between now and the fire. Ropes coil over my shoulder. They have found another troll-boulder in the woods and I head to meet them. Beside me other outlaws. We all wear masks of skulls and rotten wood. We splash across a stream and see the boulder swarming with more outlaws. I raise my hand and—

I came back to myself with great heaving breaths and pushed Hofi off of me. Bile burned at the back of my throat and I put my fist to my lips to stop from retching. I looked at Hofi's body. He was still breathing. I hung my head with relief.

For a few heartbeats, I sat still. I felt stronger, the ache in my bones faded, but knowing that it came from Hofi's soul sickened me. I wondered if this was where all Windborn got their strength. Perhaps there were secret rituals that they performed to leach the life from those they claimed to protect.

When I had stopped shaking I took up Hofi's knife and cut through the bindings on my ankles. I used whatever ropes were left to me to bind Hofi and tore a strip of his cloak to gag him with. With that done, I took up Hofi's spear, cloak, and mask and picked up my pack and crept up to the alley entrance.

I took stock of the quiet camp ahead of me. Only a few outlaws wandered to and fro with most engrossed in their activities. As I went to move out my god-speaker arm-ring clattered against the spear. I stared at it.

They had known me by the arm-ring.

I slipped it off and stared at the three interwoven pieces of wood. I couldn't help but feel a surge of pride, the same pride I had felt all my life when I looked at it. Here was the mark of what I was, both for the world and for myself. A wanderer. A healer.

I looked back at Hofi's still-sleeping body and felt sick with guilt and fear.

Whatever I was now, I wasn't that person anymore. I couldn't be that person anymore.

I put the arm-ring in my pack and closed it. Without it, my arm felt too light and my soul felt too heavy, but I had no time for self-pity.

I took a deep breath and went to save my sister.

Chapter Eighteen
Troll Stones

I KEPT TO THE EDGES OF THE CAMP as much as I could, skirting against buildings and dashing across the pathways, but before long I needed to step out into the open. The outlaws meandered to and fro performing the small acts of industry that kept any village going. People carried food across the outpost, some lounged against trees and passed pipes, more were fletching arrows or fixing torn clothing. I took a breath, trying to calm my heart as it pounded like a sailor trapped in a sinking longship. I balanced the spear on my shoulder and walked into the camp.

Fafnir and Yrsa's distant Windborn wriggle pushed at my senses but I ignored it. I needed to find Sigrun. From the looks of the buildings there were a few places where they might have taken them, most looked like workshops or living spaces so I made my way to the buildings that looked like warehouses or pens for livestock, the most likely places to keep hostages.

The first two buildings I ducked my head into were full of sacks and half-rotten barrels. I gritted my teeth and looked around. There were so many places they could be and I did not want to expose myself for longer than I had to. They had said they would put them in the usual place and all the paths seemed to meander over one another until they wove into a single track. Perhaps I would find Sigrun at the end of these footpaths.

Decided, I turned to go then stopped dead.

Three enormous monoliths squatted before me. Judging from the logs beneath them and the wake of torn and crushed foliage behind them, they had been transported here from somewhere deep in the forest. Each of the colossal stones was unique. The first tapered down to its middle and then widened out quickly like an arm flowing to the wrist with half its palm remaining. The second was fat at one end like a leg. The last was round with hollows and bumps that, in the shadowed light, looked like it could have once been a face though the details were worn by some unimaginable stretch of time.

A few outlaws leaned against them, talking, and one of them kicked at the log-wheels underneath one of the stones.

"I don't get why we have to bring them here first. We don't want them here, do we? So why bother dragging them all the way here, only to take them somewhere else?"

"Because if it's not the right kind of stone they're no good and we'd have to drag it back out again. This way, we drag them here, she comes to inspect them where it's safe, and if they're right, then we take 'em to the ritual site."

"It seems like a lot of effort."

"Yeah, well, it's worth it, ain't it?"

I ducked behind a tree, trying to figure out what they needed those stones for. I thought back to the marker that Ulfrun had made at the edge of Vidsetr. Were the outlaws forcing her to make a miniature god-stone as well as the skull-masks? The god-stones were made to protect us against the wild and monstrous things so surely that could not be it. A shiver went down my spine. Or could they be using these false god-stones to extend the shadow-creature's realm beyond the woods? Most spirits were linked to a specific place but if they could anchor the shadow-creature to one of these stones and drag it outside of the Trolbjolvid it could spread its terrible influence across the Fjalmark.

As these thoughts whirled in my mind, another outlaw came up to the ones lounging around the stones. Something flashed around their neck. I frowned. It was the first time I had seen any outlaw wearing something that wasn't smeared in forest.

"Where did you get that?" one of the lounging outlaws asked, pointing to the flash around their neck.

"I got it off the new hostages."

"It's nice."

"Thanks, I think it's an old coin from the Empire of Bones."

"Does that mean their stuff's gone?" another outlaw chimed in.

"Probably," said the coin-wearer with a shrug. "They've already carted most of them off and you know that stuff doesn't last long."

"Ah fuck. I was hoping to get a new cloak or something."

"It's like these boulders," the complainer said and kicked one of the stones. "What's the point of bringing anything here if we're moving it somewhere else in the end anyway?"

"Oh give it a rest, will you? I'm going to see if the ones that're left have anything good on them."

I squeezed the tree bark in frustration. Sigrun could still be in the camp or she could have been carted away, presumably taken to wherever they were taking the stones.

I looked around. There was no way past the outlaws milling near the boulders. They had spread out across the path, sitting on stones and leaning against trees as they talked. Neither could I see any way through the walls of congealed foliage, each one was too tightly woven for me to squeeze through.

I stood, considering my options. I would not leave without Sigrun or finding out where she was. And I had to know what was really going on in this forest. These outlaws were working towards something and had powerful magical allies. I needed to find out what they wanted and who they were working with. Without help, though, I might wander the forest aimlessly or be captured again.

The press of Windborn power against my skin. I clenched my jaw and pushed it to the back of my mind.

I watched the greedy outlaw wander away from the others lounging on the stones and followed him from a distance. We moved past people carrying bundles of sticks and trays of food and soon the outlaw came up to what looked like an animal pen at the edge of the camp. He leaned inside, spat over the fence, then wandered off.

I waited for a few moments to be sure that the outlaw wasn't coming back and then made my way over.

The ground had been dug out inside the pen, forming a shallow pit and inside were two people bound and gagged. My heart sank as none of them had my sister's golden hair, but from the way that they were all turned away from me it was difficult to tell if I knew any of them. Rotten scraps of food were scattered around and I got the impression that it was a common pastime to throw old food at their hostages. The prisoners were all deliberately ignoring me, perhaps to try and avoid whatever random entertainment the outlaws thought to inflict upon them, but eventually one of the prisoners turned to glare at me.

Nal.

Her eyes were stoked with blazing hate. Now that she had acknowledged me the other prisoner looked as well. A gaunt man greying at the temples. Where Nal looked at me with hatred, his eyes were filled with fear and sadness.

I found the pen's gate and slid down into the pit with them.

Nal snapped something at me. The words were muffled by the gag but their vicious meaning was clear from her tone and wild movements.

Now that I was out of sight of the rest of the camp I took off my stolen mask. Nal's expression changed from burning rage to a searing suspicion. The old man's fear softened with confusion, unable to comprehend why one of their outlaw captors was huddled with them in their pit.

"They wanted me to make more of those masks," I said to Nal, hoping the explanation would be enough. I removed her gag and started cutting her bonds. "Where did they take the others?"

Nal continued to glare at me, but now that I'd freed her most of the fire had gone from her eyes.

"I don't know," she said, rubbing her wrists. "Into the forest."

I gritted my teeth. I needed more information. I moved to free the old man.

"They take the strongest. Something about rituals," he said when he could. "Are you alone? Have they sent others to help?"

"Where are you from?"

The old man seemed to be unharmed and tears began to cut clean tracks through the mud on his cheeks. "I'm from Hafgata. It's by the coast. I was out hunting when these outlaws took me captive. They left me here while they took the rest deeper into the forest."

I nodded along with his explanation as my mind thrummed with possibilities. Sigrun had been taken deeper into the forest, the outlaw had mentioned some sort of ritual and they wanted only the strong, and they had left the old man and a girl that looked too young to be a fighter, though I knew how dangerous Nal was. I ran my fingers through my hair and looked at each of the newly freed captives. The ever-present press of Windborn power creaked against my ears.

"Nal," I said. "If I make a distraction can you get him out of here? Get him out of the forest?"

Her lips curled into a sneer. "I'm not leaving without my brother. Give me your spear and I'll deal with these fuckers. I'll stick them one by one."

"I'll give you my spear," I said and passed it over to her. As soon as Nal's fingers closed on the weapon her shoulders eased by a fraction. "I'll get Fafnir and Yrsa free and we'll make a distraction. You get him out of the camp and hide. Wait for us. Fafnir will be able to find you, won't he?"

Nal narrowed her eyes but didn't argue.

"Stay close to the walls. It'll be harder for them to see you. Wait for the signal then get out."

The old man nodded along to my instructions. Nal kept up her long-suffering expression and clutched at her spear. I sighed. I put on the boar skull mask and clambered back out of the pit, leaving the gate propped open.

The camp was getting busier. People returned from the forest with packs over their shoulders, nibbling on handfuls of berries and nuts. When I was forced to walk by someone I nodded at them but kept my pace quick and purposeful. It's surprising how readily people will believe you if you look like you know what you're doing.

I soon came to the long storage house where they were keeping Fafnir and Yrsa. Their Windborn power bubbled louder against my senses like a churning river.

A guard lounged against the door. She wore a deer skull mask and picked at dirt under her nails. I looked around, trying to see if there was some way to get the guard from the door. There was a gentle hum of noise all around the camp, too loud for me to distract her with an unexpected noise and at any rate no one seemed to be on alert. The outlaws had won, they weren't on the lookout for a snapping twig to alert them to an approaching enemy. People craned their necks as they passed the storage house, trying to catch a glimpse of the captured Windborn. I decided to test my disguise and try to get a look at the fresh captives.

I took a deep breath and walked purposefully towards the building. The guard turned her head to me and pushed herself off the door frame.

"You worried about her as well, huh?" she said as I came close and tapped her boar-mask.

"What?" I floundered, not sure what she meant. Then I remembered what these masks were protection against. "Oh. Yeah. I heard she can do weird stuff to your mind."

"Exactly. Frida was taking the piss, telling me they're no danger now and I can take the mask off. But why take the risk, you know?"

"Right. Do... do you think I could get a look at them? It might help me feel better, you know, seeing them tied up."

"Oh sure. Don't get too close, though. You never know what they're capable of. Windborn, right? Fucking freaks."

My gut twisted at the venom in her words. She ducked through the door and gestured for me to follow.

It took a moment for my eyes to adjust to the dim light seeping through the branch-roof. A butchered boar hung from the rafters, swinging gently, and it dripped viscous blood onto a gaggle of vines and thorns that crisscrossed over the back half of the storage shed. It looked like the building was long abandoned and the plants had become overgrown, but as my eyes adjusted to the shadows I realised that the vines were Fafnir and Yrsa's prison.

I could just make out the outlines of the Windborn trapped beneath as though they were statues in the Empire of

Bones, long forgotten and left to be consumed by the wild.

A growl from under the vines.

"Now you come to gawk. Free me and I will put on a show."

"Shut up," the outlaw drawled and bashed at the vines with the butt of her spear. "He's a big one. Not as big as our ones though."

Our ones?

"What about this new rune-weaver they've found?" I asked, sidling up to the outlaw. "What do you reckon about him?"

"I don't know why we need two," she said and tapped her mask. "Ulfrun does us fine."

"She does. It doesn't hurt to have two slave god-speakers though, right?" I was close enough to brush up against her now.

"Slave? Wait, who are—"

Before she could say anything else, before I could think about what I was doing, I grabbed her arm and pulled her life into me. The outlaw's eyes went wide and she collapsed. Strength and memories flooded my mind. I tried to push them away, along with the nausea rising in my stomach, but they overwhelmed me.

Water splatters on my cheeks as I pull on the oar. We are making good time sneaking into Ertland. Kara, the Windborn who is with us, lounges against the mast while the rest of us claw the longship upriver. She can fly. She could guide us through and she won't break a sweat. I grit my teeth and bend back to the oars.

Battle-lust, blood-splatters, and tears heat my cheeks. Somehow the Ertlanders are ready for us and now we are trapped against their stone walls. Egil and I stand shield to shield, fending off the spear thrusts of the Ertland warriors. On three we charge, Egil says to me, I'll distract them and you get away. No, I reply. We go together. Egil says nothing. Then I see Kara flying overhead. I scream her name, implore her for help. She looks at me and then to the sack of plunder in her hands. She flies on. Egil charges. I make it out alive.

When I came back to myself I was on my hands and knees, the back of my throat hot with vomit. I shook it off my hands and sat up, blinking away the tears.

"Stop pissing around and get us out of here," Yrsa hissed from inside her vine prison.

I nodded, getting shakily to my feet and stepping over the outlaw. Runa. Her eyes were open, glassy, staring into nothing. I paused and bent over her.

"What are you doing?" Yrsa fumed.

I ignored her and put my hand to the outlaw's mouth, my ear to her chest.

Runa was dead.

I had pulled too hard.

A fresh wave of nausea churned at the pit of my stomach. I swallowed sharp bile. I knew that my life as a Windborn would be different to that of a god-speaker but I had fallen so quickly. A few days ago I had been wandering the Fjalmark, moving from village to village healing people. Now, I had taken a life. And so easily.

I blinked away tears again and turned to the vine-prison. I took up the outlaw's knife and started sawing at the vines, but they were tough and thick as though they had been growing there for decades. I hacked madly at the vines, frustration overcoming caution, and woodchips flew in every direction. But when I was done and panting the vines were no closer to releasing their grip.

"You are stronger now," Fafnir rumbled. "Do not give up."

I dropped the knife and, with a glance at the outlaw's body, grabbed the vines with my bare hands and pulled on the life inside them.

Nothing happened.

There was power in the vines but instead of the blood-quick power I had taken from the outlaws, this was sap-slow. I kept pulling, squeezed harder. Thorns bit into my palms.

The power shifted, started flowing into me.

All around me: forest. Wild, primeval, endless. Somehow, I know that the world has not felt the touch of humans. The hiss of leaves shifting in the breeze fills my ears along with countless padding paws, crunching hooves, and the fluting call of myriad birds.

Vertigo seized me and I nearly fell. The vines had wrinkled

as though suffering through a drought. Their grip on Fafnir and Yrsa remained strong. I squeezed tighter, felt hot blood drip red from my hands, and kept pulling.

Thunderous footsteps. Slow and booming. My mind is stretched, flitting through a net of roots that reaches across the whole forest. Something as tall as the trees moves through the woods. I can feel the slow life of the plants all around me. The sprinting hearts of animals patter like rain as they scamper above my root-mind.

The cage of vines had withered. It was dying but was still as tough as old rope. Fafnir and Yrsa struggled. They could not free themselves and the thorns were still spearhead-sharp. I renewed my blood-slick grip and pulled as hard as I could.

Something new is in the forest. Its power distant, heavy like a hammer blow. My body is roots and leaves, pebbles and dirt. I loom over cracked boulders that are scattered across a clearing. A sadness for someone lost. In the distance the flash of blue light. Another far-off hammer blow. My body falls away, the spirit falling back into the root-mind, and I flow back to my monolith-haven.

I wake on the floor, my cheek ringing from Yrsa's slap and my mind reeling from the thoughts of the shadow-creature, the spirit that lived in a monolith.

"He's alive," she said, turning back to Fafnir as the colossal Windborn pulled dead, withered vines from his shoulders.

"Thank you, Alvir," he said. He went to offer his hand for me to pull myself up then thought better of it. "You are disguised. How many are still out there?"

"I don't know," I wheezed as I struggled to pull myself to my feet. "They wanted me to make more of those masks. I knocked out Hofi and—"

"Hofi?" Yrsa asked.

"The outlaw they left to guard me," I said. I rubbed at my eyes as though that could push Hofi's memories out of me. "I found Nal and an old man, but they've taken everyone else deeper into the forest."

"You found my sister?" Fafnir was suddenly beside me, leaning close. "Is she safe?"

"She's unhurt. I gave her Hofi's... I gave her a spear and told her to be ready to escape. I said we would make a distraction."

Fafnir shot me a knife-sharp grin, tusks twisting his face. "I am good at distractions."

"Here," Yrsa said and threw Runa's spear at Fafnir. "You'd better take this. Alvir, give me your knife."

"What? What will I use?"

"What can you use?" she snapped.

My cheeks went red. Before I entered this forest I had never charged into battle. I healed the people around me. Or I had. Now I was a Windborn who didn't know how to fight.

"Fine," I said. "You take it. I'll find a stave or something."

Yrsa snatched the knife and I ripped a chunk of wood from the vines to use as a club.

"What's the layout of the camp?" Yrsa demanded as she tested the knife's blade against her thumb.

"There's a clear space at the centre with—"

Shouts from the outpost cut me off. We straightened, immediately alert like deer who have scented a wolf. The cries were muffled from inside the storage shed. I crept up to the entrance and leaned through the door.

"Hofi's been tied up. That god-speaker must have done something to him."

"Where's the god-speaker now?"

"No one knows."

"Everyone, get your masks on. Now. You lot go check the hostages and the rest of you, with me. We're going to make sure those Windborn are still tied up."

"What if they're not?"

"You, get reinforcements. Faster!"

I retreated back into the building and shook my head at Fafnir and Yrsa.

"They know something's wrong. They're coming to check on you."

Fafnir shot me a spear-sharp grin. "Then we smash through them like an axe through kindling."

I swallowed. The withered vines seemed to wriggle and my mind returned to the visions of the primeval forest.

"I'm not sure we can—"

Something roared in the distance. The bear.

"We do not have a choice," Fafnir said. He slapped his enormous, bandaged hand down on my shoulder. Energy crackled between us and a memory flashed in my mind.

Retching, clutching my stomach as blood bubbles through my fingers. The hunt went wrong. I should never have let Nal come. My lifeblood soaks into the dark earth. This could have been Nal. The beast is dead. They are safe. I collapse. My blood pools with the boar's blood, shining in the Wind-light.

Fafnir shook his hand as I stared at him. His eyes, edged with sadness, still sparked with battle-lust. I thought of Nal out in the camp, waiting for us, and I felt an echo of the sadness and regret that Fafnir had felt dying in the forest.

"We need to get out of here," I said. "And we need to make sure Nal gets away safe. They're in a pit straight ahead of where we are. Let's make enough mess that they need every outlaw in this forest to try and stop us."

Fafnir grinned at me. "I like this plan."

He stood and stretched, his back cracked, and he twirled Runa's spear. In his huge hands it looked like a toasting spear rather than a weapon of war, but I knew before long the spear would be slick with the black-red life of the outlaws.

The shouts were louder now. The outlaws' nerves were clear in their voices as they arrayed themselves outside to meet us.

The bear roared, much closer now.

"Ready?" Yrsa asked.

I nodded.

Fafnir sucked in a breath and roared so loud that the building shook. He kicked the door to splinters then threw the boar carcass out at the waiting enemies. They cried out in fear and confusion.

Fafnir roared again and charged, shattering the doorframe with his bulk.

I gripped my wooden club and followed the screams of pain and terror.

CHAPTER NINETEEN
GIANTS CLASH

THE WORLD WAS A MESS OF BLOOD, SHARP EDGES, AND SCREAMS. Fafnir had smashed into the outlaws, throwing them aside as easily as dry grass. He charged ahead, heading away from the pit where Nal was hiding, and screamed a challenge at the entire camp. The outlaws who had been rushing to check on the prisoners swerved around to encircle Fafnir in bristling spear points.

Yrsa and I were forgotten behind Fafnir's bulk and noise. I moved out into the open space, ready to smash my club against any unsuspecting outlaws. Yrsa sprinted between the outlaws like a Death Maiden. Wherever she walked, death followed. It seemed to take the softest touch of the knife and an outlaw would collapse.

I followed.

An outlaw leapt at me, splinter-wood mask glowing, and swung an axe. I flinched, throwing up my club on nothing but instinct. The axe sunk into the club's heavy wood. The outlaw tried to tug the axe free and I let go of the club. The outlaw, not expecting me to give up the weapon, stumbled back at his strength.

"Alvir," Yrsa called.

I turned as she tossed me a sword. I fumbled the catch and scrambled to pick it up off the floor.

The splinter-faced outlaw pulled the club off the axe. He loomed over me.

I swung the sword wildly, fear lending my arm speed and strength. The outlaw jerked back, a bright red line across their belly. I smashed the sword pommel into their face.

The mask splintered in a shower of wood and blood.

Panting, I gripped the now-dripping sword tight then picked up the outlaw's axe.

More outlaws flowed in from all corners of the camp. Screams for help echoed between the trees. Yrsa blurred between her enemies leaving corpses in her wake. Fafnir smashed through bodies, tore through buildings, cracking bones with every step.

Then Yrsa ducked a spear-thrust and as she pulled the attacker off balance, sinking a knife into their neck, she called to Fafnir: "She's out. Let's go."

Fafnir roared again, a cry of victory, and turned. He set his shoulders and made another charge. This time he aimed at the walls of the camp, ready to crash through so we could flee into the forest.

When he was a couple of paces away something enormous smashed into him and he was thrown off his feet.

I stared at the brawling mass of muscle and fur as Fafnir and the bear wrestled and tore at one another. Yrsa shoved me as an arrow whistled past.

"Help Fafnir," she hissed. "Then get us the fuck out of here."

She turned back to the encroaching outlaws and began her dance again. They tried to skirt past her but she kept them at bay, tearing spears from them and twirling them round to smash them like staffs against their chests. The outlaws kept up the pressure. Yrsa's quick reflexes kept the two sides in an uneasy standoff.

I rushed up to Fafnir and the bear. Fafnir kicked the bear off of himself and it rolled past me.

It scrambled to its feet and I dove to one side to dodge a swiping paw bigger than my head. The bear snarled, lips curling back to reveal finger-long fangs foaming with Fafnir's blood. Its fur was mud-clotted and slick with algae-laden water as though it had been swimming in a bog. Another rune-necklace was bound around its neck.

Fafnir came up beside me, breathing heavy with red speckling his clothes. I wanted to reach out and offer him some support, prop him up, but I worried that if I touched him I would drain whatever morsel of energy kept him fighting toe-to-toe with this rune-touched bear.

The bear rubbed a paw against its snout and the fur came away bloody. It snarled and stood up, raising itself to its full height. With its rune-stone necklace, it looked like some ancient king of the forest. It towered over me and looked at us with contemptuous fury. Fafnir looked the bear in the eye and rolled his shoulders.

"We can take him," he said.

Fafnir charged forward and the bear came to meet him. They smashed together so hard the ground shook.

Two outlaws had managed to find a way past Yrsa and they charged at us.

I stepped in front of them, batting a spear aside with my axe and swinging at the other with my sword. The outlaw dodged out of the way of the sword and, unable to spear me through, used the shaft to trip me. As I tumbled forward I smashed the axe clumsily into his knee. He went down with a cry of pain, taking the axe with him.

The ground shook and I scrambled away as Fafnir smashed the bear onto the floor, onto the injured outlaw. The bear clawed at the earth, churning at the outlaw's body, and launched itself at Fafnir.

The remaining outlaw charged at me. I dodged his spear thrust and sliced at the spear. The spearhead toppled from the severed shaft and the outlaw dropped the now useless weapon. They whipped a knife from their belt and lunged at me. I didn't have time to use the sword and had to grab onto their arm with my free hand. I dragged the knife off course but it still scored my chest.

Teeth gritted, I pulled.

A trial. I am outlawed. I flee into the woods before the girl's father makes his own justice.

The outlaw's face went pale and they fell to the ground. Anger bubbled within me at the crimes I saw them commit in their memories and my sword sang through their neck.

Panting, I tightened my grip on the sword and looked around. The bear had pinned Fafnir and was trying to rip out his throat. Its head snapped back and forth as it tried to find a way past Fafnir's pummelling fists.

I glanced at my blood-slicked hands and charged forward. The bear took no notice of me, far too focused on the massive Windborn trapped beneath its bulk. I shoved my hands into its drenched fur and felt its fury, its thrumming vital power out of reach like a jewel trapped under ice.

I pulled.

Rope keeps me tied. I growl, try to break free. A human approaches. They smell of mud and sap. Their head all wrong. Antlers. Teeth for eyes. Behind them another. Bear-large, but human. It smells of rot. Of silt and stagnant water. Eye-tooth human raises rope and stone over my head.

I stumbled and the bear snarled, shaking its head. It swiped at me. The paw cuffed me. Pain exploded in my chest and I was sent tumbling across the ground.

As I pushed myself up I saw Fafnir had managed to get away from the bear long enough to get a spear. He held the spear-point between him and the growling bear. Fafnir lanced the spear forward and yanked it back before the bear could react. Blood began to matt the bear's fur in a hundred different places as Fafnir struck again and again, but magic stoked its rage and would not let it die.

I found an axe and readied myself to help Fafnir.

A presence along my skin: distant, writhing power.

Another Windborn.

Who? Hope blossomed in my chest. A Windborn from Konvald? No. How could they have found us so deep in the forest? A fresh terror stabbed at my heartbeat. Outlaws may not be the only thralls of the shadow-creature.

We could not stand against the bear, the never-ending outlaws, and a Windborn. We would be killed and without us, Sigrun had no hope of rescue.

I threw myself at the bear, wildly swinging the axe and sword at its furry hide. The sword slithered through the blood and algae-slick fur, cutting fresh gouts of red from the beast. The axe caught in the fur and was ripped from my grasp.

I cried out in frustration and glanced at Yrsa.

She danced through a glittering mass of spearheads and I could feel her Windborn power flaring. Fafnir's power flashed against my skin like a wildfire, blazing to give him the strength to fight. My Windborn power flickered in my chest, giving me so little, taking so much.

The bear reared back as Fafnir stuck his spear into one of its paws. Its necklace of rune-stones glittered.

I dove forward and as the bear slammed its paws onto the ground, ready to charge at Fafnir, I swung the sword into its head.

I grabbed the necklace.

The tooth-eyed human mutters. Strange words even for a human. Something flows into me and I see myself. Two minds fold into one. I am still a beast. I am more. Power flows into me through my linked human. I am given a black strength. I am given a fresh sense of the forest.

The bear wrenched itself away from me. The rune-stone necklace snapped and I ripped it off. Fafnir stood nearby, spear outstretched to fend off the bear's charge.

The bear stumbled away as the magic slipped from its mind. It bared its teeth but refused to come any closer. The beast sagged and one of its legs went out from under it. Without the runes around its neck it had transformed from a magic-fuelled monster to an animal, hurt and dying. It fell on its side and snorted, blood bubbling in its nostrils.

Fafnir went to it—the bear whimpered and huffed—and cracked its neck, putting it out of its misery.

He leaned on the bear's limp body, breathing heavily. The wind began to pick up, ruffling our clothes and the bear's bloody fur.

Yrsa rushed up to us.

"Come on," she shouted. "Let's go."

The outlaws had kept their distance when Fafnir had been wrestling with the bear, wary of getting caught in the titanic brawl, but now they slunk out of buildings and stood with spears and axes raised. Bodies littered the clearing but there were still about two dozen outlaws still standing with more sweeping in from outside the camp. They blocked both roads out of the encampment and with a sense of chill horror I saw a black-haired girl being dragged, kicking and screaming, back into the camp.

No. She was free. Nal had been free.

Fafnir saw his sister at the same time and he roared at the outlaws, blood-drenched spittle flying across the clearing.

I squeezed the sword and what was left of the rune-stone necklace and made ready to charge. We could not abandon Nal.

Yrsa tensed. Fafnir readied himself.

Then I saw something between the trees. Fear rippled throughout the camp.

I felt the press of Windborn power against my skin and from the way Fafnir and Yrsa tensed, they felt it too.

Footsteps echoed through the hard earth as something huge moved through the forest towards us. Green and blue light flickered in its black silhouette.

The outlaws all shifted, making a path for whatever this was. Nal was dragged back and out of sight.

"We have to go!" I shouted.

Fafnir did not move. He took half a step towards his sister.

Trees crunched and collapsed as this new, huge enemy closed in on us.

"Fafnir, we have to go," Yrsa said, edging back.

The enormous Windborn stomped his foot. He shook his head. He took a step back.

"We'll return for her," I said. "We have to run."

Fafnir bellowed wordlessly at the outlaws, at the colossal shadow charging towards us, then he turned and retreated. We took that as our signal. I spun on my heels and sprinted out of the camp. Yrsa followed an eye-blink later.

Terror churned in my stomach as we aimed for a gap in the walls. A couple of outlaws tried to block our path, spears lowered, but Fafnir took one in each hand and vented his fury at the loss of his sister by crushing them, squeezing them as easily as a child breaks an egg.

Then we were in the forest. Trees blurred beside us. The footsteps thudding through the ground picked up speed. It was gaining on us. Branches shook as we passed them.

"Wait."

Yrsa grabbed onto Fafnir's cloak, trying to drag him to a stop, but his bulk and strength carried them forward. I skidded to a halt.

Branches snapped and trees crunched behind us as though a boulder was chasing us through the forest.

Then something landed in front of us. It smashed into the ground where we would have been, throwing up dirt and flattening saplings.

The bear.

Whatever was chasing us had thrown the bear at us.

Fafnir and Yrsa looked at me from the other side of the bear's body.

"Come," Fafnir said and put out a hand to pull me over. "We must go."

The thudding was faster, closer. Trees bent as the colossal hunter charged between them. Wind whipped against my face, blowing dust and leaves into my eyes.

As I blinked my vision clear I saw limbs moving in the distance. It was colossal and humanoid.

In that moment I felt the weight of everything crash down on me. I was trying to find out what had happened to the shattered god-stone and save Sigrun and Ulfrun, but I had nothing to use to find them. I was a god-speaker, a rune-weaver. My strength was given to me by the gods. It was their wisdom that guided me and their power that fuelled my spells. And now I was Windborn, cut off from the gods. I would never touch their power again except as stolen glimpses from other spells. The gods would forever be silent to me.

I had nothing. I was nothing. I was holding everyone back.

I looked at the two Windborn, waiting for me, waiting to get themselves killed for me.

"You go," I said. "I'll distract it. Promise me you'll save Sigrun."

Fafnir's fingers closed into a fist. He looked at me then looked behind me. Fear lit his eyes for a heartbeat before he nodded.

"I swear. I will save her."

They ran.

I turned to watch the trees shake and snap as the monster charged.

ᚠ

Wind buffeted the trees. Branches snapped and careened through the air, caught in the unnatural gale. Another movement ahead of me. Branches and dirt swirled against the wind. A stone rolled against a branch then vines wrapped around them and in the blink of an eye it was a leg corded from the bones of the woods.

My legs shook as I realised I would have to face down two forest monsters to give Sigrun a chance to be rescued.

I clutched at the rune-stone necklace and pulled on the magic. It swirled into my blood. My exhaustion eased as I blinked away the bear's memories. They were of no use to me now. I was thankful that I would die with some memory of the gods' power in my veins.

"Hey!" I shouted over the howling of the wind.

The shadow-creature's body had finished building itself. It stood like a giant made of roots and moss and fungus and stone. Its boulder face was topped with antlers of roots and each finger whipped in the wind like willow branches.

"I'm right here!"

I swung my sword at its foot. It connected to the spirit's constructed body with a thunk but it had no effect. I swung again and again, but it was like trying to hammer a nail into a mountain. The spirit ignored me. Its gaze followed Yrsa and Fafnir. Then, with a sound like tearing fabric, it ripped its foot out of the ground and took one enormous step past me.

The ground shook under the steps of whatever other monster chased me. The earth crunched and squelched under the shadow-creature's steps.

Frustrated, I threw down my pack and looked for something to draw the magic from. Anything I could pull strength enough to get the spirit's attention.

Dried herbs, animal bones, feathers.

Useless. Then I froze. The god-stone shards. I had ignored them for fear of drawing the attention of whatever had shattered the god-stone. But what did I have to lose?

As my fingers hovered over the shattered stone I felt its

warm magic and my Windborn power reached out for it like a starving man reaching for food.

I grabbed the biggest shard and the magic flooded into me like a tidal wave. The wind died in an instant and the forest went silent. I pulled harder.

Icy gales whip through the empty forest. The world is soaked in a winter centuries old. Gods walk the land alongside beings made of magic and stone. I am the spirit of this vast wilderness. My heart beats in days and nights. My breaths are lock-step with the seasons. I do not choose a side as the gods begin to claw at each other and lock away the Winds. I protect my home.

My stone cousins help both sides of the conflict. They weave powerful magics that slay gods, empower giants, and sever souls from bodies. Their only desire is knowledge. The ancient winter is dying. The gods are winning. I protect my home.

Now, only the mortals' myths remember that ancient winter, those vicious battles. I protect my home. The gods have tethered me to a single stone. My power is couched and anchored like the mortals in their homes. A distant god approaches. A new god. Something dark and rotten.

I blinked away the visions and the god-stone shard fell from my hand. It was cold. The magic had seeped into me and I felt it pulsing through my veins. It felt like sunlight warming the first spring flowers, slow and powerful, but there was a black edge to it that hemmed in the magic like a dam on a river.

As I looked around, centring myself, I saw the shadow-creature had frozen in place. Its boulder-face turned to face me as the rest of its vine-wrapped limbs stayed as motionless as the trees around us. I felt its attention blazing down on me. The forest was still and silent except for the thudding footsteps of the monster closing in.

The shadow-creature... No. It was an immensely powerful land spirit. We watched each other. Its power rustled at the back of my mind like the whisper of the forest canopy. It was trying to tell me something. There was something it wanted me to know. Something it wanted me to do. But whatever it was trying to tell me was lost in the weakness of our connection and the disparity in the speed of our minds. A mountain-slow voice speaking to a songbird.

I reached out to touch it and that was when my pursuer exploded into the clearing.

I spun, holding my sword in front of me.

It was a troll.

It had to be.

It was made of moss and mould-covered stone, each limb a boulder tied to the next with vines and shining light. Its head and shoulders tore through the canopy as it rushed towards me. Blue and green light shone between its limbs and from the cracks of its granite body. I felt the same writhing pressure that echoed out of Fafnir and Yrsa.

For a heartbeat, the troll and the forest spirit stared at each other. Then the troll's round stone head turned to me and it rushed forward, swinging a boulder-thick arm to crush me.

I held up my sword as though that would stop it.

There was a ripping, creaking sound like a tree toppled in a storm as the spirit threw its branch-cord arm at the troll, protecting me.

The troll was sent sprawling to the side, tearing down trees as it fell. Its momentum carried it stumbling past me and it felt like I had avoided an avalanche. The earth shook as it came to a stop.

The spirit, seemingly unfazed by its confrontation with the troll, turned back to me. Again, I felt the beginnings of some sort of message grinding at the back of my mind, but the words were too quiet and too slow for me to make out.

The ground shuddered as the troll pushed itself back to its feet. I moved away from the spirit as the troll straightened. Its mountain-figure loomed over the crouching spirit and as the spirit stood, turning to face its adversary, the troll took hold of one of the spirit's arms—its fingers were stone woven together with willow-thin branches—and pulled.

A tearing, wrenching sound like a longship smashing against a rocky shore, and the spirit's arm was ripped from its body.

Using the spirit's body as a club, the troll swung at me. The spirit stepped between us and stumbled from a strike that would have crushed me.

Even as the spirit was dragged aside by the force of the blow, its body sprouted verdant tendrils. They wrapped around its disembodied arm like vines clutching a tree trunk. Suddenly, the spirit's arm writhed back into motion and clutched at the troll, trying to throw it off balance.

The troll took hold of the spirit's shoulder and lifted it up before slamming it back into the ground.

I stumbled back as the earth shook.

Insects and stones flowed into the spirit's body from the ground, bulking out its already colossal figure and birds began circling the duelling monsters. The troll wrenched itself free from the spirit's grip and began slamming its boulder-like fists into the spirit's chest. Again and again, it slammed down with the weight of a landslide on the splintering body.

Birds flew from the whirlwind of feathers and screamed at me. They scratched at my face and buffeted me until I stepped back.

Another message from the spirit at the back of my mind. This time the meaning came fast and strong.

Run.

I dropped the sword, picked up my pack, and ran. The sound of wood crashing against stone echoed behind me but I did not look back.

I found a deer trail and sprinted away from the titanic battle.

The trees and leaves became smudges at the edge of my vision.

A fallen tree. I bent to leap over it. My foot caught on a bramble.

I tumbled.

The ground opened before me. The steep slope had not been there a moment before. The world churned into a spiral and I fell.

Chapter Twenty
The Trollway

I HALF-ROLLED, HALF-FELL DOWN THE SLOPE. Sharp rocks and thorny bushes scraped my skin. The ground levelled out, then I fell as a chasm yawned beneath me. Coughing and wincing, I pushed myself onto my hands and knees. The world around me shuddered with each blow of the battle between the troll and the forest spirit. Clumps of dirt and twigs rained on me from the chasm walls.

It was as though the earth had shifted apart without me noticing and now I stood in a tear in the world. A slim crack of light above me showed how far I had fallen and the high earthen walls were thick with roots, jutting rocks, and packed earth. I remembered the old stories that spoke of the trolls and their ways of travelling unseen. They had hidden paths folded throughout the world that they could step into and then emerge leagues upon leagues later with no one able to tell how they had gotten there. Trollways. It seemed the forest spirit had unfolded such a path for me. I prayed it would win the fight and the troll would not charge after me.

As I shook the dirt from my hair, I saw the thorns had cut ribbons through the runes tattooed on my hands and forearms. Blood welled in bright droplets, turning the once-constant lines into bobbled reminders of what I once was. When I wiped away the blood the tattoos turned into black streaks across my skin. I frowned, licked at my fingers, and scrubbed at an untouched sigil on my forearm. The tattoos smudged like watered ink.

The earth shook under me, a resounding final quake. And, once the dirt had stopped dribbling down the slope and the leaves had stopped shaking, the forest went still and silent. I waited for a few moments, sure that a troll would tear apart the chasm above me, but nothing came.

I let out a breath. My shoulders slumped as my limbs went weak.

I looked again at the smudged colours all over my skin. Dark, black ink from my god-speaker tattoos and the bright red patches of blood.

I still had my pack and I tipped its contents onto the floor. I was careful not to touch any more of the god-stone shards—fearful of what might happen.

It was no longer the pack of a god-speaker. Not really. There were still some of the components I had come into the forest with—without meaning to I found myself thinking of how to replenish the herbs, where to find nests for the feathers, and where the mice went to die to find their bones—but they were outweighed by the shattered god-stones.

Worst: at some point during the fight, the flight, or the fall my god-speaker arm-ring had shattered. I picked at the splinters and tried to put the ring back together. Even if the wood had not been broken, the arm-ring had been made by hands more skilled than mine and whatever art they had used to weave the three circles of wood together was beyond me.

I stared at the shards for a long time. I had to blink away the pain of losing my arm-ring and focus on something else, anything to keep myself from falling into complete despair.

The god-stone shards were linked to the forest spirit, to the shadow-creature. It was linked to the god-stone. It was the god-stone.

It had built its body with pieces of broken forest and from what I was able to decipher from its season-slow memories, I knew it was linked to the land. Its ancient visions were older than any tree of the Trolbjolvid.

It was a landvaettir, a powerful land-spirit.

I tried to relive its memories but every time I did the thunderous tempo of my heartbeat kept me from sinking into them. I remembered the sadness, the feeling that something had come and yoked the landvaettir.

I leaned back on my heels and fell against the trollway wall. Questions circled in my mind like a flock of screaming birds, myriad and unignorable but difficult to focus on.

The landvaettir's memories hinted that the gods had tethered it to the god-stone. Bile burned the back of my throat as I thought of all the times I had used the god-stone's presence to calm me and prove to myself that the gods were with me. Were the god-stones nothing more than chained guard dogs?

What did this mean for the shattered god-stone? I had been chased by a troll. Had that troll found some way to breach the gods' shackles and enslave the landvaettir?

Was that creature even a troll?

There were tales of creatures built with magic, commanded by powerful spellcasters. That was how the Empire of Bones had spread across the world after all. The creature of stone that I had seen was nothing like that though. For one thing, the magic from the Empire of Bones was built on gristle and ligaments. And whenever the tales of distant constructs came to the Fjalmark they spoke of beings completely covered in glyphs and sigils that held their bodies together. The creature I had seen was plain and smooth like a mountainside worn by centuries of wind and rain. It was made of the troll-boulders scattered throughout the Trolbjolvid.

I tried to think of recall the tales of old stone-weavers and rune-singers. The Lofmyrk trolls who had forged powerful weapons for both sides in the god-war. They had forged the Líkrifa axe. It was the Slaidyr trolls who had given the Winds the power to change and split their forms, which they had used to kill the Warrior's wife and which ultimately led to the destruction of all trolls. Or so we thought.

The light between its limbs was the same as that from the spirit I had seen between the trees. Were the trolls pulling their broken bodies together and resurrecting themselves? Such power would not be beyond the trolls of legend. I looked again at the smudges all over my arms. Things could come back from the dead. Perhaps the outlaws had been promised some great power by the troll-ghosts and that was why they had kidnapped Ulfrun, to begin the process of their resurrection.

The more I thought of all the powerful artefacts and spells the troll-legends spoke of the more I was sure that any resurgence of their power would be disastrous for all mortals, throughout the Fjalmark and beyond. The trolls had cast rituals that sundered mountains and in so many stories the trolls used mortal blood to bind their magic. I knew the gods could hold them back, but at what cost? Many gods had died in that terrible war. That was surely why the gods had tethered the landvaettir to protect their children. They were too weak to protect us then—too distracted fighting the Winds and their armies. Now, though, surely the gods would triumph against these vengeful trolls. What of mortals? The world had nearly broken during the god-war. It could not survive another. I closed my eyes and prayed that I had not stumbled upon the opening verse of a song that would end the world.

The weight of my discoveries felt like they would crush me and squash me into the earth. I would sink down, never to return. At least, I thought, if I was to die then I would not be Windborn.

Slowly, sounds returned. Birds began to sing in the distant canopy and leaves whispered as they caressed each other in the wind.

If Ulfrun was the herald of some new era of stone then whatever rituals she was being forced to cast would need an immense amount of power.

Those outlaws had wanted the strong. They had taken the vital huskalar and left the old and young. How many others had Ormhildr said were missing? Had the troll-ghosts forced Ulfrun to sacrifice them to shatter the god-stone? Perhaps that was why the landvaettir's magic was laced with mud and rot. The trolls' inheritance for aeons spent soaking in the damp earth.

I let my head hang down brand I gripped my hair hard enough I thought I might tear it out. This all started with the shattering of the god-stone but whatever was happening was hemmed within these woods. The Forest of Broken Trolls. A forest steeped in spirits, magic, and mystery.

I growled in frustration and kicked at a stone.

This was getting me nowhere. I had nothing but questions and dirt.

I looked up and down the trollway: a looming chasm of earth clotted by roots. I picked a direction and began walking but before I had gone more than ten paces the earth shifted and the path ahead of me collapsed.

The hairs on the back of my neck stood on end. Something was watching me. I took another step and the ground shifted once more. The feeling of being watched intensified.

I stepped back and walked the other way. The pressure at the base of my spine eased. Sounds came back into the world. I swallowed, shifted the weight of my pack on my shoulders, and made my way down the trollway.

I wandered the jagged path. The gap above me, the only thing that gave me any sense that I still walked in the mortal realm, thinned and widened as I went. Once it even disappeared and I was left wandering through a pitch-dark tunnel. I hunched as I went through that place, not that I needed to as the tunnel was tall enough that a bear could have stood in it, but the weight of the earth around me oppressed me.

There was no sound. No heat from the sun.

I walked carefully, feeling my way with each boot before I took a step, and even so I felt the roots catch on my clothes as though trying to keep me in that dark place.

Then, after what felt like an eternity, the sun returned. First, as a pinprick of light when I rounded a corner, then as a glow as enticing as a winter hearthfire, and finally, in the almost too-bright slash from the gap in the chasm above.

After that the trollway split, curved, and wound its way through the earth like a mountain stream. At some points, I was forced to squeeze through gaps as the path came together. In others I had to double-back as I followed the wrong path and some rockfall or tangle of roots stretched across the trollway like a blockade.

Some hours later, I rounded a corner to find half of the trollway taken up with a boulder wrapped in tree roots.

I crept towards it, afraid that it might tear free of its

moorings and form into another troll to crush me.

The stone was covered in runes, old runes that overlapped and layered upon one another so deeply that it was difficult for me to tell which runes were which. Some of the smaller roots had leeched into the carvings, seeming to mark them with the bold emphasis of living wood.

As I approached the Windborn power in my chest sat up, took notice, and locked its hungry gaze upon the stone.

I reached out my hands.

The power within me stretched, reached out like a ravenous squid.

This boulder was a god-stone in miniature. It was like a beautiful tapestry that Ulfrun's stone at the edge of Vidsetr was desperately trying to imitate.

My fingers brushed the rough stone and my thumb caught on a root.

My mind rushed into the stone and into the memories of the land spirit.

The stone-kin teach the Winds how to forge their own mortals. Heavy browed, friends to ice. They fight with chipped-flint spears against those created by the gods. The stone-kin offend the gods in some way I cannot fathom. A god descends and stone shatters.

The trees hunch heavy under the weight of countless seasons. The stone-kin have long been broken and silent. A god-forged mortal comes. I am poisoned by another power like fungus slowly killing an ash tree. I am a river dammed. I am rootless.

I gasped as I came back to myself. Time was once again measured in heartbeats and hours, not by seasons and the withering of leaves or the fall of snow.

The spirit, the landvaettir, was trapped. Before it had been anchored to the god-stone like branches linked to their trunk, but still able to roam its domain. Now some powerful entity had yoked it and cut it off from its beating heart. The god-stone. Now, I understood why the god-stone had shattered and why it continued to crumble.

I tried to sift through the landvaettir's memories and pick out who had done this, what was responsible, but it was impossible to decipher any details in the landvaettir's glacially paced mind that smudged days into fleeting moments.

Beyond the root-wrapped boulder, which I now realised was part of the landvaettir and perhaps the reason it had not withered and died, the trollway was open and the light shone bright. I picked myself up and edged through.

I would find a way out of the trollway and when I did I would return to the dark centre of the forest. I would not abandon my sister. I had to rescue Ulfrun from her slavery and now I knew that they were not the only ones relying on me. I had to save the landvaettir and the forest.

ᚠ

By the time I clambered out of the trollway the forest was wreathed in its first, false dusk. Shadows stretched, slowly ensnaring the woods in their dark embrace. Exhaustion dragged at every part of me and hunger clawed at my insides. The sound of running water from nearby. Bright colour splashed across the bushes in front of me, berries. It was far too early in the year for fruit, so I approached with caution, yet the bush's branches were heavy with bilberries.

As I took one of the berries there was a frisson of power at my fingertips. The landvaettir. The berry was sweet and ripe. Without realising I took another and another and before long I was full of berries.

I tried to get my bearings as I wound my way to the stream for a drink. The moss-covered expanse of the forest still looked as confusing as it ever had. The trees loomed over me, breaking any hope I had to see a landmark or something I recognised.

In the trollway there was only backwards and forwards. Now the landvaettir tickled the back of my mind like fern leaves brushing against my leg. As I turned, I knew which direction was north and when I faced west I knew with unerring certainty that in the distance there were nettles crushed under mortal boots and trees butchered for axe handles and spear shafts. I could not tell if the outlaws were still there, whatever connection I had with the landvaettir did not stretch that far, but they had been there recently. I would surely find some clue to Sigrun's whereabouts, some hint of Ulfrun's slavery, and some sign of how to free the landvaettir.

I set off through the darkening woods.

True dusk fell as the tenuous link I had with the landvaettir faded and with it the surety of my direction. I caught my foot in a tree root as I skidded down a scree slope. When I got to my feet I was no longer sure where I needed to go.

I spent a few more minutes wandering in what I thought was the right direction but my confidence died with the light. I was aimless once more. Without the dull illumination from the false dusk the forest became a mess of directionless shadows.

I squinted into the darkness, hoping that might somehow illuminate the menacing trees and impenetrable undergrowth.

After I stumbled for the fourth time, I realised that I was better off trying to find somewhere to camp instead of injuring myself wandering aimlessly in the dark. Now that the sense of the land spirit had left my mind the forest was once again apathetic wilderness. It would not care if I tripped and cracked my head. I would not recover from that deathly wound a second time.

I found a tree with a large hollow between its roots and wedged myself in with my pack and cloak over the top of me. There was so much dirt on my clothes and leaves in my hair that I was sure no animal would smell me and I would blend into the muddy roots, unseen.

I tried to sleep but as soon as my eyelids began to close I heard a twig snap in the distance, some animal cried out in pain. I wriggled deeper into the root-hollow to try and make myself as small as possible.

Then, in the distance, light. I stood slowly, as though if I rushed to my feet I would scare it off.

A shimmering figure woven with sea-blue light.

A spirit.

In the night's infinite depth, it was difficult to see how far away it was and as I watched it stretched and twisted to look all around.

I took a step forward, carefully placing my feet to avoid

tripping on anything, and another figure appeared. This one shimmering ice-sheet-green.

The landvaettir had called the trolls stone-kin. These spirits, surely, were closer kin to the landvaettir than trolls. Now that I was connected to the landvaettir in some small way, would they be able to sense that, would they help me?

The spirits both seemed to be travelling in the same direction and I followed, keeping my distance. Their light flickered as they stepped between the trees. I watched with fascination as they stretched and coiled seemingly at random until one of them disappeared like mist caught in a gale.

I froze, clutching the nearest tree, wondering if they had seen me.

The ghost that remained stopped moving but its glow intensified.

Glacial light filled the night, revealing trees and boulders and swaying ferns. The spirit stood in the centre of a clearing filled with enormous stones. I craned my neck to examine the stones but I was too far away and the low, newly illuminated branches blocked my view.

The spirit walked up to one of the boulders and brushed an insubstantial hand against it. It seemed to sigh then it hunched over as though in pain.

I took a step forward. I began to reach out to it. There was a power there, shuddering in the same way the Windborn power quivered in my chest.

Then the spirit shattered, splitting like lightning and each fork splintered into different shades. The light of an ocean. A robin's egg. A clear summer sky. Each colour stepped away from the other and then there were three.

The light faded back to its muted shimmer and without a signal, the spirits walked away from each other. They circled the stones then spiralled out into the forest.

I ducked back against the tree, hiding behind the thick trunk as the nearest spirit moved past. Its bright, featureless face seemed to be searching for something as it leaned down and twisted this way and that. Before I revealed myself to these strange spirits I wanted to see what kind of stones it had found.

Once the spirit had passed I scurried over to the clearing.

Coils of rope had been left by the trees. The ground was churned by the scrape of countless boots. Deep furrows had been carved into the ground by the passage of stone.

Six boulders had been dragged into the clearing from various places throughout the forest. Every one was a troll-boulder: this one shaped like a forearm and hand, that one crooked like a leg, and that one a shoulder and part of a torso. They had been pushed together and were almost touching. They had been shoved together to make a rough humanoid shape, though there was no head.

I bent over the shoulder stone and brushed my hands along it. I had expected to feel some flicker of power like I felt with the spirits flocking around me, but there was nothing. The stone was lifeless.

My fingers brushed against something cold and wet. I whipped my hand away.

Something black and ichorous glooped from my fingers. I sniffed it. It was half rotten like stagnant silt.

I brushed it off on the ground and squinted at the nearly reformed troll in front of me. A thick, black line had been daubed across all the stones, connecting each limb to the next in a crude humanoid pictograph.

I thought back to the flickers I had felt of the god-stone's power and the black, cloying poison I had felt on it. Whatever was compelling the outlaws and had captured Ulfrun was forcing them to resurrect the trolls. The first spirits had touched these stones so gently and, I thought, with such sadness. Surely they hated that their cousin was being forced to serve some fetid master.

Lightning flashes as the spirits split apart again and again until it felt like I stood in the centre of a thunderstorm.

The more spirits that wandered throughout the forests the more I felt their power echo within my chest. Whatever magic these spirits had was something I had once known. I looked down at the smudging tattoos on my arms and shifted the god-stone shards at my back. These spirits mourned the loss and slavery of their spirit-kin and shuddered at the new power that yoked it. I felt a kinship with them then; I had been a god-speaker, a rune-weaver and now I was Windborn, chained by a power I did not want.

I grimaced at the offhand thought that I was no longer a god-speaker. It twisted inside me and left my chest feeling hollow.

I turned the thought away and looked to the spirits. Something of their power reached out to me and seemed to fill my empty chest. They would help me.

I stepped out from between the inert troll-boulders and tried to reach out to the spirits in body and soul. I pushed with my Windborn power and I felt something flow out of me.

All around me the swirling spirit-figures froze in place and as one they straightened.

Without turning, the nearest figure walked towards me. Their face and body, painted as it was in featureless light, was unreadable.

I shifted my pack on my shoulders and took a breath.

After a few steps, the spirit loomed over me. Its blue light shifted. The boulders around me were outlined in glacial colours. All except the lines of silt-black paint which seemed to absorb all light.

The spirit stood in front of me and tipped its head to one side. A question.

Whenever I had used my Windborn power before, I had drawn out memories from those I touched. If I pushed as well as pulled then perhaps my memories would be given to the spirit. It might feel something of the landvaettir's touch upon me and know I was on their side.

I reached out my hand.

The spirit stretched out one limb. Its arm ended in a twisting stub of light, glowing and fading like the Winds across the sky.

My hand brushed against its ethereal form.

I was surprised by the weight of it. I had expected the ghost to feel as insubstantial as a sunbeam but my grasping fingers felt like they were running through honey.

I pushed myself into the spirit and it flared with crackling forks of green light.

No reaction.

I pulled as gently as I could.

The raid has gone wrong. The Ertlanders ambushed us as we slept. We are trapped. In the darkness, I cannot see my friends to help. There is only the sound of wet crunches and screams of pain. The scent of blood and shit in the air. I wish I could be everywhere. I wish I could see. Something sharp stabs into my back. I smile as I fall. We have died in battle. We will feast together in the gods' halls.

Three Ertlanders pick at our corpses like crows. They talk of a betrayer. I do not know why I have not died, but I do not care. Rage pushes me from the ground. Two Ertlanders rush me. I cannot face both. I grab the spear of one as I will myself to face the other. A bright figure steps out of me. It shimmers in green and blue. My vision splits. I shake my head. The Ertlanders cry out in fear. The light-ghost hears my anger and tears the Ertlanders apart.

I blinked and stumbled back, crashing into one of the boulders. The ghostly figure in front of me flickered and then burned away like morning mist.

Suddenly, the forest was too dark. The black night too thick after the brightness of the figure in front of me. My heart stampeded against my chest as my terror surged.

It was not a spirit. It had never been a spirit. It was an echo of some distant Windborn working with whatever had captured Sigrun.

Slowly, my vision returned. Blots of light between distant trees.

The Windborn's other echoes.

I watched them. They watched me.

A heartbeat of still silence.

They surged toward me.

I fled.

Chapter Twenty-One
Echoes in the Forest

Leaves whipped against my head. Branches knocked my shins. Bushes snapped under my feet. My breath bellowed in my ears.

There were no other sounds to the chase.

The ghostly figures or Windborn echoes or whatever they were kept their silence as they hunted me.

I tried to keep sight of them as I sprinted through the forest. They were everywhere. Their squirming blue light was enough for me to see by and dodge around the trees to keep ahead of them. But they gained on me.

Whenever I charged through a thicket of gorse or stumbled through a patch of nettles, the ghosts slid straight through them. The world flickered as they passed through it, leaving speckles of light on the leaves like mildew, but they did not slow.

They spread out and one curved in to cut across my path. I twisted mid-step to sprint off in another direction.

The rest came on, relentless.

Another ghost cut across my path and then another, each time the rest kept at my heels and forced me to find the one path away from them. They hunted me like a pack of wolves.

I cried out in frustration as I was forced to stop. My lungs burned and my legs shook. I could not run forever. I could fight. If I could absorb another ghost perhaps I could take its strength and use it to—

"I don't know what you did, god-speaker," a voice called from somewhere in the darkness, "but you're on the wrong side of this."

A flare against the Windborn power in my chest as blue light blossomed ahead.

A new ghost took shape and stepped into the world, moving away from a scrawny man with a scraggy beard and dark clothes.

He shivered as the ghost stepped away from him then straightened and faced me.

The air around us thrummed with Windborn energy as the man's power echoed from his ghosts like a whisper bouncing in a cave. I shoved my Windborn power down as hard as I could and prayed that he would not realise I was Windborn.

"I don't know what the fuck kind of spell that was," the man continued. "Ain't no one knocked out one of my boys like that."

"I am a powerful rune-weaver," I said and immediately regretted it as my voice quavered, betraying my fear and exhaustion. "I have the gods with me and they will help me save the people you have taken. You are on the wrong side."

The man grinned, his teeth a shining blue slice in the night.

"I have gods with me too."

He stalked behind the blue fire-flicker of his... Ghosts. Echoes. Not gods. They stood silent and full of churning light. I felt the Windborn power in them, but the stranger sounded so confident.

"These things aren't gods," I scoffed. "Are they?"

"Ha, these things?" He swung a hand through the nearest one as though swatting away a fly. The ghost's torso broke apart then flowed back together like a stone-splashed reflection. "No, we got all sorts of other gods with us. These things... They're echoes. Part me, part something else."

Disgust laced his words and I edged away as he glowered at his nearest echo.

"Don't do that," he said with a sigh. "I've already chased you once. I can't be bothered to do it again."

"Then let me go."

"Nah, it's not gonna work like that. I've got orders. Another rune-weaver would be helpful so you've gotta come with me.

It's going to happen sooner or later so either you come with me now, nice and easy, or you can run into the woods. I'll catch you again, but I'll be in a bad mood."

I looked at his ghosts. They shifted slowly from side to side like grass in the wind. As the silent moment dragged on and I tried to decide if I should run, they stilled, one by one. Their featureless faces all locked on to me and I felt the intensity of their gaze, the tension in their frames, ready to chase me. I looked beyond them at the night-dark forest. There was no way I could outrun them, especially in the dark. They were too close and I was too exhausted.

"Fine," I said. "If you answer my questions."

The man scowled and pinched the bridge of his nose. "Alright, you come with me and we'll walk and talk."

He stepped aside and swept his hand back, gesturing for me to walk with him.

I ground my teeth and moved up to him, pushing down my Windborn power as much as I could. It felt like trying to walk silently across a room covered with eggshells and I sent another prayer to the gods that the shivering power of the ghost-echoes would keep the Windborn man from sensing my true nature.

He nodded as I came level with him and he turned to lead me through the forest. As one, the ghosts moved with us. They fell into a loose circle a few paces all around us, illuminating the foliage with their sickly shimmering.

"See, ain't this much nicer? We get to have a nice stroll through the woods. And I've even got you an honour guard," the Windborn said and shot me another vicious green-flicker grin.

I grimaced. It felt more like a tightening noose than an honour guard. As we trudged through the forest in a ring of wavering Wind-light I found myself clenching and unclenching my fists. It felt like we made no progress through the infinite trees yet the Windborn seemed to be in no hurry. He began to whistle.

"Why do you need another rune-weaver?" I asked, praying that Ulfrun was still safe.

"Spells are complicated," he said with a shrug. "I guess it's easier with two of you."

Relief washed over me. If Ulfrun was still alive then maybe they had not completed whatever ritual they had taken Sigrun for.

"What kind of spells?"

"How the fuck should I know? Do I look like a rune-weaver to you?"

I glanced at him and silently agreed that he looked nothing like any rune-weaver I had ever seen. Lit by the ghost-light, I could see the scars across his face, the patchy beard, and the knife scabbards lining his belt and chest.

One of the echo-ghosts stepped through a tree and something about the way its light forked around the stubby branches reminded me of the troll that had chased me from the camp.

"Did you force Ulfrun to make that troll?

The Windborn choked as he whistled which turned into spluttering laughter.

"Did I make Ulfrun do it? Brother, it was Ulfrun's idea."

I froze. He took a couple more steps before he turned to me, grinning.

"You kidnapped Ulfrun from Vidsetr. You're forcing her to work for you."

"I ain't done anything. I told you we got all sorts on our side, Ulfrun among them."

That couldn't be right. Surely Ulfrun was being forced, complying for fear of her life and the lives of her friends. I blinked, trying to block out the light from the shimmering figures. I had been wrong about the echo-ghosts. Could I be wrong about Ulfrun? What else was I wrong about?

No. Ulfrun would not help them willingly. A god-speaker would not deliberately break a god-stone. The gods had gifted us with them to protect us. How could a god-speaker do such a thing?

"What about the shattered god-stone? The forest spirit?"

That same flicker-knife grin.

"I told you, god-speaker: we got all sorts. We got the forest on our side. We got these new troll things on our side. And something strong, something dark."

"Why?" I shook my head, unable to find any purpose in all this. "Are the trolls forcing you to do this? I can help you be free of them. Let me help you."

"You can help us, god-speaker, but you'll be doing what we tell you. We ain't being forced to do anything by anyone. We're here to make sure that things get put right. The High King used to have it right, but he's gotten all twisted. Whatever happened up north this past couple of years. You hear about that? Some fucking Windborn saves the day and then the High King is using them, getting them to swear to him again." The disgust in his voice, the self-loathing, sent a shiver up my spine. "We're going to remind him that the only power that's worth swearing to is the gods. Now, get moving, Ulfrun wants to do this tonight."

I watched him, waiting for some hint of uncertainty, anything that might give me a crack I could wedge open and twist him into an ally.

"You're Windborn," I said. "Why would you want to force the High King to abandon them? You could have whatever you wanted if you went to the High King, to any chieftain, and swore loyalty to them."

"Whatever I want? What I want is to be feasting in the gods' halls with my raid-brothers," he spat in a voice full of rage and loathing. "Just because I'm Windborn doesn't mean I don't know that Windborn are wrong. Fucking freaks. They're already dead and damned but they don't know it. We're cut off from the reward we were promised and forced to fight for shit-for-brain lords and kings for money and power.

"You know what the Empire of Bones used to do? They made soldiers. Really made them. They fused them together with I don't even know what. Everyone knows that was fucking wrong.

"Windborn are fused together, souls caught in the heartbeat after death and stolen from the gods. How is using Windborn any different to what the Empire of Bones was doing? Better they're all wiped out."

His rant reached a crescendo then crashed down into a mournful tone of self-pity. He turned his face away from me and stared into the distance, deliberately looking between his echoes and at the darkness.

Part of me—the part that was still a healer and prayed for this all to be a dream—wanted to reach out and tell him that it would be okay and we would find a way to fix him. Another part—one that was slowly saturating my every pore—knew there was no solution. I had so desperately wanted to fix my Windborn soul, I had run through so many incantations in my mind, but I knew it could not be done. It would have been so easy for me to fall into a spiral of self-hatred like he had, but I had Sigrun.

We were brothers in our resurrection. We were forever lost to the gods. We were Windborn.

I reached out to him, flicking my wrist so that my sleeve fell to expose the sigil tattoos on my arm. I prayed that in the darkness he would not see that they had smudged.

"I understand," I said.

"How can you understand?" he snapped and whirled to face me. "I worshipped the gods. I said all the prayers and now I've been abandoned. Those dead soldiers who fought for the Empire of Bones had a choice. At least that bloody bog-water monstrosity chose their path. What about Windborn?"

He stared at me, eyes glittering with furious tears, and I felt my eyes well up watching him.

"We need to show the Winds that we don't want nothing to do with their fucking powers. Maybe then they'll let the gods take their faithful without getting in the fucking way."

I kept my arm outstretched to him. I clenched and unclenched my fist.

"I understand," I said again and took a step towards him. I replayed his memories and felt the knife-twist of betrayal when he'd realised he was still alive. I blinked away tears. "It's not fair the Winds took you. When you died on that raid the gods should have swept you into their hall to feast and fight. You should be standing with the gods when the world ends, shield to shield with all your raid-brothers."

"How did you... How did you know how I died?"

His eyes rounded with fear and confusion now. He stumbled away from me, but I took a pace to follow him. The ghosts did not move and kept their silent vigil a few paces away.

"That doesn't matter. What matters is that I can help you. Take me to Ulfrun. Together, we can unravel your Windborn power and you will be free to join the gods as you should have."

He watched me, eyes still wide with confusion, but I could see how badly he wanted to believe me. He so desperately wanted a god-speaker to sift through his soul and draw the Windborn poison from it.

He took a step towards me.

"Can you really—"

He stopped. The ghosts were still a few paces distant, illuminating the forest with their glacier-blue flicker. The haze of power that his echoes had threaded through the air was distant. There was nothing between me and him. Our Windborn powers squirmed and reached for each other.

"No. You... You're—"

Before he could finish I dove forward and grasped his wrist. Shock widened in his eyes as I pulled at the power within him.

It was like shoving my hand into a churning blizzard, icy power whipped within him and I clawed at it. There was more strength in him than in the outlaws or the god-stone shard. I pulled and pulled and still there were depths of strength in the Windborn maelstrom within him.

The echoes blinked out like candles in a storm. I drew harder on the strength of his soul and his memories flowed into me.

My son is becoming a man. Later, we will feast in the mead hall. Now, a quiet celebration for us. We sit together at the shrine behind our home. We light the kindling together and offer a prayer to the Warrior. The gods have protected me on my raids and now we ask them to do the same for my son.

Sweat beaded my brow, my breath came heavy, my chest felt like it would explode.

The longship crunches into the sand of Ertland. We prepare for our attack. More longships slice into the beach. My son leaps onto the sand. He grins, the wild smile of the young and reckless, but it falters when I am ordered elsewhere. My son will be with the raid proper while I, along with a select few, sneak into the stronghold. I slap my son's shoulder. Do not worry, I say, I will find you whether on this world or in the hall of the gods. His grin returns.

We fell to the ground. My hand came away from his sweat-slicked wrist and I wretched. The power in my chest coiled and twisted like caged snakes with each scale a spear-head slicing my heart.

He lay next to me, half covered in mud and leaves and breathing heavily. His eyelids flickered as he fought to remain conscious.

"I'm sorry, Nori," I coughed between bile-soaked breaths, his name now floating through my mind along with his memories.

His eyes fluttered closed and he went still.

I lay next to him, but I could not tell if I had taken enough to kill him. Windborn power fizzed in my veins. It was going to explode if I didn't use this energy.

I put my hand to the ground and pushed myself to my feet. Without meaning to, I let some Windborn energy flow out through my fingertips and some of the brown, mulchy leaves under my hand hardened and turned a crisp green. Mushroom heads speckled the ground.

I stumbled to my feet, took one last look at the Windborn I might have killed, and ran aimlessly into the dark.

CHAPTER TWENTY-TWO
A RITUAL INTERRUPTED

I STUMBLED THROUGH THE FOREST UNTIL MY BREATH BURNED white-hot. No ghosts or echoes or Wind-light illuminated my path or the distant tree trunks. I slowed my hurried, panting flight and leant on a tree. The fresh, virulent power still writhed in my chest, but my awkward flight had eased its insistence against the inside of my ribs.

I squinted into the darkness, trying to decipher where I was. Everything was painted in shades of black and nothing was recognisable. I gritted my teeth in frustration. Along with some of the memories from the ghost-summoning Windborn I had gained a rough sense of the forest, or this portion of it. If I could find some landmark then perhaps I could aim myself at the outlaw's camp and finally find Sigrun.

I unslung my pack and slumped against the tree. The rough bark tore at my sleeve as though urging me to stay upright but I ignored it and sat on the wet ground.

The Windborn had said that Ulfrun wanted to work a spell that night. I couldn't wait for morning. Sigrun was in danger.

I shook my pack and heard the clatter of stone and slithering shift of my irreparably broken components, the unfixable arm-ring, and the god-stone shards. I looked inside the pack and chewed my lip. I had killed—or nearly killed—several people when I drew from them. What harm would I do to the landvaettir?

I looked around. I could barely see anything in the depths of the night.

Hesitantly, I pulled out a stone about the size of my palm. Its power was warm against my skin, but it was fading like heat from a coal on a long-forgotten fire.

I pulled on its power.

Mortals hunt through ancient forests. Fur clothes flap. Flint-tipped spears flash. The scent of moss and freshwater. The cool comfort of dirt inside my skin.

The god-stone shard went cold. My senses returned and with them something else.

I dropped the stone then turned to the tree I had slumped against. It was a spruce tree, its bark was cracked like dried mud, and it had been growing in the forest for an age. When it was a sapling, barely sprouted, the world was still settling from the tremors of the god-war. It had witnessed the first mortal feet to tread the Fjalmark and had sprouted not long after the god-stone had first been carved. Its roots snaked deep through the dirt, not far in the eyes of the landvaettir, but they were entwined with the fingers of fungus that stretched out for miles around and connected this singular tree to the entire forest.

I placed my hand on the rough, scaled bark and closed my eyes. I pushed myself into the wood, through the sap and into the heartwood, in the same way I blended my vision with the ravens' eyes. My breathing slowed to match the slow stream of air around the branches and needle-leaves.

The world flitted around me, rushing by with the speed of a blackbird's heartbeat, and I shivered as my awareness expanded.

I no longer stood in the forest. I was part of it.

I felt the shift of leaves as an owl made its silent perch on a nearby branch. I knew the ground sloped down to a stream which wound its way past boulders furred with moss. I knew that in that direction the earth was scarred by the fresh passage of troll-stones that had lain still since I was a sapling.

I took my hand from the bark and blinked myself back into rhythm with my heart.

With both the vague sense of direction from the Windborn's memories and the sure knowledge of the forest from the tree's senses, I knew where I needed to go.

I hurried down the slope, towards the place where the troll-stones had been taken. Those tracks would lead me to the outlaws and then I could join them and we would destroy any Windborn in our way. No. That wasn't right. I shook my head, pulling my mind from the memories and desires of Nori, the ghost Windborn. I needed to find the outlaws to save Sigrun. I grabbed the charm from my belt and ran my thumb along its rough ridges.

I darted through the forest. With the tree's knowledge of the forest lingering in my mind, I knew exactly where the rocks and roots lay in wait. I ran as graceful as a deer.

Then, lights in the distance. Bright, clean.

I slowed and darted from tree to tree, hiding behind their low branches and the feathered ferns.

People moved in a clearing. Some shouted instructions. Others grunted with exertion.

In the light of lanterns and torches I saw a group dragging at ropes and pulling stones along the ground. Beyond them, there were about six straight-backed figures each with a mask of bone or wood. Some shouted and cajoled at the people hunched to their tasks.

I crept closer, trying to make out the workers' faces and see who they were, but the torches and lanterns showed me that the workers were ragged, a mix of men and women and panting with exhaustion. They each wore a heavy, pendulous necklace and I thought back to the first body, Arvid, which seemed an age ago, and the necklace that hid him from scrying eyes. All other detail was hidden in the night. I cursed under my breath. I could not tell if Sigrun was there without giving myself away and though Nori's strength still thrilled through my veins I had no weapons.

"Come on, you lazy arseholes." The outlaw closest to the workers shoved at them, waving a hand to show where he wanted the stone. "Put it there. Quickly. It can't be that heavy. That's it. You happy with that, Virun?"

"Yeah, that'll do. Finna, Skuta, stay here. We'll take these back for her to decide which she needs. We'll be back with the god-speaker."

There was some muttering amongst the workers, which was soon cuffed out of them, as they gathered the ropes before they were led away from the clearing. They left one of the torches for the two remaining guards but took all the rest, clearly marking their passage through the trees.

I waited until their lights had disappeared and then crept forward.

It took me some time to move up to the edge of the clearing. My sense of the forest was fading as the landvaettir's magic diluted within me and I had to squint at the ground to avoid snapping twigs or crunching pebbles underfoot.

The two remaining outlaws had already grown bored with their loops around the boulders. They both wore masks, one a boar's skull and the other a patchwork of wood and leaves. Bone-mask yawned and stretched, staring disinterestedly out into the forest. Wood-mask leant over the stones to examine them.

From where I crouched behind a fern, I could see a sliver of the sky. It was a clear night with the stars sparkling on their velvet bed. I craned my head from side to side to see if I could spot the Warrior's constellation, to take some comfort from the immutable canvas of the night. I saw two stars that might have been the edge of the Warrior's hammer, but as soon as I spotted them something shimmered across the sky. A coil of blue-green light. I scowled. The Winds.

"It's going to be a good night for it," Bone-mask said, gesturing to the sky.

Wood-mask grunted and straightened. They turned to face Bone-mask as they sat on the stone they had been examining. "I don't get why we need another one anyway."

"This one's for the god-speaker. That's why we're doing this so far away from—Hey!" Bone-mask cried out. "Don't sit on the stones."

"Why not?"

"You know how long it takes the god-speaker to paint them up right. If she finds out your arse smeared all those runes she'll use your guts to hang you."

"Whatever."

Despite his nonchalant tone, Wood-mask stood up quickly and—after a quick check of the stone he'd been sat on—moved to stand with Bone-mask.

If I could examine the rune and sigils painted on those

stones then, if I could not stop the ritual entirely I might be able to unpick the magic holding the landvaettir captive.

I moved closer, pushing through the undergrowth. A thorn caught on my sleeve and before I could stop it the bramble whipped back into place with a snap.

"What was that?" Bone-mask asked, their spear ready.

"Probably a fox," Wood-mask replied. "Do you think they'll be long? Thorunn brought back a deer earlier. I want to get back before Runa eats it all."

"I'm going to check."

Wood-mask sighed. "Whatever. Don't go far and don't moan to me when you step in fox shit."

"Keep an eye out," Bone-mask snapped back. "There was an attack on the camp, wasn't there? What if it's one of them?

"You know anyone who's stupid enough to run straight back to their jailers? I'm telling you it's a fox or a rabbit or something."

Bone-mask grunted then made her way out into the forest.

I was hidden well enough by the shadows and my mud-covered clothes for now, but once Bone-mask was close enough, she would spot me.

I pawed at the ground and found a small stone. I waited as Bone-mask crept towards me, my heart hammered so hard I thought it would break free of my chest. Once Bone-mask reached the edge of the torchlight and their glinting spear seemed close enough to touch, I threw the stone into the forest.

The stone plunked off a tree trunk then clattered through the undergrowth.

Bone-mask's head snapped around and she crept towards the noise. I waited a moment and then followed. I moved close enough to grasp at her cloak. I glanced back at Wood-mask who was picking at their fingernails with a knife.

"Maybe it was a fox," Bone-mask muttered.

As they turned around I leapt at them.

"What the—"

She shoved her spear between us on instinct. Thank the gods that I was close enough to knock the spearhead aside. I grabbed hold of her cloak and tugged, pulling Bone-mask off balance. She dropped the spear and, in one fluid motion, drew her knife and slashed at me.

I cried out as the blade sliced across my forearm. My other hand lashed out and caught the outlaw's arm. I pulled.

The Fjalmark isn't safe anymore. We herd our pigs through the forest like we always do and there is always someone watching, someone ready to take them from us. The dog growls. My bow-string creaks. They attack. We lose another pig. Fucking outlaws.

The attacks are worse now. I seek out the god-speaker. We cannot go on like this. She nods. She agrees. She says it is because people no longer fear the gods. They no longer fear consequences. What can I do, I ask. She says I can help her. She has the power to remind the world of the gods' true strength, then no one—not spirit nor king nor mortal man—will dare to break the gods' laws again.

We lose two more pigs. On the third we fight back, I kill one, but they kill my dog and my husband. Fucking outlaw scum. I seek out the god-speaker. Let me help, I say. She nods and leads me into the forest.

The outlaw tried to cry out but her voice was only a wheezing whisper. She slumped to the ground and went still.

"What's going on?" Wood-mask called over. "You stepped in shit didn't you?"

I couldn't risk them getting up. Fucking outlaws. I took up their knife and slashed their throat. As the hot blood bubbled over my fingers I felt my mind shift, becoming mine again. I shook my head. Bile rose in my throat even as the fresh strength and power thrilled through my veins.

"Astra?"

Wood-mask had reached the edge of the torchlight, their spear lowered and ready.

I tried to regain Astra's memories, remember what it was like to be them.

Wincing, I pitched my voice to try and fool Wood-mask. "Yeah, it was a fox. It startled me is all."

"Huh? Come back here. Nice and slow."

I picked up Astra's spear and bone mask, cursing at myself through gritted teeth, and moved slowly to the torchlight.

"Easy now. That really you, Astra?"

I didn't risk answering. I waited until I was a pace outside of the flickering light, enough that Wood-mask could see me but not realise who I was.

Spear-lowered, I charged.

I was Windborn-quick, but Wood-mask had battle-honed reflexes. They dodged to the side of my clumsy spear thrust and whipped their spear out to stab me. The blade sliced through my billowing cloak and scraped along my ribs.

With a cry of frustration, I took my spear in two hands and swung it like a club.

The move took Wood-mask off guard and they were knocked off their feet as the spear shaft slammed into their shoulder.

I dropped the spear and leapt on them.

We rolled in the dirt, fists pummelling each other. I tried to grab hold of Wood-mask's arm, their face, neck, anything that would let me draw out their strength and overpower them. Every time my fingernails clawed their skin they squirmed out of my grasp and knocked me off balance with a well-placed fist.

Then Wood-mask was on top of me. They had a rock in one hand and brandished it like a hammer. Instinctively, I covered my head with my arms as the stone smashed into them.

Again and again, the stone slammed into my arms. My bones strained under the pressure of each blow and I knew that if I had not been Windborn I would not have survived.

Eventually, Wood-mask grew bored with their assault and grabbed my arms to pry them off my head. As their naked fingers clenched around my skin the Windborn power within me swirled with glee and I pulled on them.

The god is gone from the water. We still throw offerings into the bog, but the power is gone. It has disappeared across the ocean. I cannot stay knowing my prayers are unheard. I pack my things and travel to the Fjalmark.

Wood-mask whipped their hand away for the briefest moment, but it was enough. They were shaken, weakened, and I threw them off.

Fresh strength roared through me and I grabbed Wood-mask by the throat, lifting them clean off the ground and slamming them onto the nearest boulder.

They writhed and clawed at my fingers, but my grip was iron.

As I pulled on their strength Wood-mask's struggles weakened. I pulled a knife from their belt and stabbed at them. And again and again.

The woods are damp. Mud squelches underfoot. It is comforting to feel the cold, wet earth push between my toes. I follow the colossal bulk of my god through the forest. The sweet-sick scent of rot drifts over me. My god turns and—

Searing pain as a knife drives into my belly. My hot blood mixes with the cold damp ground.

I am so far from home and the reassuring quiet of the marsh. But it is quiet here also. The strange northern gods are silent and the forest is yoked under our power. I watch the slaves drag the stones together. A smile tugs at my lips knowing they are building their barrows. Limbstitcher calls to me, telling me—

The knife stabs me again, clumsily now, so it drags across my belly and draws out my insides. I try to scream but my lungs are empty. I cannot breathe. I feel the damp earth and my hot blood and the cold.

When I resurfaced from Wood-mask's pain and memories I was on the floor. My clothes were splattered with dirt and gore and my forearms were drenched in bright, smeared crimson. I pulled myself up using Wood-mask's legs, dragging them from the stone as I did so. There was still heat in the body, but no strength to draw from. The soul was gone.

I buckled, retching and vomiting onto the corpse I had made, then looked around and cursed.

In the scuffle, we had smeared all the painted sigils and there was blood splattered across the stones, dripping down and obscuring the rest of the runes. Whatever hope I had to glean the weave of the magic was lost.

I stood and stared at the stones as my breath slowed, my heartbeat quietened, and the small noises of the forest returned.

These stones were the same as the others I had seen in the forest. Each boulder was a troll-stone that had been dragged with great effort to recreate the form of a colossal humanoid.

I walked around the stones, letting my fingers trail along the crook of a granite elbow and marvelling at the time-worn hands. The outlaws had piled vines and roots in the gaps between the stones like arboreal ligaments. At first, I thought that they had been haphazardly thrown onto the stones, but as I looked closer I saw that they had been carefully placed so that they nestled between the painted runes and sigils.

For the runes and sigils that remained across the stone body, I could decipher perhaps half of them. There were runes for healing—presumably to knit the body together—and sigils for protection—to keep the power caged—but there were still more that had been written in a language I didn't understand. It looked like a cross between the ancient script from the Empire of Bones and the constantly shifting tribes that had inherited its ruins. Those strange symbols were painted with a gritty, black substance and they snaked through the god-given runes like rivulets of rotten water. Whatever ritual Ulfrun planned here was beyond me.

As I rounded the shoulders of the inert figure I saw another stone set a little way apart from the rest.

It was smaller than the others, flat, and looked to have been washed clean.

I stared at it, uncomprehending. All the other stones had been draped with vines and dragged into that rough humanoid figure. This one a few paces away. Perhaps they had brought it to be used as a head stone if the other was not suitable.

Then I noticed the grooves cut into the stone that led into the ground and ran all the way to the half-formed troll in front of it.

An execution block.

This was a blood ritual.

The magic here had a steep cost and Ulfrun would pay for it with a life. My heart lurched and my hand went to Sigrun's charm.

I fell to my knees and scrabbled at the ground, smearing the grooves and runes placed so carefully on the floor. It wouldn't stop Ulfrun, but it would slow her down, perhaps long enough for me to figure out a plan.

Something pressed against my mind and it felt like my head was being wrapped in an oily mist.

I looked out into the dark wood and saw a flicker of light in the distance.

Pressure against my mind again. The power in my chest responded.

Windborn.

ᚠ

I hurriedly dragged the body out of the torchlight. I grimaced as the corpse carved lines in the soft ground, messing the carefully marked sigils and clearly showing where I had moved the body. Once it was outside of the circle of weak lantern-light, I grabbed their mask and cloak and put them on.

The flickering of Windborn power pushed stronger against my senses. The distant light now brighter, closer.

I dashed over to the lantern and moved it as far as I could from the now-bloody boulder. There was no time to disguise the fight, but I could do that.

They were close enough now that I could make out their black silhouettes against the lanterns they carried. I squinted but couldn't tell how many there were.

If I could convince them I was Wood-mask—the name Siggut bubbled up from his memories—then perhaps I could get close enough to free Sigrun and escape into the forest. I looked at the blood under my fingernails. I could fight us out if I had to.

I adjusted the mask, took a breath, and looked up. There was a small patch of sky visible, the stars glittering bright against their sable backdrop and I felt some tension leave me. Whatever happened, the stars would continue, the gods would watch over us. Then the Winds snaked across the sky like a shimmering green tentacle. I scowled as another reaching tendril of light stretched across the sky and soon the stars were drowned in blues and greens.

I wanted to scream at them, decry them for their greed, demand they free all the souls they had stolen from the gods.

Footsteps in the clearing.

My head snapped down and I watched the procession wash up against the execution stone.

It was a motley group, led by an old woman—reed-thin, with animal teeth braided into her hair, runes tattooed all over her skin, and a necklace of wood and stone bouncing against her chest—there were five or six masked outlaws and three other figures tugged along behind them, hands bound and heads hung low.

One of the outlaws stepped away from the group and walked up to me. Between her mask and the stolen memories I knew her as Virun—one of the outlaws' leaders.

"Where's Astra?" she asked.

I gestured vaguely behind me and pitched my voice low and gruff, "Taking a piss."

"Fine." Virun leaned around me to try and stare into the forest's shadows, then called, "Hurry. Ulfrun wants to get this started. Come, help us with the sacrifices. You know they always start struggling after the first one goes."

My stomach lurched. I swallowed, nodded, and followed her over to the rest of them.

The old woman, Ulfrun, was examining the execution block, muttering to herself and drawing fresh lines on it with a chunk of coal.

"Which one first?" Virun asked Ulfrun.

The god-speaker waved her hand behind her, disinterested. "Whichever, just leave the warrior till last. Hurry, we must do this whilst the Winds are strong."

Panic wrapped around my throat. I walked to the prisoners. I looked them over, feeling as though I were a butcher picking a pig for slaughter. Two of them I did not recognise. The first was a woman, barely more than a girl, with mud-caked hair and tear-tracks down her dirty cheeks. The second was an older man, standing tall but shaking, nonetheless. The third—I sucked in a breath—was Erri. His shoulders were slumped and he stared at the ground. I expected him to throw me off of him as I took his arm, guiding him a little way away from the others, but he followed me like a collared dog. Resigned. All the fight gone from him.

Relief washed over me now I knew that Sigrun was not to

be sacrificed, but it was quickly quelled by guilt and pity for Erri and the others.

"Take this one," one of the outlaws said, pulling the woman roughly forward. "Then she'll stop crying."

I kept my hand on Erri's arm, caught between my desire to help him and save the woman. I twisted, using the stolen cloak to hide my movements, and slipped my knife free. I pushed it into Erri's hands. The huskalar's shoulders tensed as his fingers tightened on the knife's handle, but he kept his head down.

"I will stop this," I replied. "Free yourself and we will escape."

I joined the group before he could reply.

The woman was dragged, screaming, towards the execution stone.

Ulfrun started to sing, a deep guttural note that reverberated between the trees. She dipped her hand into her bucket. It came out dripping in black tar and as she sang her wordless song she flicked the sludge onto the execution stone. Once, twice, thrice. She raised her hands. Her voice rose in pitch. Something shifted in the air.

I watched with my mouth open in horror.

My soul shrivelled inside my chest as she marshalled the magic of the gods. I glanced at the smudged tattoos across my fingers and forearms and tears welled at the corner of my eyes.

I could not believe that a god-speaker would betray the gods for this. The gods were there to help us. Their runes for us to keep ourselves safe. My knees shook as I watched the ritual unfold.

The woman screamed again as she was strong-armed to her knees.

"May the gods bless this ritual," Ulfrun said. "We call upon the—"

I could not let this happen. I stepped forward, pulled the mask from my face. "You cannot do this."

Confusion, then fury rolled across Ulfrun's face like storm clouds.

"I cannot? I should sacrifice you instead?"

"This is wrong. You cannot bind the landvaettir like this. I know you want to prove to the High King that he does not need Windborn, but this is—"

Ulfrun's face was a frozen picture of confusion, then her eyes raked over the tattoos on my cheeks and she let out a thin, wheezing giggle. The runes on her skin wrinkled as she laughed.

"You're the rogue god-speaker are you? Come to lecture me have you, young one?" She flicked her hands and the outlaws moved to surround me, spearheads low. "Perhaps you do not appreciate what is happening. The gods fall ever out of favour. The people must be reminded of their power."

"The gods are not forgotten," I said, pleading. "I have travelled all over the Fjalmark. I am always welcomed and the gods are always given their due."

"When you are present, perhaps. What of when you leave, god-speaker? Do you think they tell stories of the gods and the god-war? No. Now they are obsessed with the stories of the Windborn. Have you seen how eagerly the children sit by the fire waiting for another saga of those poisoned warriors?"

I frowned at her, trying to think of when I had last heard a skald sing a legend from the god-war. It had been in Konvald. Not on a recent journey, but years before. All the tales I had heard skalds sing in longhalls and distant homesteads since then had been sagas of the Windborn.

She laughed again. "You see? You know I'm right. Help me and we will remind the High King of the true power of the gods. We will show him that he cannot forsake the gods for Windborn."

I looked at the troll-stones and the vines draped over them. "This is not the way, Ulfrun. You are draining the landvaettir of its strength. It will unbalance the land. The forest will die."

She waved her hand, batting my arguments away like I was an unruly child.

"The god-stones are there for our protection, are they not?" she snarled. "What better way to protect us all than to remind the High King of the gods' true power? I will use the landvaettir to show him we do not need the Windborn. The Windborn must be snuffed out. Destroyed."

She stepped towards me, spittle glistening on her lips and

fury shining in her eyes. She stood, back straight, and watched me. Once her breathing had calmed she smiled, a gentle smile that might have been reassuring if the sobs of the soon-to-be-sacrificed woman did not nearly drown out our conversation. Ulfrun reached out a hand to me.

"You must understand what I am trying to do. I am trying to save us all from the horror of the Windborn. Will you not help me?"

I swallowed and for a heartbeat I did understand. Had I not felt much the same about Windborn a few days ago? Gods, was it only days? Surely it would be better for the people to remember the gods and forsake the Windborn, even if it meant that I would be destroyed as well.

Then the woman's sobs started again. I thought of Fafnir's soft words to me when I had felt lost and alone. I looked around, at the masked figures standing in the deepest part of a cursed forest, willing to burn it all down in some misguided sense of justice.

"I cannot help you."

Her expression splintered into a scowling annoyance. "Take him."

The outlaws surrounding me pounced. I leapt back out of the way of the fists and grasping hands and towards Erri. I swung my spear around, freeing some space around me.

Erri ripped himself free of his bonds and slashed at the nearest outlaw with my knife. The outlaw cried out and fell back.

"Don't kill the warrior!" Ulfrun screeched. "I need him alive."

Two outlaws, one injured and one hale, charged Erri. He tried to fend them off with the knife but as he turned to face one the other slammed their spear butt into his stomach and he doubled over.

The other three outlaws came for me. I jabbed at one. He fell back and the other two lunged. They grabbed me by the shoulders and forced me to the ground. My spear went flying. I got my hands under the chest of one attacker and threw them off me. Their body flew back and smashed into the execution stone with a crunch.

A fist pummelled my stomach.

Instinctively, I grabbed their neck and pulled.

I have made a small shrine to the gods on Ertland's shores. It reassures me that they watch over me on the raid. A shout interrupts my worship. We are ambushed. As battle is joined the Windborn with us throws an Ertlander like a stone. They land on my shrine, drowning my offerings in blood. I confront the Windborn after the battle. They do not care.

The outlaw went limp. I shoved them off me and leapt to my feet, grabbing a knife from the ground ready to take on whoever came next.

The outlaws had a knife to Erri's throat.

"Drop the knife, god-speaker," Ulfrun said.

I gritted my teeth and looked from Erri to Ulfrun. The huskalar shook his head. His eyes begged me to keep fighting.

"I understand your reluctance, god-speaker. I was the same." Ulfrun stepped slowly towards me, hand reaching out. "But the gods are with us, and not only our gods. We—"

Her fingers brushed my arm and my Windborn power clawed at her soul.

The Windborn behind the throne sneer at me as I beg the High King to prove his faith, abandon these godless revenants. His voice echoes around the hall. He curses me for my impudence. I am thrown out. The gods are abandoned.

Ulfrun whipped her hand away from me.

"Wait..." She squinted at me then her eyes went wide and she smiled. This time a vicious smile as sharp as wolf's teeth. "You are tainted. You are part of the rot. Then I name you Poisoned One. I name you God-Bane. I name you Forsaken. I am sorry to see you fall so low, but I see now why you cannot stand with me. Kill him."

The outlaws rushed me. Someone burst out of the dark foliage into the clearing. A flash of iron, the glitter of spraying crimson. An outlaw dead.

Before anyone could move, Yrsa had stabbed the outlaw holding Erri and killed the one standing next to him.

"Stop this, Ulfrun," Yrsa growled.

The old god-speaker glared at the Windborn warrior. "You are interfering with powers beyond your understanding, girl.

Surrender and I will be lenient."

Yrsa said nothing. She passed an axe to Erri and pulled a knife from her belt.

"So be it."

Ulfrun clutched her necklace of wood and bone and I felt something shift around me. Sorrow slithered beneath the earth and the forest bowed under a sudden gale.

Yrsa leapt to attack Ulfrun but a branch fell between them.

Another branch fell, then a root-wrapped stone lifted from the ground and within a heartbeat the landvaettir loomed tall in the clearing.

"Fuck," Erri breathed.

The creaking colossus of moss and wood swung its root-antlered face around the clearing. Its gaze found me. A sense of sorrow fell upon my shoulders along with a chained frustration. The landvaettir stood tall but its living body wilted as I watched. Its fern-leaf mantle burned at the edges with brown rot and the root-antlers drooped.

I glanced at Ulfrun, who had her necklace in a white-knuckle grip.

She pointed at Yrsa and the landvaettir swung a tree-thick arm at the Windborn. Yrsa had enough time to throw up her arms but the blow still sent her flying through the clearing, snapping branches as she went.

Then Ulfrun waved a hand at Erri and me.

The landvaettir groaned like a ship caught in a storm as it took a step towards us.

Roots exploded up from the ground and wrapped Erri's feet in their oaken grip.

I sprinted to him, diving to rest by his feet. I put my hands on the roots and pulled. They shrivelled and retreated back to the soil.

A shambling black creature crosses my forest. It smells of rot. I cannot turn it away. It limps towards my standing stone. It is a clear day, but the thing drips with fetid silt-water. It has the power of a god. It reaches for my heartstone.

Ulfrun screamed behind the landvaettir. Her outlaw minions were unwilling to step any closer and risk an errant blow from the looming monstrous construct.

The spirit looked from Erri to me. I stared back.

I felt the verdant pressure against my mind, like a nearby Windborn but broader, slower, and more powerful. It was trying to show me something more than those brief snippet-memories but its language was as slow as summer and I could not understand.

I stepped towards the landvaettir. It groaned again and bent towards me.

Ulfrun screamed behind it, but I could not make out the words.

Branch-fingers reached out to me. I brushed the leaves with my fingertips.

A blast of power from Ulfrun: *Take me and flee.*

I took a step towards her, following her command, then the power faded and I was myself again. I blinked as the landvaettir twisted itself around and scooped up Ulfrun in an enormous branch-basket hand. I felt its power rest on me once more before it sprinted off into the forest.

The outlaws fled with it, fleet as deer with the landvaettir's borrowed power.

The forest spirit's figure was swiftly lost as its silhouette merged with the reaching tree limbs and bushy ferns, but the thump of its steps and the snapping of branches carried on for some time.

Erri put a hand on my shoulder, snapping me from my reverie.

"Thank you, Alvir. I don't know what I would have done without you. I don't know what they're trying to do here, butvwe can't let them do it. Is there anything we can do to stop this ritual?"

I looked around at the boulders and the lines once so carefully carved into the ground and now churned and broken like the world after a landslide.

"There is no magic to break," I said, my words coming slowly at first then speeding up as I fell into rhythm with my heartbeat. "The ritual was not truly begun and the fight has ruined the sigils."

"Is there anything more we can do?" There was a desperation in his voice, eagerly hoping we could ruin this ritual permanently and make sure no one would be sacrificed.

"We could move the boulders."

He looked at me and cocked an eyebrow. "I don't think we have the strength for that."

"No," I agreed.

Instead, we freed the other prisoners. We tried to reassure the crying woman, but she was still in shock and could not be consoled. The older man was more receptive and took up one of the spears that the outlaws had left behind.

Yrsa soon appeared, panting and with mud smeared on her cheeks and broken twigs in her hair. She looked after the thudding footsteps of the landvaettir and then walked in the other direction.

"Let's fucking go," she growled through gritted teeth.

Erri hurried after her, urging the now-freed prisoners along ahead of him. I stared at the shattered troll-boulders for a few heartbeats more and followed.

Chapter Twenty-Three
The Forest's Black Heart

Yrsa led us from the ritual site. She gave me directions so that I could clear a path as she propped up a limping Erri. He had tried to lean on me, but I had flinched away. I would not risk drawing on his strength and soul.

We came upon the camp as the heat of the morning began to warm the air.

A huge figure rose ahead of us. For a heartbeat, panic gripped me then Fafnir's rumbling voice cascaded over us.

"You are safe, thank the gods, I heard such noises. You found Erri! And Alvir!"

He ran over, leaves swept in his wake, and hovered over us. He reached out his hands, then lowered them again as though unsure if his enormous hands would harm or help us.

"Are you hurt? Do you need help?" He bounced between me and Erri, looking us over and sniffing.

"I'm fine," I said. "Erri, how are you?"

The huskalar smiled as Yrsa helped him to sit on a tree stump.

"A little shaken, but unharmed."

"You must eat," Fafnir said and bustled over to a torn pack. He pulled out some dried meat and passed it to us along with a waterskin as Yrsa slumped down against a tree.

"What happened after we were separated?" I asked between bites of meat.

Fafnir looked to Yrsa, but she had her eyes closed and was breathing slow.

"We escaped. The creatures did not give chase. We thought you were slain." He grinned at me, his tusk-teeth moving his face in strange ways and I realised that despite his looks I had missed his enthusiasm. "I have tracked the outlaws but could not find their camp again to rescue the others."

I frowned.

"It's this fucking forest," Yrsa said, with her eyes still closed.

Fafnir nodded and rumbled his agreement. "Each time we find them and try to follow we get lost or the path is blocked with thickets and we must turn back. Twice we have chased them and almost caught them but the outlaws fade into the forest and I cannot pick up the trail. It is like the trees do not want us tracking them."

"They don't," I agreed.

Yrsa opened her eyes and the others shot me concerned looks as though I were going mad. I pursed my lips and shifted the weight of my god-stone-laden pack. "They have found a way to chain the spirit of the forest. All those runes that Ulfrun's given the outlaws are linked to it. She's forcing it to keep them hidden, give them the power to sprint through the woods unimpeded so that we cannot follow."

"I knew it," Fafnir growled. He looked over at Yrsa. "I told you she has betrayed us."

Yrsa sighed and her shoulders slumped. "You're sure she's responsible?"

I nodded.

"She's leading them," Erri said. "Her and... something else. I didn't get a good look at it. It was huge, grotesque. The camp went quiet whenever it shuffled about. Even the birds stopped singing."

"Maybe she's being forced by this thing, then?" Yrsa asked, her voice strained with hope.

"No," I sighed. "Ulfrun is a driving force behind these outlaws. I tried to speak with her earlier, before you arrived, to get her to stop this. She wouldn't. She's..." I paused and glanced at Yrsa. She had closed her eyes and hung her head, resigned to whatever I had to say. "She said that the High King has forgotten the power of the gods and she intends to remind him."

"She hates Windborn," Yrsa whispered.

"Well..." I paused. Yrsa looked at me. Her eyes shone with

the hope that she was wrong, but from the tightness in her shoulders and the press of her lips I could tell she knew the truth. "Yes. I don't know what she's lost, but she seems to blame Windborn for it. She said she'll show the High King the true power of the gods and destroy all Windborn."

"Ulfrun's got no one to blame but herself," Erri said. "The High King called her to Konvald when his god-speaker travelled, to interpret the gods' wisdom or to look after his daughter if her pain was particularly bad.

"The last time she went there, she saw the Windborn wandering about and blew up at the High King. Named him God Traitor. The High King threw her out and, from what I heard, she was lucky to get out alive."

I gasped, stunned. "The High King wouldn't have killed a god-speaker, would he?"

"That's what saved her," Erri said. "Even the High King wouldn't kill a god-speaker, but I heard he came close."

"It is an easy thing for a god-speaker to hate Windborn," Fafnir said. He looked pointedly at me.

"What?" I felt heat rushing to my cheeks. "I don't hate Windborn."

Yrsa scoffed and Fafnir waved a meaty hand in dismissal.

"It is fine, Alvir. A god-speaker pulls on the threads of the gods' power. Windborn have been woven with the power of the gods' enemies. You saw us and wondered if we were puppets to the Winds, didn't you? If we would turn on the gods if given the chance?"

"Perhaps for a little while," I said, trying not to look at Fafnir or Yrsa. "But I don't—"

"I did too," he said. "When I first became Windborn and changed into... this. I thought: how can the gods allow this? I am a monster, I thought."

I opened my mouth to protest, but Fafnir held up a twin-fingered hand to stop me.

"Now, I do not think so. I am stronger. I have helped so many in Vidsetr with this new strength, my fresh senses. Now I wonder if the gods allowed the Winds to grant us these gifts. Are we the repayment of the blood-debt the Winds owe to the gods? Is our strength, our power, reparations for the god-war?"

Fafnir nodded as he spoke, staring into the middle-distance. When he finished I saw the peace in his eyes and the gentle warmth that lit his face as he thought of those he had helped in Vidsetr. I looked down at my hands and felt the unrelenting hunger of the Windborn power in my chest.

Could that be true? Could the gods have allowed the Winds to take me and give me these powers? It was a comforting thought, but one I was not sure I could believe. Before, I had been able to call upon the power of the gods themselves. Now, my soul hungered for the life and strength of others.

As I turned my hands over I felt my Windborn power writhe and reach out for Fafnir's strength, Yrsa's speed.

I clenched my fists and shook my head.

"You have all known Ulfrun for years," I said. "Is there any possibility that we can talk her out of this? Can we get her to fix what she has broken?"

The others looked amongst themselves, sharing expressions of helplessness and inevitability.

"When Ulfrun sets her mind on something she does it," Erri said. "Nothing will get in her way."

"It's not just that," Yrsa said. "It's worse if Ulfrun thinks she's been singled out. Ulfrun's always been quick to anger when something doesn't go her way, but there are things that she will hold on to and never let go. When... when I became Windborn it felt like she blamed me for it. We never talked after that. Not really. Whenever I went to see her, to gossip like we used to, she'd always tell me she was too busy and wave me away."

She slumped down against the tree again. Fafnir went over to her and put a hand on her shoulder. Yrsa sighed and put her hand on his. I made my way over to them and reached out, then realised that I couldn't offer consolation without risking my Windborn power draining Yrsa of hers. Instead, I offered her the waterskin. She smiled weakly and took it.

We stayed like that, the Windborn caught in consolation and the newly liberated prisoners eating as much as they could. As we waited, perhaps hopeful that we could stay in this moment, the sunrise burned away the last of the night.

Eventually, Erri came over to drink from the waterskin. Fafnir and I moved away from Yrsa and found our seats.

"Then what now?" rumbled Fafnir. "We came to find Ulfrun. Now we've found her and she does not want to be saved."

Erri looked at the Windborn and shook his head. "What can we do? You may be Windborn, but what about those creatures that Ulfrun has chained? The forest spirit? The stone creatures? That black monster? We need to go and get help."

I looked over at Erri. His clothes were torn and stained with shades of blood and dirt. Fafnir and Yrsa were slumped over, leaning against a tree for support. Bits of wood and leaves stuck out from their clothes at all angles. I felt the Windborn power within them, but it was slow and dull like a snake just woken from sleep. My energy felt much the same. My body ached from myriad scrapes and cuts that would likely have killed me if I were not Windborn. I felt the weight of the last few days pressing on my bones and could have slept for a week. What I would have given for a soft bed and a warm home.

My thoughts turned to Sigrun. To her home. To her family.

I wondered how she must be feeling. Was she hurt? Had the outlaws bound her and the other captives?

"We can't leave them," I said. "I won't abandon Sigrun."

"And I will not leave Nal," Fafnir said, the ground rumbling as he growled out the words.

Erri threw up his hands. "What do you want us to do? You said the forest keeps throwing you back. We've all seen what monsters Ulfrun can throw at us. How can the four of us go up against that?"

"We may not be completely alone." I sat and pulled one of the god-stone shards from my pack. It was the size of a clenched fist and had sharp edges where it had shattered from the god-stone proper. I kept myself from pulling on its power, like holding my breath, though some of its warmth seeped into me.

"What's that?" Erri asked.

"This is a piece of the god-stone. It's linked to the forest spirit. When I draw the power from it I am connected to the forest."

Erri rolled his eyes. "I don't think you being at one with the forest is going to help. We need weapons. We need warriors."

I ignored him and turned to the other Windborn. "You said that whenever you tracked the outlaws it was like the forest was turning you back, wasn't it?"

They nodded.

"I think that I can use the power of this stone and force the forest to let us follow them. Whatever magic Ulfrun has shackled the forest spirit with is not as strong as its connection to this stone. We can use it to get to their camp. We can free Sigrun and Nal and the others and then we can go and get help."

"Are you sure?" Erri frowned and looked at the chunk of rock in my hand. "That thing will help us get to everyone else without the outlaws noticing?"

"Yes, I think so. The spirit wants to be free," I said. "It's bound to Ulfrun, but only to a point. Didn't you see that it wouldn't attack me?"

"It hit me pretty fucking hard," Yrsa growled.

"He's right, though," Erri said, chewing his lip. "She screamed at that tree monster to kill Alvir, but it just looked at him."

The huskalar rubbed at his eyes and sighed. "What do you think?"

Fafnir looked at the stone in my hand then met Erri's gaze, challenging and unafraid. "We must save them."

Erri's shoulders slumped a little, but he nodded as though that was what he had expected. "And you, Yrsa? What do you think we should do?"

Yrsa leaned forward, putting her elbows on her knees, and stared at the god-stone shard. "What if Fafnir, Alvir, and me save them and you get help, Erri?"

"I'm not leaving you. Ormhildr put me in charge and I won't abandon you to go face the darkest parts of the forest." He looked up and smiled, a white slash through the muck and blood on his face. "I'd miss all the fun."

Yrsa smiled back and Fafnir laughed, a snort that echoed around the trees. "There is my shield-brother."

I put the god-stone shard away and looked at them.

They were all covered in dirt with blood splatters all over their torn clothes and suddenly I felt the weight of our situation. My breath came shallow and too quick. I closed my eyes. I clenched and unclenched my fists. They were long used to this, but my fights had left me shaken.

I couldn't let Sigrun's family lose her. I couldn't lose her. I couldn't walk away.

What hope did I have to survive this? Was that the gods' plan when they made me Windborn? Was I simply a sacrifice? A means to get the true warriors into the enemy's lair so that they could fight their way out whilst I died in battle?

"Breathe." Fafnir's deep voice from next to me.

I felt his two massive fingers wrap around my shoulder. Our Windborn souls sparked and fizzed against each other. He squeezed. I tried to stop it but my Windborn power sucked hungrily at his strength and warmth.

Fafnir grunted but kept his hand in place.

I walk through Vidsetr. My face is covered by my hood. I wave to people with bandaged fingers. They know becoming Windborn has ruined me, turned me into a monster, but we all play along. I wear the bandages. I keep my hood up. They smile at me.

Olga's wagon has overturned. She chases the bolted pony as others struggle to drag the tipped wagon from the sticky mud. I rush over, rumble that I will help. They smile. They shift uneasily next to my bulk.

I strain and the wagon comes free with a sucking pop.

Cheers. People slap my shoulder. They thank me, no longer uneasy. Then someone rushes from the trees at the edge of town, cloak billowing. They run up to us.

"Outlaws in the forest! They're taking the cattle."

People look to me. The familiar battle-fear settles in my gut, cold and sharp. I stand tall and my figure rises high above everyone else.

I cannot be who I once was, but I can still protect those I love.

"Stay," I say. My teeth—tusks—stumble over that simple word. If I can catch the outlaws in the forest out of sight of

my friends, then perhaps I can still their fear of me.

I take up my spear and go to fight.

He lifted his hand. My fear was gone, replaced by an iron certainty and a serene conviction. I opened my eyes and looked at him. His expression was both kind and serious. Lines crinkled at the edges of his eyes but the set of his warped, tusk-filled mouth was firm.

"You are not alone, brother," he said. "Fear seeks us when we must tread dangerous paths. We all feel it. The fear will not win. I will stand with you. We will seek our sisters and we will save them."

I looked into his eyes. There was fear there, glinting deep, but there was also something harder. A fierce and righteous rage that Fafnir stoked so he could charge into battle to save his loved ones.

I took the seed of his certainty and planted it deep in my chest. Its echoes thrummed through my blood.

"Yes," I said. "We will save them."

ᚠ

We slept for most of the morning. Fafnir took the first watch. By mid-afternoon, we had all had time to rest and Erri had explained what had happened since he had been captured. Most of the captives had been taken deeper into the forest and thrown into a rough-dug pit that was already crowded. Tjorvid had been taken on the first morning and it was not long before Erri was taken for the ritual that Nal had been thrown into the pit, captured after our escape attempt. Fafnir growled to hear of Nal's capture and the knowledge sat heavy in my belly. I swallowed and tried to harden the guilt into resolve as we made ourselves ready to leave.

The forest was still bathed in shadows as the canopy caught the sunlight, but there was a green dimness that extended into the distance. Once again, I felt how far we were from civilisation and any help. I looked to my companions and I felt Fafnir's iron resolve surge in my chest. It was decided that the recently freed prisoners would wait at the camp until the next morning. If we succeeded in our rescue

mission then we would return for them and if we did not…
they would try to find their own way out of the forest.

Our meagre warband—three Windborn and a single
warrior—collected what few weapons we had and made our
way out into the wilderness to track down our loved ones.

Fafnir and Yrsa led us over a small hill. The trees thinned
as we climbed and for a brief moment we were gifted a vision
of the forest from above. The endless trees huddled together,
clinging to the landscape like verdant spear-tips. They rolled
up and over the mountains with bright blue rivers and
streams slicing through the swaying canopy. It seemed to go
on forever like the fur of some world-straddling beast.

I squinted into the distance and saw the glistening blue of
the distant fjord which led to Konvald and the seat of the
High King.

"Where's Vidsetr?" I asked, wanting to see where this had
all started.

"There," Fafnir said, pointing. "Between us and Konvald."

I strained to follow the aim of Fafnir's finger but I couldn't
see it.

We pushed on and before long we were turned back by the
forest twisting our path.

I frowned as I clambered over a fallen tree, grimacing as I
pricked my palm on a snapped branch and I realised that we
had been this way before. It all looked the same as it always did.

Trees, moss, ferns, stones, fallen branches.

Something had changed. The air felt heavy like it had
folded in on itself.

The others had gone on ahead, but they stopped when
Fafnir hissed between his teeth.

"What is it?" Erri said, crouching and lowering his spear.

"We have been turned away," Fafnir grumbled.

"Fuck. He's right. We passed that stone half an hour ago,"
Yrsa added.

Erri looked at me and I nodded. "The air is different here.
I will see if I can find where the border is and push us
through."

I went to examine the familiar boulder. It was rusted with
moss and fungus, but otherwise smooth. No runes. I pressed

my hand against it and closed my eyes, hoping it would reveal some hidden power.

The stone was cold against my hand. I grimaced and called on my Windborn power, drawing on its ravenous hunger. The boulder did not react, though I felt Fafnir and Yrsa take a step away from me.

I was about to give up when my senses touched upon something, like the warmth of a fire from across a room. It came from the ground.

I opened my eyes and bent down, waving my hand across the base of the boulder and praying I would sense something.

The ferns and undergrowth withered as my skin brushed up against them. When my fingertips touched the mushrooms clinging to the base of the stone I felt a rush of dizzying power.

A monster wanders through my home. It drags its foot. Not crippled but badly made. I am chained. Its foot scars the ground and marks the earth black. I am commanded to weave a subtle barricade.

I gasped and whipped my hand away.

"That's it," I said between breaths. "These mushrooms are linked to the landvaettir somehow. I think it's what's keeping us out."

The mushrooms were a pale yellow with flat heads and forked ridges on their undersides. They poked through the mulch of dying leaves and pine needles from a patch of wet, black earth. I looked around us and saw the pale yellow fungus formed a stuttering line along the trees and I thought of the tales of god-speakers painstakingly growing circles of mushrooms as places to speak with ghosts.

One of the nearby trees had a stain of yellow mushrooms at its base like the high tide mark on a mooring post. I watched some leaves swirl around us, caught in a sudden gust of wind, and gasped as they flowed past the tree trunk and disappeared.

I tipped my head and realised that the view on one side of the tree was different to the other.

This was the border.

If I could break the chain of fungus then we should be able

to get through to find Sigrun and the others.

I took a handful of dirt and mushrooms and, instead of pulling on its power, I pushed myself into it.

My senses flowed beneath the ground and I felt the ending power of the landvaettir and what had chained it. Surprise at my sudden presence in its domain whipped at me like a branch in a storm. Then I felt the cool forest breeze brushing against my skin, ruffling my hair, but I also felt the familiar, cool darkness soaking against my roots and the sunlight warming my upper leaves.

I could stay like this. Time meant so little couched between sap and bark. I would be protected beneath the ground and the trees would breathe for me. They would take in the sunlight and I would be safe under the dirt.

No. I needed to save Sigrun.

I tried to push myself into the landvaettir's senses and keep myself centred in my body, but it was suffocating and dizzying. My heartbeat slowed. I breathed out, matching the wind. My lungs were empty but the wind did not stop. Panic thrashed in my chest like a trapped bird. I couldn't inhale. A slow echo of alarm came from the landvaettir, a warning come too late.

I ripped my hand from the mushroom.

I fell back and sucked in a deep breath of cool, life-giving air.

The others had gathered around me with expressions of concern etched on their faces.

"I'm alright," I said. "I need to use the god-stone shard before I try that again, that's all."

"Are you sure?" Erri asked.

"Yes. Just give me a minute."

I sat, trying to figure out what had gone wrong. I had pushed too hard. I'd nearly lost my soul to the forest. Before, when I had shared the forest spirit's knowledge and power it had been because I'd drawn on the god-stone. The shards were small pockets of power, too small to overwhelm me, but strong enough to give me what I needed.

I pulled a shard out of my pack, closed my eyes, and pulled.

I am too strong for any mortal to yoke me. This is not mortal strength. The black silt and death drapes over me and, fast as an opening flower, I am chained. Yet I have power still. They cannot see all in the forest. There is a piece of me lost in the secret pathways of the stone-kin.

When I came back to myself the forest felt different.

My senses stretched out to take in the ferns' long-fingered fronds, the shivering boughs of the treetops, and the skittering paws of squirrels scratching at the trees. This time, though, I was not overwhelmed. Rather than forcing my mind out into the forest, this felt like I was being guided by the landvaettir's kind hand.

I closed my eyes and let my mind wander along the roots beneath my feet.

The dirt was cool, dark, damp.

Worms churned through the darkness, eyeless and determined. Beetles scurried under the leaf litter covering the ground.

And there: a sharp chasm where there should be smooth and subtle earth.

Cold water saturated the dirt in a jagged, curving line across the forest. Within that flooded ground nothing grew except for the pale yellow mushrooms.

On one side of the fungal border, there was an expanse of forest that thrummed with life. On the other, I could sense darkness, rot, and blood.

If I could pull enough power from the black earth then I could break the connection long enough for us to slip through into the forest's dark heart.

I reached out, my fingertips a hair's breadth away from the sodden earth and looked at my companions.

"Are you ready?" I asked. "I will disrupt the power and then the forest ahead of us should change. You will need to move quickly."

They looked at each other, then to me, and nodded.

I plunged my fingers into the earth, gasping at its chill. Power tingled against my senses as the dirt clogged my fingernails.

I pulled.

Bog water in my lungs. I cannot drown. I am already dead. My shoulder feels tight from my new limbs. The ritual is only a few days past. The ache will fade and my strength will grow. The thanes of the Daendrec will be protected by my might once more.

I felt, more than saw, the others dash forward through the forest. I tried to pull away and hurry after them, but something rushed up to me like a bubbling spring of rotten water.

You think by drawing on my power you can affect the chains on the landvaettir? Foolish. It will not last.

Oh, you are Ulfrun's Poisoned One. Do not try to pull away, Forsaken. You are a thorn in our side and I would look at you.

My lungs were heavy. I tasted silty water at the back of my throat. Panic wrapped around my heart and I frantically tried to pull away. I thrashed but my hand was locked in the wet, black earth.

It seems you are just another one of them. You borrow power. First from your estranged northern gods and now from your Winds. Do you have any strength of your own, I wonder?

God-Bane she names you. Do you deserve such a name? Can you earn it?

The landvaettir saved me.

Tiny tendrils wrapped around my fingers. Roots from the mushrooms and ferns and trees and brambles. They snaked around my hand over and over until it encased my arm like a living glove.

The connection shattered. I fell backwards, panting.

My hand dripped with chill bog-water and I felt the warmth of my blood seep down my arm from the places the brambles had wrapped too tight. I coughed out a sound that was halfway between a sob and a laugh.

"Come on," Erri shouted.

I looked at them.

They stood in a shadowed part of the forest, spots moved around them like mould floating in the air. I scrambled forward even as the weight of the weave reasserted itself. The forest border was closing. I could not be on this side. I could not face that thing again. I could not be alone.

I stumbled over a stone and felt a fizz against my skin as Fafnir grabbed my arm. He yanked me forward as the magic slammed shut behind me.

I landed on my back on a pile of rotting leaves and stared at the canopy. The leaves were wilted and discoloured. Some of the branches drooped and their ends had snapped, though they were still connected to the branch and wavered like dislocated limbs.

The ground squelched as I sat up.

"Are you alright?" Erri said, putting his hand on my shoulder.

I nodded. I had no words.

"What the fuck is that?" Yrsa hissed, pointing at my arm.

Roots, tendrils, and brambles coiled around my fingers, my hand, up to my elbow where they sprang away from my skin like torn up tree roots. I clenched my fist. The roots bent with my fingers, but as the landvaettir's magic faded they grew dry and brittle and as I opened my fist they snapped and fell away from my hand.

"I don't know. I think it was the forest spirit. There was… something in the earth that took hold of me and wouldn't let go."

"It was that black monster, wasn't it?" Erri said, his expression grim.

"Yes, I think so. It spoke to me, then the landvaettir cut the connection with this." I gestured to the roots scattered on the floor with my half-covered hand.

"This monster is killing the forest," Fafnir rumbled.

"I think so," I said as I pushed myself up. The slick ground shifted under my hand and black water bubbled up between my fingers.

"It is killing the forest," Fafnir said again, gesturing all around us.

Within this final barrier, the forest had changed. Gone were the moss-speckled trees and bright green ferns that nestled at their roots. In their place was a shadowed realm of slanted and tumbledown trees stained with black mould. Before, we had been able to gaze out into the forest and look between the straight-backed trunks but now our vision was blocked by the rotten boughs of hunched trees and wilted shrubs. Even the leaves were sickly. Their vibrant emerald shine, that had been a constant companion even in the dark paths we had wandered, were now dried brown, yellowed and shrivelled.

"Gods help us," I whispered.

Behind me, the others muttered prayers and oaths of their own.

"Which way?" Erri asked, grip tightening on his spear.

I opened my mouth, closed it, and shook my head.

The magic of the landvaettir faded from my senses and with only two god-stone shards left, I did not want to waste them. Something told me, as I stared at the rotten forest ahead of me, that I would need more strength before this was over.

"It is hard to say," Fafnir said. He sniffed at the air. "The rot is thick. There is something this way."

He pointed with his spear tip. Erri nodded and gestured for Fafnir to lead us deeper into the woods.

I stared after them, swallowed down my fear, and walked into the forest's rotting heart.

CHAPTER TWENTY-FOUR
TROLL GRAVES

THE AIR GREW DAMP THE FURTHER WE VENTURED. We were forced to take careful steps as the ground sloped and took us down a wide, deep valley. With every footstep we fought against the slick, saturated ground and more than once I slipped and slid down on my arse.

The others fared a little better. Erri used his spear for support, sinking it into the squelching earth before each step. Yrsa walked in Fafnir's shadow, resting a hand on his back as the enormous Windborn's bulk kept him from going over. He sank ankle-deep into the ground yet was still taller than any of us.

We passed the cracked trunk of an ancient oak tree. I put my hand out to let it take my weight as I stepped over one of its fallen branches.

The bark under my palm sloughed off like slow-cooked meat.

I cried out, slipping, and tumbled forward headfirst.

Fafnir whipped out a hand to catch me but I was too far.

For a few heartbeats, my world was a spinning mess of muck and mulch until my shoulder slammed into something hard and unrelenting.

I sucked in a breath at the pain, shook my head, and bent to see what had saved me.

A stone.

It was about the size of my torso and as I pushed myself to my feet, black mud now caking my clothes, I saw the boulder had a strange protrusion at its middle and worn, sunken sockets beside it. A nose and eyes.

The others slid down next to me.

"Are you hurt?" Fafnir said.

I shook my head, mute, and pointed at the troll's head in front of us.

"Another rock," Yrsa scoffed. "So what?"

"Look," I said. "It's a troll's head."

The others shifted. They had lived next to the Trolbjolvid for years, Yrsa had never lived anywhere else, but it wasn't until we ventured into the forest's darkest depths that anyone had seen a troll move and that one had tried to kill us.

I pressed my hand against the rock. It was cold, smooth with age. I pulled as gently as I could, hoping for some echo of the troll this had been but wary that the black god might somehow capture me once again.

Nothing.

Only stone.

I let my hand fall with a sigh.

"Alvir, look," Erri said, tapping my leg with his spear.

We were near the bottom of the slope and Erri gestured out over the valley floor.

It was littered with countless boulders. Every one had the mark of a troll-stone: the crook of an elbow, the smooth line that spoke of a mouth, a hand with two half-shattered fingers. It was at once awe-inspiring and terrible. My mind reeled to think of the figures that had once been built of these fragments as my stomach lurched at the horror of this mass grave of trolls.

"We must be getting close," Erri said. "Keep moving but be careful."

He edged around the boulder I had crashed into and made his way into the maze of troll-stones. The Windborn followed in his wake.

I ran my hands over the stones as we walked, no longer afraid that my touch would rekindle any connection between me and the black godling. Now that I had glimpsed the landvaettir's memories I could appreciate more than ever the aeons that stood between the troll's life and this moment.

A few of the troll-stones were sunk deep into the mud and looked to have been there for some time, unmoving.

Most, however, had been dragged from elsewhere in the forest. There was a lattice of deep furrows in the ground and some of the boulders had bright halves splattered lightly with mud. One of these bright boulders caught my attention and I swerved over to it, careful not to move too far from my companions.

It had once been a hand. The fingers, fused together, had been smoothed by time and speckled with moss and lichen, but the back of the hand, bright and clean, was crowded with swirling symbols and patterns.

I trailed my fingertips in the patterns, feeling their rough texture scraping against my skin.

There was an ethereal beauty to their configuration that reminded me of the ocean. The longer I stared at the markings the more I made sense of them like a picture seen from a strange angle. There was magic hidden in these patterns, or there had been once.

Troll-runes.

Here, excavated and abandoned, were the secrets of the trolls laid bare. Beautiful, powerful, unknowable.

My heart ached and a sob wrung itself from my throat. I wasn't a god-speaker. I would never rune-weave again. If I had found this stone a few days ago then I could have lost months studying this patch of swirling lines. But I was Windborn now. I would never be able to understand them.

I blinked away tears and abandoned the troll's hand. The others had made it to the bottom of the valley, too focused to notice my swift detour, and had found several tracks. Fafnir bent low and sniffed at the ground as the others ducked behind the troll-stones.

"Which way?" Yrsa said as I slid down to join them.

"I do not know." Fafnir clenched his fists and bared his tusk-teeth. "The scent of rot is strong and these paths are well used."

We stared at the churned mud, hoping that there would be some sign of which path to take. I studied the nearby boulders. Perhaps there would be some furrow to show where they had taken the troll-stones that would lead us to their base.

Distant branches snapped and undergrowth crackled as something rushed through the forest.

We flattened ourselves against the troll-stones and readied our weapons.

"This way!" A voice called. A woman's voice. "We'll lose them in the boulders."

It was Sigrun's voice.

My sister.

I leaned around the troll-stone, a toppled foot, and squinted out into the black forest. Through the confusion of dying trees I saw the leaves twitch.

More shouts. Indistinct. A cry of pain and rage.

I had heard that cry before. That same shout had echoed back to me in my nightmares, reminding me of my failure to protect my sister.

Sigrun cried in pain.

This time I ran to it.

"Alvir, no!" Erri hissed, trying to stop me. "We need to—"

Sigrun was in danger. I would not be stopped.

My feet stuck in the wet ground and I bounced between troll-stones as I drew my knife.

I burst out from the troll graveyard and saw the skirmish.

A pack of masked outlaws chased five muddy figures like vengeful spirits and in the middle of the battle: Sigrun.

She clutched a spear that was sunk in her leg. She strained against the outlaw trying to impale her, teeth bared with red and black streaks all over her face.

Everyone froze and turned to me.

They did not know what I was: a strange figure caked in black mud.

Within that frozen heartbeat, Sigrun ripped the spear from her leg and threw a punch at her opponent.

Her fist crunched into the outlaw's jaw, sending their mask flying, and they fell to the ground.

That broke the spell and the outlaws charged, reigniting the battle.

I rushed up to help Sigrun and pushed her out of the way of a swinging axe.

The outlaw came on, their bone mask's relentless grin

taunting me. I dodged their next swing and sliced my knife across their chest. The outlaw shrieked and stumbled back.

I followed.

A spear flashed towards me.

I leapt too slowly to dodge it entirely and the spear carved a line across my back.

As I hissed in pain the first outlaw came at me again. I managed to grab their hand, stopping the axe from cleaving into my chest, and I pulled as hard as I could.

Our life is kept in our longship. A family cradled by the smooth curves of wood and waves. We are camping on the shore. My children giggle and run circles around their father and me. A crash. Something slams into the beach, throwing up a cascade of sand. A Windborn. Another follows an eyeblink later. They fight like titans. We push the children behind us. One Windborn tries to fly away. The other grabs our ship, strains, and throws it after them. The longship, our life, sails through the air. It does not hit its target. It lands on the opposite shore and cracks apart. Our livelihood is splintered. The Windborn flies after his prey. He has not even noticed.

The outlaw dropped dead.

Life and power crackled through me. The world seemed to slow.

The spear-wielding outlaw leapt for me, iron flashing. I moved in, leaning to the side, and gripped the spear shaft. The outlaw's eyes went wide from within their wooden mask as I pulled the spear from them.

Before they could move I twisted the spear around and stabbed it through their chest. Their ribs crunched as the metal punched into the body. Blood sprayed onto the outlaws behind them.

The other outlaws, wary now, circled around me.

Masks of wood and bone stared at me with sightless eyes.

They lowered their spears.

I lowered mine, still dripping with the gore of their companion.

The closest leapt forward, wolf skull mask caught in a silent, endless snarl and stabbed at me. It was like he was moving through water. I knocked away the spear, stepped forward, and swung my stolen, gory spear around. The spear butt, now club, crunched through the wolf skull and smashed into the human skull beneath.

The outlaw fell.

The others shifted, tensed. My muscles tingled as the outlaw's stolen strength faded from me. The spear felt heavy in my hands and the blade drooped as I struggled with its weight.

An outlaw with a mask of shattered wood shifted their foot forward. I gripped the spear tighter and turned to face them.

A rock flew through the air, flying out from the troll-stones to slam into the outlaw's chest.

Fafnir roared and charged from behind the troll-stones with ground-shaking steps. Yrsa sprinted alongside him and in a heartbeat she was beside me, axes raised.

The outlaws, realising they were outmatched, edged away and at some hidden signal they fled. They darted between the dead trees and we did not bother to chase them.

As the forest fell to silence we huddled around Sigrun and her companions. I helped to ease Sigrun onto the floor as the others looked at us with a mixture of relief and fear.

"Alvir?" Sigrun's voice was strained through the pain. "What are you doing here?"

"What am I... I couldn't leave you. You saved me before. I came back to rescue you. We all did."

Emotions warred on her face. Pain. Confusion. Anger. "I wanted to save you, Alvir." She clenched her eyes shut against a fresh wave of agony before she continued, "I wanted you to get out and save yourself."

I frowned. "I know, but I—"

"You don't understand," she said. "There's something here. I don't know what the fuck it is. You need to go and get help. Get them out of here and leave me. I'll just slow you down."

Sigrun gestured to the rest of her group, the ones she had been protecting. Drifa was there. I didn't recognise the other three. All of them were dirty and exhausted.

I put my hand on Sigrun's shoulder, careful not to come into contact with her skin. My Windborn power shivered and gnashed its teeth in anticipation of the energy it could draw from Sigrun. I forced it down and looked my sister in the eye.

"I will not leave you, Sigrun." She stared at me and tears welled in her eyes. I pulled her children's charm from my pocket. "I brought this."

Tears flowed freely as Sigrun snatched the charm from me and pressed it against her chest.

"Thank you," she whispered between sobs.

I squeezed her shoulder then stood and turned to everyone else.

All of the dishevelled escapees looked like they were ready to drop dead from exhaustion. Drifa nodded at me, her hand bandaged and myriad bright scratches all over her. Beside her was a young man, barely out of boyhood and hunched over in fear, an old man with twigs caught in his silver beard, and a blonde-haired woman with her arms around the old man.

"These others were kidnapped by the outlaws," Sigrun said. "They're from Holtsker."

"Please," the woman said. "Will you take us home?"

Sigrun tried to stand, to say something more, but the pain forced her back to the ground and gritted teeth dammed her voice. I crouched to help her but Sigrun waved me off.

Fafnir brushed past us, nearly knocking me to the ground. His chest heaved. He whipped his head around, looking in every direction.

He stopped and his shoulders slumped, his fists clenched.

"Where is my sister?" His voice thrummed with a rising panic. "Where is Nal?"

Chapter Twenty-Five
Reunion and Parting

WE HID OURSELVES WITHIN THE TROLL-STONES, in case the outlaws returned. Yrsa had stayed at the edge of the troll-grave to keep watch. The rest of us found a clearing behind an enormous troll-stone, a chest as large as a longship. Fafnir hunched at the end of the boulder, his gaze bouncing from us to the trees and then back to us as he fought to keep himself from charging headlong into the forest to find Nal.

I was with Erri, tending to the countless wounds of the rescued. Most were small things, scratches from brambles or skin scraped against a tree as they fled. Some, like Sigrun's spear-wound, required deeper attention. I did what I could with my healer's skills, but I was fearful to touch anyone and Erri had more experience with battle-wounds.

We were all silent except for the hissing breath of a cut pressed too hard and the rip of clothes to make bandages.

Fafnir approached, casting a deep shadow over us. He clenched his fists, opened them, and clenched them again. I glanced at him as I ripped another strip of cloth from my cloak. He was torn between demanding answers and not wanting to interrupt us.

"Why did you leave Nal?" Fafnir growled when he could no longer contain himself.

Sigrun's shoulders slumped. She tried to stand and face the giant Windborn but with a wince she collapsed back against a boulder. "We didn't leave her, Fafnir. She chose to stay."

"What do you mean?"

"When we escaped the outlaws were chasing us from the camp. There was no way we were all going to get away."

Sigrun sighed but she met Fafnir's gaze with her tear-stained eyes. "I told them all to go. I ordered them to run. I thought I could hold the outlaws back for long enough to let them get away."

"You thought?" Fafnir asked, leaning forward with fists clenched.

"There were too many." Sigrun shifted and pulled herself up against the troll-stone. "They kept coming out of the woods. I told them to run. Nal snatched my spear out of my hands and told me she would hold them off."

Fafnir clenched his jaw and his tusks ground together. "You could have stood and fought. Nal cannot be bested with a spear."

Sigrun shook her head again. "There were too many, Fafnir. Nal stopped them from coming after us. She gave us time to organise but there were too many."

Fafnir growled and this time Yrsa came up to him and put her hand on his shoulder. I felt their Windborn power spark.

"We will go and get her," Yrsa said.

"What?" Erri stood up and shook his head. "You know what we're facing in there. We need to get help."

"I will not leave my sister." Fafnir took a hulking step towards Erri, fists clenched and knuckles cracking.

I stepped between them. Erri was the leader of our expedition, but we were inside the dying heart of the forest, far from any whisper of civilisation. If he tried to command Fafnir to leave his sister then any semblance of order would break down. Our tenuous fellowship would shatter.

I held up my hands, palms facing each warrior's chest. Erri flinched. Fafnir remained in place.

"We will not leave her," I said. "Fafnir, Erri needs you and Yrsa to help get everyone out of here. Look at them."

I gestured to the bloody, exhausted people around us. They had done well to get themselves free from the outlaws' clutches, but had found themselves rushing around inside this rotten core of the forest. They could not find their way out. Without help, there was no way they would make it back to Vidsetr.

"If you leave them on their own then they're not going to

make it. I know she's your sister, Fafnir." I glanced at Sigrun whose intense gaze was locked onto me. "Believe me, I know what it's like to have to leave your family, but I will go. I must go into the outlaw's camp and free the landvaettir, or else this rot will spread throughout the entire forest, and Vidsetr even. I will save Nal for you."

The tension in Fafnir's shoulders eased a little, but it did not disappear. "Thank you, Alvir, but I cannot leave her."

"Fafnir," Erri said through gritted teeth. "I will—"

"I will save my sister," Fafnir said as he stretched to his full height.

I looked between them again, torn between the three things that needed saving. Sigrun was dirty, ashen-faced, and wounded. Nal was missing, and I could not stop thinking about the execution block we had seen before. And the landvaettir was dying, the forest withering with its spirit, and who knew what strange powers would try and fill the void it left behind. Before, I had always had the power of the gods on my side. I had never been alone. I looked down at my hands. They were covered in dirt with flecks of moss caught under my fingernails and my tattoos—the markings I had once been so proud of and that had been the conduit for the gods' power—were fading and smudged. Now, I was a single man. What could I do?

I looked at Fafnir again, his muscles quivered as he held back his anger. I looked to Yrsa. She watched the standoff with narrowed eyes but seemed unwilling to take a side.

Their Windborn power shimmered at the edge of my senses, reaching out to me, beckoning me.

I was severed from the gods, but I was not truly alone. I was stronger in myself than I had ever been and I had allies, friends, and I could help them all.

"Erri," I said. "I need to stay. I have to help the landvaettir. I will help Fafnir."

"But the black—"

"I know. But I still have to go."

I looked over at Sigrun and caught a flash of hurt across her face before she hid it under a grimace.

"Sigrun." I gestured for her to follow me and she hopped

beside me to take us out of earshot of our companions. "Sigrun... I am sorry that I abandoned you. I should have been there for you when you were growing up. And I am sorry that I cannot stay with you now, but I can't let Fafnir go on alone. Though I can still help you." I held out a hand, hovering my palm over her skin. "Do you trust me?"

She looked at my hand, then to me, a question writ large in her frown. I saw Erri tense at the edge of my vision, taking half a step forward.

Sigrun nodded.

I pressed my hand against her skin.

I have to leave. The house is empty, echoing with the memories of a father who could not show me he loved me. I hoped my brother would stay longer after the funeral. I look around the house but there is nothing for me to take. What would I want to remember? I close the door and smile. Ljota waits beyond the cluttered remnants of lobster traps and fishing nets. I run up and kiss her. I take her hand and we run out of town, laughing. This is what I want to remember.

I slammed down on my Windborn power, stopping it from drawing in any more of Sigrun's energy. I glanced up at my sister. Her eyes were wide and I thought her skin looked a little pale against the bright blood and dark mud on her cheeks. She did not pull away.

Carefully, I pushed my strength into her. I tried to siphon off the wriggling power within me and not shove my consciousness into Sigrun, like I had with the mushroom barrier, but it was difficult.

I have to leave. My family died with my mother on that distant shore. I bore the brunt of my father's grief and rage, but the gods saved me. Floki taught me runes and prayers and how to weave a spell. It was the only time anyone showed me I had value, but my runes were not strong enough. They could not save her. I looked at my hands. Scrubbed and washed so many times. They still felt sticky with a mother's life-blood. Floki told me to look at my sister. I had saved her, he said, be glad of that. I have not yet finished my apprenticeship, but I have begged Floki to send me to another god-speaker. Reluctantly, he agrees.

I stop in one final time to see my father and half-sister. She is still swaddled in cloth, bawling, my father looks at me but does not greet me. His eyes are full of disgust when they look at me. I have to leave.

Sigrun's eyes went wide. The colours returned to her cheeks. She sat a little straighter. Tears rimmed her eyes.

I slowly lifted my hand.

"How do you feel?" I asked.

"Better," she said, slowly. Her mouth was no longer pressed together in pain and her eyes had lost their hardness. "I feel better, thank you, Alvir."

She squeezed my arm. I put my hand on hers. For a moment we stayed like that—brother and sister—and I wished that moment could have been stretched out like the memories of the landvaettir where moments felt like seasons.

I blinked away my tears and stood to face the others.

"I will stay and help Fafnir. Erri, you go and muster Vidsetr. I can gift some strength to anyone that needs it."

The huskalar who, days ago, had led his band of warriors into this forest, dressed in the best war gear the village could muster, now looked to me dressed in rags and dirt with a mixture of frustration and confusion.

"You can't possibly hope to win, Alvir. I don't want to leave Nal any more than you do but she knew what she was doing. She may be young, but she's a warrior. She's a huskalar. She did what she did to save everyone else."

I held up a hand to stop Fafnir from taking another step.

"Then let us do this to save you all."

Erri looked at me, exasperation clear on his face, then looked past me to Fafnir.

"Fine," he said. "We're wasting time here. If you want to charge off and get yourselves killed that's your business. The rest of us are going to warn Vidsetr."

"I'll stay with them," Yrsa said.

Erri sighed and his shoulders slumped. "Fine. Make sure they don't get themselves killed by doing something stupid."

Sigrun shifted from where she sat against a boulder, pushing herself to her feet. "It barely hurts," she said. "I think I'll be okay."

She tested her weight on her injured leg and winced in

anticipation of the pain, then her eyes went wide and she smiled. I smiled back and it felt like the first time I had ever truly been able to help my sister.

"Does anyone else need some help from Alvir?" Sigrun said. "It's good stuff."

The old man limped over to me, his scalp was crusted with blood and his cheeks were covered in hair-thin scratches. I took his hands in mine, careful to stop my Windborn power before I touched him, and gently pushed.

The power trickled from me like meltwater flowing from a glacier. I watched the old man's expression soften, his posture straightened, and the cuts on his cheeks began to close. After a few heartbeats, he no longer looked like a ragged victim, but a capable woodsman.

He thanked me and I moved over to Drifa, but she waved me off.

"Aren't we forgetting about the actual getting out?" she asked. "We couldn't find our way out of the forest. There's something that's keeping us in. It keeps throwing us back in here."

I nodded. "Ulfrun's chained the forest's spirit."

"You got us through last time," Erri said to me. "Can you come and get us out?"

I bit my lip and looked back at Fafnir. The huge Windborn was pacing from side to side like a caged wolf. I did not think he would wait the hours it would take for us to trek back to the mushroom border before traipsing back here.

"We cannot risk delay if we're going to save Nal," I said and felt Fafnir pause behind me. I bent to the ground and drew the rune *journey* into the mud with a finger. "Go and see if any of the outlaws have stones with this rune on it. That is what is letting them slip through the landvaettir's magic. If you can find those stones then you can get through the barrier without me."

"Right. Drifa, let's go."

The huskalar and the huntswoman jogged out of the clearing to find the runes they needed. Yrsa went with them to scavenge whatever equipment would give us the best chance to save Nal and the forest.

Those of us who remained prepared ourselves for our journeys. Fafnir had stayed, both to give us some protection and because he was content with his spear, though it still looked like a child's toy in his hands. I moved from one escapee to the next, checking them over and offering them strength once more. No one needed any of my Windborn-gifted strength, but I was able to use some of my healer's skills. As I tied the dark-haired woman's sprained fingers together I felt a sense of peace wash over me. Not everything I had learned as a god-speaker was tied to the gods' power. There were some skills, small healings or the way that I had learned to talk to the grieving, that I still had and I could still use. I offered a reassuring smile to the dark-haired woman as she winced at the tight bandages.

Then there was nothing to do but wait.

I sat with Sigrun.

She looked at me and smiled.

"It's good to be with you."

I tensed. Had she not heard that I was staying in the forest? Had she hit her head? My mouth opened and closed as I tried to find the strength to tell her I was leaving her again.

"I mean right now," she said with a laugh. "Your face. I'm glad you came back for me and I'm glad you came to Vidsetr."

I pulled back on my Windborn power, reining it in like a bucking horse, and squeezed Sigrun's hand. "Me too. I'm sorry it took me so long."

"It's okay." Her mouth pressed together into a sad smile and she shrugged. "I always thought you hated me for stealing our father. I thought that's why you never came back."

It was my turn to offer a half-smile. "Only at first. I was young when they sent me away and I got this idea in my head that once I left he was different. That he was happy with you. I couldn't bring myself to come back and see how happy you were together. It was stupid."

"It was stupid." Sigrun chuckled and punched me playfully in the arm then she grew serious. "He never recovered from my mother's death. I was raised by everyone else in the town as much as him. It was hard to leave them, but not so difficult to leave him."

"I know what you mean."

Comfortable silence enveloped us. We watched Fafnir pace back and forth and listened to the swish and crackle of the trees.

Eventually, the others returned. Erri and Drifa cradled armfuls of stones which they poured onto the ground in front of me. I sifted through them with a stick, careful not to touch them and picked out the ones with the right runes painted on them. There were three. I looked at the group. Sigrun, Erri, Drifa and the three ragged escapees.

"You'll have to make the trip through the barrier more than once," I said as I flicked the right necklaces out of the pile. "Is this all there were?"

"That's all," Erri replied.

I looked at Sigrun. She met my gaze with the iron-hard eyes of a seasoned warrior. She nodded.

"It will be fine, Alvir," she said. "We've got two strong huskalar thanks to you. One of us can stay and keep everyone safe whilst the other leads them through."

The pit of my stomach twisted at the thought of Sigrun standing alone unable to pass through the barrier and a troll barrelling through the forest towards her, or the black, rotten god coalescing nearby. But there was nothing I could do. And she was right. Between her and Erri, and with Drifa too, there were seasoned fighters amongst them. I glanced at her leg. She stood straight, putting her weight on the once-injured leg.

It would be fine.

It had to be fine.

"Okay," I said. "Just put them around your neck and then you will be able to step through the barrier."

Erri nodded and turned to Sigrun, Drifa, and the others shivering with fear. "Time for us to go."

I looked back to Sigrun. She was putting one of the necklaces around the old man's neck. She saw me watching her and came over.

"Stay safe," she said. "We've got a lot to catch up on."

I reached out but let my hand fall. "You, too. And if we don't make it out, make sure Vidsetr's ready to face whatever comes out of this forest."

Her eyes hardened and she nodded. Erri called for them to move. Sigrun squeezed my shoulder.

They clambered between the troll-stones caught on the slope, helping the captives to make the muddy climb.

Then they were gone.

Only the Windborn were left to face whatever hid between the rotting trees.

Yrsa had brought back a bundle of spears and axes which she'd piled up against one of the troll-stones. Fafnir came and examined them. He hefted one of the larger axes and nodded before slipping it through his belt, then he toyed with the spears. His arms were a blur as he stabbed, swung, and twisted them through the air. A few did not pass his inspection, but soon enough he had two that he was happy with and he passed one to Yrsa and then gave the other to me.

"It is a good spear," he said.

The wood was smooth under my fingers, light and well-balanced. I twisted it through the air, adjusting my grip under Fafnir's tutelage. Once he was satisfied, he turned to his own needs. He wrapped some of the outlaws' cloaks around him. On him, they were little more than scraps of cloth tied around his arms, but they helped to break up his outline and camouflage him in the dripping forest. My heart swelled. I had found friends and allies in this dying forest and I would not let them down.

I gripped my spear and looked at Fafnir and Yrsa.

"I'm ready," I said.

Fafnir's tusk-grin split his face. "Then let us save my sister."

Chapter Twenty-Six
Rune-Trees

THE SCENT OF OUTLAW WAS THICK ON THE GROUND and Fafnir soon found their tracks. We made our way through the dripping, fetid forest, squelching through the black earth and after a couple of hours we caught sight of a group of masked figures rushing through the trees. Yrsa gestured for us to hide, we couldn't risk a battle. We were too close to Ulfrun's stronghold yet too far to rescue Nal. We ducked behind a hunched, rotting tree and waited for them to pass. I counted about six outlaws that moved by with preternatural speed and I prayed that Sigrun and the others would be able to defend themselves.

We waited for a few, long minutes after the outlaws disappeared behind half-dead leaves and sinewy branches but they did not come back and we pressed on.

Soon, we came upon a boulder wedged into the ground. At first, we ignored it, thinking it another troll-stone hauled from elsewhere in the forest. Then, we realised that it was too regular in its circular curves and too calculated in its carved patterns.

I edged up to it as Yrsa and Fafnir kept watch.

The stone was sunk deep into the earth though it was clear from the crater around it that the outlaws had tried to excavate it. Its top was the rough, worn surface that showed on any boulder, likely why the outlaws had thought it a troll-stone, but the lower, freshly revealed sections were too straight. It took my mind a moment to parse the straight sides and curve at the top: an archway. A weave of jagged lines was etched across the stone that blossomed outwards before the archway was hidden beneath the earth.

It was an entrance. It had been buried and lost for countless years, but this was the top of a door, half-hidden in the dirt.

I slid down the side of the crater. Loose dirt tumbled down with me as I fell.

"Alvir," Fafnir growled. "We do not have time."

"Just a moment," I said, waving him off.

The door was blocked by earth, but as I put my hand against the weave of carved lines I felt the echo of a long-dormant power. It rippled outwards and with it I could feel the hint of some vast network like colossal hollow roots that stretched under the entire forest. The feeling was similar to how I felt when I shared the landvaettir's power and I thought I knew where it led.

"This is a doorway," I said as I scrambled back to the others.

Fafnir glared at me and shifted his weight from foot to foot, eager to be on our way. "You stopped for a buried door?"

"This door might be as old as the god-war. I think it leads to the trollways."

Both of the Windborn looked unimpressed. I could tell that they wanted to tell me the trollways were just stories, but we had seen so much in the last few days that their scepticism was kept in check.

"Come," Fafnir said. "Night falls."

He moved without waiting and Yrsa went with him. I glanced back at the trollway entrance, but I had to follow. If we survived then there would be time to investigate.

The forest darkened as we pushed on. Without the weak amber sunlight that had filtered through the withered canopy, the forest looked even more foreboding. The leaning, moss-covered trees leapt suddenly out of the darkness. I twisted my grip around my spear, hoping that no outlaw nor troll would swipe at us from the shadows.

Then, something squirmed against my mind.

The others pushed ahead. They had not felt it.

"Wait," I hissed.

They stopped and looked at me.

I stretched my senses out. The squirming was faint, like a

worm twisting through the earth, but it was close. I gingerly stepped over fallen branches and brown, withered ferns until I came to a tree. The squirming whisper came from the tree at about head height. The tree itself was covered in long fronds of sallow yellow moss that looked to have once covered the entire trunk, but now there were clumps of it on the floor and the moss had been replaced with splotches of black mould.

I circled the tree and saw it: a sigil carved into the trunk at eye level. Parts of it were similar to symbols I knew of, mostly for keeping ghosts and spirits tethered during rituals but there were smaller runes that matched the ones the outlaws had on their necklaces. There was a stone hammered into the centre of the sigil. Those other parts that I did not understand reminded me of the script of the Daendrec and the old alphabet first used by the Empire of Bones, though it had since been taken up by most kingdoms south of the Fjalmark. Was Ulfrun using some forgotten magic that she had found in those ossified ruins?

I reached out my hand and brushed my Windborn power against it, getting a sense of its power and purpose.

I felt the gods' power, a hint of Windborn strength, and something black and wet.

The magic led from this tree to countless others. One such tree was a few paces away and I knew that if I went over to it I would see a similar rune carved deep into its trunk. It was a lattice of magic, thin and strong like an iron spiderweb, and it was meant to keep the landvaettir tethered to the whims of Ulfrun and her lackeys.

"What is it?" Yrsa said.

"Part of what's keeping the forest spirit under Ulfrun's thumb." I showed them the sigil. "It's linked to other trees, one over there, and many others."

"Can you destroy it?" Yrsa asked.

"I think so," I said, flexing my fingers and feeling my Windborn power aching to absorb the sigil's strength. "If I do then they will know we're here. They will know we're coming."

"But the forest will be free?" Fafnir rumbled.

I chewed my lip. "No, I don't think so. The landvaettir will still be trapped but it won't be forced to do whatever Ulfrun wants. I think she'll not be able to summon it anymore."

"Good enough for me," Yrsa said. "If we don't have to fight that tree monster, I'm all for it."

I looked to Fafnir. He nodded.

"We will have one less enemy."

I took a breath and reached out to the sigil carved into the rotten trunk. The power within me slathered for it. My skin brushed against the wood's wet fibres and I let my Windborn hunger feast.

The mortals have chained me. Trapped between runes and the soul of a foreign god. They drag the shattered corpse of the stone-kin. They have found a way to breathe life into—

Fury fires my blood. The High King turns away in favour of his poisoned warriors? They should be dead. I will prove the strength of the gods to him and then—

God-Bane? Are you brave or stupid? No matter. You are too late. Night is fallen. The ritual is—

I am drowning. Forever drowning. A fresh ritual sends ripples through my pool. A new death. I am pulled free of the bog, my worshippers replace a limb. The fresh sacrifice gives me new power. I—

Enough! These memories are not for you, God-Bane. Come, then, and test your new name.

I blinked against the confusing mix of thoughts and memories and the press of the black god-monster against my mind.

For a moment, I stood shivering in the cold forest. Shaken by the attention of whatever had allied itself to Ulfrun and the sensation of still water filling my lungs.

Dark sodden power drenched my hand. My fingers were wrinkled as though my hand had been submerged for hours. The tree was now dry, brittle, any memory of mould or moisture gone.

The skein of magic shattered and the power that flowed through the intricate network of rune-marked trees became too much for the spell. Power buffeted my senses as the power of the landvaettir fled back into the world and for a brief moment my mind was carried with it. I flowed out along the net of sigils and runes that reined in the forest spirit to

Ulfrun's desires. My mind bounced from one tree to the next until it ended at a boulder surrounded by boggy water and runecraft.

The top of the god-stone.

A sudden gale raged from the centre of the forest, kicking up a wave of pine needs, moss, and twigs. It blew from the tip of the god-stone. The landvaettir was no longer forced to do Ulfrun's bidding but it was still chained to this place.

Yrsa and Fafnir watched me as I shook the water from my hand.

I looked up, through the gaps in the canopy, and saw the stars beginning to shrink against the blossoming light of the Winds.

"We need to go," I said. "Nal is in danger."

Without waiting for an answer, I sprinted off in the direction of the god-stone and the troll-corpse waiting for its resurrection.

Chapter Twenty-Seven
A Final Ritual

We ran.

Fafnir's feet thumped the ground like the beat of a war drum as Yrsa and I crashed alongside him. Branches snapped. Leaves hissed as we sprinted by. The forest seemed to quiver as we rushed to the shattered tip of the god-stone.

The forest knew we were coming. The outlaws knew we were coming.

The foliage around us came alive with the movements of our enemies.

Masked outlaws leapt from between the trees as we came to a clearing.

One crashed into me and sent me tumbling across the black mud. More appeared, forming a loose battle line at the other side of the clearing, spears lowered. Their movements seemed clumsy, slow. They had lost the deer-footed grace the landvaettir's stolen power had given them.

As I rolled to my feet Yrsa's axe whipped out, viper-fast, and took off the head of the outlaw who had attacked me.

Three more charged.

Fafnir roared.

He fell upon his enemies with a rage that the Trolbjolvid had not seen since the Warrior stalked the world and gave the forest its name.

A deer-skulled outlaw lunged for Fafnir. He smashed them aside with a clenched fist. The outlaw flew back and crashed into a tree, cracking the trunk in half. The other two outlaws swarmed up to Fafnir but before they could get close he ripped the broken tree from the ground. He swung it like a club, crushing both outlaws with a single swing.

Five outlaws left.

One came for me. Fafnir and Yrsa fell upon the others.

The outlaw swung their axe overhead. I rolled to the side. The axe blade sunk deep into the wet earth. They let go of their weapon and leapt at me with raking fingers and pounding fists.

I used one arm to shield my head and shoved at them with my other hand.

My Windborn strength sent them tumbling back. I grabbed their axe, leapt forward, swung it into their chest. A crunch. Blood spurting, then bubbling, then nothing.

The sound of fighting continued for a heartbeat more before they ended with a sudden, final snap.

I pushed myself to my feet. We were alive, unhurt. The outlaws were dead.

"Which way?" Fafnir said. His clothes were sodden with blood and he still clutched his tree-club in one hand.

As I looked around to get my bearings I realised that the night air felt heavy. Not just the moisture hanging in the air, but something else, something charged.

"We have to hurry. They're starting a ritual."

"What ritual?" Yrsa asked.

I was already running, but I shouted over my shoulder: "One that needs a sacrifice."

They needed no more encouragement and once again we crashed through the forest.

The canopy thinned above us as the trees had become too rotten, too damp to hold their own weight and had toppled over. The stars shone down, making me feel exposed after so long under the safety of the forest canopy, and the Winds snaked out across the sky. We leapt over the fallen, mould-ridden trunks and clambered up a rise.

Then we saw it.

There was a clearing ahead with enough space for a prison cell and a ritual.

One side of the clearing was peppered with troll-stones. Most had been dragged together into a humanoid shape and covered with vines and painted runes. Ulfrun muttered and sang by its head, her eyes closed as she focused on the ritual, with a gaggle of masked accomplices and bound captives beside her. On the other side, the tip of the god-stone was trapped inside a ring of fallen trees that had been dragged around it like the nest of a colossal bird.

Power radiated from the barrier around the landvaettir. A sorrowful fury smouldered within the god-stone. The weight of the ritual's power hung in the air.

None of those pressed as hard against my senses as the power dripping from the black-stained figure that turned to watch us from the centre of the clearing.

It towered over Ulfrun, even hunched as it was. One arm was withered and pulled close to its chest whilst the other hung too low beside its body. Water dripped from its clothing as though it had just stepped out from a river. Dirt clung to its cheeks and its wet hair was plastered to its head. The black figure's smile flickered green in the light from the Winds.

"God-Bane," it said. Its voice bubbled with intrigue and delight. "You came."

I had heard that voice in my mind and, briefly, felt its memories. I shivered as I recalled the feeling of cold, still water around me, seeping into my pores and saturating my lungs.

I edged down the slope, slipping through the dark mud.

"Stop this," I said. I prayed that I would be able to end this without bloodshed, but I knew the gods weren't listening. "You are killing the forest."

The hulking black-stained figure twisted to look at the landvaettir's prison. It was too stiff to twist its head and had to move its whole body to see it.

It shrugged. "All great magic requires sacrifices."

The Winds burst into bright colour above us like blood falling into water.

Fafnir stomped up beside me. Wood creaked as he squeezed his tree-club in a death grip.

"Who are you?" I called over. The few masked outlaws in the clearing had begun to shift, moving to surround us. Yrsa pulled her axes free and glared at them but held herself back as I tried to talk to the monster before us.

"It doesn't matter," it said. "It has been so long since anyone said my name that I have forgotten."

It edged towards us around the troll-stones with limping steps. As the Winds began to dance more furiously the details of the black-dripping figure became clear. Its oversized arm was bulky and furred whilst the other was skinny and withered like a corpse-arm dredged from a river. It was difficult to see its legs properly as its clothing shone with moisture and its cloak hung heavy over it, but they looked similarly mismatched.

"What are you?" I breathed.

"I was a man once. A long time ago." Water dribbled from its open mouth with each word. "Now... mostly man, but more."

I racked my brain trying to think of what spirits or demons or constructs I had ever heard of that could be this powerful and this... patchwork.

Fafnir moved up to stand beside me.

"This thing smells of bogs and lies," he growled, then to the un-man before us: "Free my sister or I will kill you."

The black, bog-stained thing glanced back at Nal, at the captives, and then to Fafnir.

"You are a big man, but you cannot kill me. I have already survived more deaths than you, Windborn."

The words caught in my mind and I remembered Eylis describing the dead, drowned gods of the Daendrec. Sacrificial victims drowned in bogs then, sometimes years later, dredged up to be joined with the bodies of other victims and it did not matter if those bodies were human or animal.

I felt, more than heard, Fafnir's growl of rage.

"Wait!" I cried. He was already gone.

He charged at the dripping figure, Yrsa a few steps behind, and swung the tree-club with his colossal, Windborn strength.

The figure's arm came up to block it. I winced in anticipation of the crunch, but it never came.

Their white-furred arm, a snow bear's arm, caught the tree-club mid-swing. Fafnir's power sent the monster skidding through the mud and it strained against Fafnir just holding him at bay.

Fafnir roared, let go of the club and—

The figure kicked with a misshapen leg—a horse's leg—and Fafnir flew back.

As Fafnir slammed into the landvaettir's tree-prison, the other outlaws charged. Yrsa leapt forward, axes flashing in the Wind-light. Some retreated, others fell limp, and then they blurred into a churning mass of blades and blood.

I rushed to help Fafnir. Yrsa had faced outlaws before, but Fafnir had never faced a god. The enormous Windborn leapt forward again, hands out to try and pull the god apart. The black-drenched figure smashed the tree-club at Fafnir and sent him flying once more.

"I know you northerners like your names," the god said as it examined the tree-club as casually as I would have examined a broken twig. "Especially of those about to kill you. I have long forgotten the name I had, but my people call me Thrice-Killed. Your Ulfrun has named me Bimyrr, Bog Dweller. So choose whichever name you like. That is who killed you."

It hefted the tree-club over Fafnir as he tried to right himself.

I slid across the mud beside them and grabbed hold of the Thrice-Killed's leg. It was human, but sallow and cold. A long-festering corpse. I pulled.

The Fjalmark raiders have learned to avoid my waterways. Their petty prayers cannot protect their longships from me. I splinter their hulls, drown their warriors, take their plunder as offerings. A rage boils within my cold chest for those few that slip my grasp and raid my worshippers.

I speak with my priests. A plan is made. I will slip through the water, raise myself on the Fjalmark, and destroy them from within.

Bimyrr Thrice-Killed faltered. The tree-club fell from its bear-paw grasp. Fafnir leapt up, putting his shoulder into Bimyrr's chest and threw it backwards. Together, they smashed through the forest, splintering trees as they moved in a great boiling mess of claws, fists, and tusks.

The strength of the god-like power sent me to my knees.

Cold moisture dripped across my skin and I vomited silt-grained water.

Ulfrun's voice reached a crescendo and raised the ritual's power to new heights. The air pressed so heavily against me, I was forced back to the ground as I tried to stand.

Colossal shadows crashed together in the forest as Fafnir tried to claw his way past the Thrice-Killed and back to us. Fafnir threw himself at the dripping god, but even from a distance I could see the power of the ritual was crushing him as well. The Thrice-Killed batted away Fafnir's fists then used its monstrous arm to throw Fafnir at a heavy, thick oak tree. The trunk buckled and fell as Fafnir crashed into it.

Ulfrun raised her arms to the sky, eyes obscured by her teeth-laden headdress. The old gold-speaker gestured and I felt something shift in my chest. Whatever she was weaving called to my Windborn power. Above us, the Winds circled the clearing like blood in a whirlpool.

I tried to move to the landvaettir's prison, but between the weight in the air and the ritual's pull on my Windborn soul it was all I could do to push myself to my feet.

Yrsa struggled to fend off the last two outlaws facing her. I saw her try to shake off the effect of the ritual as she swung an axe wildly at her closest opponent.

I turned to Ulfrun. She grabbed at one of the captives and shoved them down against the execution block. I tried to see if it was Nal's throat she clutched at, but my vision blurred.

"Ulfrun, stop this!" I screamed to be heard over her shrieking voice and the cacophony of creaking, snapping wood as Fafnir battled Bimyrr. "The landvaettir will not survive this. You will kill the forest."

She paused, one hand pressed hard on the throat of her victim and the other held high, a blade flashing bright in the Wind-light.

"Do not speak to me, Poisoned One." Her eyes burned with hatred. "It is because of you that I am driven to these lengths. The Windborn disease must be driven out of every hall across the Fjalmark. I will use the god-stones to protect everyone from the likes of you as the gods intended."

"We can help you." I took a step forward, stretched out my

hand. "Windborn power is not—"

She plunged the knife down.

Everyone except Ulfrun was thrown to the floor as the ritual's captured power exploded out.

The sky shattered. The Winds cracked. Then a single tendril of blue light snapped down like a whip and into the troll-stones.

All at once, the pressure pulling me towards Ulfrun vanished. My vision cleared. I blinked and looked over to Ulfrun. Her first victim lay on the ground with their life-blood shining over stone and rotten roots. In the bright Wind-light, I saw Nal. She was behind Ulfrun bound and gagged, but struggling still. My chest flooded with relief.

It was short-lived.

The troll-stones had begun to glow. A low blue light slithered across the runes carved along the boulders and a sickly green light flowered across the vines and tar-paint. The green light grew stronger and I realised that it was being pulled from the landvaettir's prison like water guzzled by thirsty roots.

"What have you done?" My voice was a whisper but it still carried to Ulfrun in the fresh silence.

Victory danced in her eyes as well as rage. "I have put the Winds in their place. My ritual summons them and so I will use their power. To protect the gods and their people. As it should be."

My stomach twisted when I looked at the glowing troll-stones. The Windborn part of me reached out to whatever Ulfrun had created. There was power there, but it was unguided, unfocused, useless. An ember floating on the breeze in search of kindling. The sacrifice of one human soul had drawn the Winds to earth and the power of the landvaettir and the Thrice-Killed kept it tethered to the troll-stones. Horror drenched by bones as I realised Ulfrun needed another soul to fuse to the Wind to give it a mind, to make it a Windborn in all but body.

"Give me the girl," Ulfrun said to someone behind her.

"No!" Yrsa and I screamed it together.

Yrsa sprinted across the clearing, knocking outlaws out of

her way as she tried to get to Ulfrun and Nal. More outlaws threw themselves at her and she was forced to face them to save her life.

From outside the clearing: a roar. The Thrice-Killed tumbled into view as Fafnir charged through him like a boar charging a wolf. Rage and panic shone bright in Fafnir's eyes as he ran to his sister.

I was too far away. I would never get there.

But I was by the landvaettir's prison.

Somehow, Ulfrun was using the forest's power to anchor the Wind to the troll-stones. If I could free the landvaettir then the ritual would fade. Ulfrun would not need to kill Nal. We could save spirit and sister both.

The nest-cage around the god-stone was made of thick tree trunks. I could see runes carved into the wood, but they were too high for me to reach. I fell to my knees and clawed through the clots of moss and brittle twigs on the ground.

Memories sparked in my mind as my fingertips tore through the dirt. The mud was saturated with the power of the landvaettir, Ulfrun, and the Thrice-Killed.

The gods rattle their spears at one another. We retreat to the forest to wait out the war.

My lungs fill with bog-water. My neck is raw from the noose's embrace. My ribs scream with the spearhead still snug between them.

The High King turns away from me. He whispers to a Windborn. He ignores the gods for those with rotten souls.

My fingernails tore as they suddenly clawed at hard tree bark. I whipped my hand away from the pain and with my other hand I scraped the mud from the tree. My palm came away sticky with black tar that seared my skin and I realised that I had found the edge of the spell. This was the tar that many rune-weavers used to extend the power of their spells. It was the only thing that could hold magic to a Windborn and it burned me.

I pressed my hand against the black tar and pulled.

No memories. Only the searing pain of wildfire in my veins.

My ribs creaked as my Windborn power bucked in agony inside my chest.

I screamed and fell away from the spell, clutching my smoking hand.

For a long moment, there was only pain, white behind my eyes, and then the world was dark again.

I pushed myself up to my feet, cursing. The tar wasn't only there to hold the enchantment in place. It was there to stop someone breaking it.

I cursed again and looked around. Yrsa was fighting her way to Ulfrun. The god-speaker had been forced to hide behind her servants as the Windborn warrior clawed her way to the execution block. Yrsa was too far to help me, too deep in the blood of our enemies.

Behind her, the forest was lit with the green light of the captured Wind and something else. Blue ghosts sprinting through the distant trees.

Fafnir wrestled with the Thrice-Killed. He had caught the god's monstrous arm and was trying to twist it, snap it, before the monster could bring it to bear on him.

"Fafnir!" I shouted. "Throw him at the god-stone! If we break the spell they can't sacrifice Nal."

The colossal Windborn grunted but could not get any purchase on the slick ground.

A laugh bubbled from the Thrice-Killed's throat as it slowly straightened its arm and forced Fafnir onto his knees. "Weak. You cannot stop a god."

I tried to stand, but my legs gave way.

As I fell, my pack crashed to the ground beside me and a god-stone shard tumbled free.

I grabbed it.

There was hardly any power left but it was enough to push me to my feet and give me the strength to stumble towards Fafnir.

Before I had taken two steps, the Thrice-Killed snapped its head around, black watery eyes glaring at me.

"What—"

Fafnir twisted its white-furred arm. The Thrice-Killed's eyes widened with surprise as Fafnir pulled, tusks bared in furious effort. A slick pop and rending flesh. The arm was wrenched from the Thrice-Killed's unbalanced body. Black, bloody water sluiced from the wound, covering Fafnir in a dark flood. As the god screamed in fury and pain Fafnir grabbed it and with a scream threw it at the god-stone.

The god's body flew through the air before crashing into the ground where it slid like a rockslide into the rune-carved trees, exploding the landvaettir's prison into knife-sharp splinters.

"Ulfrun!" Fafnir's roar shook the earth. "Give me my sister."

The ground shook as Fafnir charged at the god-speaker. Figures of blue-shivering light sprinted out of the forest and threw themselves at Fafnir. He faltered like a man caught in a blizzard and screamed with fury.

I twisted and looked back at the god-stone.

The Thrice-Killed still reeled from its dismemberment, clutching a withered hand to the gaping hole where its bestial arm had been.

I clambered over it, feet slipping on the bloody tree trunks, and leapt into the heart of the landvaettir's prison. With the whisper of forest power in my veins I could hear the screams from the god-stone.

The landvaettir cried for freedom. It demanded revenge.

I kicked through the runes and sigils that had been carefully placed around the shattered tip of the god-stone. With every displaced sigil I felt the weight in the air shift.

The ritual weakened.

The landvaettir shed its chains.

"I am disappointed, God-Bane." The voice growled from behind me like the burble of a rotten stream. I turned to see Bimyrr Thrice-Killed raising itself to its feet. "I thought you might understand what we are doing here."

I stumbled away from the god until my back bumped up against the god-stone.

I had nowhere to go.

"All you're doing is manipulating her," I said, gesturing to Ulfrun. "You are using her hatred for your own ends."

The rotten, dismembered god took a shaky step towards me. "I have given her the power she needed. Without me, she could not have broken the stone housing your precious forest spirit. I have taught her the true power of death. I have such a lesson for you."

I pressed myself against the god-stone.

I pushed my hands against it.

I pulled.

An ancient, overpowering rage blossomed in my chest.

Roots wrapped themselves around my legs and raised me from the ground even as they snaked around my chest.

Bimyrr snarled and lurched forward, withered arm outstretched, but the ground shook under its feet and it had to abandon its attack to keep its balance.

My senses unfurled and I felt a wave of nauseating vertigo as I saw myself standing beside the god-stone but also felt my senses spread throughout the forest. I felt the firm, languid touch of every tree root digging into the earth. My breath moved in time with the wind. I felt it brush against every leaf. I felt Fafnir's footsteps trample moss and stamp on branches as he battled the blue ghosts to get to Nal. I felt the queasy power trapped in the troll-stone slowly fading as the landvaettir's power, now unchained, no longer kept it tethered.

My body was wrapped in vines and moss and stones. The landvaettir's power swirled around me as it built itself its massive avatar and kept me armoured at its centre. My forest-body straightened and I grew taller than the Thrice-Killed.

I stepped forward, to go and help Fafnir, and the forest-colossus moved with me.

Thrice-Killed snarled again and leapt for me.

I swiped a branch-woven arm at it. Wood creaked and splintered as it smashed into Bimyrr's side and it tumbled out of my way.

My forest-body was heavy, each step needed to be unrooted before another could be taken, but I hurried over to Fafnir and Yrsa and the ghosts swarming over them. Ulfrun reached back to take hold of Nal.

Another tree-thick swipe through the ghosts. I felt their cold power scrape over mine and the landvaettir's arm. Some of the wood withered as though in a winter frost. Nevertheless, the ghosts shimmered and some went out.

Something smashed against me from behind.

Tearing, wrenching, snapping. Pain flared against my

senses as the Thrice-Killed pulled chunks of branches and stone from the landvaettir's back.

I tried to turn, to face Bimyrr, but I was trapped in the wooden body.

Another blaze of pain.

The roots and vines holding me in place withered and I fell forward onto the wet ground. As I scrambled away, the forest around me rumbled and moved, gathering itself around the landvaettir. In the blink of an eye, the landvaettir's body was thick and verdant, bulky with stones and broken wood. It charged at the Thrice-Killed.

The ground shook as the two monsters came together. Rotten water drenched the vital roots of the landvaettir and thorns ripped through Bimyrr's bloated skin.

I stumbled away before I was crushed under the feet of one or the other.

Fafnir screamed as a fresh flood of ghosts washed over him.

I sprinted to him, grabbing a ghost and draining it. It blinked out. The other echoes flickered and turned their attention to me.

"Go," Fafnir roared, swiping at the ghosts, rending one of the ghosts in two like a knife through cloth. "Stop the ritual. Save Nal. I will deal with these."

He pushed forward, through the shimmering figures, and threw a stone at the ghost-summoning Windborn at the edge of the clearing. As Nori leapt out of the way his spectral minions faltered, unsure whether to keep up the attack or save their creator.

With the ghosts distracted, I sprinted across the clearing. I dodged outlaws as they stabbed at me with spears, swiped with axes, then Yrsa was there. Slashing and killing, keeping the outlaws at bay.

The air grew heavy as Ulfrun began to hum, adding a throaty hum to the cacophony of battle bouncing around the clearing.

"Ulfun, stop!"

She ignored me, desperate to finish the ritual before its power faded. There were three outlaws with her, masks expressionless in the face of the horror Ulfrun wove in front of them. As I skidded through the black mud two of them peeled off to face me, the last kept their captive close.

The outlaws lowered their spears, but I was flush with the power of the forest, stolen ghost-strength, my Windborn power.

One of them stumbled on a root as they lunged. Their blade dug into the ground by my feet and I danced over it, wrenching the man's head around with a crunch as I moved past them.

The other outlaw swiped at me with a woodcutting axe. I couldn't move out of the way in time. I managed to twist the outlaw's arm, but the axe came on. The edge of the blade sliced through my forearm, bouncing off the bones near my wrist.

I howled in pain. I kicked at the outlaw's knee. It snapped backwards and he went down with a scream.

I sprinted forward as the last outlaw dragged Nal towards the execution block.

Ulfrun was lost to her ritual. She was too far. I could not stop her.

Nal fought against her captor, but she was forced to her knees. I could get to her. I had to reach her.

I grabbed the outlaw and pulled and—

I chew my lip as I collect the ravens for this strange god-speaker. He says he can use them to find Ulfrun. I wonder if I should tell him that Ulfrun does not wish to be found. He is a god-speaker. He will understand, won't he? I come to Ulfrun's house and see him with Sigrun and the wretched Windborn. My stomach settles. A god-speaker he may be, but he won't understand.

I whipped my hand away.

"Tjorvid?"

The outlaw shoved my chest, forcing me to stumble back, and then pushed Nal's head down onto the execution block.

"Tjorvid, no!"

It was too late.

Ulfrun's hand swung down and smashed Nal's skull with a stone.

Fafnir screamed in rage and grief.

The troll-stones glowed brighter. They began to move.

CHAPTER TWENTY-EIGHT
THE THRICE-KILLED

ALL THE MAGIC WAS SUCKED OUT OF THE AIR and into the shifting troll-stones. The vines draped between the boulders' joints shifted and tightened like ligaments as the creature came to life.

I stood, amazed and horrified at the rising monster. Ulfrun had somehow managed to summon the Winds and bind them into these troll-stones with a human soul. This was not simply a stone-clad Windborn that raised itself in front of me.

It was more than that: it was Trollborn.

It tottered on uneven granite feet and I saw the massive legs trip towards me but I could not move, I was rooted in shock.

Yrsa crashed into me and we both tumbled out of the way as the Trollborn found its balance.

"What the fuck is that thing?" she hissed.

"It's..." I could not take my eyes from it. It raised two boulder-hands and looked at them, then looked to the clearing. "I think it's Nal."

Ulfrun cackled, raising the gore-stained stone high in exultation. She opened her mouth to call to the monster but was cut short as Fafnir charged towards her.

The great Windborn trailed shimmering ghosts, but they could not slow him.

Fafnir arrived at the execution block like an avalanche. Ulfrun was thrown back by a backhanded swipe, crashing into a nearby tree with a crunch. Without taking his eyes from the body of his sister, Fafnir reached one massive hand to the last outlaw—to Tjorvid—and crushed his head with an idle squeeze.

He cried out in hurt and grief, as he slumped down in front of his sister. He slid his hands under her limp body and cradled her as though that would bring her back.

Sobs shook his shoulders and for a long moment grief was all that filled the clearing. Then he lay Nal down on the ground as a mother would lay down a newborn child.

Fists clenched, he stepped over her and put himself between Nal's body and the Trollborn.

"What have you done to her?" he shouted, looking from Ulfrun to the Trollborn. Neither answered him.

His words twisted together into a roar of rage and he charged. The Trollborn took a faltering step away from Fafnir's pummelling fists, trying to protect its face behind a monolith-arm. None of Fafnir's blows seemed to be doing any damage but the Trollborn fled from his attacks, nonetheless.

As Fafnir threw himself at the living troll-stones, the rest of the world came back into focus.

Dead outlaws littered the clearing, their blood sparkling in the light from the Winds and the shimmering echo-ghosts. Ulfrun groaned. The ghosts loomed at the edge of the clearing, circling and ready to pounce, and at their centre I saw their summoner. Behind us, the landvaettir had caught the Thrice-Killed in a cage of roots and stone, but it would not hold. The god strained at its confines and the roots snapped like tearing cloth.

Yrsa bared her teeth and looked around, unsure which way to point her axes.

"Keep the ghosts off of me," I said. "Maybe Ulfrun knows how to fix this."

She nodded.

I ran to Ulfrun.

Yrsa sprinted ahead of me, axes flashing through the shimmering ghosts. They broke apart like mist sliced by a longship but most flowed back together and whipped out formless arms to sear Yrsa's skin. She cried out, but pain only spurred her fury and her axes slashed faster than my eyes could follow.

I slid down beside Ulfrun.

She was covered in blood and dirt with splinters and leaves

in her hair. Her eyelids flickered as I propped her up.

"Who?"

"It's... I'm a god-speaker. Ulfrun, what have you done? Tell me how to reverse this and kill this abomination."

Her eyes went wide and then focused on me. A cackle escaped her which became a scraping cough.

"You are the abomination, Poisoned One. I have made this creature to demonstrate that we do not need the likes of you. We do not need Windborn."

"You're wrong, Ulfrun. You've been manipulated by the Thrice-Killed. It's using you to weaken the Fjalmark."

"No. Do you not see? These are not saga-hungry warriors, God-Bane. These creations are simple weapons." She smiled, the bloody spittle covering her teeth, lips, and chin. Her breath ragged and shallow. "They are better than Windborn. They are bound to my will. I will show the High King what he has forgotten. The gods are supreme and will not be ignored."

She waved a stone at me. The same one she had used to sacrifice Nal. It was saturated with dark blood and there were strands of hair and flecks of bone clung to it. It was not a simple stone. It was a piece of god-stone wrapped in vines and daubed with tar.

She could control the Trollborn. It was the same as the rune-sticks I had used to control the ravens what felt like a lifetime ago.

I grabbed for the stone.

Ulfrun tried to jerk it out of my reach, snarling, but she was too weak. As my fingers closed around her wrist my Windborn power blossomed, I tried to hold it back but either its hunger was too strong or Ulfrun's remaining strength so small that before I could stop it she was gone without a hint of memory flickering in my mind.

I pulled the stone from her grasp and gagged at the power within the stone. It was soaked through with the Thrice-Killed's rotten touch and still echoed with Nal's last throes of fear and agony. I tried to push my senses through the stone, to see through the Trollborn's eyes as I had with the ravens, but this magic was not made for Windborn and it was like trying to dive into a frozen lake. I sensed that there were two more of the troll creatures coming towards the clearing, shadows beneath the ice racing closer. Now the ritual was done, they could come without worrying that the magic would somehow unravel the weave soaked into their stone bodies. I could not break the spell.

I looked to my friends.

Yrsa was cloaked in shimmering ghosts, barely staving them off with her blurred axes. Sweat shone across her face and her breathing came hard.

Fafnir chased the Trollborn around the clearing. He kicked and punched at it, picking up stones and tree trunks to smash against its granite hide, but the Trollborn backed away like a whimpering dog.

More ghosts stretched into existence between the rotting trees and though most went for Yrsa, like wolves targeting an injured deer, some broke away to stalk Fafnir, to hunt me.

We could not stay.

"Fafnir, Yrsa," I called. "We have to—"

A great rending, screaming of wood. Broken branches rained down over me.

The Thrice-Killed was free.

It roared as it stomped over broken trees, each one shattering under its uneven gait. I scrambled back, trying to get out of its way, but it ignored me and aimed straight for Fafnir.

The enormous Windborn, breathing hard, turned to face his new opponent with iron determination in his eyes.

The Thrice-Killed put its hand on the Trollborn.

The stone in my hand shuddered. The quality of the magic changed, like a river suddenly roiling, blackening from a landslip. My sense of the Trollborn, all three, flickered. Faded. Disappeared.

When I looked to the Thrice-Killed and the stony creature beside it, the magic glowing within it shifted. Before it had mirrored the Winds, a slow writhing glow the colour of deep glaciers. Now, the Trollborn's limbs dripped with murky water and the light glittering across it looked like algae clinging to a stagnant lake.

"Kill him." The Thrice-Killed gestured at Fafnir and turned

to face me in the same motion. "I will take care of you."

I pulled on the power of the stone, praying it would break the connection and Bimyrr's control over the Trollborn. The magic drained from the stone. Nothing happened.

The weave was broken, subverted.

With the trickle of power from the god-stone shard itself, I felt the mind of the landvaettir swimming through the soil, cautious after its body had been broken by Bimyrr. It had been drained for weeks to fuel Ulfrun's rituals, but it was not yet done. I clenched my fists and willed it to rise, to charge, but this was a spirit used to measuring time in days, seasons. This was happening too fast. It wanted to wait until the stain of poisoned mud was washed away by the rains and seasons. It could afford to wait.

"It is a shame you must die, God-Bane," Thrice-Killed said as it shuffled towards me. "You have done me a service killing that petty god-speaker. No contest, then for me to claim these stone warriors. I will test them on the god-speaker's home and then on Konvald. I will kill you now as payment for that service."

I scrambled to my hands and knees, crawling through the slick mud to try and reach the tip of the god-stone, pull on its power, to beg the landvaettir to join the fight.

Viper-fast, Bimyrr's cold, wet hand closed around my ankle, its grip as strong as death. Before I could try and pry myself free it yanked me back and threw me across the clearing.

The world spun. I slammed into the granite back of the Trollborn. White pain exploded behind my eyes as my arm, crushed between my body and the living troll-stone, broke. I fell to the ground.

"This was never about your absent gods or the favour your withered king gives to Windborn. This is about destroying the Fjalmark." The Thrice-Killed shook its head as it shuffled towards me. "You are so easily drawn out. A few shaking spears and thumping shields along the sea and your king cannot resist doing the same. And so I bring the strength of death and stone to you. When your king returns to see his shattered home these trolls will lay waste to him and his warriors. And, if he survives, he will be the lord of splinters and corpses."

Bimyrr's lopsided, bog-water grin faltered as he caught sight of the Trollborn behind me.

"What are you doing? Kill him."

I turned.

Fafnir had collapsed onto the ground, exhaustion finally claiming him, waiting for the final blow.

The Trollborn loomed over him but did not move. It shook, seemingly unable to overcome its fear of the Windborn. Dark droplets of water rained on Fafnir.

"Kill him!"

Bimyrr staggered over to the Trollborn and shoved it with their remaining hand. The stone colossus staggered forward, stamping a foot down next to Fafnir's arm, but it refused to act.

I tried to drag myself toward Fafnir, determined to help, but could not find purchase in the slick mud and with every jerky movement my broken arm screamed in fiery protest.

I was too heavy.

My pack still hung from my shoulders with ragged straps. I yanked it off and it split open.

Plants, twigs, and stones tumbled into the mud. One of the stones was the size of my head. The god-stone shard.

Without thinking, I shoved my good hand onto the stone, toppling over as my other arm gave way. Agony ripped through my side and I bit my lip so hard I drew blood.

The shard was warm under my fingertips.

I pulled.

Power flowed up my arm, rooting itself in my blood and muscles with a furious vitality.

I bit down on a scream as the sudden surge of power tried to heal my unset broken arm. The bone fused together awkwardly. Cuts closed. Bruises healed.

Beneath me, the landvaettir took notice. I felt it begin to shift in the ground, reaching out towards everyone and everything in the clearing.

I pushed myself to my feet, awkward with my wrong-set bones. Energy thrummed in my blood and I ran to Fafnir.

A question within the earth. Roots stretched out, ready to ensnare. I pushed them away from an exhausted Fafnir and kept them from Yrsa, now captured by her ghostly opponents.

I came up behind Bimyrr as it shoved the Trollborn out of the way. It snatched a spear from a dead outlaw.

"I will kill you myself."

The landvaettir's tendrils broke the surface of the bog-clogged soil.

I threw my shoulder into the Thrice-Killed. The blow sent a shiver of agony down my barely-healed arm, but it shoved Bimyrr off balance and the spear sunk deep into the earth instead of Fafnir's chest.

"Enough, God-Bane. I will see to you soon."

I slid in beside Fafnir. He turned his sorrow-thick gaze to me. Grief was carved deep in his face and he looked like he would have welcomed the release of the spear.

"We have to go," I whispered. "We need to warn Vidsetr."

"They know what lurks in the woods," Fafnir said, each word a battle. "They cannot stand against this."

He tried to gesture behind me. To the Trollborn. To the Thrice-Killed.

The mud around their feet swirled with reaching roots. As Bimyrr put the spear butt into the ground to push itself up the landvaettir struck. Brambles and vines engulfed the Thrice-Killed and pulled it back into the mud. Bimyrr's furious cry was swiftly drowned as its head was shoved into the wet ground. It screamed still, its rage-drenched voice bubbled up around its head.

"We cannot abandon them," I said. "They have a chance if we warn them."

I put my hand on Fafnir's shoulder. He flinched, knowing what my Windborn hunger could do, but I held it in check. The hairs on the back of my neck stood on end as our Windborn powers pressed against each other, flaring like a freshly kindled fire.

Then, I pushed some of the landvaettir's strength into him.

The colour returned to Fafnir's cheeks, his breathing evened out, and then his eyes went wide.

"A gift from the forest," I said and pulled Fafnir to his feet.

The Windborn stood, fists clenched and ready to battle the Trollborn once more.

"No," I said. "We need to get Yrsa and get out of here."

Fafnir paused, staring death at the Trollborn, then nodded.

We left the shuddering Trollborn as it was slowly wrapped in vines, as though we were watching centuries of growth overtake it in mere moments.

On the other side of the clearing, the ghost-summoner strained against his bramble-bonds. His ghosts still clogged the air around him. Those few that were not keeping Yrsa captive fretted over him though they could not help him.

We sprinted past the broken god-stone and the shattered nest-prison. Fafnir picked up one of the tar-drenched tree trunks as we ran, hefting it as easily as I would have picked up a walking stick.

He crashed into the ghosts with the power of an avalanche and swiped through the shimmering figures with the tree trunk. The ghosts tried to move out of the way but the sweep of Fafnir's attack was too great and they flickered out as they touched the tar-covered tree.

I helped Yrsa to her feet, pushing the landvaettir's power into her.

She gasped at the sudden influx of fresh strength and grabbed her axes from the ground, baring her teeth at Nori. I held her back.

"We have to go."

She turned to argue. Something huge crashed through the trees, just out of sight of the Wind-light.

Another Trollborn.

CHAPTER TWENTY-NINE
FLIGHT BENEATH THE EARTH

YRSA GROWLED AT THE DARKNESS. Fafnir panted from the effort of carving through the ghosts. I had given my friends some of the landvaettir's strength, but it was not much. We could not stand against this.

We backed away from the forest as the sound of splintering trees grew louder and the canopy began to shake.

"Can we outrun that thing?" Yrsa asked.

I looked around, trying to find something that would slow down the Trollborn enough to let us escape. All I could see was wreckage. Shattered trees. Troll-stones. Dead bodies.

Even the landvaettir's senses revealed nothing.

The thick network of roots under the clearing quivered under the strain of keeping the Trollborn and the Thrice-Killed locked in place. I pushed my senses deeper into the earth, hoping for an answer, but felt only the cold dirt and the echo of stone-kin memories long lost.

The curve of one of the troll-stones caught my eyes and I had a flash of inspiration.

"Come on," I said, already starting to run. "We need to get to that ruined archway."

"What? Why?"

Before I could answer, the trees ahead of us exploded as the new Trollborn charged into the clearing. Splinters sliced through the air. Yrsa dove out of the way of the massive column-legs. The few remaining ghosts withered under the onslaught of splinters before they were smashed out of existence by the careless Trollborn.

Fafnir's face was covered in tiny slices but he blinked them away and set himself in the mud, ready to stop the charging monster.

The Trollborn ignored us, instead stomping to the Thrice-Killed and clawing at the brambles and vines keeping it trapped. The monster's stubby stone hands had trouble pulling the constraints from Bimyrr, but they tore and snapped all the same. It would not be long before it was free.

I turned, shouting for the others to follow me.

I didn't look to see if they followed, but from the sense of their Windborn power and the magic of the forest that connected us, I knew they were not far behind.

We ran and circled around the god-stone shard and made for the other side of the clearing, to the half-sunken arch and the trollway.

A Trollborn crashed out of the woods beside us. We wove around the massive stamping legs and ducked the swiping boulder-hands. Within a heartbeat, we were past it.

We would get free. We would warn Vidsetr. I would keep Sigrun safe.

This Trollborn kept after us. Its stamping feet shook the ground as we tried to run. I stumbled. Fafnir grabbed me by the scruff of the neck and kept me upright.

We sprinted out of the clearing, dodging past trees, over logs, and around moss-covered stones. The landvaettir's magic lent our steps the speed and surety of deer. We knew the ground underfoot as though we had lived in the forest all our lives. We dodged every stone, every bramble, and every hollow.

Even that was barely enough.

We danced through the dangers of the forest. The Trollborn ignored them.

The woods behind us were churned under the Trollborn's feet, leaving a chasm of splintered trees and mud.

There was only the forest and the deafening crashes of the Trollborn. The sounds faded slowly, too slowly for us to stop and rest, but we were gaining ground.

We ran and my lungs burned.

We ran and my legs ached.

We ran and my vision blurred.

We came to the graveyard of troll-stones.

The Trollborn was not far behind us, but its crashing was distant. It was enough.

"What now?" Yrsa panted.

Fafnir sucked in huge gulps of air but said nothing. He looked back to the forest. The trees shook as the Trollborn got closer.

I leapt into the crater with the archway and ran my hands along it and closed my eyes to feel its energy and the landvaettir's power around us.

The forest quivered in fear at the poisoned colossus charging through it.

The landvaettir's strength had grown thin. It needed to rest or it would be stretched beyond repair like a dying plant too long without water or sunlight. I pushed some of myself into the landvaettir. It was like trying to rekindle a wildfire with a single, fluttering ember, but a fresh awareness of the forest blossomed in my senses.

The poison in the Trollborn came closer. It snapped trees and infected the ground where it stood. My stomach roiled at the thought of it.

"Come on," Yrsa mumbled.

Around us was infinite life. Bugs and small creatures scuttling and burrowing through the earth. Countless plants and fungi rooted in the soil around us. And there: something forgotten. It stretched out beneath the forest like the roots of an enormous tree, but cold as a cave.

The trollway.

I pushed myself into that dark, cold thread. The soil shifted.

The ground shuddered as the Trollborn came closer.

"Any time now, Alvir."

There was a gap. Enough for a beam of light. No more.

I pressed power down into the earth and coaxed it into the forgotten trollway. The ground moved a little more. A hole opened up beneath the archway.

"Now!" I cried.

Yrsa leapt into the hole without hesitation. Fafnir looked back at the Trollborn's hulking silhouette as it shoved the forest aside. His fists clenched.

"Come on, Fafnir," I said through gritted teeth, still clutching tight at the stone or else the way would close. "We have to save everyone."

He bared his tusks at the Trollborn, then at me, and lurched down into the trollway.

The Trollborn crashed through the trees. It kicked the troll-stones out of its way.

I shoved a burst of power into the trollway. The hole beneath me widened.

The Trollborn leapt forward, swiping its enormous granite fist.

Air buffeted me as the Trollborn's fist missed my head by a hair.

The ground swallowed me, closing almost too soon and caking my hair in mud.

I fell.

ᚠ

The trollway was cold, dark, and still. After the heart-pounding battle and chase through the forest it felt strange, almost unnatural. Where were Fafnir and Yrsa? Should I not have been able to see them, feel them? I half-expected something to emerge out of the blackness and swallow me whole. I edged back until I felt a hard wall of dirt at my back.

I blinked as my eyes adjusted to the dark.

This trollway looked much the same as the other. It was a huge tunnel of dirt carved under the earth. Now that I had seen the troll-stones fitted back together and seen how large the Trollborn were, I realised that even the trolls must have had to hunch when they wandered these subterranean holloways. Roots jutted out from the walls at every angle and mushrooms, echoing with the landvaettir's power, sprouted from the dirt by my feet.

As the features of the trollway came into focus I saw Fafnir and Yrsa's lumpy silhouettes. They had moved away from the trollway entrance and their heads were bent together in fervent conversation.

I walked up to them, my legs still unsteady after the sprint through the forest. They straightened as I got close and stepped apart.

"Is everything alright?"

Fafnir turned to face me and loomed over me, his hulking form blocking the massive trollway.

Yrsa grimaced and shook her head. "Let's get moving."

I nodded and made to go past Fafnir, but the enormous Windborn did not move.

I looked up at his shadowed face. "We need to go, Fafnir. We have to save Vidsetr."

Dirt shook free from the walls as Fafnir's low growl rumbled and echoed up the trollway.

"We could have saved her."

"What?"

"We could have saved her," Fafnir repeated. His words came thick through his tusks and weighed heavy with grief. "You could have saved my sister. You stood next to her as the stone came down. You did nothing."

He took a step towards me. The air in the trollway chilled as he leant down and shoved his tusk-filled face up to mine.

"Tell me why you saved your tree spirit and not my sister."

"I tried to save her." I took half a step back from Fafnir. "I grabbed the person holding her. It was Tjorvid and—"

"Lies!"

He roared the word and slammed a balled fist into the wall.

Stones and dirt fell on top of us as the trollway shook under Fafnir's rage.

"You let my sister die." He followed me as I tried to move out of reach of his clenching fists. "You are in league with Ulfrun. Did she send a raven for you? Did you drag us into the forest to be sacrificed?"

I looked at Yrsa. It was difficult to see her behind Fafnir's shaking form, but I could see she kept her distance. She was not coming to save me. She wanted to hear my answers.

"No, never," I said. "I was sent to Vidsetr by Eylis, the High King's god-speaker. She had not heard from Ulfrun in some time and wanted to know what was wrong."

"This forest is wrong," Fafnir growled. "No good ever

comes from this place. You forced us to come here. You kept things from us. You saved your sister and let mine die."

My mouth opened and closed. The barrage of accusations pelted me like a rain of arrows and my exhausted mind struggled to find an argument that Fafnir would accept. The sorrow and fury that filled him would seek to deflect any explanation. Now that we were safely away from the Trollborn, he had a target for his misery. And I would not be able to stop him taking his justice.

"I tried to save them both. It was my fault Sigrun was captured in that first ambush and when I tried to save her it literally got me killed. She saved herself before we found her with Drifa and those others."

I forced myself to look into Fafnir's deep, glittering eyes. "I thought if we could get the landvaettir free then the ritual would collapse and Ulfrun wouldn't need any sacrifices. That wasn't true. I tried to save Nal, Fafnir. I went right up to them and tried to kill the outlaw holding onto Nal. But when I realised it was Tjorvid... I hesitated."

Fafnir began to growl, but I raised my voice to talk over it.

"That hesitation was all it took and I am sorry, Fafnir. I am sorry."

Fafnir's tusks shone in the dim light. His breathing was deep, ragged, and he stared at me for a long time without moving.

"Fafnir," I said. "I swear to you that I am not working with Ulfrun or that monster Bimyrr. Didn't you see the hate in Ulfrun's eyes when she looked at me? Can't you feel the power that links us? I was never working with Ulfrun, Fafnir, and now I'm Windborn. I will do whatever I can to protect the people of Vidsetr. I know it can't make up for failing to protect your sister, but please, please don't let this stop us from saving all the sisters and brothers and daughters and sons of Vidsetr."

He still didn't move.

Yrsa sidled up beside him and put a hand on his arm. She nodded at me and then looked up at Fafnir. The boar-built Windborn still glared at me with his spear-sharp gaze. I looked back and tried to imagine how I would have felt if

Fafnir had left Sigrun to die.

"If you want to kill me, to take the blood-price for Nal out of my veins, then I won't stop you."

Fafnir shifted, took half a step towards me. Yrsa shoved her hand against his chest. I did not move. If Fafnir decided he wanted me dead there was nothing I could do to stop him. I could fight, but I was tired, body and soul, and he was a seasoned warrior on the precipice of a berserk rage.

"I won't stop you," I said again. "But do it once we have saved Vidsetr. You've seen what is coming for them and they will need our help."

For a long moment we stood, still and silent except for Fafnir's heavy breathing. My heart pounded and I closed my eyes so that I would not see death come for me.

"This is not over, Betrayer," Fafnir shrugged off Yrsa's hand and began to walk off along the trollway. "We save Vidsetr, then there will be a reckoning."

Relief flooded through my limbs and I slumped, shaking, against a dirt wall.

"You better get us home quickly," Yrsa said. "If we can't save Vidsetr then gods only know what he'll do to you."

I pushed myself off the wall and nodded to Yrsa.

"We'll stop them. I won't let those monsters take anyone else."

She shook her head and turned to follow Fafnir.

"I don't think that's up to you, Betrayer."

I watched them go. The name Betrayer stuck between my ribs like a knife. I grimaced against it, but let it come. No matter what they thought of me I would not let Vidsetr fall to these undead trolls and this poisoned god.

I saw the pain in Fafnir's eyes. I would not let that same pain settle in my soul.

I would save my sister and protect my family.

Chapter Thirty
A Shattered Family

Our journey through the trollway took hours. I had almost forgotten how deep we were in the forest but as we trudged endlessly beneath the earth, I was reminded of the vastness of it. Whenever I glanced up I thought of Sigrun and the others running above us. I urged the landvaettir to give them strength and speed, but I did not know how much power was left to it.

Yrsa and Fafnir were silent and I only spoke to direct us through the trollway's forked paths. They had long lost their connection with the landvaettir's magic and trudged beside me, their exhaustion clear on their faces. Whenever we came to a split in the path, I reached out my senses. The forest above us was full of life but every creature was on edge. They had all felt the rising of the Trollborn and knew that poison and death had soaked into the heart of the forest. For its part, the landvaettir lay deep beneath the earth barely moving. It had done all it could and it needed to rest or else it might fade completely. My connection to the landvaettir remained, tenuous, and with it the knowledge of which path to take. Then the landvaettir told of the forest above: it showed me the shuddering of the earth as the Trollborn moved through the forest, but their footsteps were slow and heavy, marching not chasing as the trollway kept us hidden; then it showed me birds and deer bursting out of the undergrowth as panting humans charged past them. Sigrun. Through the landvaettir, I felt the connection to the stones they had taken from the outlaws. Small things with limited power but it was enough for the landvaettir to urge them on like a gust of wind caught in a sail. They had already covered much of the distance to Vidsetr. I stumbled when it showed that to me, but I could not stop, we had to keep moving.

The trollway changed as we lumbered through it. At first we moved through deep burrows near pitch-dark and clogged with wet roots and crumbling dirt. In parts we crept through small ravines and as we splashed through trickling streams we saw the sky. The night was still lit by the Winds, shifting and stretching over the stars as though they were tasked to find us. No matter where the trollway took us, we were always far beneath the surface of the earth. There was no way out. Nothing could reach us.

Eventually, the winding troll-road sloped upwards and the bruised light of dawn filtered down. I squinted against the soft light, harsh after so long so deep in the earth, and saw leaves quivering overhead. The path opened up and we ducked beneath a fallen tree. The dirt beneath us became hard-pressed and well-trodden by beasts and men.

We were back in the forest. We were near the edge.

I turned to Yrsa and Fafnir.

"Are we close?"

Fafnir lifted his head and sniffed. "It is not far."

I let them lead and we hurried on through the thinning trees. Now that we were free of the closeness of the troll-way we had a fresh energy. We were free. We would soon be amongst friends.

Then, I saw houses in the distance. Woodcutters' sheds. We were close.

We picked up our pace and ran to the edge of the forest.

More buildings beyond the trees.

I saw hills, their overgrown slopes climbing to mountains, and then a pink sky. So much sky.

My breath caught in my throat. I had never thought to see so much sky again. The world was open once more. The cage of trees and undergrowth was nearly behind us.

As we sprinted out of the forest, finally free, there was a cry ahead.

A lone arrow whistled past us and sunk into the ground by my feet.

I cried out and leapt aside. Fafnir and Yrsa raised their hands and called out to the village.

Between the buildings at the edge of town, stood two huskalar. Both had bows, one with an arrow nocked and the other with an arrow half-pulled from their quiver.

"It's us, you idiots," Yrsa shouted.

The huskalar who had shot at us said something to his companion and then ran off. The other lowered his bow and beckoned us closer.

We ran past the imitation god-stone that Ulfrun had set into the ground. Something about it tugged at the Windborn power in my chest. I slowed, the others sprinted ahead while I examined the stone. A shiver whispered up my spine as I imagined the troll it had once been part of. The stone looked the same but it felt different. The magic was obvious to me now that my Windborn power was hungry for it. When I was a god-speaker I had needed to raise my second sight to see the pattern of the weave, but now I could taste the magic in the air without effort. The stone was a barrier, a magical defence like those we had slipped through in the forest. It seemed that even in the depths of her fury Ulfrun did not wish harm on the people she had spent her life healing and protecting.

Yrsa called for me and I sprinted to catch up with them. As we reached the huskalar and caught our breath, I looked out into Vidsetr. The town was beginning to stir as bright morning stretched across the sky. People yawned as they wandered out of their houses and collected tools or leaned against a fence to talk with their neighbours.

I frowned. I did not have much experience with raiding or war, but this was not the welcome I had thought to receive. Where was the horde of spear-wielders? Where was the shield wall?

"Snorri," Yrsa asked the huskalar. "Where is the chief? Where's Erri?"

"Inga went to fetch her. She'll be here soon. Isn't Erri with you?"

I stared at him, open-mouthed, but before I could say anything a shout caught my attention. People were calling out. Ormhildr rushed up to us with a small crowd in tow just as a ragged band rushed out of the forest behind us. Sigrun, Drifa and Erri leading the other escapees. They all looked like they were about to collapse with exhaustion but they did not stop.

Ormhildr's group slowed as they reached us but Sigrun and her companions did not. They sprinted across the final stretch to safety. Erri and Drifa collapsed onto the ground. Sigrun sped up and threw her arms around me. For a moment, I didn't know what to do. I worried that my Windborn powers would drain her, that if I returned the embrace it would be too much and she would throw me off.

"You're safe," she whispered, her voice choked.

I shoved my Windborn power down as far as I could and wrapped my arms around her, squeezing gently. A sob shook her shoulders then she shivered and wouldn't stop. I let go of my Windborn power and eased it into Sigrun like a warming blanket. Slowly, her shivering stopped and we pulled ourselves apart, our vision blurred with tears.

Ormhildr scowled at us.

"Well?" she said, looking between us. "Where's Nal and Tjorvid? Where are the others?"

"Nal is dead," Fafnir said, his voice thick. "He says Tjorvid betrayed us."

"What?" Ormhildr looked from me to the massive Windborn. "Tell me what happened."

We explained as best we could. Ormhildr's expression was dour throughout our retelling, in parts she looked to Erri, Sigrun, and Drifa as though to confirm what we were saying. They nodded grimly. When we had finished and the others had corroborated our story the chieftain looked between us all with her mouth set in a deep grimace.

"And these trolls are going to smash through Vidsetr?"

Everyone looked at me.

"I don't know," I said. "The Thrice-Killed wanted to use Vidsetr as a testing ground for the Trollborn, but I think that Ulfrun has built a safeguard to protect you."

Relief washed over their faces. I pointed to Ulfrun's imitation god-stone.

"She has woven a spell into that boulder. We had to cross

similar barriers in the forest, but I think this one has been cast to keep these new trolls from overrunning Vidsetr."

"Will it work?" Ormhildr asked.

"I don't know. Ulfrun was a talented rune-weaver. But this Thrice-Killed... it is something else entirely. Even with all our strength and that of the forest spirit, it was still able to break Ulfrun's hold over the trolls and take them for itself.

"Her barrier might weaken the Trollborn, but I don't know if it will stop them."

Ormhildr looked around. The people before her were bedraggled, tired, and covered in mud and wounds. Any sense of hope and vitality that we had had before we went into the forest had been beaten out of us. Ormhildr had the look of a woman being asked to stand up to a pack of wolves with nothing more than determination and a blunt knife. She glanced back at Vidsetr and when she turned back to us I saw something bright and hard in her eyes.

"Then we cannot rely on this barrier to protect us. We must defend ourselves. How long until these... things reach us?" she asked.

"I don't know. They nearly kept pace with us when chased us. But once we got away they slowed." I looked at Fafnir and Yrsa and then back into the forest. "I would hope we would have a few hours, at least."

"Fine." Ormhildr nodded. She waved at us. "Get some rest. Snorri, I need you to—"

"I will help," Fafnir said, stepping forward. "I do not need rest."

Ormhildr looked him up and down. "My boy," she murmured, "you look like you can barely stand. You need to sleep, eat, get yourself rested. We can prepare for whatever is coming. You need rest. What if you collapse from exhaustion in the middle of the fight?"

"But—"

"Fafnir." She held up a hand. "You have always put others before yourself, but this time I am telling you... No, I am ordering you to go and rest."

The big Windborn looked like he wanted to protest but Yrsa put her hand on his arm. All the running and fighting and grief caught up with him and his shoulders slumped. A sob shook his chest. Yrsa took his enormous hand in both of hers and led him away.

Ormhildr turned to her crowd, urgently discussing what they could use to protect the town, how to gather the townsfolk, who could fight, and what to do with those that couldn't.

I waited awkwardly nearby, unsure where I should go. Sigrun had begun to move away but I worried our relationship was still too tentative for her to want me to join her in what could be the final moments with her family. Briefly, I thought I should turn and go to Ulfrun's, the house was separate from the town and I had always been separate from those I had visited. Perhaps I would find something useful in the house for the coming conflict.

As I turned, Sigrun touched my shoulder.

"Where are you going? Aren't you staying with me?"

"I didn't know if you would want me to," I replied.

She looked at me as though I was mad for thinking anything else. I smiled at her, grateful that our family was finding its way back to itself.

"Alvir, you're family."

We walked together through the town. The relaxed atmosphere of the town shifted as word of the impending attack spread. The people who had, moments before, been chatting amiably to their neighbours were suddenly being asked to flee or else take up arms against a strange and powerful foe.

Pity warred with nervousness at the base of my stomach. I had seen what these Trollborn could do, the hideous strength of the Thrice-Killed, and I would not wish it on any of these people. I also knew I was not abandoning them. I had some strength and I would stand with them. But I had never felt the sickening, quiet tension of a place before a battle. It soaked into me and with each house I looked at I began to shake at the thought of these resurrected trolls smashing through them as easily as a child kicks over an anthill.

My heart lurched when I saw Sigrun's home. The crossbeams with the dragons carved into it. The turf roof with spots of moss and wildflowers.

How much would survive?

Sigrun ushered me through the door. The warmth of the hearthfire was a welcome relief and the smell of breakfast lifted my heart. Inside, this was a sanctuary of love and family. The children dozed in their beds as Ljota stirred a pot of porridge over the fire.

She turned to us as we came in and her worry-soaked face exploded into relief and joy and love. She dropped the spoon and rushed over to her wife. Ljota leapt at Sigrun and they would have fallen over if they'd not collided with the door.

I edged around them, ignoring the tear-soaked whispers of their reunion. They were not for me. We may have been reforging our family, but this was a moment for Sigrun to have with her wife and children.

For my part, I went over to the pot and kept it from spilling over. Sigrun and Ljota woke the children and more tearful joy echoed around the house. Once they had gone quiet, the initial shock and joy now calmed, I set the food out on the table and invited them to join me. The children refused to be parted from Sigrun and squeezed themselves as close as they could get to her on the bench. Sigrun couldn't get her arms free to feed herself but she did not seem to mind and pulled Ama and Raggi in for a hug at every opportunity.

Once again we gave an account of the last few days, although this time we skated over the details for the children's sake. Ljota was ashen-faced by the time we had finished. Her lips pressed together in a thin line.

"Ormhildr is organising a defence," Sigrun said. "She's told me and Alvir to rest, but you will need to get the children away from here."

Ljota frowned. "You're not coming with us?"

Sigrun shook her head. "I'm going to stay."

"But... I heard what you said about those... things. Why aren't we running?"

"If those monsters get through Vidsetr then they'll head straight to Konvald," I said. "Who knows what kind of destruction they will cause when they get there? The High King and his warriors are away. We need to stop them here."

Ljota looked at Sigrun for a long moment, her eyes wide and blurring with tears. Then she looked to me. "Are you going to stay?"

I half-reached out to her before I let my hand fall away. "Yes," I said. "I am going to stay and I swear to you I will not let anything happen to Sigrun. The gods themselves won't stop me from protecting her."

Ljota looked between us again. She looked like she wanted to protest, but she must have seen the desperation, exhaustion, and pleading in our eyes. With a sorrow-heavy sigh, she nodded.

"You have to rest. I won't have you running off to face those things without any sleep. I'll get you a bed ready, Alvir."

We finished our food in silence. Now that I had finally stopped, that I was no longer trapped by the ever-present foliage and looming presence of the landvaettir, my limbs felt heavy and sleep scratched at my eyes.

I breathed in the heady scent of a home well-lived in. A welcome change from the cloying smell of dirt and sap. Ljota got up from the table and gathered belongings for their flight as Sigrun nestled between her children and told them how much she loved them.

Too soon, the beds were made and Ljota was ready to go. She wanted to stay, urged Sigrun to come with them, but my sister shook her head.

"You need to get as far away as you can." She stood and finally managed to slip free of her children. "There's no telling when those things will get here. I need you to get to safety."

The two women embraced, arms wound tight around each other and squeezing as though that would make everything all right. I prayed that it would. Behind them, the children began to shift nervously. I wondered if they had ever seen their mothers look so frightened.

"Hey." I beckoned them over. "Do you remember the runes I showed you?"

Ama kept her younger brother's hand tight in hers as they came over to me, eyes shifting back to Sigrun and Ljota.

"I remember your stones," Ama said.

"That's right. I lost those out in the forest. Do you want to help me make some new ones? We can make something to keep your mothers safe."

Ama's eyes lit up whilst Raggi looked confused.

I told them to find something important, something big enough to draw a rune on, and we would make it magic. The children bustled off and brought me back a toy boat and some wooden animals: a rabbit, a raven, a deer, a fish, and a wolf. The fish and the rabbit were too slim and small so I took the boat and then asked them to each pick their favourite from the rest. The deer and the wolf.

"You're going on an adventure with Ljota, right? So we'll make this boat into a charm to keep you safe on your journey. Then you can each put a rune onto an animal to summon their spirits and keep Sigrun safe. Does that sound good?"

Mute nods.

I had them fetch a piece of cold charcoal as I warmed a knife in the fire then used the hot knife to draw a rune onto the boat and asked them to copy it on their animals. *Protection*. The boat's rune was carved deep with smoke curling up from the wood whilst the runes on the animals were crude and shaky.

"Will they work?" Ama asked, looking sceptically from her rune to mine.

"Of course," I said. "It doesn't matter how straight the lines are. All that matters is how pure the intention is when you set the spell. Now, close your eyes and focus on how much you love your mothers and how much you want to keep them safe."

They screwed up their eyes and grimaced. I smiled and took the toys in my hands. I didn't know if this was going to work, but I needed to try. I took a deep breath and gently pushed some of my power into the toys. The wood soaked up the magic and I heard the toys creak in my hands. I eased back and stopped the Windborn power after a trickle had fed into the toys. I opened my hands. The wood was warm, but only from my Windborn power. The runes were unaffected.

Another piece of me broke in that moment. Here was a final confirmation that I was never going to be a god-speaker again. I was Windborn. My life, what remained of it, would be measured in blood and sharp edges.

I cleared my throat. "Okay. Open your eyes."

Ama's eyes snapped open. Raggi slowly opened one eye, then the other.

"Did it work?" Ama asked.

"You tell me."

I passed them the toys and their eyes lit up.

"They're warm!"

"It's hot!"

I smiled at them. "That means it works. Why don't you give them to Sigrun? And don't forget the boat, too. That's for you and Ljota."

They hurried off to the other side of the house as Ljota and Sigrun reluctantly pulled themselves apart. Their sorrowful faces quickly changed into expressions of delight as the children gave them the newly runed toys. I smiled as the children explained what they had done and how the magic worked.

All too soon the moment was over and Sigrun passed Ljota her pack and the family edged to the door. Ljota smiled at me as she left the house and mouthed a thank you. I nodded, but I had no energy to stand.

Then they had to go.

My heart broke to see Ljota lead them from their huskalar mother. She would be fine, Ljota said, but Ormhildr needed her strength. You know how strong mummy is, she said. Tears rolled down Sigrun's cheeks, cutting through the forest grime still caked there. She gave each of them one last bone-creaking embrace and then they were gone.

I clenched my jaw as my sister's family shattered, at least for a little while. I would not let this be the last time they saw each other. My knuckles cracked as I clenched my fists. I would not let another family lose a mother.

Sigrun stayed at the door, watching them go. I turned back to my half-finished porridge and stared at it as I ate to try and give her some semblance of privacy.

Eventually, she came to sit beside me.

"Thank you," she said and held up the animals in her hands. "They were so happy to have helped."

I smiled back at her.

"I have found that most people want to help, especially children. Even if it doesn't seem like a lot."

"It is a lot," Sigrun said, still looking at the toys. "I'm going to try and get some rest. I pray that it takes those trolls a few days to reach us. Maybe then we'll be ready."

I nodded, unsure how to respond, and fell into the bed Ljota had made for me. It was blissful to sink into a proper bed with a blanket and frame instead of sleeping on packed earth and twigs. When I closed my eyes I could feel the distant writhing of Fafnir and Yrsa's Windborn power and, more distant still, I could feel the drained and near-spent power of the landvaettir.

Outside, people called to each other. I heard lumbering carts and shouts about a barricade. From the sounds of it most were trying to shepherd the livestock and children away to safety.

None of that could contend with my exhaustion and my eyes closed as soon as I hit the bed.

In the moments before sleep took me I felt a shiver run through the earth. Something had shaken the landvaettir's power. The spirit was still there but shrunken even further and retreating to the furthest reaches of the earth.

The Thrice-Killed had shattered the barrier deep in the forest.

The Trollborn were coming.

CHAPTER THIRTY-ONE
ATTACK ON VIDSETR

THEY DID NOT WAKE US UNTIL THE AFTERNOON. My aches and exhaustion had washed away and the many scrapes and slices gifted by branch and bramble had all but healed, leaving only bright lines across my skin. The wonders of being Windborn.

My bittersweet joy was short-lived as the huskalar pounding on the door cried out for us again.

"We're awake!" Sigrun shouted back. She groaned and pulled herself out of bed. "Gods above, I'm not sure I'm up to this. How are you feeling, Alvir?"

"I don't think I'm ready," I said, examining the smudged tattoos across my arms.

"No one is ever ready," Sigrun said as she stretched, her back crackling. "But you found me in the forest and you fought your way out. We'll get you some proper gear this time too. And you'll have me. Come on, let's go find out what's happening."

She offered me some food and changed into her huskalar gear as I ate. I winced at every clink of metal as I imagined what battlefield injury the armour had been made to prevent. I prayed that we had done the right thing staying in Vidsetr.

By the time I looked up, Sigrun was transformed. My sister stood before me like a Death Maiden, the gods' battlefield servants. Chain rings glinted underneath her tunic. Her spear, its ash shaft standing high above her, ended with a long shining blade. She held a shining helm loose in one hand and smiled sheepishly at me.

"A true warrior," I said as I stood, my voice full of awe. "Vidsetr will be well protected with you in the battle lines."

Sigrun smiled, then her eyes widened and she dove over to an old chest. She rummaged through it, throwing old clothes into the room, and pulled out something wrapped in a faded, dusty blanket.

"This is for you," she said and reverently passed it to me.

It was heavier than I expected. I frowned at her and unwrapped the bundle.

Metal glinted in the light from the dying hearth. A worn handle, a hilt covered in engraved spirals, a dull blade with runes running along the middle.

"You're giving me your sword?" I said, incredulous. "Do you trust me with it?"

She looked at the sword, a strange expression etched into her face, then she met my eyes. "I found it after Dad died. It was wrapped up in a cloth bundle under his floorboard. I think it was your mother's."

Something twisted in my gut.

I dropped the blanket to the floor and held up the sword. A chill ran up my spine as my fingers found the place where someone's fingers had worn grooves into the grip after long use. Where my mother's hand had been.

Tears welled in my eyes. How many years had it been since I had lost my mother? How many times had I wished I could take her hand one more time? I squeezed the grip and the old leather creaked.

I looked at Sigrun. She had stepped back and hunched her shoulders as though trying to hide from me, perhaps unsure of how I would react to this gift.

"Thank you," I whispered. "Thank you, Sigrun."

I put the sword on the bench beside me and grabbed Sigrun, pulling her into a fierce embrace. Quiet sobs wracked my frame and with each one Sigrun's chain shirt shook. It was a long moment before I could pull myself free and even then we looked into each other's red-rimmed eyes, feeling perhaps for the first time like we were truly family.

"Come on," Sigrun said, her voice husky with emotion. "Let me show you how to put it on."

She helped me belt up the sword and gave me a few tips on how to use it before we left the house.

Vidsetr was ghostly quiet. Anyone unable to fight had long since left and those that could fight had been summoned to the edge of the forest. The closer we came to the dark edge of the Trolbjolvid, the noisier the gathered host became.

A ramshackle barricade crossed the ground a few paces beyond the houses. Upturned carts, rough timber, barrels, and crates had been tied together and a crowd of people—huskalar and armed townsfolk—gathered behind it, trying to prepare.

Fafnir and Yrsa were already there, Fafnir's huge frame loomed high above the barricade as he stared into the forest whilst Yrsa stalked along the crowd, barking advice to the inexperienced. Their presence seemed to be invoking equal parts consternation and relief. It seemed that people were pleased to have the Windborn with them, but it looked like they would rather not be fighting and those awkwardly clutching spears and shields would rather have fled.

This was not something that could be run from. Bimyrr Thrice-Killed would charge its creatures through Vidsetr like an avalanche and if there was any hope of saving it then we had to make a stand.

I took a deep breath as we approached the crowd. Everyone turned to look at us: Sigrun, clinking metal with every step, and the once-god-speaker beside her.

I felt inadequate in only my tunic and cloak with my mother's sword on my belt. Sigrun walked like a warrior, a saga-worthy hero. I felt like a man broken and stitched back together. I was uncertain of my role here. I was not an experienced fighter like Sigrun and the other huskalar, but neither was I like the townsfolk with a spear shoved into their hands and who had the gods to look after them.

I was Windborn.

Sigrun took us to Erri and Ormhildr. The two leaders talked together in hushed tones but stood to face us as we approached. In the heartbeat before we reached them, Sigrun squeezed my shoulder.

"You'll be okay," she whispered. "I'll protect you."

I nodded but could not force any words through the clog of fear in my throat.

"Welcome to the battle line," Erri said, a grim smile on his face. "Alvir, fetch a shield and a spear. It's all we can spare."

I nodded, grateful that there was anything for me at all, and found myself the equipment.

"The others have told me what to expect," Ormhildr said as I returned. "We have decided our best tactic is to try and hold them here, hence the barricade. There are stones for us to sling at these trolls as they come for us, larger ones for the Windborn to throw."

"Where do you want me?" Sigrun asked. The quaver in her voice was gone. My sister, whom I had shared an emotional embrace with in her home, was gone. Now she was huskalar truly, battle-ready.

Erri directed her along the barricade as calmly as though he were giving her directions through town. The ease with which he spoke of placements before the battle made the hairs stand on the back of my neck.

Ormhildr looked me in the eyes, pulling my attention away from Sigrun as she walked away. "Your task is the same as Fafnir and Yrsa. You are to throw yourself wherever the fighting is thickest, defend my people and kill their enemies. I will not let these monsters destroy my town, Windborn. I expect you to do everything you can to protect these innocent people."

Fear squirmed at the pit of my stomach and rose like bile at the back of my throat. I swallowed it down. "Of course, Ormhildr. I will do whatever it takes."

"Good."

She nodded and turned away, returning to her conversations with Erri.

They continued like that for a while, discussing plans within plans and escape routes should the worst come to pass. With every passing moment, my fear soaked into my bones like a night's winter chill.

I wandered up and down the barricade, trying to pull on my experience as a god-speaker and give some sense of comfort to the nervous levy. They smiled at my prayers, but I saw the glances at the shield and spear and my blurring tattoos.

I told them the gods were with us.

They did not believe me.

The light of the afternoon began to fade, sunlight charred to a deep red, and the forest darkened.

All idle chatter stopped.

Erri clambered onto the barricade, stepping into the last shafts of light before the sun dipped behind the mountains.

"Friends," he called. "Do not fear. I know some of you think that this is a fool's task, to stand here and face these broken trolls, but I ask you: do you know me for a fool? Of course not. I know what marches through the forest and I stand with you.

"There may be trolls and foreign monsters shambling through the forest, but I am not afraid. Do you know why?

"I am not afraid because I know that the gods are with us. I know that you are all by my side and we cannot fail.

"We stand here to protect those we love. We stand here to show this poisoned godling that the warriors of the Fjalmark fear nothing and will not be defeated.

"Show me your strength, friends. Cry out and show these monsters that you are to be feared!"

A ragged cheer.

"Is that all you have? You don't cheer for me. Show me your battle-cry! Shout to show the gods our devotion and these monsters how they should fear us! You are powerful. Show me your strength!"

A roar: ground-shaking, spirit-stoking, war-mongering.

The cry echoed out into the forest, bouncing between trees until it was lost in the ferns and moss and stone.

I half-expected the Thrice-Killed to charge out of the forest after our challenge. Hearts thumped and adrenaline thrilled through the veins of Vidsetr's defenders. We were all eager to set ourselves against the monsters of the Trolbjolvid.

ᚠ

We waited.

The trees shifted in the breeze.

For a long time, there was only silence.

All eyes locked onto the darkness in the Forest of Broken Trolls. Feet shifted as minds began to conjure images of what might be coming for them.

Then the trees shivered.

The ground thumped in time to heavy, slow footsteps.

People huddled down against the barricade, caught between wanting to hide and the need to see what was coming.

Hulking forms appeared between the trunks. Three massive shapes took up all the space under the canopy with heads that jostled the low branches. At first they were only shadows, hints of the blocky Trollborn as they shoved their way to the edge of the woods. Then they began to glow. Shimmering Wind-light glittered across their boulder-limbs although it was stained with the black streaks of the Thrice-Killed's power.

I gripped my spear until the wood creaked.

"Get your stones ready," Erri called. "This is when we show the gods what we're made of."

People gathered their slings and rocks. Fafnir stomped over to a pile of boulders as big as barrels that had been dragged to the edge of the barricade. Yrsa ushered me over to a similar pile, though our stones were smaller than Fafnir's.

We waited.

Tension chilled the air like winter.

The Trollborn stopped at the edge of the forest and stood stone-still as though waiting for us to make the first move.

Whispers from along the barricade. Now that the enemy was here, they wanted the battle to start.

"I thought they'd look like that Stoneskin Windborn, you know?"

"What are they waiting for?"

"They're bigger than I thought they'd be."

In the fading light, it was difficult to tell where the bulky silhouette of one Trollborn ended and another began. As I squinted at them I realised that they had stopped a little way behind Ulfrun's god-stone. Its power pushed against them, spluttering as it brushed against the power trapped in those living boulders, and the poisoned light shining from the

Trollborn flickered in irritation.

A darker power appeared behind them. Like a clot of blood falling into a clear stream, the Thrice-Killed's presence blossomed. Its wet silhouette shone in the light from its monstrous minions.

The Trollborn parted to let the shambling figure through.

Compared to its boulder-built followers, the Thrice-Killed looked small, though there was someone beside it who was smaller still. It looked like two children hiding behind their parents, but I knew the two smaller silhouettes were as dangerous as the Trollborn, if not more so.

Bimyrr's skin was pale, still shining with moisture, but it no longer blossomed with mud and mould and its breathing seemed to be shallow, laboured. A chill went up my spine as I saw that the snow bear arm was somehow reattached. I prayed that it would be weakened outside of its rotten domain.

It said something to the figure beside it, holding out its withered hand to keep them back, then it shuffled up to Ulfrun's god-stone.

It reached out and pressed its dripping corpse-hand against the painted stone.

Even from a distance I felt the magic of the Thrice-Killed press against Ulfrun's protections. It felt like two waves crashing together with neither being able to overpower the other.

The Thrice-Killed leaned into the stone, stained teeth bared, until its whole body was pressed against the dry paint and stone.

The air sizzled. A clap of magical power. A cry of agony.

The Thrice-Killed staggered back, smoke trailing from withered fingers. It clutched its hand to its chest and snarled something at the Trollborn behind it.

"Stones ready," Erri called as he took up a sling.

The monsters stepped froward, then jogged, then built to a charge. They barrelled forward, rolling their shoulders as though trying to break through a locked door.

Slings were loaded with stones and began to spin. The air began to hum as the stones whirled in their leather cradles.

The Trollborn shuddered as they slammed into Ulfrun's barrier. The Wind-light dancing across their stone bodies stuttered and flickered like lightning.

Another snap of power through the air.

They stumbled forward like dazed drunks.

They were weakened by Ulfrun's magic, but they were through.

"Loose!"

A hail of stones flew from the barricade. The Trollborn raised their arms as chips of stone were blasted from their limbs.

I picked up one of the stones around me, each about the size of a skull, and threw it as hard as I could. My Windborn power surged and sent the stone whipping through the air. It smashed into the nearest Trollborn's foot, knocking them to their knees.

Fafnir roared. A boulder soared through the air and crashed into the hobbled Trollborn. Its body pushed against the falling boulder then its Wind-light flashed once, twice. The Trollborn fell backwards and as its body shook the ground the troll-stones rolled apart. It was dead once more.

The Trollborn could die.

A cheer from the barricade. Fresh stones rained down as everyone took up their slings with fresh vigour.

More chips broke away from the two remaining Trollborn but whatever weave had tried to hold them back, that had torn and incapacitated the Trollborn, was evaporating. The stuttering Wind-light shining between their limbs shone clear once again. One of the Trollborn took a firm step forward, then another. It looked at the barricade and I felt the weight of its gaze.

Fafnir threw another massive stone. It arced towards the Trollborn's chest.

The Trollborn raised its arm and smashed it out of the air.

"Aim for the middle one," I called as I threw my heavy rock at the still-shivering Trollborn.

My stone soared through the air and smashed into the Trollborn's chest. It rocked half a step backwards as more slingstones chipped away at its stone flesh. The light dancing across its chest flickered and its stone limbs drooped as its magic faltered.

I glanced down the barricade and saw Fafnir wrapping his arms around one of the boulders, ready to throw it at the weakened Trollborn.

He put his shoulder under the wagon-sized stone, ready to loose, then heard the call to aim for the other Trollborn. His eyes went wide and he twisted strangely as he threw. The boulder bounced along the ground like a rock in a landslide.

It carved craters into the earth with every tumble.

The boulder whistled past the standing Trollborn, close enough to clip it and send shards of rock flying, then with a crack like thunder it slammed into the shoulder of the shivering Trollborn.

Stone exploded as the Trollborn's arm was torn from its body.

Trees and branches snapped as the shockwave of shattered stone crashed into the forest.

The Thrice-Killed screamed as spearhead-sized shards sliced into its bloated body.

It shuffled forward and slapped a hand down onto the arm-less Trollborn.

The air shivered, the Wind-light faded, black mould spread over the Trollborn like morning frost.

The Thrice-Killed shouted something to the blackened Trollborn in the rough tongue of the Daendrec. It straightened and shuffled on, looking like a stone-built imitation of its master.

I threw another stone. It arced high and I prayed that it would find its mark in the Thrice-Killed's skull.

The black Trollborn shifted and took the hit on its chest without flinching.

I cursed and went to find another stone but the ground started to shake.

"Hold!"

I looked around in time to see the first Trollborn smash through the barricade.

Bodies, screams, and splinters flew through the air.

Warriors surged forward with spears and shields raised.

They stabbed at the monster. Their blades bounced from stone skin.

The Trollborn turned its fury onto its attackers. It fell upon them with wide, sweeping blows of boulder-fists.

Shields splintered. Ribs cracked. Bodies flew.

Fighters, huskalar and levy both, sprinted to join the fight. The chaos suffocated me, even from a distance. Bones crunched under heavy stone feet. Axes pinged from moss-mantled limbs.

I had spent so much of my life trying to heal, to preserve life, but here I stood, spear in hand, as it was snuffed out in front of me as easily as beetles crushed underfoot. Fear rooted me so deeply I could do nothing.

Erri appeared beside me and shook my shoulder. He gestured to a group of huskalar behind him with grim faces, "Alvir, take these warriors and deal with that monster then help us kill this one." He leapt onto a piece of the once-barricade, waving his spear. "With me! We have the Warrior's strength and we will kill this troll!"

With a scream he charged the Trollborn and a tide of warriors went with him.

I watched them for a heartbeat as they washed up on the Trollborn's feet like the surf against a cliff. Fafnir and Yrsa charged out from the crowd like frothing waves, but nothing slowed the Trollborn. How could we win now?

One of the huskalar grabbed my shoulder and spun me round.

"Come on, Alvir," a familiar voice said. "We promised we would protect them."

I looked into Sigrun's eyes, hooded under her helm, and tried to smile.

"We did," I whispered. In that moment, I saw her children, her home, and all the others who had been forced to flee. I looked at the huskalar behind her and called, with a confidence I did not feel, "Let's go kill that thing."

We sprinted towards the shuffling black Trollborn. I winced at the screaming we ran away from, but the best thing I could do was try to stop this Trollborn from joining that fight.

The Thrice-Killed shuffled on but the Trollborn outpaced it and there was a healthy gap between them.

Some of the huskalar threw their spears as we got close. They pinged uselessly from its stone hide.

"What do we do?" Sigrun asked, breathing heavy.

I stammered as the crippled Trollborn limped on, towering over us even from a distance.

"Shield wall," Sigrun yelled, unable to wait for my decision.

The huskalar fell into line in an instant, shields locked and eyes forward. Spears lowered to make a bristling line of steel and wood.

I stood behind them, my spear held loose in my hand. This wasn't going to work. The barricade had splintered as easily as kindling. Bodies would be no obstacle.

The Trollborn picked up its shuffling pace and aimed for the centre of the shield wall.

"No," I cried. "Space yourselves, encircle it. Fight like wolves."

They looked back to me, then to Sigrun. She nodded and they broke formation a heartbeat before a monolithic foot swept past with enough force to shatter shields and snap bones.

The huskalar circled around the Trollborn and as it turned to face one of them, the warriors on the opposite side of the circle leapt into slash and stab and bludgeon.

It swept a massive arm at its attackers, but they had already dodged back.

I sank my spear butt into the ground, to free my hand, and moved in to join the circle. Black water splattered across me as the Trollborn spun around again.

Another clatter of arms against the Trollborn's back. The poisoned light across its body flickered in irritation and it twisted again. This time it clipped a huskalar's shield and they went flying through the air.

It followed the huskalar and as it stomped past me, I lunged.

My hand slipped on the slick stone then my fingers caught in a crack and I was dragged along with the Trollborn's leg.

My Windborn power shifted eagerly under my skin as it

scented the strength inside the Trollborn.

I pulled.

The Trollborn's power was cold, furious, poisoned.

Its strength burned through my veins. My heart pounded and with every beat the pain spiked through my entire body.

The Warrior is come. His fury will destroy us all. We mourn for deaths we have yet to face.

We are imprisoned in the sky. The world feels small beneath us and we are cursed to see it only in darkness.

The outlaws grab my neck and force me to my knees. The Winds have cracked above me. The stones glow ahead of me. The glint of a knife. Sharp agony.

Black sweat began to bead on my skin and mould blossomed from my fingertips.

The Trollborn slowed, stumbled.

The damp vines and mud that joined its stone limbs slackened, leaving gaps between its boulder chest and monolith arms.

I stumbled back, clutching my cold-burning, blackening hand. The huskalar, warriors down to their marrow, leapt forward. They stabbed spears and clubs into the thin gaps between the Trollborn's rocky limbs. They leaned against them, grimacing as they pulled and stretched the stone limbs apart.

Magic ripped up my veins like poisoned thorns. A cry of pain from the Trollborn. My bones creaked under the power I had taken. Blood leaked from my nose. A scream ripped free of my throat.

A thunder-loud crack and the Trollborn's leg was ripped from its body.

It tumbled onto its side, holding its one remaining arm up to keep it free.

The huskalar danced in. The Trollborn's pained swipes threw up clods of mud as its arm carved through the ground.

The huskalar dug their weapons back into the gaps even as the stone limbs began to knit themselves back together.

I had taken too much from the Trollborn.

I felt every spear tip between my bones. Pain erupted under my kneecaps, a searing slice within my wrist, my spine felt like it was falling apart.

I tried to scream but I had no breath.

I fell to the floor, curling into a ball. My skin, darkened by bog water and black mould, twitched as my bones creaked under the weight of the Trollborn's death throes.

The husksalar were too distracted with their killing to notice my agony,

I was too taken by pain to see the Thrice-Killed grab one of the huskalar.

Then the Trollborn died.

Its limbs gave way, flying out like an avalanche. Most of the huskalar dodged out of the way but some screamed as their arms or legs were crushed under the weight of the tumbling troll-stones.

The pressure in my flesh eased. With the Trollborn gone, I no longer felt its pain though its power still whirled through my veins. The memory of it kept me shivering, but I was able to push myself to my knees in the slick mud.

"God-Bane indeed," the Thrice-Killed growled.

I swung a heavy head to look at it. It had a huskalar by the neck, their legs kicked as it held them high.

"I had hoped to bring these three monsters to bear on Konvald so that I could watch from a distance. No matter. I will use what I have left to tear down its walls and I will raze the city myself."

Those huskalar that could stand pushed themselves to their feet.

Two charged, spears levelled.

The Thrice-Killed let them sink their spears deep into its side. It snarled at them and batted them aside with its matted, bear paw. They flew back, rolled in the mud, lay still.

"This one's blood smells like yours, God-Bane." He shook the huskalar in his hand and they wriggled like a caught fish.

Ice-terror in my veins.

Sigrun.

"If you let me pass I will not kill her. No one else here needs to die."

"Don't—" Sigrun's words were cut off as the Thrice-Killed threw her to the ground and stomped on her chest with a hoof-foot. Sigrun cried out in pain. She clawed at the unnaturally thin leg pinning her to the floor but she could not move it.

"A simple choice, Betrayer. You have felt my power. It festers in your blood, even now. You cannot stand before a god."

It raised its voice to carry past me. I heard the nervous shifting of the huskalar behind me. I wanted to reassure them, to tell them it would be okay, but I could not take my eyes from Sigrun as she was pushed further into the squelching mud.

The power of the Trollborn writhed within me. It bucked and kicked like a frenzied elk. I couldn't think properly. I pushed it down; I wanted to throw it like lightning from my fingertips. The dirt-ridden sweat and mould on my skin shifted and dripped down my hands. The hairs on the back of my arms twitched as the Trollborn's strength collected in my fists.

I looked at the Thrice-Killed. They stamped harder on Sigrun's chest. I heard the chain shirt ping as some of its rings popped.

"Answer quickly, Betrayer."

I drew my mother's sword. My fingers slid into the grooves where her fingers had been.

I pushed the Trollborn's strength into my legs, my sword arm.

"Very well," the Thrice-Killed drawled. "I tried to—"

The world blurred as I sprinted forward, powered by a Trollborn's soul.

The Thrice-Killed's eyes went wide.

It swiped its snow-bear arm at me, red-stained claws slashing at my face.

My mother's sword flashed.

The sword slowed as it bit into fur and flesh. The power of the Thrice-Killed stopped the blade. I pulled deeper, drew on my strength.

The sword sliced through Bimyrr. Its monstrous arm fell to the ground, spurting dead blood.

It snarled. Its other hand curled into a fist that slammed down at Sigrun's head.

Without thinking, I pushed all my stolen power and the strength of my beating heart into my other hand. I shoved the Thrice-Killed back, away from Sigrun.

It flew back with the force of a tempest. Trees snapped as it crashed into the forest.

All my power was gone. My limbs felt hollow, my muscles like water, and I collapsed onto the churned ground beside Sigrun.

The huskalar behind us, those that were left, cheered. As their voices faded I heard again the crunch and screams of the battle still raging beside Vidsetr.

She coughed, pushed herself up onto her elbows. "Alvir, what... I told you not—"

"I will not abandon you." I rolled onto my front and raised myself to my hands and knees with shivering limbs.

The huskalar came to help us to our feet. I nodded and looked to the forest.

Branches tumbled from the canopy where they had shattered as the Thrice-Killed smashed through them. Somewhere within the forest I felt the Thrice-Killed begin to stir. I did not have the strength to face him again.

I glanced over to the battlefield. The Trollborn swayed and swiped at the minuscule warriors around it. Fafnir stood tall above them. As I watched he caught a blow from the Trollborn, tried to catch it on his enormous shield, but its strength was too much. He was thrown back, smashing into a house. The wall splintered inward and the thatch tumbled down onto him.

"Come on," I said, forcing myself to stand straight even though my body screamed at me to lay down, to sleep, to die. "This isn't over."

ᚠ

Bloody, bruised, broken we ran.

Water splashed across my face and within a few heartbeats the hiss of rainfall swept over us.

We sprinted to the battle. I pushed through the crowd, most of them the conscripted fighters who were staying well out of reach of the Trollborn's boulder-fists.

Someone had gotten a rope around the Trollborn's neck and whilst Yrsa and Fafnir kept the Trollborn's attention, a team of fighters tried to topple it.

The Trollborn leaned back and it looked like it would work. Its head twisted. Too far. All the way around. Then with a shiver of its stone limbs it was somehow facing the other direction, leaning over the rope-wielding warriors with furious intent.

Some of them managed to drop the rope. Most were caught in the downward strike of earth-heavy fists. Bones cracked as stone thumped into the mud, sending a spray of dirt and blood into the air.

The rope trailed from the Trollborn's neck like a failed noose. Warriors tried to grab hold of it, but the strength of the stone monster was too much and they were thrown off their feet as it bucked this way and that.

"Yrsa, Fafnir!" Erri's voice. It cut across the carnage with the long practice of screaming over battlefields. "Get hold of that rope!"

The two Windborn rushed forward. Yrsa danced between the earth-shaking blows of the Trollborn like a bird dancing through a wolf's jaws. Fafnir charged forward and smashed his shield into the Trollborn's leg, making it stumble long enough for Yrsa to leap and grab the rope.

She wrapped it around her arm and tugged. The Trollborn lurched back but kept its footing. Fafnir leapt forward and put his weight on the rope as well. This time, the Trollborn whipped back and as it strained against the rope another was tossed over its neck. Then one over a leg as it tried to stamp down on one of the huskalar.

People swarmed over the ropes and began to pull. The Trollborn began to shift itself around, to face Fafnir and Yrsa, but its leg slid in the mud, throwing it off balance. It wasn't enough.

I sprinted over and grabbed hold of the rope on its leg. My shoulders shivered with exhaustion and my fingers began to tingle with cold. I heaved on the rope.

Its foot shifted again.

We pulled again and the leg was dragged out from under the Trollborn.

The ground shook as the monster slammed onto its back, mud exploding up around it like a geyser.

More ropes flew out from the crowd as we tied it down. The Trollborn squirmed, but between the wet mud and the ropes still holding it, it couldn't right itself.

"Tear it apart," Sigrun shouted. "Get between the stones and pull."

I kept hold of the rope, keeping the Trollborn captive. I looked over to the forest. The Thrice-Killed shuffled towards us, limping through the trees with teeth bared. Power radiated out from it like a tidal wave saturated with rage.

Behind it, figures of blue light flickered into being.

Ghosts.

The echoes floated forward like morning mist. Their forms shifted as they moved. In one moment they swelled as several ghosts came together then they broke apart and stretched like reflections on a raging river.

I lurched forward as the Trollborn kicked to try and dislodge the huskalar pulling apart its limbs. Its soundless scream of agony shivered through the air.

"Take hold of this rope," I shouted to the nearest warriors. They turned to me, confused, from where they were trying to pry the Trollborn's leg from its body. "Now!"

Whether it was some vestige of my god-speaker's authority that still clung to me, or fear that they had seen me take down the other Trollborn, I didn't care. They fell from the Trollborn and took up the rope.

I waited for their calloused hands to take up the slack then let go.

As soon as the rope left my hands, the Trollborn's leg began to buck. It kicked out and the warriors clinging to the line were dragged this way and that. But they held on.

I moved towards the Trollborn.

Its leg jerked again. It clipped my shoulder, the barest touch. I flew aside. Agony ripped through my chest as my arm was nearly wrenched from my body.

Before I could let myself give in to the pain, I clambered

up and rushed back to the Trollborn.

Another kick.

I ducked and the stone foot sailed over my head.

I lunged and pressed my hand against the Trollborn's body, held still by the myriad ropes across its torso.

The stone was hot with rage, shivering with barely contained power.

Another wrenching kick from the Trollborn. My hand slipped. As it was slammed back down my fingers sliced on a crack in the stone. I winced then shoved my fingers deep into the crack. Steam poured from my hand as the heat of the Trollborn burned my blood away.

Fury and frustration pressed against my skin.

I pulled.

The landvaettir sleeps. It will not stand against a god and without it the stone-kin cannot. I charge through the forest, crushing trees in my haste. The Warrior hunts me. The trollway is ahead. If I can reach it then I may escape. The entrance is—

The mortals fight amongst themselves as though their lives have any meaning. We watch from the sky. Sometimes, a death leaves a splinter-crack in our sky-prison. Is this by design? A trap by the gods? After an age one of us slips through the crack and resurrects the mortal with its power. Windborn, they call them.

My brother is finally teaching me how to wield a spear. He shoots me a lopsided smile as he brushes blond hair from his eyes. "Come on then," he says. I charge, whipping my staff forward in a feint before whirling it around to strike his leg. Fafnir slaps my staff aside with his and moves his leg back. "You can do better than that, sister." That smile again. I smile back. I charge again.

I whipped my hand away and looked with horror on the captive Trollborn.

Somewhere, soaked into the stone and woven into whatever remained of the trolls and Winds, was Nal's soul.

I looked over to Fafnir. His face was contorted by rage and effort as he struggled to keep the Trollborn tethered to the ground.

I swallowed my nausea, pressed both hands to the

Trollborn and drained it of all its power and memories.

My brother hasn't sparred with me since he came out of the forest. He hides his face beneath a hood and barely says a word. I want to show him that I don't care what happened, what he looks like. I still want to spend time with him, spar with him. He's my brother.

Pain rippled through my skin, squeezed my bones, and boiled my veins as the Trollborn fought me.

It wanted to live.

I did not stop. My arm wrinkled and blackened.

The Trollborn slowed.

Its power faded.

Its limbs were torn apart.

The Trollborn died. A wave of power exploded outwards and everyone was thrown back.

I rolled through the mud as the stolen power and memories overwhelmed me.

I looked over to my brother, so changed once he became Windborn, and my heart broke to see him so battered and broken. His chest rose and fell with great heaving breaths as he pushed himself to his feet.

No. I shook my head and closed my eyes.

"Sigrun," I called for my sister as waves of freezing agony crashed against my bones like countless knives.

Someone pulled me to my feet. I looked at them as I stood. One of the gods' new mortals.

A sense of vertigo. I should tower over this bag of flesh and blood. Fear should run through their thumping heart. I clenched my fist. I would teach this meat-thing fear.

"Alvir?"

I shook my head and looked long and hard at my sister. Her eyes were ringed with exhaustion and worry.

"Alvir, are you alright?"

"I'm fine." I tried to smile, but the pain clawing under my skin turned it into a grimace.

"That thing is coming back and he's brought company."

I turned to see the Thrice-Killed walking over the corpses, its eyes locked onto me. A rush of feelings surged out of the maelstrom in my chest. Fear at the Thrice-Killed's power.

Anger at what it had done to me.

All around him the ghosts rushed forward, moving through the barricade as though it was no more than mist.

The Thrice-Killed stopped. It kept its eyes on me as it tore the sliced stub of the snow bear arm from its own body with the rip and pop of tearing gristle and bone. Then it lifted one of the dead huskalar from the ground by the forearm and, with one foot pressed down onto her chest, it ripped the arm free.

Bimyrr held the limb aloft and I felt its power surge through the air as black mould covered the arm like a sudden frost. The Thrice-Killed shoved the freshly stolen, newly poisoned arm onto its body and once again it was whole.

"Get behind me." Sigrun's voice shivered with fear, but she still shoved me behind her as the ghosts charged the battered defenders of Vidsetr.

She stabbed her spear into the nearest ghost as it reared up to attack. The blade cut through its chest and the ghost's light flapped like a torn sail.

It did not care. Its arms slammed down. Sigrun raised her shield.

The shield caught the shining arms. I thought we were safe. Then the arms flowed through the shield and flesh sizzled.

Sigrun screamed and lurched backwards. The ghost followed, arms raised.

I shoved the mixed memories and surging power within myself to one side and lunged with my mother's sword.

The blade sparkled with blue light as it sliced through the summoned ghost, cutting it in two.

The ghost turned away from Sigrun as its body knit back together.

It swiped at me, trying to bat me aside. I grabbed for its wrist and felt my flesh burn, then I pulled on the ghost.

It flickered out.

I howled as the ghost's power mixed with the Trollborn's strength and my Windborn power. It felt like I was drowning, my lungs full and bursting. I looked around to see the ghosts swarming over what was left of Vidsetr's defenders. I could not stop.

The Thrice-Killed had nearly reached the battle. Erri had gathered a couple of huskalar and tried to resurrect the barricade to give them some protection. They stabbed at the Thrice-Killed with their spears and cried defiance with battle-hoarse throats.

The Thrice-Killed ignored them, it let the spears sink into its already dead flesh and rammed a fist into the barricade. It hit like a battering ram. Splinters flew. Warriors screamed. The way was clear.

I looked around and saw the ghosts spreading through Vidsetr like wildfire. Weapons flew through their incorporeal bodies, slowing them but not stopping them. If they could not be killed then they might reach the children. I heard the Thrice-Killed roar and then a sickening crunch of wood and bone.

"Fafnir." I called to the massive Windborn and saw him trying to swipe through several ghosts with a charred roofbeam.

He looked over to me and in that moment one of the ghosts lunged and wrapped a tentacle-like arm around Fafnir's wrist. The Windborn bellowed and dropped his smouldering club.

The other ghosts moved forward and began to whip him. I sprinted towards him. The splattering sizzle of flesh grew louder.

I grabbed at the ghosts and pulled. One by one they blinked out. For each ghost that I dragged into myself, I felt my ribs creak and splinter from the inside. I screamed and pulled another ghost into myself. And another.

Then the world went dark.

The ghosts were gone.

Fafnir shivered on the ground and looked at me with begrudging gratitude. He pushed himself to his feet and I saw a weave of burns all across his skin.

"You need to fight the Thrice-Killed," I said.

Fafnir looked from me to the god shuffling towards us. "I have not the strength. You hurt it before. Do it again."

I glanced back at the Thrice-Killed. His slimy flesh shone in the light of countless ghosts.

"I can give you strength," I said and held out my hand. "Then I can deal with these ghosts."

Fafnir looked at me, scepticism clouding his brow.

"Please, Fafnir. Let me help you." I held out my hand. "For Nal."

His expression turned stormy at the mention of his sister. His jaw clenched, pushing his tusks out to the side, but he nodded and wrapped his massive hand around mine.

For the shortest moment, my Windborn power tried to pull on Fafnir's strength. Fafnir's eyes went wide and he fell to one knee.

Then I pushed my stolen power into Fafnir.

I gave him the strength of the Trollborn. I found Nal's life trapped in my chest. I found the deep love Nal had for her brother and the joy she felt when she sparred with him. I found the memories of riding on his shoulders, pretending to hunt monsters in the forest. All of this I gave him.

I thought of my sister and the joys and time we could have spent together, if I had been stronger, braver, and had returned to her. Fafnir could protect her. If I gave him everything then he could defeat the Thrice-Killed and keep my sister safe.

I pushed. I gave him everything.

It felt like I stood under a waterfall but with every passing drop of water part of me was torn away. Clumps of me fell away like a cliff into the sea.

It stopped.

Fafnir took his hand away.

My body was cold. I fell to my knees, shivering. I felt hollow and brittle.

I looked to Fafnir.

He stood taller than I had ever seen him. His cheeks were flushed. Wind-light shivered across his skin.

He looked at me.

"Thank you, Alvir." There were tears in his eyes. "It is such a gift to see my sister again."

I nodded, words would not come. Fafnir grabbed my arm, deliberately wrapping thick fingers around my skin, and pulled me to my feet. I could not stop my power from drawing back some of what I had given to Fafnir. It was not much, but it stopped my shivering and gave me the strength to stand.

"Now, you can fight," he said to me.

He picked up the roofbeam he had been using to fend off the ghosts, hefting it as though it were as light as a willow switch.

"Let us see if this god will survive a fourth death."

He roared, the sound shook the ground and left a ringing in my ears. Then, with all the fury and strength of the Warrior, Fafnir charged the Thrice-Killed.

CHAPTER THIRTY-TWO
KILLING GHOSTS

THE BATTLE STOPPED. Everyone turned to watch the troll-strong Windborn fight the Thrice-Killed god. They came together like a landslide meeting a tidal wave. Fafnir bunched his barrel-sized fists and slammed them again and again into Bimyrr and with every blow the ground shook.

I forced myself to turn away, I wanted to help Fafnir, but others needed my help.

The ghosts overran Vidsetr. Many loomed over cowering figures, whipping them with incorporeal arms. Flesh singed with every swing. A few ghosts had pressed their limbs against buildings that smouldered at their touch. It was as though the Winds themselves had descended to set fire to Vidsetr. Rippling ghosts of green and blue flames sprinted between burning buildings, silent as death.

My whole body shivered. I felt brittle and hollow. My bones ached and my skin burned. Cuts, bruises, and red raw lines littered my arms where my stolen power stretched my skin from the inside. I took a breath and stood straight. I gripped my sword tight. I felt the memory of my mother's hand in mine.

I ran to the fight. Two ghosts whipped their arms at some warriors huddling behind their shields even as they were pushed against a half-collapsed building. They sliced and stabbed at the ghosts, whose bodies grew tattered and flapped in some non-existent wind, but they were at a stalemate. As fast as Vidsetr's defenders could attack the ghosts their bodies rebuilt themselves.

I swung my sword into the legs of the nearest ghost. Its legs broke apart and twisted like smoke, then shifted and became whole again.

It turned to me, batting an arm at me as though I were a nuisance fly. As its arm brushed my shoulder, I pulled. For a heartbeat, my skin burned at the ghost's touch, then it flickered out and its power flowed into me.

My muscles swelled, pressing against my creaking bones. I fell against the building and screamed as my skin stretched with this fresh strength. My mind buzzed. I blinked away spots behind my eyes.

When I looked up, the defenders had fallen on the remaining ghost, slicing it apart with renewed ferocity until it evaporated like morning mist.

"Are you okay?" one of them asked.

I nodded and waved them off without looking. "Go. They need your help."

They took me at my word and rushed off to find another ghost to vanquish.

Eventually, I managed to push myself up.

Vidsetr was overrun.

Fafnir fought the Thrice-Killed. Every blow shook the rain around them. Warriors slashed recklessly at the ghosts. Yrsa danced between the blue flickering figures, leaving tattered, fading silhouettes in her wake. For every ghost they slew two warriors fell and did not get up. And with each passing moment, more ghosts rushed out from the forest.

We needed to kill the ghost-summoner.

I looked around and saw Sigrun trapped against Ulfrun's house.

Her helm had been knocked loose. She screamed at an echo leaning over her, teeth sparkling in the glittering ghost-light and the flame of a torch in her hand. The ghost cocked its head as she swung the torch in front of her, trying to keep it at bay. It stepped forward. She plunged the torch deep into its stomach. The ghost blossomed with purple light as the raging flame mixed with its Wind-light body.

It did not care.

My eyes flicked to the house behind her and a plan fell into place in my exhausted mind.

I rushed over to Sigrun, tripping on the rain-slick ground.

Sigrun screamed as the ghost wrapped long arms around her. It lifted her from the ground. Rain hissed and spat against the ghost. Another tendril-arm extended from the ghost's shoulder. It reached for Sigrun's throat.

"No!"

I scrambled forward, hands outstretched. I missed Sigrun, but my momentum carried me across the wet ground and as I slid to a stop my fingertips brushed the ghost's leg.

I pulled. I screamed.

Power flowed into me like a flooded river and it threatened to rip me apart from the inside.

An echo of fury from the Windborn at the forest's edge.

A wet thud as Sigrun fell to the ground.

I shivered in my rain-soaked clothes and dragged myself over to my sister.

"Are you alright?" I asked, my throat hoarse from screaming.

Smoke curled from her shoulders. Her cheeks were too pale beneath the dirt and mud. She blinked slowly as her eyes struggled to focus.

"Sigrun." I took her hand and pushed a little power into her. My body shook as I emptied it. "It's me, Alvir. It's your brother."

Colour rushed into her cheeks, flickering blue before they flushed red.

"Alvir. Is it over?"

"Not yet," I said and wiped her dirty cheek with my cloak. "Stay here. I'll be back soon."

I propped her up against the house. She tried to pull herself to her feet, but I pushed her back down with soothing words. Then I turned back to the battlefield. I saw Yrsa and cupped my hands to my mouth.

"Yrsa," I shouted. The lightning-quick Windborn glanced at me, winced as a ghost slashed across her back. "I have an idea. We can stop this."

I tried to send her some mental signal but had no way to tell if she understood me so I beckoned her over. She turned to the ghost behind her and attacked it with bestial fury.

I could not wait. I dashed into the house.

ᚠ

The sudden quiet was unsettling. The cacophony of battle was reduced to muffled thumps and stretched out noises beneath the thundering of rain against the roof.

Without the light from the ghosts or the flames I had to squint to penetrate the darkness inside. The table was still covered with a jumble of objects that could be used in any rituals. Bones, feathers, plants, bowls filled with dirt and eggshell. I ran my hands along them, trying to find what I was looking for.

My fingers brushed against an old bucket. A shock ran through me like a spear made of ice as I touched the tar-like substance inside.

This was it.

Yrsa burst into the room, bringing with her the flickering Wind-light from the ghosts chasing after her.

"This better be good." Her sweat-soaked hair was plastered to her head. Her cheeks and neck were covered in red-raw burns and there were charred holes seared into her sleeves.

"Give me your axe."

She looked at me with a mixture of curiosity and uncertainty but did not have the energy to argue. She flipped one of the axes and shoved its handle at me. I took it and dipped its head into the bucket, letting the tar flow right up to the handle. The tar tried to keep hold of the axe and there was a sucking sound, then a pop as I pulled it out.

The tar-covered axe glittered like the night sky.

"Hurry the fuck up."

Yrsa's voice was strained with urgency and exhaustion. The Wind-light grew blinding as the ghosts closed in on the door. My heart lurched as I realised that they might ignore us and choose easier prey. Sigrun.

"Here." I tossed the axe back to her. "Use this."

Yrsa took a split second to examine the axe, brow furrowed, then she sprinted out the door.

I followed after her with the bucket swinging from one hand.

She was already surrounded.

Her axes flashed as she spun and slashed at the two ghosts: one, a bright flash like lightning; the other, a dim flicker like shark's eyes.

Each axe carved chunks out of the ghosts. This time, instead of knitting themselves back together, wherever the dark, glittering blade ripped through them their wounds smoked and sizzled. They did not heal.

Yrsa yelled in triumph as the ghosts shrank back from her. Their screams were high-pitched mournful whistles like poisoned wolves.

Within a moment, the ghosts were torn into ragged shreds that floated away and all that was left was Yrsa, breathing hard and grinning.

She turned to me and lifted her bright axe. "Now, do this one."

"Be careful," I said as we dipped her other axe in the black tar. "This is made to keep Windborn in check. This stuff will stick to you and drain your power."

"I've been using these axes for years, Alvir, and never hit myself with them."

I shot her a look, but she ignored me as she pulled her axe free.

She took a moment to examine it, glittering as though it was covered in ichor. Then she shot me a feral grin and ran out the door. She sprinted to join the battle with fresh vigour and fury. The ghosts turned to face her and she cut them down.

Still more flowed out from the forest.

I grimaced. The tar was already low. I turned back inside. I knew there was more somewhere inside.

I scattered bones and plates and cups and half-rotting food as I searched the pitch-dark house. Then my foot stuck against the floor as I stepped in something sticky. I looked down. A barrel had fallen on one side and leaked a viscous black liquid. I tore my foot free and pressed a tentative hand against it.

Pain.

This was it.

As I carefully rolled the barrel across the room a figure

appeared in the doorway.

"Alvir," Sigrun said, leaning against the door frame with a spear in her hand. "Let me help."

"You've done enough, Sigrun," I said.

"My home is burning," she growled.

Her exhaustion was writ large in her pale face, her shivering limbs, but my body felt hollow and brittle and I would not stop. Her home burned. I could not ask her to rest. I nodded and gestured to the barrel.

"Help me get the lid off." As we wrestled the barrel open I explained what it was and how it would help. The tar inside seemed to blink at us as we looked at it. My stomach twisted in a mix of fear at the pain this would cause me and hope that this might save Vidsetr. "Get everyone to cover their weapons in this. It will kill the ghosts."

She nodded. "I saw what Yrsa did to them."

We found some knives and coated them in the tar before we moved the barrel to the door then dipped Sigrun's spear blade into the Windborn-killing ichor. I looked from her to the spear. I could not bear the thought of her trying to fight so exhausted. I stepped away and took up Tjorvid's old hunting bow from the corner and passed it to her.

"Here," I said. I dipped a handful of arrows into the tar. "Use these. Keep yourself safe."

She looked like she wanted to argue but she could not summon the energy. She took the bow from me with a nod then rushed back into the battle, flush with an armoury of Windborn-killing blades and arrows.

I watched her go and took a breath. The air burned the back of my throat, the inside of my lungs. I was spent.

Another ghost flowered in the forest and moved into the town.

I gritted my teeth, dipped my mother's sword into the tar, and ran to meet it.

CHAPTER THIRTY-THREE
A FINAL DEATH

MY HEART POUNDED AS I RAN FROM VIDSETR. The woods were picked out with bright colours by the burning town and the Wind-bright ghosts.

I charged at a ghost rushing from the trees. Its lolloping steps carried it quickly from the darkness under the canopy. It hissed when it saw me and charged. I gripped my sword until the leather creaked. I clenched my free hand, knowing how easy it would be to absorb the ghost, but also knowing that if I inhaled any more power I would shatter like a clay bowl. Instead, I held my sword in front of me, ready to slash.

The ghost—unafraid of mere steel—reared like a bear made of glacial flame. It brought its hands together to form one club-like limb and slammed it down at me.

I met it with my black blade.

It screamed as its arms tumbled from its body, writhing and fading like a bonfire's final flames. The tar coating my sword cauterised the ghost's wound and it held up its stump-arms in front of it as though it did not understand.

I hacked at its legs. It toppled to the ground. I fell upon it, my sword flashing black against the ghost's light until it flickered out forever.

I stood, panting.

As I stared into the dark forest, squinting to try and make out Nori, the last Windborn, he stepped forward. His eyes and teeth shone in the light of the burning town as he offered me a wolf's grin. His Windborn power, still fresh and vital, called to my battered and stagnant strength.

"I'm impressed," he said. "Who'd have thought a god-speaker would be such a pain in my arse?"

"I told you, Nori. The gods are on my side. You can't win."

"Nah." He waved a hand, dismissing me. "The gods aren't with you anymore. You should have realised that by now. You're the same as me. Outcast." He waved to Vidsetr. "They only want you as long as you're useful."

"Call off your ghosts." I took a step towards him, pointing my sword at his chest. "It's over."

"What are you going to do? You can barely stand, God-Bane. But me?" He gestured to himself, his body glowing with Wind-light. "I can go all night."

A fresh ghost pulled itself out of Nori. It stretched high then sprinted for me.

I cut at the ghost but it reared back well out of reach.

As I widened my stance to take another swing, something slammed into my head. My ears rang as Nori punched me again. I stumbled to the side and slashed wildly with my sword.

I blinked stars out of my vision. Nori stood at the edge of the forest flanked by his flickering echo. He picked dirt out from under his fingertips with his knife.

"I couldn't face coming home when I became Windborn," he said. His tone was conversational, as though we were old friends talking over a campfire. "I went south and found some ruins from the Empire of Bones. They got me thinking about the power of death. Did you know some of their monsters are still there? I couldn't find any of those old spine-priests though, but the Daendrec had the Thrice-Killed. It showed me a few things in exchange for bringing it up here, all quiet like. So I did. I brought the Thrice-Killed here and it has opened my eyes."

"You brought that thing into the Fjalmark?" I all but screamed at him. Behind me, buildings crackled and snapped as their walls collapsed under their own burning weight. This was all his fault. All those lives lost under the Trollborn and he did not seem to care.

Nori frowned at me as though I was a child upset at nothing. "I did. I knew what Ulfrun was like, heard the stories. You know, how she tried to stitch those things together? Sounds a lot like Bimyrr to me. It can give us what we want, god-speaker. The gods will never take you into their halls now. You're tainted with the Winds. But the Thrice-Killed?"

Nori's arm fell to his side and his eyes slid in and out of focus as he stared into some perfect, imagined future.

"The Thrice-Killed will take you into itself. You saw all its different parts. If we give ourselves to it then it doesn't matter if we're Windborn. We can become part of something bigger than ourselves. We will be gods."

My mouth fell open and I shook my head. "No. You won't. That... monster is nothing like our gods. It—"

"Our gods? What loyalty do I owe your gods? I worshipped them all my life," Nori snarled. "I devoted myself to them. I died in battle screaming their names. I did everything I was supposed to do and then what? Because I'm Windborn they're going to cast me aside? No. I have found a god that will have me and I will join it."

Nori shifted his feet, his knife coming up.

"Listen to me, Alvir. This is your chance to get what you deserve. I thought that if anyone would understand it would be you. How deeply have you devoted yourself to the gods? Do you think that makes a difference now? With what you are? No. They will discard you.

"There is still a god that will embrace you. Help us and you can have a life after death like you were promised." He paused to let his words sink in.

My mouth hung open in disbelief.

"Do you think that there will be anything left of you when the Thrice-Killed takes your strength?" I asked, incredulous. "I don't know what lies it has told you, but I have seen it. All that is inside that creature is rotten flesh and poisoned water. You will be swallowed by it like a stream flowing into a river. Anything that you were will be gone."

Nori bared his teeth. He grinned with a sharpness that mixed fury and pain. He shook his head. "I thought you would understand."

He glowed, shivered and another echo shook itself free.

"Let's get this over with," he said. "Then we can take Konvald."

The ghosts sprinted forward.

I planted my feet and raised my sword.

The ghosts moved around me to catch me between them. I lunged at one and sliced its reaching arms from its body. As it screamed that too-high scream, I turned to face the other ghost. It swerved clear of my next sword swing and circled me cautiously.

Behind the ghosts, Nori paced like a waiting wolf.

The armless ghost screamed at me again and a third arm ripped itself free of its torso. It lurched forward, fury sizzling in its features.

It was sluggish from its injury. The blow came slow but deliberate. I let it come. As the arm came down I met it with my hand and pulled on the ghost's power.

Strength and pain bounced up my arm. My vision blurred, my head pounded as though my mind was trying to force itself out through my eyes. I stumbled back, blinking. Blood trickled from my nose. Skin all along my arm stretched and split.

The other ghost lunged. I swung my sword wildly, no method, only hope.

Something sharp and cold bit into my leg. I screamed as Nori ripped his axe free. His figure was a black blur behind the ghost, already falling away. He dodged back, well out of reach of my sword swing.

The ghost pummelled me, keeping my attention. I tried to swat at it with my sword, but was too clumsy. My leg couldn't take my weight and I tumbled to the ground.

For a moment, the world was lost in searing blue light. I held up my arms to keep the ghost's arms away from me, trying to slash at it, but my thoughts were blurred against the smell of cooked flesh and the bright pain in my leg.

After what felt like an age, the ghost stopped its searing attacks. It stood over me like a giant then stepped away. Nori snorted from somewhere nearby.

"Is this how you thought this would go?"

I gripped my mother's sword and glared at him with all the fury I could muster.

He came to stand over me. I tried to cut him. Clumsy. Slow. Tired. He dodged it easily and calmly swung his axe at my hand. The blade bit into my fingers. I could not hold on to my mother's sword. It tumbled out of my grip. Nori stamped a foot on my chest. I cried out as I felt something crack.

His summoned Wind-light silhouette leaned over him like a curious child.

"You charge up here all alone expecting... what? Some saga-worthy ending? That you're going to take me on all by yourself? You think that's going to make them forget what you are?"

He kept his foot pressed hard on my chest as he slung his axe back into his belt. The ghost behind him cocked its head. Something tore a hole through it and the ghost began to burn away. Then another hole appeared and another and within a heartbeat the ghost was gone.

Nori was transfixed on my sword, watching it as though to figure out what caused it to destroy his precious echoes. His expression smoothed as he saw the tar and then he smiled at me. The smile a cat reserves for a trapped mouse.

"They will never accept you," he said. "You're useful now, but when this is over? What are you to them then, God-Bane? A broken god-speaker. Tainted. A Windborn that drains the life from anyone he touches. What place could you possibly have in their world?"

I grunted as I tried to prise his foot from my chest. My mud-slick fingers slipped from the leather as he shoved me harder down against the ground.

"Easy there." He picked up my sword, grinding me further into the mud as he did so. "A neat trick with this tar stuff."

He raised the blade, ready to swing, and watched the tar shimmer as it moved.

"I would say see you in hell, but we both know there's nothing left for you now."

Nori's shoulder twitched. He screamed.

An arrow impaled his shoulder and his arm hung loose at his side. My sword fell onto the ground.

"What—"

Another arrow bit into Nori's chest.

The force of them pushed him back and I rolled out from under his boot. A third arrow flew overhead, missing Nori by a hand's breadth as he fell, and I clambered to my feet, my injured leg burning.

Nori tried to push himself up, but his impaled shoulder gave way.

I scooped up the sword and swung it at him as hard as I could. The blade caught before it sliced through skin, flesh, cartilage, bone, then air.

His head fell free of his body, picking up mud as it rolled along the ground.

I bent over, panting and wincing at the pain in my chest. Looking back at Vidsetr I saw Sigrun, bow in hand, rushing over.

"Alvir, are you alright?"

I offered her a pained smile. "I'll be fine."

She helped me up and I winced against the pain in my leg. "Is it over?" I asked.

She smiled at me as she took my weight. "Almost."

She nodded at Vidsetr.

The town was illuminated with bright orange flames, but the shimmering blue and green from Nori's ghosts was fading. Whatever power had driven them was dying along with their creator. Without ghosts to fight, Vidsetr's defenders rushed to help Fafnir, though they kept a healthy distance. The Thrice-Killed was pushed back against a burning building like a deer cornered by a pack of wolves.

I looked at the skin of my ripped arm and my sliced fingers, sighed, and wiped the blood from my nose with my sleeve. "Then let's finish this."

Sigrun nodded and we limped back into battle together.

ᚠ

The crowd parted for us as we hobbled up to the trapped god. The defenders, huskalar and levy both, were covered in mud and worse. They held spearheads snapped from their hafts, black-tarred knives and axes, and all of them—despite the exhaustion on their faces—looked ready to charge the Thrice-Killed.

Fafnir was visible above the heads of the assembled defenders, his furious eyes locked onto Bimyrr. As we came to the front of the crowd he glanced at us then returned his guarded gaze to the injured god.

During the fight, the Thrice-Killed's stolen arm had once more been ripped from its body. Spears pierced it from every angle, pinning it to the house. One side of its chest had been crushed and pushed inward like rotten fruit.

Yet still, it stood.

It watched us with fiery hatred burning in its eyes. Its black, bog-water blood spluttered from its gaping shoulder and the spear wounds glittering across its chest. The rotten blood soaked into the ground and I shuddered as I thought back to the poisoned heart of the forest.

Fafnir stood straight despite his countless bruises and cuts. One of his fingers was snapped at an unnatural angle and he had lost a tusk. His breath came heavy but he did not look away from the Thrice-Killed.

Yrsa came to stand beside us. Her shoulders drooped and her left eye was crusted shut. Her axes still glittered with tar and a fresh coating of slick, black blood.

"It won't die," she said. "Fafnir's ripped off its arm. We've stabbed it with the tar weapons. It's not slowing down. This is the best we could do."

I nodded and pulled away from Sigrun, testing my wounded leg. I sucked in a breath at the pain but it held so I hobbled up to Fafnir.

The Thrice-Killed scowled at me as I came forward, its neck twisting to see me from its pinned position. "God-Bane. I had hoped Nori would have killed you. He always droned on about his prowess in battle."

I smiled weakly. "He would have been too much for me alone."

"Ah, yes. That is the problem with you northerners. You huddle together like sheep, safe in your herds, and you think that somehow makes you strong. I have proven you wrong. Your abomination"—he gestured to Fafnir with his withered, lacerated hand—"cannot stand against me. None of you can stand against me. Even your mustered strength is not enough."

I looked back at the crowd. There were only twenty or so

fighters left. Each bloodied but still standing and still willing to fight. Sigrun caught my eye and took a step to join me but I shook my head. The Thrice-Killed was cornered but not yet defeated. I would not risk Sigrun. Her eyes filled with confusion and worry but she stayed in the crowd.

"How is your strength?" I asked Fafnir.

The enormous Windborn took a deep breath then turned his head towards me without looking away from the Thrice-Killed. His tusks gleamed in the dull embers falling from the town around us. "I am nearly spent, Alvir."

"I have nothing left to give you," I said.

He finally looked away from the Thrice-Killed and to me. His eyes darted to my rupturing arm, my bloody leg, and my pale cheeks. "You gave me strength. My sister's memories. Your memories and strength."

It was not a question, but I felt the weight of it, nonetheless. I had not pulled away from Fafnir when I was pushing the strength of the Trollborn into him. I nearly gave him everything. I had not wanted to stop.

"Yes," I whispered. "Vidsetr needs someone who can protect them. A real warrior. They don't need me."

Fafnir rumbled his disagreement. "We need you."

I smiled, but there was no warmth to it.

I looked over to the Thrice-Killed. It was pulling spears from itself, expression blank as each blade sliced back through the skin. As it dropped another onto the pile at its feet it saw me watching and grinned.

"Come then, God-Bane. Another victim to be remembered by the snap of their bones in one of my legends. Or do you think you can earn your name?"

"I can't..." I said, too quiet to carry to the Thrice-Killed, but loud enough for Fafnir. "I can't kill him. I can weaken him. I can make him vulnerable and you will have to finish him."

I looked down at my arm. My skin was red-raw, stretched, ripped apart from the inside.

"This might... I... Please take care of Sigrun. She deserves a better brother than I have been."

Fafnir's eyes softened. He placed one massive hand on my shoulder and his tusks shifted as he smiled. "She does. You will have time to make amends, Alvir Einarson. You have a strong heart, a good heart."

As Fafnir's words sank into me I felt some of my exhaustion melt away, my shoulders did not seem so heavy, the burning in my soul not so fierce. I smiled at Fafnir then turned back to look at Sigrun one last time. She stared straight back at me, the same panic and worry etched on her face. I nodded to her. She would understand. She had stayed behind to protect her family and now I did this to save her.

I turned away from my sister and walked towards the Thrice-Killed.

ᚠ

I stopped a few paces away from the dripping, undying god. Even though he only had one arm, his reach was still far longer than mine.

"You look spent, God-Bane. Mortals are so easily spent."

"I offer you this chance to leave. Enough blood has been spilled here and I do not wish to deprive the Daendrec of their god, as foul as you may be."

The Thrice-Killed shook its head and dragged another spear from its spongy flesh. "I will leave soon enough. Without my creatures, it will be too much effort to destroy Konvald. I will leave this wretched village a pile of corpses and rubble. Let your High King know then how brittle his strength is."

Leather creaked as I squeezed my mother's sword.

"I will not let you harm anyone else."

"Let me? God-Bane, you are nothing. You live by my grace and you are beginning to irk me."

I took a step forward and raised my sword.

"Leave now. Or, by the gods, I will strike you down."

It laughed. The sound like bubbles in mud.

"Come then." It yanked another spear from its chest and threw it at my feet. "Perhaps you will find it more useful than its previous owner."

I kicked the spear away and raised my sword. I tried to grip it in both hands, but my ruptured arm would not respond.

I charged at the Thrice-Killed, yelling a wordless war-cry and raising my sword high.

The undying god lurched forward to meet me. Before I could react, its massive hand wrapped itself around my throat and lifted me from the ground. I made to swing my blade down. The Thrice-Killed shook me until my teeth rattled in my skull and my sword flew from my hand.

An arrow thunked into the Thrice-Killed's torso. It sank into the pallid flesh all the way to the feathers. Bimyrr shook its head and gave another burbling laugh.

"You still do not understand." It squeezed. "I have already died. By the blade, by the noose, by the still waters. There is nothing that you or your gods can do to stop me."

I clawed at the wet hand as it crushed my throat. I pulled away one finger but the others tightened.

My vision blurred. The Thrice-Killed's bloated corpse-white face would be the last thing I would ever see. I focused on the bright arrow jutting from its chest. Three white feathers being slowly stained by Bimyrr's never-ending dripping. I wrapped my hand around its wrist, prayed to the gods to keep Sigrun safe, and I pulled.

Poisoned power cascaded up my arm like a flooding river.

I screamed in agony as my bones splintered. My hands and arms blossomed with blood and black mould.

I am bound. The priests around me watch with hard expressions. The rope lies light around my neck. The fibres scratch like a new woollen shirt. They chant. I can't make out the words through the pounding of my heart and my panicked breath. A nod. The noose tightens and I am dragged high, kicking, unable to breathe. The priests look so small.

I die.

The Thrice-Killed's eyes were wide with fury.

My throat crunched.

I drew deeper.

Water filled my lungs and I coughed up silt-laden water. Algae and moss blossomed on my bloody arms and I began to shiver as the heat left my body.

My breath comes hard, as painful as the rope-burns around

my neck. The chanting is louder. I am curled on the wet ground, half-sunk into the mud. One of the priests draws a knife. Its bronze blade gleams like crystallised sunlight. He looms like a giant. The knife plunges between my ribs.

I die.

The fingers began to loosen on my throat. I grasped the Thrice-Killed's arm as hard as I could. My fingernails dug into the soft, rotten skin and my fingers sank into Bimyrr's flesh to the knuckle.

The Thrice-Killed began to scream. It tried to shake me off but had no other hand to pry me loose. It slammed me into the building and I felt my ribs crack, another note in the chorus of pain that had become my existence.

I kept pulling.

With every breath, I feel the knife between my ribs. The rope-burns on my neck flare as I turn to the priests. The chanting is deafening. Every syllable echoes through my body. It takes four priests to lift me and carry me to the pool of stagnant water. Their feet echo on the wooden planks they use to keep themselves dry. The chanting stops. Silence. I fall. Bog water fills my lungs.

I die.

The Thrice-Killed collapsed, unable to bear its own weight. Our bodies tumbled together as it tried to drag itself away from me and I clawed my way up its arm with broken, dying hands.

Someone roared, the sound coming from impossibly far away. I held the power of an undying god within me and it ripped me apart from the inside but without it, the Thrice-Killed would finally face a death it could not survive.

The ground shook as Vidsetr's defenders charged.

My vision blurred as though I had fallen into a river. My lungs were heavy with water. My body cold. I fell into darkness and silence.

Chapter Thirty-Four
An Invitation

The world returned in shades of pain. Aching muscles. Heavy blood. Sore bones. My body shivered with an echo of agony that clawed through me with every heartbeat. Sharp pain up my arms as my skin tried to patch itself together. With each breath, my chest crackled and I felt every splinter in my ribs as they desperately tried to hold me together.

Noise clattered somewhere in the distance. Unknown smells crawled past the mix of mud and blood crusting my nose.

I was lying down. On a bed.

I forced my eyes open and the world slowly swirled into focus. Blankets hung from roof beams.

"Where..." My voice caught in my dry throat and I coughed which sent fresh waves of pain kicking through my chest.

A chair scraped. Something clattered to the floor.

Sigrun's face above me, creased with concern and a hint of relief.

"Alvir," she said as she sat on the stool by my bed. "Are you alright? How do you feel? Can I get you anything?"

Her face was bruised and covered in small cuts, still bright and unhealed. There were deep rings under her eyes. She reached out as though to grab my hand then pulled back. I smiled and rested my hand on hers. It was all the movement I could muster. As our fingers brushed against each other, my Windborn power twitched to pull some of her strength into myself. I held it back without thinking, finally accepting it as part of myself.

"Water," I rasped. "Some bread?"

She nodded and rushed off. Plates and cups clattered. Then she was back, skidding onto the stool with a sloshing jug of water, a cup, and a chunk of bread. I pushed myself up on the bed, wincing at the pain, and took them gratefully.

"Did it work?" I asked once I had managed some of the meal.

Her eyes went distant before she answered. "It did. Those tar-covered weapons did a little, but once you'd weakened it Fafnir did most of the work. He ripped that thing apart." As her eyes came back into focus she shot me a reproachful look. "Why did you do that?"

"Do what?"

She chewed her lip not quite willing to voice the question. "I could have lost you."

I squeezed her hand and tried to smile, but it turned into a grimace. "I couldn't put you in danger. You've got your family to look after, Sigrun. They need you."

Tears shone in her eyes. "And I don't need you?"

Before I could answer, Ljota leaned in from outside and caught Sigrun's attention. My heart sang to see Sigrun's wife whole and healthy. If she had returned to Vidsetr then the danger was well and truly past. Sigrun shot me a look to say that this conversation wasn't over and went outside. A hushed exchange. Sigrun's voice turned sour as she tried to shoo someone away, but they would not be swayed.

She sighed and said, "Fine, but you two stay outside. He's only just woken up so make it quick."

When Sigrun returned she was followed by a woman with dark hair. She wore travelling clothes, mud-stained but well-made and had an embroidered belt tied around her waist. Several necklaces bounced across her chest as she walked and a thin band of metal on her head glinted in the sunlight. Her cloak was the colour of glaciers and pulled at an angle over her chest so that it completely covered her left arm.

"Alvir," Sigrun said as they came to me. "Do you feel well enough for visitors?"

I swallowed a half-chewed chunk of bread.

"Yes, of course." I pushed myself further up in the bed, wincing as fresh needles of pain lanced through my chest.

Sigrun shot me a worried look, but let the newcomer take over her seat. Sigrun offered her a drink but she declined. Hesitantly, Sigrun left me to my conversation and went to clear up. Even so, she kept glancing back at us.

"What brings Vigdis Ragnasdottir to my bedside? Surely I do not warrant such attention."

The High King's daughter smiled. A stately smile wrapped in warmth but tempered with concern and restraint.

"All of this." She gestured to the door and the world outside. "We came as quickly as we could. Well, once we managed to get the story out of the exhausted messenger. It caused quite a stir. Bandits, trolls, dead things in the forest. It was almost too much to believe."

"And yet you came."

"We can't have monsters running around, especially when my father's away. How do you think he'd react if I let Konvald be destroyed as soon as he left me in charge?" Her eyes sparkled with mischief.

"Not well," I admitted. "But I am still not sure what you need with me, Your Highness?"

"Vigdis, please," she said then brushed some crumbs from my blankets. "I've spoken with your sister and the others who went into the forest with you, but I wanted to get a god-speaker's perspective about what happened."

She must have noticed the pinch in my expression, the echo of sadness behind my eyes, and my glance to my smudged tattoos. She offered me a kind smile.

"Don't worry, I know about your situation, but you were instrumental in understanding exactly what happened and how the magic was woven. I'd like you to explain it all to me."

I swallowed, took a sip of water, and told her as much as I could.

Her expression darkened as I told her of the kidnappings, of the rituals, and the power that had been used to shatter the god-stone. When I came to something she did not understand she asked me questions before she would let me continue. And when I touched upon any part of the tale about my transformation into one of the Windborn, I kept the detail as faint as I could manage.

Once I had finished my story, Vigdis nodded and leaned back in her seat. I was not sure how long it had taken me to recount the details, but a chill had begun to seep into the air and the light outside had dimmed.

"Thank you, Alvir," she said, looking into the distance. "We clearly need to take care to hunt down these forest outlaws. Perhaps if we had then we would have known what was going on.

"And there are no more of these remade trolls moving around in the forest?"

"I cannot be sure," I said. "But I do not think so. There is a strength to casting a weave in threes and we killed three of them. If there were more, the Thrice-Killed surely would have called them to battle."

Vigdis nodded along with me, still in thought.

"Could another rune-weaver work from her rituals? Continue the work she has done?"

I frowned. It was possible. Then I thought back to Ulfrun's home and the grotesque tapestry of limbs, gristle, and tendons pinned to her wall. There had been rumours of Ulfrun's gruesome obsession for years. If there was another rune-weaver with the knowledge that she had, I would surely have heard of them. I told Vigdis as much.

"Good," she said. She seemed satisfied and leaned forward in her seat. "We must still purge the woods of any trace of her rituals and the foul magics from this Thrice-Killed. You say it claimed to be Daendrec?"

"It did. I saw some of its memories." I shuddered as the feeling of a noose closed around my neck. "I saw the ritual that made it. It was an ancient place, but it looked like one of their sacred, flooded groves."

"I fear the Daendrec have made the opening move in a bloody game." Vigdis' expression twisted then softened and the stately façade returned. "Will you help me, Alvir? We could sorely use your help. Will you swear your Windborn oath to the throne?"

Noise flooded the house before I could answer. The high-pitched squeals of children bounced from the roof a moment before Ama and Raggi bounced in themselves. They sprinted up to Sigrun, who was preparing something in the hearth, and tugged on her sleeve. Both talked over each other in their eagerness to tell their mother all about the strange things they had seen in town.

"I saw seven men with big shields and spears and they had swords and one of them said hello to me and—"

"Well, I saw something gross and dead. It was so huge. Bigger than Fafnir even. He said he ripped its arm off! Did he really? Could you rip someone's arm off, Mum?"

I smiled as Ljota appeared in the door. She leaned on the frame, panting. "I told you to wait out here!"

"Must I answer now?" I asked.

Vigdis followed my gaze and gave a small smile of her own as we watched the children run between their mothers, stick swords waving above their heads and questions filling the air.

"No. By law, a Windborn must swear loyalty before the next Althing, whether to a chieftain or the throne, so you have a couple of months." She turned back to me and cocked an eyebrow. "I must admit, I was not expecting you to decline, Alvir."

"Please, do not misunderstand. I am grateful for the offer, and I am not necessarily declining, but I would appreciate some time with my sister. Some time to be a family."

Vigdis nodded and her lips twitched into a smile as the children rushed past her. "A worthy choice. Enjoy the time with your family, but I hope we will be able to greet you in the halls of Konvald before long. Now, I will leave you to your rest, Alvir Einarson."

Vigdis bowed her head and stood. I returned the gesture and shifted myself in my bed. Pain still lanced through me, but it had softened. Vigdis said goodbye to Sigrun and Ljota and swept out of the house.

The evening had crept in through the door and, despite the blankets, I felt a chill over my arms. I looked down and saw the mess of scrapes and stretchmarks covering my skin. My Windborn power had healed most of my injuries, leaving dry scabs and red raw skin. The deep slices across my fingers had droplets of blood on their sharp lines which began to split as I clenched my fist.

My god-speaker tattoos were undecipherable beneath the wounds from my battles and the bright marks where my skin had ballooned from absorbed power.

I sighed and wondered where my god-speaker's arm-ring was now. No doubt buried deep in the forest. If it was lucky, perhaps it would be taken by a raven to build a nest.

Across the room, one of the children clapped and giggled.

I shivered and pulled my sleeves down my arms. It was a price gladly paid and I would do so again.

The fire crackled beneath the cooking pot. Its warm light danced over my sister, her wife, and their children. It looked inviting. I stretched for a spear leaning against the wall beside me and, with the spear's help as a walking stick, I was able to shuffle out of bed.

The children's eyes lit up as I hobbled over to the fire. Ljota had to hold them back so that they didn't topple me over with their enthusiasm.

Sigrun helped me into the seat closest to the hearth. I smiled at her and squeezed her hand. She smiled back and we held each other's hands, unwilling to let go just yet. Then Raggi crashed up to us, holding his boat charm up to me, desperate to explain how it had kept them safe on their adventure. He knelt in front of me and pointed to the smeared rune on its side. I smiled and nodded along to his babble and explanations.

For a long time, I warmed myself by the light of the fire and with the embrace of my family.

Epilogue

AFTER TWO DAYS OF TRUDGING through the forest, Auden was beginning to feel like this journey would be the end of him. The straight-backed trees had snagged his clothes with snapped branches. The groping gorse had scrabbled at his shins with thorny claws. The winter-wilted ferns had hidden grimy puddles that made him slip and fall. And now, with a burbling squelch, his feet were sinking into a patch of mud that had once been a stream.

Auden's face pinched with disgust at this latest indignity. These were new boots. Bought and paid for with some of the best sagas sung across the Fjalmark. As he tried to pull his foot out of the quagmire, the other sank in, and he was forced to stamp on his cloak to get free.

Auden took a deep breath and reminded himself why he had ventured so far from the warm, clean embrace of civilisation: rumours of a Windborn who had once been a god-speaker. The promise of a tale that would straddle the worlds of the gods and the Winds had lured him to the town of Vidsetr and, from there, the townsfolk had pointed him to the forest.

If he could pay the price of some scuffed boots and a muddy cloak, if he could survive a little longer, then Auden could craft a new saga that would make him a legend. He would earn the kind of glory that could buy the best boots and the finest cloaks in the Fjalmark. As Auden tried to stamp the mud from his boots, he glanced at the massive figure beside him: a Windborn of colossal proportions with a face twisted by the tusks jutting from his mouth. The Windborn was a man of few words, but then, Auden supposed, he would be, too, if he had to slur sentences through those twisted lips.

"Are we almost there, Fafnir?"

The Windborn looked down and shot him a crackling smile. "We are close."

"Great."

It took perhaps another hour until Auden sensed a shift in Fafnir's mood. His steady gait lengthened into an excited march and Auden struggled to keep up with the Windborn's enormous stride. As Auden panted, praying they would arrive once they crested the next rise or once they reached that tree, the forest seemed to become animated and watch their progress. Branches twisted in the wind as they passed. The canopy opened like parting curtains to let them walk in the sunlight. Birds hopped from branch to branch alongside them, heads cocked to keep Auden in sight.

Auden cleared his throat, about to ask Fafnir what was happening, when he heard distant voices and saw the hint of habitation over a rise ahead. A large tent—no, three smaller tents—a well-used fire pit, and people moving between the trees.

"We have arrived," Fafnir rumbled.

Auden nodded and brushed down his cloak, trying to dislodge as much muck and forest from the fine material as he could.

He clambered up the slope behind Fafnir and let out a gasp when they reached the top.

The forested valley ahead of them was gnarled and lush. It was a mishmash of crooked trees, half-fallen but now growing again, and between their bent trunks was a tapestry of saplings and fresh undergrowth, glittering green in defiance of winter. It looked like this part of the world had fallen to rot some time ago but was now well on the road to recovery.

More than that, Auden was in awe of the countless boulders that littered the hidden valley. People wandered between them—some bent close to examine the stones and others scraped them clean of moss and dirt—and these curious caretakers gave the boulders a sense of scale, making it clear that even the smallest was as big as a horse. Auden grinned.

He had seen the odd troll-stone in his travels, but they were always half-sunk into the earth and barely recognisable as the legendary creatures they had once been. These boulders, though, crowded the fresh green forest with hands and arms and legs and faces. Whether or not the Windborn he sought was willing to give up his story, these troll-stones would serve as worthy inspiration for a few songs.

"Come," Fafnir beckoned, and started forward.

As Auden followed his enormous guide into the valley, the campsite came clearly into view. The straight tent poles were sunk into the valley's soft slopes in brazen, rigid contrast to the ancient trees' curling boughs and the time-softened edges of the troll-stones. Auden's eyes followed the tents' straight lines down to the barrels and supplies placed neatly around an area cleared of undergrowth, and there Auden saw two figures sat beside the fire pit.

The man and woman laughed together as they tried to coax the fire back to life, finding humour in their failure. Their easy manner and high spirits told of long years of close companionship. The man was silver-haired and cradled a staff with fresh leaves blossoming from its head, whilst the woman was perhaps a decade younger and dressed in well-worn travelling clothes, with a spear and shield beside her. A familiar thrill shivered up Auden's spine as he sensed his chase coming to a close. This had to be him. Auden would finally be able to weave another Windborn's saga and, while he listened, he could clean the muck from his boots.

Fafnir called out to them, hand raised in greeting, and they stood to meet their old friend and this new stranger.

"I have brought you a skald," Fafnir said.

The man and woman frowned, confused at their unexpected guest, and looked to Auden. Now that they were closer, Auden could see a few grey strands in the woman's hair and the scars and stretchmarks on the man's arms.

"Greetings, friends," Auden said, giving them his warmest smile. "My name is Auden Leifson and I wish to speak with the Windborn Alvir Einarson."

The warrior-woman took half a step forward, putting herself between Auden and the scarred man. "What do you want with him?"

Auden offered another smile. "I wish to hear his tale."

She glanced back to the scarred man and stared at him for a long moment.

The man twisted the leaf-laden staff in his hand. His gaze flicked from Fafnir to Auden. "You have come a long way to find me, friend skald. Chieftain Ljota would have been glad to host you until I returned."

"He was keen to see you," Fafnir said with a shrug of his giant shoulders. "I was glad to guide him."

Auden's smile nearly faltered. It was not quite a dismissal but neither was it a promise of a story. Still, he had squeezed sagas from frosty Windborn before, and he could do it again.

"Well met, Alvir." Auden stepped forward and held out his hand. "When I heard you were in the forest, I knew I could not pass up the opportunity to see the legendary Trolbjolvid for myself."

Alvir glanced down at the proffered hand but ignored it and instead gestured for Auden to join him by the fire.

"Do we have any more of the mead from the Black Lakes?" Alvir pitched his question to the woman beside him.

"Most of a barrel," she replied. "Want to give me a hand, Fafnir?"

Alvir thanked her as she and Fafnir wandered off to find the mead. Auden settled himself on a log that had been dragged up to the fire pit, and Alvir did the same on the other side.

"Who are those people around the boulders?" Auden asked. He did not want to press the matter of the Windborn's saga too soon. People were often more willing to tell their tales if their tongues were already warmed by idle conversation.

"Some are warriors from Vidsetr, but most are rune-weavers," Alvir said, glancing at them. "There is much to learn from these troll-stones. Our hope is that we might regain some of the trolls' storied rune-craft."

Auden's eyebrows shot up. "There is some very impressive magic in those old tales."

"It may come to naught, but we lose nothing to try."

They sat in awkward silence. The canopy gossiped in the wind. A songbird chirruped, flitted down to rest on Alvir's knee, then flew off in a burst of wings. Auden looked to the staff cradled against the Windborn's shoulder. The wood was worn smooth from long use—even now Alvir's fingers idly stroked a knot in the grain—but from the leaves sprouting from its end, Auden would have guessed Alvir had cut it from a tree mere moments ago.

"I came down from Konvald," Auden said, not taking his eyes from the fresh buds on the staff. "You have made an impressive shrine at the shattered god-stone."

Alvir smiled. "It has grown since we first built it. Then it was merely a pile of broken shards. Any credit to its current size goes to the rune-weavers that leave offerings on their way to see the troll-stones."

Before Auden could enquire further, Fafnir lumbered over with a barrel cradled under one arm. The woman—Alvir introduced her as his sister, Sigrun—grinned at them as she held up four cups. The mead sloshed as Fafnir thumped the barrel on the ground, and it was not long until they each had a full cup of the sweet drink.

The fire between them spat and Sigrun appeased it with fresh kindling.

After a long moment, Alvir looked at Auden and smiled with tight-pressed lips. "You honour me, Skald Auden, that you have come so far to speak with me, but you can see the scars of my saga linger on me still." He raised an arm and the stretchmarks glittered in the firelight. Then he sighed and gestured to Fafnir and Sigrun. "Perhaps you would rather hear a tale from my sister? Or Fafnir?"

Auden looked to the others. Sigrun still looked cautious as she sipped her mead whilst Fafnir looked disinterested, craning his head around to stare at the rune-weavers and their guards as though looking for someone.

"Fafnir has had enough of me after these past two days, I am sure. And though I do not doubt, Sigrun, that you have many daring tales, it is your brother's story that I have come for. I would hear the tale of the man who entered the forest a god-speaker and came out a Windborn."

"It is usually enough for me to hide away here," Alvir said through his brittle smile. "Not many skalds are willing to traipse so deep into the woods to find me."

"I am not most skalds," Auden said with a grin. "I seek only to tell your story, Alvir, to immortalise you in song."

The scarred Windborn frowned.

"I have already withstood death once, had the briefest taste of immortality, and I did not care for it then."

Auden's smile faltered, but he persevered, softening his expression with a hint of regret. "I am sorry, Windborn Alvir, I have ambushed you here in the forest. I had hoped this secluded place would give you some measure of privacy to tell your story, but I can return to Vidsetr and we can speak there."

They stared at each other for a long moment, until Alvir's stern expression gave way to a sad smile.

"I can see, friend skald, that you are not a man to give up easily." Alvir passed his empty cup to Fafnir and, as he waited for the Windborn to refill it, he looked out into the forest, smile faltering and eyes unfocused. "Perhaps this would be the best place to tell of what happened."

Alvir took his now-full cup from Fafnir and sighed. He looked at his sister. She put her hand on his sleeve, careful to avoid touching his scar-stained skin, and squeezed. Alvir smiled softly at her and then nodded.

He took a deep draught of mead and stared out at the once-rotten trees beyond the firelight. He sat like that for a long moment, looking from the marks on his arms to the troll-stones all around them and then back again.

The once-god-speaker turned his attention to Auden, his expression serious once more, and took a deep breath.

"My runes were too weak to save her."

Author's Note

Thank you so much for reading *Trollgrave*.

I hope you liked it and that you'll consider leaving a review.

Reviews are so important, especially for indie authors like me, even a short one will help and you will have my eternal gratitude!

If you'd like to be the first to find out about my future books and get occasional freebies then please subscribe to my newsletter by heading over to my website.

www.alexsbradshaw.com/newsletter

You can also find me on social media as @AlexSBradshaw to get in touch and see what I'm up to.

I'd love to hear from so please get in touch!

ACKNOWLEDGEMENTS

This book has been a long time coming, so thank you to my readers for their patience as this fresh Windborn Saga has made its way into the world!

Behind every book is the continued and priceless support of friends and family and I am so grateful for every drop of it as it's kept me going.

Thank you to my brother for his relentless encouragement to finish this book and his enthusiasm when he (finally) got to read the early copy. Thank you to my wife for her endless support with my writing and everything else. And of course thank you to Pippin for being the best pup.

Thank you to Timy, Jenny, Anne, and Matt for reading an early version of the book. Your thoughtful notes were invaluable and more than that I count myself lucky to know you and call you friends!

Thank you also to my amazing editors, Sarah Chorn and Nathan Hall, whose notes have wrung every scrap of story from every page and paragraph and word of this book. It is a much better book because of you and I am so grateful.

Thank you to Raph and Shawn for their peerless work on the cover and design of Trollgrave. I cannot overstate how thrilled I am with how the book looks and that is all down to your amazing talents.

And finally, my heartfelt thanks to you for reading Trollgrave. I am indebted to you for joining me as we hear Alvir's story.

I hope you enjoyed it!

CREDITS

Beta Readers:	Timy Takas
	J.E. Hannaford
	Anne Mattias
	Matt Duke
	Matthew Bradshaw
	Rachel Bradshaw
Editor:	Sarah Chorn
	www.sarahchornedits.com
	Nathan Hall
	nathanhalledits.wordpress.com
Cover Artist:	Raph Herrera Lomotan
	www.artstation.com/raphlomotan
Cover Designer:	STK Kreations
	www.stkkreations.com